Maxxed Out

David Collins

Maxxed Out

WILLIAM MORROW

An Imprint of HarperCollins*Publishers*

MAXXED OUT. Copyright © 2009 by David Collins. All rights reserved. Printed in the United States of America. No part of this book may be used or reproduced in any manner whatsoever without written permission except in the case of brief quotations embodied in critical articles and reviews. For information address HarperCollins Publishers, 10 East 53rd Street, New York, NY 10022.

HarperCollins books may be purchased for educational, business, or sales promotional use. For information please write: Special Markets Department, HarperCollins Publishers, 10 East 53rd Street, New York, NY 10022.

FIRST EDITION

Designed by Kate Nichols

Library of Congress Cataloging-in-Publication Data has been applied for.

ISBN 978-0-06-145619-0

09 10 11 12 13   OV/RRD   10 9 8 7 6 5 4 3 2 1

To Claire and second chances

Too much for what I do, too little for what I could do.

—Mozart, on being asked what his
wealthy patron was paying him

Prologue

Anyone who reads the papers, or watches TV news, or browses the blogs, or even goes out to a dinner party now and then will be familiar with at least the bare bones of the story I am telling here. The scandalous fall and stunning murder of Robert Maxx, after all, made headlines from New York to Tokyo, and were as likely to be discussed in the pubs of London and cafés of Paris as in the luncheonettes of Brooklyn. These were events that resonated everywhere, not only because of their intrinsic drama and lurid complications, but for what they told us about the world we live in, a world defined by wealth and debt, power and envy—and, occasionally but unforgettably, by sudden shocking collapses that are so destructive and so messy that they can only end in violence.

Pundits and talk-show personalities couldn't get enough of the case. Gossip writers who had fed for years on Maxx's affairs and feuds and lawsuits took a gloating, finger-wagging tone at his demise. Wrote the *New York Post,* "He died where he lived—at the noisy and treacherous intersection of Celebrity Boulevard and Easy Street." *The Economist* put a European spin on his obituary, calling him "an icon of everything the Old World loathes and loves about the New—the arrogance and the energy, the barbarism and the zest."

Even the sober *New York Times* weighed in with an editorial assessing Maxx's significance with a certain grudging admiration. "If he seemed at times little more than a coarse bully with deep pockets," opined the Great Gray Lady, "in other ways he must be deemed a visionary. Like the robber barons of old, he left his mark on the landscape by the sheer force of his will."

The business press weighed in with its own postmortems. On CNBC, in *Forbes* and *Fortune* and the *Journal,* the same tough questions were asked—and never really answered. How was it possible that Maxx's financial empire had come unglued as swiftly as it did? How had he been allowed to run up such massive debts in the first place? Where was the oversight? These prudent bankers with their somber shoes and muted ties—didn't they realize the wild recklessness of the loans they kept making? As to Maxx himself—was he an unfortunate casualty of the deadly worldwide credit crunch that was wreaking havoc everywhere, draining wealth and destroying storied firms? Or was he simply a monstrous example of a compulsive spender whose resources, however vast, could never quite keep pace with his cravings?

Whatever the reasons for the galloping fiasco, the shakeout from it was ugly, and it was felt from Shanghai to Berlin, from Moscow to Buenos Aires—everywhere Maxx had built skyscrapers, or shopping malls, or golf courses, partnering with local investors who'd trusted him, on projects that supposedly could not miss. When Maxx finally went down, vast amounts of money seemed simply to have disappeared. Nest eggs vanished. Lives were ruined. Careers were wrecked, and reputations were sullied beyond repair. And someone took it personally enough to murder Robert Maxx.

Assuming, that is, that it was money that drove the killer. But there were other grudges, too, more intimate in nature. Sexual betrayals. Soured relationships with sometimes invisible and unsavory allies. Long-ago insults that festered for decades. Robert Maxx had lived so largely and so abrasively that, in the matter of his slaying, nothing and no one could be ruled out.

I know . . . because I was a suspect myself.

And the fact is, I could have murdered Robert Maxx; I *might* have murdered Robert Maxx. I had the opportunity—a perfect opportunity—and a compelling, if secret, motive as well. On the night he died, he showed me a side of himself that was cruel and vindictive and petty, and I was angry enough to wish him dead. He was unconscious when I left his apartment.

That I saw Maxx on the night of his death was not surprising—I had complete access to him during the last weeks of his life, and I probably spent more time with him than anyone during that turbulent autumn. You see, we were writing a book together. Or, to put it more accurately, I was writing a book for which Maxx would get the entire credit as well as 98 percent of the money. No use complaining; that's just how it is when you're a ghostwriter; you cash the check and try to make your peace with it. Still, it leaves a bad taste sometimes. Was the mere fact of Maxx's name on the jacket worth fifty times as much as my labor and my talent, such as it is?

The police, at least, might eventually have figured out that I had good reason to be unhappy with the deal, and their logic would be hard to fault. Alive, Robert Maxx would glory in the publicity and gobble up the profits from my work on our tell-all volume, *Maxxed Out;* I would remain the anonymous and ill-paid scribe who put words in his mouth and made him sound more thoughtful and clever than he was. But Maxx's death, as it turned out, voided our contract, freed me from a strangling and unjust nondisclosure clause, and left me with sole ownership of the story you're about to read—a story that only I could tell.

People, I suppose, have killed for less.

Chapter 1

I'm superstitious. I admit it. I have a lot of superstitions. Some of them are pretty standard; others might be all my own. Now and then I get a new one; I don't know how this happens. It just shows up one day, like a moth hole in a sweater. But, though new ones come, the old ones never go away. They just accumulate.

Most of the time I don't mind my superstitions. I actually sort of like them; they're like tiny warning signs that help me navigate the real and imagined dangers of the day. Sometimes, though, I wish my superstitions weren't there. It would be nice to believe that life and people are more reasonable than that. But life isn't, and people aren't, and that's just how it is.

On the day that set the stage for my association with Robert Maxx, I woke up at an unlucky time. Given my line of work, I rarely have to be anyplace special in the morning. So I seldom set an alarm clock. But, as the old saying goes, habits are the shackles of the free, and my habits shackle me plenty. Alarm clock or no, I almost always wake up between 7 and 7:30. That morning, I cracked an eye and the first thing I saw was 7:13.

I slammed my eyes shut quickly, but not so fast that I could kid myself that I hadn't seen the dreaded number. I lay in bed until I was sure that at least a full minute had passed, then I knocked wood to counteract the effect of having seen the inauspicious digits, and only then did I get up.

Considering the lousy start, the morning went okay. I made coffee, read the paper, pissed around with a little essay about the creative use of boredom. Then the phone rang. Before I answered it, I looked down at the clock in the bottom corner of the computer screen. It was 10:13. What were the odds?

The call was from my agent, Paul Hannaford. I love Paul. We've been together for a dozen years, through thick and thin, though most of the thick part was a while ago. What I cherish and admire about Paul is his ability to live and function in a constant and unremitting state of unspoken conflict. At heart, my agent is a profound pessimist, a man of serene dejection whose worldly disillusionment is so thoroughly ingrained as to seem almost French. He knows deep down that most books won't sell, that reviewers will generally be invidious and snide, that publishers will often break promises. He accepts these things without umbrage or surprise. At the same time, in his role as a salesman, a peddler of goods, he has no choice but to be cheery, optimistic, upbeat, to do that whole Willy Loman thing complete with the smile and the shoeshine. He's very good at this, and I have no idea how he does it. His looks probably help. He's got sandy, reddish hair and a scattering of yachtsman's freckles, and while he must be in his early forties, he could pass for twenty-eight.

In any case, I looked away from the computer clock, knocked wood again, and said hello.

"David," Paul said, "got a minute? I just had an interesting call from Marcie Kanin over at Porter."

My ears perked up. I've known Paul long enough to understand that the word *interesting* in this context is his code for the possibility of money changing hands. It's not a usage I'd heard very often lately. "Talk to me," I said.

"She wanted to know if you're available. I played it coy, let her think you might be drowning in offers."

I said, "Maybe I would be if I had a better agent."

"You might be drowning. But it wouldn't be in offers. You know Marcie?"

I didn't, which was actually surprising. Publishing is a small village, and if you stick around awhile and don't get fired once too many times, you'll pretty much meet everybody, generally over lunches that are all the same. They start with rather stilted chitchat before looking at the menu, then move on to a main course of industry gossip and schaden-freude, which leads in due course to that deflating moment over demi-tasse when editor and writer gaze hopefully at each other and realize more or less simultaneously that the other has not brought a brilliant book idea to the table.

"Well, no matter," Paul said. "You'll like her. She's a grown-up and a survivor. And she just got into business with Robert Maxx." He put an almost salacious breathiness into the mention of the name, then let it hang suspended for a moment.

If I was supposed to be instantly impressed, I wasn't. "Robert Maxx? Oh, great. There's a prestige project. Musings of a fucking egomaniac parvenu with an infantile obsession about putting his name on build-ings. It's like graffiti at a higher economic level."

"David," he said, "Robert Maxx's name recognition is right up there with the president's. He can get on *Oprah* with a phone call. Larry King *begs* him to appear."

"Okay. Big celebrity. But he does schmucky business books. Crap for middle managers and neo-yuppies. I don't want to do that. Get some hack from *BusinessWeek*."

"Marcie doesn't want just any hack. She wants a hack who can tell a story."

"Is that supposed to be flattering?"

"I've done some homework. Over the last twenty years, Maxx has published half a dozen books, each one with a different ghost. They've all been bestsellers, but every one has sold fewer copies than the last. What does that say to you?"

"For starters," I said, "it tells me he's either a real dick to work with or impossible to please."

"Probably both," Paul admitted. "But that's not the point. The point is that there's magic in his name. Always has been, always will be. But the straight business-book vein was tapped out years ago. Marcie wants this to be a different kind of book."

"Oh? What kind of book does she want it to be?"

I would have put money on the answer that was coming, and I would have won the bet.

"She doesn't really know. Not advice. Not anecdotes. Something with a narrative."

"A narrative. A nice self-congratulatory, name-dropping, wallet-sniffing narrative. Sounds fucking awful."

There was a pause. I could picture Paul working that little blue squeezy ball he keeps on his desk for exasperating moments with temperamental clients. Finally, he said, "You turned forty yet?"

"I'm forty-two," I said. He knew perfectly well how old I was, the bastard. He also knew that my boyish brown curls no longer covered quite as much of my forehead as they used to, and that the very first wiry gray strands had recently shown up at my temples.

"You have a trust fund you're not telling me about?"

He knew damn well I didn't. I'm a public-school kid from a crummy tract-house suburb in New Jersey. My father owned a hardware store. When it went belly-up, he took a job with one of the giant chains that had driven him out of business. He ended his working life as a stooped guy in an orange apron full of carpet tacks and picture hangers. Trust fund? Hell, it took me till my middle thirties to finish paying off my college loans.

"Is there some point you're making?"

"I'm just wondering," he said, "how you can afford your snobbery."

"Okay, I'm a snob," I said. "So shoot me. I happen to believe that a book should have something inside it, not just some celebrity asshole's name embossed in foil on the cover."

He sighed and I vaguely realized that I was being perverse and difficult; but if Paul didn't want to deal with people who were perverse and difficult, he shouldn't have been a literary agent.

At last he said, "David, listen. Little reality check, okay? You haven't worked in almost a year. Your fiction didn't sell. You've earned yourself a solid reputation as a ghost. That's the good news. But you're not the fresh young face anymore and you're not the flavor of the month. If you want to stay in this business, I think you need to get over yourself a little bit."

I guess I deserved that. Still, it stung. But here's the thing. I wasn't just being cranky and a snob. There was more to it than that. I have protested and bitched and moaned on the threshold of every job I've ever taken. I have marshaled persuasive arguments in favor of rejecting every single project. The details of my reluctance are different every time, but the root cause of it is constant, and it is neither more nor less than the terrifying fear of failure. Embarrassing but true—for all my cockiness, I secretly tremble that each new book will be the one I cannot write, the story that doesn't speak to me and that I can't make work.

Paul seemed to figure out what I was wrestling with, and he softened up his tone. "This is gonna be a big book, and no one could do it better than you. Marcie Kanin thinks that and so do I."

He was patronizing me. I knew it. Far from minding, I was grateful. Already, in some dim, half-conscious way, I was beginning to work on this new project, wondering how to craft a voice for Robert Maxx, how to distill his personality or invent one if I had to, to make him live as a character on the page.

By my very silence, Paul knew that he had me. "Marcie's holding an appointment for you," he said. "Three o'clock this afternoon."

I hung up the phone, rubbed the lucky baseball that I'd once caught out at Shea, and headed for the shower.

Chapter 2

It was late October—for my money the best time of the year. In the natural world, spring, of course, is the season of renewal, but in New York, it's the fall. The city comes into its own, reawakens, as the natural world dies back. The summer torpor lifts; people who fled town on summer weekends now hunker close to home, hoping for glimpses of greatness in the theater or the concert hall. The first northwest breezes blow away the haze, clearing the mind as well as the air.

Heading for my appointment with Marcie Kanin, I came out of my building into mild sunshine that was the orangey yellow of caramel. I live in a third-rate co-op way up on the Upper West Side, one of those buildings where the floors haven't been sanded since Abe Beame was mayor and there are still faint and flickering fluorescent lights in the alcove with the mailboxes. My immediate neighborhood is an island of funkiness that has somehow been left high and dry by each successive recent wave of gentrification. Where I live, building facades haven't been tarted up with glass and brass. You won't find fresh marble in the lobbies; you won't find calla lilies.

But call me unhip and call me nostalgic, it's still my favorite part of the city. No, I'll go further: to me, it *is* the city, the last bastion of certain types of characters who constitute the real Manhattan, who make it different from anyplace else. Ancient Jewish violinists, four-foot-eight, shuffling in galoshes; Puerto Rican supers listening to transistor radios as they wrestle inexpertly with faulty pipes and wires; culture vultures on a budget—retired teachers, students from Taiwan—working the system for half-price tickets to off-Broadway shows and standing-room deals at the opera. And of course the yentas, little old ladies who stand by day and night, ready to open their doors just a crack at the first syllable of conversation in the hallway.

This was my New York. And as I walked down Broadway, past the fruit stands with their terraced ranks of oranges, past the headless parking meters, the Greek coffee shops with their hand-scrawled, misspelled breakfast specials, I couldn't help thinking how wildly different my city was from Robert Maxx's.

His Manhattan gleamed in the lambent sunlight just a couple of miles south. In his New York, everything was new and tall and shiny; people in uniforms kept it all buffed up and free of smudges. Elegant buildings puffed and strutted to outdo one another, like aristocratic ladies at a ball. Elevators rose as fast as rockets; the people who mattered lived and worked far up off the ground. There were no dun bricks and flaking mortar in Maxx's version of New York; rather, there were sheets of aluminum and titanium, alloyed so they bore postmodern tints of green and blue. It was hard to grasp that Maxx's city and mine occupied the same planet, let alone the same fragile strip of rock and soil along the Hudson River. It was as if the Flintstones and the Jetsons were living side by side.

As I looked at these two Manhattans, something else occurred to me as well: Robert Maxx was fundamentally an enemy of the city I loved. This wasn't a matter of ill will or even greed, exactly, but of something deeper and more intimate, impossible to change or reason with; it was a matter of temperament. Robert Maxx lived to knock down old things and put up new ones in their place. This wasn't a choice, and it wasn't right or wrong; it was simply who he was. In his bones he lusted after big, untarnished monuments; he couldn't help but despise and dismiss the weathered and the flawed.

It so happened that I—also by temperament, not by reasoning or choice—am just the opposite. I love the old, the dinged, the dented. I find new and shiny things irredeemably vulgar and somehow sad. New things will decay just as surely as old ones; but as with the young of every species, they just don't seem to know it yet, and therein lies the heartbreak. In any case, this basic temperamental difference made me want to hate Robert Maxx before we'd even met. In light of what happened later, I wish I hadn't felt this way. I wish I hadn't entertained the fantasy, however fleetingly, of somehow becoming the person who would stop him.

M aking sure to avoid the bad luck that would certainly result from stepping on blue lines or wheelchair-access stencils, I walked all the way to midtown, to the building in the East Fifties that housed Marcie Kanin's office.

I knew the building well. A dozen or so years ago, back when I was a promising young novelist and Porter & Kraft was an independent house of modest profits and more than middling prestige, I'd actually published a book with them. Much had changed since then. Porter had been taken over by an international conglomerate whose executives promulgated the droll if not preposterous notion that a publishing house should be run as a business. The patent hilarity of this was unfortunately wasted on the editors who lost their jobs and the writers who were thereby orphaned— but hey, things change, media evolve, and that's just how it is. You get with the program or you find a different line of work.

Marcie Kanin—unlike more than a few of my friends—was one of the veterans who'd made the cut; I admit I felt a petty impulse to resent her for that, but I realized in the first moments of our conversation that I wouldn't be able to hold her professional survival against her. She was savvy, she was nice; she had humor and an edge. On her desk was a framed photograph of two kids—girls, maybe ten and eight—but no spouse or partner, and I wondered if she was a single working mom, someone who was a solid pro because she had to be. In any case, she quickly and gracefully dispensed with the usual blah-blah-blah about how much she enjoyed my stuff, and got right down to business. "So. Robert Maxx," she said. "How much you know about him?"

"Nothing except what everybody knows," I said.

"Have you read his other books?"

I tried not to make a face while admitting that I hadn't. Then, like a high schooler hoping to avoid a particularly onerous assignment, I added, "Do I have to?"

Marcie Kanin gave a little laugh. I looked at her more closely. She was right around my age, dark hair with reddish glints piled on her head, quick and lively hazel eyes against the pale skin of a person who made her living reading. Either I'd been on my own too long, or there was something undeniably fetching about her—some of that shake-loose-the-hairpins-and-go-wild sort of librarian appeal. "Probably just as well you don't," she said. "They're just full of business platitudes. Predictable stuff. What I'm hoping we can do together is something very different."

So there it was again—that fond, vague hope for a new concept, a fresh approach. I sat there, waiting her out. If I was flunking the audition, so be it. I really had nothing to say.

Then Marcie Kanin surprised me; amazed me, in fact. She leaned forward on her elbows, fixed me with those hazel eyes, and all at once she was on fire.

"Look," she said. "I've got this off-the-wall idea. Maybe it's terrible but maybe it's good. The other evening I'm watching TV with my kids. *Animal Planet.* The show's about a baboon troop, the struggles for status and power and sex. Fascinating! So human. There's shifting alliances. Bullies and suck-ups and jokers and sneaks. And all of a sudden I think, 'Jesus, give these monkeys briefcases and silk ties, and they're businesspeople.' And then I thought the way to do the Maxx book—the way to make it real and alive—is to look at this guy's life like you're going on safari. What he does—forget that it's business, forget that it's happening in privileged places in New York. Bring it back to the elemental. Turf. Territory. Life and death. I want it to read like it's happening in the jungle. Fists and fangs. Cunning. Domination. Let me smell the sweat when things get tight. Make me cringe at the humiliation of the guys who get outmaneuvered or pushed around. Make me cheer when the worm turns. What do you think?"

"I love it!" I said.

For everything that's changed in publishing, there are some few things that haven't. One of them, thank God, is the excitement that sparks when an editor and a writer click on an idea. Adrenaline spurts; there's a warmth in the belly as from a swig of scotch; a book starts to seem possible, maybe even worth the trouble. I leaned way forward, matching Marcie's posture, narrowing the space between us, and blathered on. "The primitive rituals of the alpha male! The limo as sedan chair. The power tie as both phallus and shield. The firing as human sacrifice. Gotta find some way to work cannibalism into the mix . . ."

We were on a roll, having a fairly sexy kind of brain fun, but then I had a troubling thought that stopped me cold.

"But wait," I said. "Why would Maxx let us do this? I mean, we're not talking advice or safe little anecdotes here. He'd have to let me in on all kinds of confidential stuff. He'd be totally exposed."

Marcie leaned back in her chair and with quiet assurance she said, "I think he'll go along. I'm almost sure he will."

She paused. In the silence I noticed for the first time that her office smelled like paper. That's another thing that hasn't changed about publishing—the dusty smell of manuscripts and the electric smell of printer ink and the waxy smell of new laminated covers. To me those bookish aromas are as homey as the bouquet of baking bread. "But why? Why would he?"

"I've met with him a couple times," she said. "He's a very interesting man."

Her face changed slightly when she said this, her pallor took on just the palest flush, and I understood at once that there was a component of sexual attraction in her response to Robert Maxx. *Animal Planet* indeed! There seems to be something hardwired into us that inclines women—even smart women—to be drawn to swaggering jerks with power, some atavistic voice that whispers, *Fuck this guy and your off-spring will be well protected and your DNA will prosper.* It's unthinking and irrational, but no more so than the stab of jealousy I felt upon seeing the color in Marcie's cheeks and the slight squirm in her posture.

"He seems to understand," she went on, "that at this stage of the game, it's almost incidental that he's a businessman. What he's really become is a public entertainer. He provides spectacle. He spins off controversy. Look, he's an epic or a farce or a soap opera just waiting to happen, and I think he'll let you as far inside as you dare to go."

She broke off. My head was spinning. Somewhere in my mind I was already roughing out scenes, imagining fraught exchanges. Rather absently I asked, "What's the pay?"

"That's between you and Maxx," she said. "He pays the writer out of his advance."

"What's he getting?"

Marcie looked away, picked up a pencil, tapped the eraser on her blotter. "Sorry, but I can't tell you that."

"Okay, I know you can't. You didn't. So what's he getting?"

She glanced toward her open doorway and spoke very softly. "Five million."

I stifled a wow. This was publishing, not Hollywood or Wall Street or Dubai. In our quaint little village, five million bucks was still a lot of money.

"It's a big bet, but we think he's worth it." Then, as an afterthought, she threw me a bone. "And we know you'll deliver something exceptional."

Exceptional? That was a stretch. But I believed by now that I could deliver a workmanlike product, and it would have a celebrity's name stamped on it, and if it sold even half as well as Porter & Kraft was wagering that it would, it would provide some restorative luster, a face-lift, to my slightly faded and slightly sagging résumé. I went home to study up on Robert Maxx.

Chapter 3

The skeleton bio went something like this:

Robert Maxx was born in Southampton, New York, in 1946. Contrary to his posturing as a rough-and-ready self-made man, he was a millionaire many times over from the instant he slipped out of the womb. Stubborn and combative as a kid, he was kicked out of several private schools before being sent off to a Virginia military academy where he did well enough to gain acceptance to a so-so college; he transferred after two years to a better school, from which he earned a bachelor's degree. That was as far as his formal education went; he didn't have an MBA, though he never corrected people who assumed he did.

Straight out of college, he joined the family business—a quite substantial, though virtually unknown, real estate company. Almost immediately, he set about upgrading the company's holdings and raising its profile. No more apartment buildings in Cincinnati or warehouses in Pittsburgh! Now it was skyscrapers in New York, wildly expensive office blocks in Tokyo, speculative dabbling in a Berlin that was still divided.

Clearly, the young Maxx was intent on becoming a player on the worldwide stage—and he did so by burdening the family business with vast amounts of debt. On two occasions—well reported at the time, but later nearly expunged from the record—he came very close to bankruptcy, but avoided ruin by quietly shifting ownership of many properties to his bankers, leaving other investors and creditors to absorb substantial, and in some cases catastrophic, losses. The full details of these arrangements were never publicly revealed.

In the mid-1970s, he married a Polish fashion model, Kasha Swiatkowski. Six feet tall and famously blond, she seemed to be the Heisman of trophy wives, but the marriage didn't last. Maxx began a dalliance with a former Miss Kentucky, then another with a Romanian countess, then another with a highly telegenic business journalist, and so on down the line. According to the tabloids, his current squeeze was a lissome television actress—known equally for her smashing looks and her sometimes ill-considered candor on the talk-show circuit—whom he'd originally met when they were both judges at a beauty pageant in Bangkok.

By the 1980s, Maxx had somehow become, both at home and abroad, an emblematic figure of American enterprise—a questionable honor he had never yet surrendered. His name was stamped on hotel stationery and casino chips; his face had adorned the covers of *Time* and *Paris-Match*. From Dublin to Sydney, everyone knew his carnivorous smile that was never far from a snarl.

But for all of that . . . who was Robert Maxx, *really*? I sat at the computer in my bathrobe, a mug of tepid coffee on my left, a good old-fashioned yellow pad on my right, and I had to admit that I didn't have a clue. The Web offered literally millions of references to him, but in some strange postmodern way this avalanche of information resulted not in comprehension but in a highly detailed fog. Every so-called fact was larded with a heavy coat of hype and spin and punditry and bullshit; every purported insight was undermined by a contrary opinion. The human being within the celebrity husk remained hidden in broad daylight.

Take the simplest of questions: Was Robert Maxx a good or bad businessman? After a quarter century in the public spotlight, you'd think the answer would be clear. But it wasn't. Not even close. Maxx had been called everything from an entrepreneurial wizard to a one-man third-world country. When things were going well, the business press fawned on him for his boldness and imagination. When he went into the tank, those very same approaches were labeled recklessness and greed. That he was a brilliant salesman who was very handy with other people's money was unquestioned—but did that make him a visionary or a con man? It was really a case of take-your-pick.

In his personal life, too, everything was inference and interpretation. Was Robert Maxx the suavest of men-about-town, drawing beautiful women by his charm and witty conversation? Or was he just a leering pussy hound who used his wealth and fame in a pathetic effort to get back at the cheerleaders who wouldn't date him when he was a nobody in high school? Opinions ran the gamut; there were even occasional suggestions that his showy squiring of gorgeous women was nothing but a mask for being gay.

Even his family background—a settled matter, you would think—seemed open to wildly divergent readings. The official version presented Maxx's forebears as models of Scotch-Irish prudence, piety, hard work, and thrift. Other researchers told it rather differently.

According to one account, Maxx's great-grandfather—born Eamon McDermott—had fled the Ould Sod for America just one boat ahead of being transported to Australia for petty theft. By the time he reached Ellis Island, the patriarch's name had become Edward Maxx, and life had granted him a do-over. Working with a pick and shovel on the fabled New York aqueduct, he developed a knack for poker as well as an eye and an appetite for New World real estate, picking up muddy rural parcels as his winnings allowed. His son—Maxx's grandfather—became a builder and a landlord, slapping up so-called workers' housing, not to say slums, on the gradually appreciating land. By the time Maxx's father came of age, the workers' shacks had become low-rent apartment buildings in half a dozen cities, and there was something of an empire to be managed—albeit a shabby empire, devoid of glitz or grandeur, excellent for cranking out money but rather useless in terms of the social-climbing ambitions of

Maxx's stiff, forbidding mother. Mutually disappointed, the parents seem to have lived a life of polite and prosperous misery.

Robert was their firstborn son. Although he would grow up to work closely with his father, it seemed that he had far more in common with his mother. Like her—according to some accounts, at least—he never really respected his old man; like her, he looked down on his father's satisfaction with safe and stolid riches. Maxx *père* seemed to see himself as merely the steward of an existing fortune; he played defense, shunned risk, avoided debt as something intrinsically unclean. But what the older man saw as prudence, Maxx saw as a despicable lack of nerve and failure of imagination. In this, Robert was a throwback to the earlier Maxxes—the flamboyant gamblers whose natural impulse was to double down on every bet, borrowing a stake whenever necessary. The clash between father and son was fundamental, almost biblical. Maxx was goading the older man, elbowing him aside, before he himself had even come of age.

Then there was the imperfectly kept secret of Maxx's younger brother, Anthony.

Very little had been written about the only sibling, in part at least because, early in adulthood, he'd shed the Maxx name and gone back to the original McDermott. Whether this was simply to preserve his privacy or to dissociate himself from his famous brother, it seemed impossible to say. Either way, he'd managed to live his life mostly below the radar. All that was known about him was that he was a painter of no particular distinction, as well as an art collector and sometime patron of talents larger than his own. It had also been reported—though details were few and far between—that he'd spent a fair bit of time shuttling in and out of discreet and extremely costly mental institutions. As to his relationship with his older brother, there didn't seem to be one; reading between the lines, it appeared that Anthony's name change and voluntary disappearance were nothing but a relief to Robert.

In any case, I spent the afternoon, the evening, and the next morning wading through this stuff, and as I read I found myself thinking of Jay Gatsby, aka The Great, another business potentate whom no one really knew. In a time when privacy was still possible, Gatsby had crafted his own disguise; he seemed to understand that if he merely hinted at being the person he wished he was, and looked the part at every moment, then the expectations of others would do the rest, because people wanted to believe. This was an insight and a stratagem that, consciously or otherwise, Robert Maxx seemed to have adapted to the information age. He gave the press and the bloggers everything they wanted, and the result was that everybody *thought* they knew him; this, paradoxically, turned out to be the perfect cover. People rarely trouble to look past what they already think they know.

For better or worse, however, I had a book to write, and if there was to be any chance at all of making it a worthwhile book—a book, for starters, that would keep *me* entertained during the months that I'd be living with it—then I had to get beyond the image, chip away at the heavy varnish that had been slathered on the icon, and get back to flesh and blood. That wasn't going to happen while I was sitting on my ass in front of a computer screen in the threadbare comfort of my own apartment. I would have to leap into the fray—or, as Marcie Kanin had put it, the jungle.

I called and told her that I had done my homework and was ready to meet with my new subject. She said she'd call his office to get me an appointment.

I assumed this would take some days or even weeks, but Marcie called me back within the hour and told me that I'd be seeing Robert Maxx at 4 P.M. next day.

"Tomorrow?"

"He seems really hot to trot on this," she said.

"Why?"

"Who knows? Maybe he's hard up for the advance."

At the time we both thought she was kidding.

I cleared my throat, already getting nervous at the prospect of the meeting. "Any advice? For how to deal with him, I mean."

She thought that over for a moment. Then she said, "Leave your ego at the door. He has enough for both of you."

Chapter 4

Robert Maxx's office was on the fifty-first floor of a glass box that bore his name very near the southeast corner of Central Park. I took this as a good omen, as fifty-one has long been one of my lucky numbers. Don't ask me why. It struck me as lucky many years ago and so it has remained.

Sixteen elevators glutted up the building's lobby, but only one of them went all the way to Maxx's floor and it had its very own security guard stationed in front of it. I got cleared for takeoff and rocketed upstairs.

The elevator door opened in front of a sort of rosewood podium where a receptionist sat. She wore a wireless headset and had a charming, if slightly suspect, British accent. She directed me to a small waiting area, where I plopped down on a leather chair that was as soft as a newborn puppy. After a few minutes an assistant appeared. She was a young black woman, over six feet tall and gorgeous in mid-height heels. She had latte-colored skin, shocking yellow-green eyes, a small nimbus of fluffy hair like an Afro dandelion, and very cool glasses—narrow rectangles of magenta wire. She extended her arm in an assertive handshake and introduced herself as Jenna Cole. She led me to the most gigantic office I had ever seen in all my life.

It was smaller than, say, Carnegie Hall, but not by a hell of a lot. Huge windows on two sides let in more light than I'd believed ever fell on Manhattan. There was a conference table with a dozen baronial chairs as well as several living rooms' worth of sofas and lamps. Potted palms and ficuses flourished under the twenty-foot ceiling. Off in the distance, raised up, altarlike, was the platform that held Robert Maxx's acre of desk. We approached, our footsteps alternately ticking on the hardwood parquet or melting into Oriental rugs.

And now I had my first in-person glimpse of the famous Robert Maxx. He was wearing a powder-blue shirt with an immaculate white collar and a burgundy silk tie. His dark brown hair seemed strangely brittle—too much coloring? too much spray?—and it cantilevered well beyond the contour of his scalp. I couldn't immediately see his face. He was looking down, sucking what seemed to be an enormous soft drink through a straw. He kept on working it until the liquid was nearly gone, and there came that rasping, plumbing sound of air being inhaled through the dregs of the ice. He moved the straw around to slurp the last of it, then he looked up.

He half stood behind his desk and extended a soft hand, a hand with the tender consistency of a rare filet mignon. "Robert Maxx," he said. "Thanks for coming in."

I took a moment to study him. He wasn't bad-looking but he wasn't handsome, either. He just missed out because of a certain thickness in his features. He had a big chin that was a bit too heavy for the clean, square line of a really handsome jaw. The eyes were dark, alert, but somehow muddy, ringed, and pinched by pads of flesh that made them look a little piggy.

"David Collins," I said. "Thanks for taking the time."

He motioned me into a chair, offered me Pellegrino or coffee. I declined. Jenna disappeared without a sound.

"So, Dave," he said, settling once again into his high-backed chair, "Margie Kanin thinks you're pretty good."

This was a bad start, twice. You'd think that a $5 million advance would have been enough incentive to get his editor's name right; but okay, that was Marcie's headache. But I had this Dave thing to deal with. No one calls me Dave. Dave is a name for a bait-shop owner or the worst guy on your bowling team.

"I prefer David," I said.

"Sure. Whatever. She sent over a couple of your books. I see you did one for Mike McIntyre."

"Yeah," I said. "Six, eight years ago."

"Small world. He was a friend of mine. What'd you think of him?"

I wasn't sure if he was easing in with chitchat, or if I was being tested, or if Maxx just felt the need to remind me that he was in the tight club of famous big shots. The late Mike McIntyre had virtually invented the sports-agenting industry. You couldn't put a game or tournament on television without slipping him his vig. He was a selfish, ruthless, jock-sniffing sociopath. Coward that I am, I said, "Interesting man."

"Total prick," said Maxx, with finality but not rancor. "Brilliant, but a prick. I read a few pages of your book. You made him sound like a really nice guy. You always do that?"

"Depends on the job."

Maxx raised a finger toward me. It was a very small gesture, not threatening in any obvious way, yet there seemed to be a whiff of violence in it that unsettled me. "Well, I don't want you doing that for me," he said. "I don't need to come across as nice. I'm way past that. People do business with me because they need me, not because they think I'm nice."

While I took that in I glanced around the office. On a nearby wall was a cluster of posed photos. I counted Robert Maxx with four mayors, three governors, and two presidents. "So how *do* you want to come across?" I asked.

He considered that for a moment, then gestured toward his own well-padded rib cage. "Like I am. Like a guy who says what's on his mind. Like a guy who finds a way to win."

I took a small notebook from my pocket. It's a good thing to hide behind when I'm about to ask a question that might be touchy. "But winning means different things to different people," I said. "What does it mean to you?"

He looked at me like it was the dumbest question he'd ever heard.

I said, "If I'm going to get your voice right, this is the kind of thing I need to understand. Is it just about money? Or is it more than that?"

He pinched his fleshy lower lip. "Usually it's money. Of course it is. But there's also the satisfaction of convincing people, having an idea and seeing it happen." He seemed unaccustomed to explaining things and grew suddenly impatient. "But look, if you need to worry about what winning is, you're probably a loser. You know it when it happens. You feel it in your pants."

There was a pause. Not being that interested in what happened in Robert Maxx's pants, I looked away. Beyond the privileged windows, the late-afternoon light was growing more viscous and golden. From where I sat, I saw nothing but a naked and luxurious swath of atmosphere. In teeming New York, the empty space was beautiful.

"Anyway, you're coming on board at the perfect time. I have some big stuff coming up. Huge stuff. All strictly confidential. That's rule one. Understood?"

I nodded that it was.

"Handled right, it's gonna make a terrific book."

I scratched my neck, then said, "Excuse me, Mr. Maxx—"

"Robert."

"Robert. Maybe I'm missing something, but I don't see how things can be strictly confidential and also put into a book that we hope will be read by millions of people."

This seemed to me a pretty basic paradox. But, as I would learn, contradiction was so much a part of Maxx's personality that he really couldn't see it. As a businessman, he was compulsively secretive—secretive to the point of paranoia; but as a celebrity and public entertainer, he craved being talked about. So he was always doing this coy little dance, both revealing and concealing, teasing and withholding. If his name vanished from the papers for a while, he was miffed; if tidbits leaked out beyond his control, he was furious.

"Look," he said, "things are confidential until I say they aren't. Stuff comes out on my schedule, no one else's. Margie talk to you about the way she sees the book?"

Once again, I played it cautiously. I really didn't know what the editor had said to Robert Maxx, but I doubted that she'd pitched the project to him as a jungle story populated by would-be alpha primates jousting for first dibs at the bananas and the females. "I know she wants it more immediate—"

"Like a memoir, but a memoir of the present. That's how she put it to me, and I think it's pretty damn good. Think you can do it?"

This was the part of the audition I'd been waiting for. I mentioned a while ago that I am nearly paralyzed with fear at the start of every project. That's true. But it's also true, if a seeming inconsistency, that writing books is the only thing in life that I am truly confident about. Here was my chance to voice that confidence. "Robert," I said, "I can definitely do it. The only question is how you want it done."

"Meaning?"

"How much do you want to be involved? How much time do you want to give it? You and I can have three conversations, I disappear for four, five months, call in with a question now and then, and you end up with a book that sounds pretty much like you. It would sell and it would be plenty good enough. I'm guessing that's how your other books were done."

He didn't respond to that, and he didn't have to.

"If that's what you want," I said, "I'm fine with it. Easy for you, easy for me."

I paused. Maxx had cocked his head and seemed to be looking at something just over my right shoulder.

Then I did something really dumb; I kept on talking, I'm not sure why. Maybe I was just echoing Marcie Kanin's wishes, trying to be a good scout and give my editor what she wanted. But I think it was more than that. I think I was goaded on by some tattered remnant of adolescent belief that I was born to write something someday that might actually be of consequence. I mean, a fascinating if rather odious billionaire, as seen through the eyes of a ghostwriter who did not have to pretend that his subject was a nice guy. This could actually be good. This could actually be worth more effort and more passion than the usual half-ass ghosting job.

"Or we can try to do something better than that. Something real. Something with some heart and guts in it. Something that—excuse me—isn't one more bullshit business book."

He didn't seem to take offense. In fact he looked intrigued. "And that would be . . . ?"

I was winging it. I knew I was digging myself a deeper hole. I couldn't seem to stop. "If we really want to do this right, I move into your life and really observe. So I don't have to fake it. I take things down first-hand. Like reality TV, okay? And I'm the camera."

Maxx leaned back in his enormous chair and locked his fingers behind his head. After a moment he said, "You're *here*? You watch? You listen in?"

I nodded.

"Jesus. Sounds like a big pain in the ass."

"It would be. For both of us."

With each heartbeat I was starting to realize just how much of a pain it would be. What the hell was I doing to myself? Meetings. Suits. Shaving first thing in the morning. I tried to edge away from the brink, move back toward the safe and lazy and conventional way to do this job. I said, "It's probably a bad idea. I'm just thinking out loud. "

He didn't seem to hear that. His eyes had gone out of focus and something interesting was happening to his face. The flesh of his fore-head was softening, his mouth was easing toward a slightly cockeyed smile that was smaller but more genuine than the meat-eater's grin he saved for the media. There was mischief in the smile, boyish zest; it was my first inkling of how seductively likable Robert Maxx could be at rare unguarded moments.

"The bankers would shit," he said, and he gave a quick bark of a laugh.

"Excuse me?"

"The cash guys. The equity guys. The great minds of the lending business, sub-prime and otherwise. They'd shit if they knew there was a writer in the room."

I took the opportunity to backpedal. "You're right. I guess it's really not a good idea. I mean, you and I could just *talk* about those meetings."

But it was too late. The billionaire had caught the contagion of my ill-advised enthusiasm, and he was on a roll.

"You can't tape," he said. "That's out of the question. Tapes are like a loaded gun. Just notes. And we can't say you're a writer. We'll need a cover for you. Special assistant. Confidential secretary. Something vague like that."

By now I was really squirming. I felt like I was being sentenced—no, that I'd sentenced myself—to however many months as a prisoner in Robert Maxx's life, a life that was unimaginably different from the serene and tiny life that I was used to. "Robert," I said, "please, let's back up a step or two. This could be wildly impractical. I really think we need to think it over."

"Definitely," he said, though I didn't believe him for a second. "We'll think it over, sleep on it. It's not like anything's signed. But while you're here, we should talk about the fee."

More out of my depth at every second, I said, "I usually let my agent handle that."

He gestured like brushing lint away. "Agents fuck things up. Here's the deal. They're giving me a million. I'll cut you in for ten percent. A hundred grand."

Professionally, I try to pass as a reasonably savvy, street-smart guy, but the truth is that in many ways I have led a very sheltered life. I didn't have much experience of someone looking me in the eye and lying through his teeth. The odd part is that he didn't have to do it. He could have simply said he was willing to pay a hundred thou, period. In my line of work, that's a pretty decent payday, and I would probably have taken it without question. But who knows—maybe the bullshit was part of what made it fun for him. Part of the nasty pleasure he felt in his pants when he believed that he was winning.

I took too long to respond. Maxx may have suspected that I knew he'd lied to me. If so, he didn't seem to care. Maybe he even wanted me to know, because in some alpha primate way, he wanted to send me a message of dominion. Like he'd said, people didn't do business with him because he was nice, but because they needed him; and the fact was that he could find another out-of-work writer a whole lot easier than I could dig up another celebrity billionaire. Struggling to save face, I said, "My agent will go nuts if I agree to something without involving him. I'm sure you understand."

"Sure, sure, whatever," he said, and then he smiled. It was the phony smile, the official one, stiff and rote and toothy, nothing like the small amused one that had made me almost like him just a few short moments before. As I would come to know too well, this was vintage Maxx. He pulled you in only to remind you that you counted for nothing, that no one held a place in Robert Maxx's inner circle except Robert Maxx himself. I tried not to take it personally. He probably did it with everyone.

He extended his hand to let me know that the meeting was over. And before our fingers were even disengaged, his eyes got restless, like he was already on to the next project, the next negotiation, the next chance to prove himself a winner. "Think about it, Dave. I'll think about it, too. We'll be in touch."

I slipped my notebook into my pocket and took the long walk through the giant office.

Chapter 5

After my sit-down with Robert Maxx, I badly wanted a drink. I'm not, God knows, above drinking alone, and I can't believe that any writer is, but generally it's not my preference. So I headed north and west through Central Park, got clear of the filtered din of rush-hour traffic, took out my phone, and called my ex-wife.

Claire and I were married for six years and we've been divorced for eight. Since splitting up, we've both dipped toes into other relationships, but we're still each other's closest friend. You might think that's fucked up, and you might be right, but please don't judge too hastily. Nobody knows anything about anybody else's marriage, and the same goes for their divorces. We had a youthful marriage that was very sweet for a while, then smashed against certain realities and turned bewilderingly sour. Our divorce, on the other hand, started off bitter and has only gotten more sweet, caring, and maybe even grown-up. You tell me which trend is healthier.

Her line was busy. I put the phone away and kept on walking.

It was around five-thirty. The afternoon was still quite mild, long shadows stretched away from the sycamores and willows. The park was mobbed. All around me there was a flow of humanity so massive and purposeful as to seem almost Chinese. Tens of thousands of worker bees—men and women, young and old, black and white, straight and gay—were fleeing midtown in sneakers, carrying their shoes in brief-cases or canvas totes, rushing home to cramped apartments to feed cats, walk dogs, snip limp leaves from housebound plants; to be them-selves in the part of the day that was their own.

This world of nine-to-five had always been a foreign country to me. I'd observed it on occasion as if I were a tourist or an anthropologist. Suddenly I was being pulled into the human tide, becoming a part of the lemminglike march to midtown and the slouching exodus back home. If this book went forward, I wouldn't just be going on safari with Robert Maxx and his club of big shots. I'd be entering the actual world of work, getting a taste of what most people had to do to pay the rent. What had I done to myself?

I tried my ex again and this time I got through. I asked her if she'd like to join me for a cocktail. She thought it over then said she didn't feel like going out, why didn't I come by for a glass of wine. Frankly, this is what I'd hoped she'd say. I still like being alone with her. I still find her company soothing.

So I walked to her apartment, in the middle of a park block in the West Seventies. It was a place she'd had since her student years at Juil-liard. As Manhattan real estate went increasingly crazy, it had become far too good a deal to give up. Plus, there was the problem of the piano. Claire had a Steinway grand that took up about three-quarters of her living room. The instrument had had to be largely disassembled to get it up the two flights of narrow stairs and through the grudgingly pro-portioned doorway. Its dark bulk in such a modest room had some of the glorious improbability of a sailboat in a bottle; getting it out again was almost inconceivable.

I rang the front doorbell and entered on the answering buzz. Claire was standing in the hallway when I'd made it to her landing. At the first glimpse of her, I felt what I always feel but try to deny: I felt like I was coming home. It's a stupid and self-lacerating thing to feel about a person you're not married to anymore, but there it is.

Claire isn't classically beautiful, but I have always savored the sight of her. Her looks remind me of a cartoon character. Not any character in particular—just the way those hand-drawn figures always seem to have a few characteristics that are endearingly exaggerated and make them instantly distinct. With Claire it was mainly her eyes and her hair. Her eyes were dark saucers, sometimes almost liquid-seeming, and wider open than most eyes—so wide that they seemed taller than they measured across. Her hair was chestnut brown and very thick. Parted in the middle, it hung down shoulder length in tight curls like fusilli pasta. She was very thin—too thin, really, as even she would sometimes admit. She ate fine. It's just how she was made. Her hipbones stuck out, she had little points on the tops of her shoulders, and when she gave me a hug, I could feel her bottom rib and also feel her heartbeat, which was right there on the surface.

We went into the apartment. It smelled like that tea that women love, the one with clove and orange. Aside from the huge piano, the living room held only a tiny dining table with two spindly stools, a lumpy-looking chair for reading, and a munchkin-size settee with a coffee table in front of it. Call it artsy-fartsy-spartan. It was the only kind of decorating in which I felt truly at ease. A bottle of red wine was breathing. There were two glasses and a candle. This wasn't meant to be romantic—just civilized. Claire poured and we clinked.

"So, what you been up to?" I asked.

She lifted her thin shoulders in a shrug. "Nothing much. The usual. Lots of teaching. A couple of my students are doing really well. I've got a Russian boy who's off to conservatory in Tokyo, and a Korean girl who's being taken on by Pommier in Paris. She's really good, especially her Chopin. She's got a real shot at a career."

"Ah," I said, and restrained myself from saying anything more, because if I said more it was bound to come out rueful or maudlin or bitter or sarcastic. The ever-elusive musical career. That was one of the two things that had poisoned our sweet little youthful marriage. The other was the ever-elusive literary career.

When Claire and I first got together, we fancied ourselves—as did so many young couples with big dreams and at least a modicum of talent—as a golden duo, a supernal pair who would be written up in magazines, recognized in restaurants. Not rich, necessarily, but successful, accomplished, respected. Claire Martell, concert pianist. David Collins, major novelist. If the fantasy was naive and grandiose, it was not entirely far-fetched. Claire was a stunning musician, transcendent, a favorite of her world-class teachers, who were grooming her for the most important competitions, the Tchaikovsky and the Cliburn. As for me, I was doing honors work at Columbia, finishing up a master's thesis on point of view in the later works of Joseph Conrad, while also bleeding out the coming-of-age story that would become my first published novel. We were both on the launchpad of great things. We married, and our marriage bed was like a great, fluffy, fair-weather cloud, sun-shot full of hope.

And then things didn't quite work out. Not for her. Not for me. Nothing terrible happened; we just came up a wee bit short, and the narrowness of the miss only made it more bewildering and excruciating. Claire performed beautifully at the competitions, and didn't win. Her recitals in New York drew favorable notices but not the kind of raves that led to bookings in the bigger venues. Meanwhile, my first novel came and went, and neither my life nor the literary universe was much transformed by it. On my second outing the critics were less generous. We'd both hit the wall.

It was probably inevitable that we blamed each other. In some dim, inchoate way, I was holding her back. In some equally vague manner, she was thwarting me. Or so we imagined. There were arguments, recriminations. We worked very hard at being angry with each other. But as we came to realize only much later, we weren't angry. We were embarrassed. The dreams we once shared mocked us. Our ambitions, because we'd fallen short of them, seemed conceited and ridiculous. We were a constant reminder to each other that we'd failed to do the things we'd hoped we would. It was less galling to part, to lick our wounds in separate corners.

Claire's voice pulled me out of my thoughts. "And you?" she said. "What's been going on with you?"

I sipped some wine before I answered. "Well, I've just come from a very interesting meeting with one of my least favorite people in the whole wide world."

"Ann Coulter?"

"Robert Maxx."

"You serious?"

I nodded. "I may be writing a book for him."

"Wow," she said. It was just one syllable—spontaneous, maybe even impressed, and no doubt meant to be supportive; absurdly, though, I read my own ambivalence into it.

"I think it could actually be good," I said, as if someone had suggested that it couldn't be.

"I'm sure it could. That boardroom-drama stuff. You could write the hell out of that. I mean, write it like it was a novel."

"The editor's idea is sort of business as a primal ritual. Monkeys with boners in Armani suits."

Claire laughed. I love her laugh. It's soft and low-pitched, but it carries. "I can hear the sound track now," she said. "Cash registers playing *Rite of Spring.*"

She made slow drumming gestures, like beating hollow tree trunks or playing tympani. Then she reached for her wineglass and two completely unexpected, flabbergasting things happened.

The first was that she spilled her wine. Somehow her fingers failed to grasp the stem of her glass, knocking against the bowl instead. The glass teetered, tipped, and fell with a dull clink, spreading wine in a dark puddle.

This was shocking only because Claire is the most graceful person I have ever known. She moves deliberately, she flows like music. There's a quiet in her motion that begins with the skill of her hands. Her knife and fork make no sound when she puts them down. She makes buttoning a button seem a tiny act of Zen perfection. Now she recoiled from her fallen glass with a kind of shame and horror.

The second thing that happened was even more surprising. She started to cry. Claire is not a crier. She didn't cry when she lost the crucial competitions. She didn't cry when we pointlessly argued and spewed blame at each other. But, now she cried, and seemed mad at herself for doing so. She tried to squeeze back the tears that welled at the outside edges of her eyes and spilled down along her cheekbones.

Baffled, I reached clumsily toward the coffee table, picked up the glass, and chased spilled wine with a paper napkin. "It's okay," I said. "It's just a little wine."

Looking down, she shook her head. It didn't seem like she was disagreeing; more that she was fending something off, trying to push away an awful thought.

Awkwardly, I touched her shoulder. "What is it?"

She sniffled, labored for a deep breath that racked her thin body, then looked up at me. "My hands," she said. "I'm having trouble with my hands."

I didn't get it. It didn't register. I said, "What kind of trouble?"

She held them up between us. Slender and sinewy wrists. Long pale fingers ending in spatulate tips and short, neat, unpolished nails.

"I don't know. At times it's like I don't know what they're doing. Like they're not a part of me. I can't tell if my hand is closed or open. I think a finger's moving, and it isn't."

I sat there, utterly helpless. I tried to think of something comforting to say, but I couldn't. A long moment passed. Claire wiped at her eyes. Struggling for control, she made a tiny sound, barely audible, but in its soul it was a shriek.

"David," she said. "I'm scared. I'm really scared."

I took her hands in mine. To me they felt as they had always felt, precise and strong. "Have you seen a doctor?"

She bit her lip. "I've seen two," she said. "I've had an X-ray and an MRI. They haven't shown anything."

Stupidly, I said, "Well, that's good, right?"

"No," she said, "it isn't. If they found something, they could fix it. I'm supposed to see another specialist next week."

She paused, then pulled her hands away and retreated against the back of the settee. "But, Jesus, I didn't mean to burden you with this. You've got better things to—"

I interrupted her. I think I must have been in shock. I mean literal, clinical shock, because my sense of time and memory was all screwed up. It was like a bunch of years and a thousand things just hadn't happened, and I very nearly said, *Claire, hey, you're my wife.* Instead, I caught myself and said, "Claire, hey, I'm your friend."

By the time I left the old apartment with the huge piano, my head was spinning and my emotions were a tangle. I'd caught Claire's fear. I felt the corrosive anger that goes with helplessness.

But along with the crap, I felt something unaccustomed and disarmingly nice. I felt gratitude. It was odd—the specter of something going very wrong made me realize in a flash that I'd been insufficiently thankful or attentive to all the things that had gone right. Okay, I wasn't a famous novelist and Claire wasn't a superstar on the concert stage, and we weren't married anymore. But we'd had the great good fortune to be in love for many years and to share a passion for the things we'd tried to do, and we'd even been able, so far, to make our livings from our respective crafts. We were way luckier than most.

I touched every tree along Claire's block, making silent wishes for the health of her hands.

Chapter 6

First thing next morning, I called Paul Hannaford and filled him in on my meeting with Maxx. He was pissed, of course, but only in his usual calm way, that the billionaire had tried to exclude him from the negotiation.

"That's not the worst of it," I said. "You know what he's getting for this book?"

"I asked Marcie. She said she couldn't tell me."

"If that's your story, you stick to it. I think she told you. She told me, too. Five mil. Maxx just flat-out lied about it. He wants to pay me a princely two percent of the advance."

Without the slightest uptick in tone or volume, Paul said, "The guy's a greedy dick, but we knew that going in. Still, I think we can do at least a little better. Lemme call his contracts guy."

We hung up and I went to the computer. Once there, I performed one of the many small but essential rituals by which a project becomes incrementally more real to me: I prepared to create a new folder.

The folder needed a name, and this got me up and pacing. The

name was important. I'd see it every day for as long as I was working on this book; in some subliminal way the name would steer my
thoughts. A bad name would be an annoyance and a distraction. A
good name would keep me believing, keep me pumped. The blue-
sky scenario was that the folder name would prove right and dura-
ble enough to end up as the title. So I paced and pondered but tried
not to force it. I looked out the smudgy window at the building
across the street. I took a dust sample from the sill with my thumb.
I paced some more, straightened a stack of magazines, and then it
came to me.

Maxxed Out.

False modesty aside, I liked it from the start. It was catchy. It was
terse. A weak pun, true, but puns are almost always weak. Still, it resonated; it nailed some things. Maxxing out—and not just for the
billionaires among us—was how we lived: maxxing out on dreams
and ambitions, on caffeine and credit cards; maxxing out on giddy
confidence when things are going well, and on scattershot blame when
they were going badly. We didn't measure; we maxxed. So *Maxxed
Out* it would be.

I created the folder.

Then, feeling that I'd done a pretty good day's work, I closed it and
picked up a magazine.

A while later, Paul Hannaford called back.

Unflappably, he said, "These people are really scumbags. They won't
budge on the basic fee. I got them to put in a best-seller bonus. Twenty-
five thou for anything short of number one. Fifty if you make it to the
top. That's the good news."

I put my feet up on the sofa. "I'm ready for the bad."

"Zero up front," he said. "Zip."

"That's ridiculous."

"It's more than ridiculous. It's unconscionable. They don't care.
Apparently, on the early books, they used to do the standard thing, a
third or so on signing. Then a writer got fed up halfway through a

project, and walked. Maxx went berserk at the thought of being fired by a writer. So now they pay nothing unless you finish the job."

"What if he fires me?" I asked.

"Kill fee's twenty-five," he said. "But it's payable only on the eventual publication of the book. Assuming he gets someone else to finish it."

"That sucks," I said.

"It really sucks," he concurred. "But we're Bambi and they're Godzilla, and this is basically a take-it-or-leave-it offer."

He paused. I could almost hear the air wheezing out of his little blue squeezy ball.

"David," he resumed, "I know I was pushing for this at the start, and the upside is for real. But the truth is that it's a crappy deal. The risk is all on you, and I don't blame you at all if you decide to pass. In fact, it would make my day to call this guy back and tell him in a genteel and businesslike manner to go fuck himself. You want to think it over?"

We hung up and I thought it over. Mainly what I thought about was how accidental life is—a game of inches and moments. For instance, if Paul had called back before I'd thought of *Maxxed Out* and performed the totemic act of naming the new folder, then this unfair and shitty deal might have provided just the out I needed. I might have passed, feeling completely justified, and been finished forever with Robert Maxx. But a certain balance had shifted. I was a small but crucial notch more committed to the project. The fetal book was taking on a heartbeat, and it was much more difficult to walk away.

Make no mistake—I knew that I was getting hosed. Hosed on the fee, hosed on the payout, hosed on the contingencies. I wasn't yet consciously adding up my grievances against Robert Maxx—that would come later—but the grievances were already beginning to accumulate. I comforted myself with two arguable but soothing beliefs. The first was that the risks were moot, because this book was going to happen, if not because I would write a masterpiece, then because the people with the power—the publisher and Maxx himself—wanted it to happen.

The other leap of faith was more personal, less tested, but more stubborn. In a vaguely Buddhist sort of way, I happened to believe that underdogs had a different kind of power, that the advantage was not always where it seemed to be—that sometimes the Bambis of this world ended up with the last laugh. I called my agent and told him I would take the deal.

To ease my pique and my ambivalence, I went out for a run in Riverside Park.

The day was mild, but there was something melancholy in the air, some indefinable but certain sense that change was on the way, that the inevitable winter was edging closer. The sunshine seemed a barely perceptible fraction less robust than it had the day before. The leaves were not yet changing color, but quite suddenly appeared fatigued and brittle. I ran as far as the handball courts at Seventy-second Street, stopped a minute to watch some old guys playing, then headed north again.

Back at home, I found that the day's affronts were not over. I had a phone message from Marcie Kanin. I showered, then returned her call. She told me that Robert Maxx's people were running a background check on me.

"A background check?" I said. "What is this, the fucking CIA?"

"No," she said. "The CIA has frequent leaks. The Maxx Organization doesn't. That's why they do background checks."

"But they can't just—"

"David," Marcie interrupted, "relax. Let them have their fun. They're like kids in a tree house. They have to have code words and secrets. It's part of the game. Background checks, nondisclosure clauses—makes it seem sexy, no?"

"Makes it seem fascist."

"It's just some assistant covering his ass. It's not that big a deal. They want to talk with some of your past editors, some of your previous collaborators. They just want to know that you're discreet."

I stewed, and Marcie no doubt realized that I was stewing, so she moved to change the subject.

"The meeting went well?" she asked.

"It went all right," I said.

"It went more than all right, or they wouldn't be moving ahead this fast. Did you tell him our idea?"

"About him being the number one baboon? No, I didn't go there in as many words."

"Not that. About getting up close. Being in on the action."

"Yeah," I said. "I brought that up."

"And?"

"And you were right. He seemed to go for it."

Marcie savored that for a moment. Then she said, "Did you get to see the B smile?"

"Excuse me?"

"You know, the private one, that little sideways smile. The one that doesn't look like an ad for a denture adhesive."

"Oh Christ," I said. "You think that's a put-on too?"

"I didn't say it's a put-on. I mean, I don't know. Maybe it's fake. Or maybe it's as close as he lets himself come to connecting, to taking off the mask. In my limited experience, he seems to allow himself one of those per meeting."

I said, "There was one thing he was very clear about. He doesn't want me to make him sound like too nice a guy."

Marcie considered that a moment. Then, a little cautiously, she said, "That's really kind of funny, isn't it?"

I said, "I think it's a fucking riot."

Chapter 7

A few days passed, the weekend came and went. I lost a couple of squash matches, made a half-assed attempt to pick up a woman in a much too hip bar over on Amsterdam. But my heart wasn't in it and I guess it showed. The truth is that I was thinking about Claire. She hadn't called. I was afraid to call her. Superstitiously, I feared that if I asked about her hands, the very act of asking might call forth something bad.

On Monday morning I heard from Jenna, Robert Maxx's gorgeous assistant. She had good news. Or, at least that's what she called it. Mr. Maxx was ready to proceed. I guess my background check came back with no big black slashes on it. Contracts were being drawn up. Did I mind coming in that afternoon to go over some procedural things and to meet with Mr. Maxx again?

So, after lunch I put on my best and only suit, and headed for the subway. In the lobby of Maxx Tower I got clearance for the private elevator up to fifty-one. This time, Jenna was waiting to greet me at the elevator door.

She looked fabulous in a midnight-blue jacket and pants. She gave me another of her firm and well-schooled handshakes, and said, "Welcome to the team."

This was an absolutely pivotal moment in my relationship with Jenna, because if there had been no irony, facetiousness, or subversion in the simple words she'd uttered, I'd have known that we would never be friends. So I wanted to believe that I heard a delicate hint of sarcasm, the merest whisper of sedition, a faint acknowledgment that *team* in this connection was just a shade away from *cult,* and that this year's Christmas bonus could be next year's Dixie cup of Kool-Aid. I searched her wild yellow eyes behind the cool magenta glasses for some kind of confirmation. I was pretty sure I saw a twinkle, reinforced by just the slightest curling of full and purplish lips. I provisionally concluded that Jenna would be an ally. I strongly suspected I would need one.

She led me through a maze of corridors to her office. I tried to read the corporate codes to figure out where she stood in the empire. She was no mere assistant, because she *had* an assistant—two, in fact, both of whom sat outside her office in cubicles whose low walls were padded in pearl-gray cloth. Her own space was more than comfy, if not resplendent. It had a big window that looked out over the park, a very handsome desk that was topped with green granite, and a couple of upholstered chairs for visitors. She ushered me in and closed the door behind us.

"So," she said as she motioned me into a chair and settled in behind her desk, "our new writer."

"That's me," I said. "But I thought it was supposed to be a secret."

"It will be," she assured me.

"But you know," I pointed out.

"Of course I do. But that's my job. To know things." She studied me a moment, then added, "And even if I didn't know, I'd know."

"Know what?"

"That you were a writer."

"How?"

"No offense, okay? Your suit doesn't fit that well, your tie's too wide, you should probably have put in a fresh blade when you shaved this morning, and I noticed when you got off the elevator that you're wearing brown shoes."

Ordinarily, I consider myself a fairly natty dresser, and decently groomed to boot. I spend good money on haircuts. My tortoiseshell glasses may not be the hippest in a downtown kind of way, but I maintain that they are arty classics. I've managed to stay reasonably lean, and my pants fit more or less the way they show them in the catalogs. My confidence shaken, I rubbed a hand over my mouth and chin. "Oh, great. So you're saying I look like shit?"

To my surprise she leaned close to me and dropped her voice. "No. I'm just saying you don't look like every fucking B-school clone around here. But don't worry about it. No one else is gonna notice. At worst they'll think you're a computer guy or a finance geek."

She reached into a desk drawer and came up with a magnetic-strip ID card, complete with clip and laminated holder. Handing it to me, she said, "This'll save you the hassle at the elevator. Opens up the bathrooms, everything."

I looked down at the card. It said *Dave Cullen*. "That's not my name," I pointed out.

"I know," she said. "But I thought it might be good to change it just a little bit in case anyone remembers your earlier books—the novels, I mean—and puts two and two together."

Ruefully, I said, "I think it's unlikely in the extreme that I'm going to be meeting anyone who's read my early books."

Almost shyly, her yellow eyes averted, she said, "I have."

Before I could choke back the words, I said, "Part of the background check?"

"No. I read them when they first came out. I thought they were really good."

I was stunned, disarmed. I felt an insane and preposterous urge to weep with gratitude, or to tuck away those kind and simple words as the last thing I would ever hear and throw myself out the window. Instead, I said, "Thank you . . . thank you. Cullen's fine. But this Dave stuff has to stop. It's David. Please."

"Sure," she said, "I'll have a new card made up."

"Think there's any chance you could help Maxx remember?"

She cocked her head. "Oh Jesus, he's still doing that?"

"Doing what?"

"The whole first year I was here, he called me Janet. I must have corrected him twenty times. Was he trying to insult me? Who knows? Maybe. Anyway, if you ever get to the point of mattering to him, he'll get it right. It's like a graduation."

"Maybe I should call him Bob a couple times."

Apparently that was so outré that she didn't even bother answering. Instead, she said, "About your cover story. We're calling you a special strategic assistant. That means nothing, so it's perfect. You've just finished your training in Singapore."

I held up a hand. "I've never even been to Singapore. What if someone—"

"David," she interrupted, "you're an assistant and you don't have tits. Don't worry, no one's gonna talk to you."

"Can we please make it someplace I've been, at least? Montreal maybe?"

She agreed to make it Montreal. Then we sat quietly for a moment. I looked at her in her perfect suit, perched behind her classy desk, sunlight filtering through the edges of her fluffy hair. She was awfully pretty, but what I was thinking about was her poise. She knew how to play this game and I did not. I felt a sudden, silent, first-day-of-school kind of panic that put a metallic taste at the back of my throat. "Do you really think this is going to work?" I asked. "I mean, I've never been a good liar."

"You write fiction."

"Yeah, but not with people watching."

"And no one's going to watch you here. Let me tell you how these meetings work. The focus is always on Robert. Always. Either people are hanging on his every word or they're falling all over themselves to impress him. As long as you keep quiet, you're not a threat. You're not one-upping anyone, not pushing anyone aside. You're just some new guy with a notebook. You're furniture."

"Furniture," I said. "Okay."

"You ready to go in?"

I nodded and stood up. Jenna rose and came around her desk.

"Do you mind?" she asked me, and moved very close. I smelled a faint, piney sort of perfume, and for one deranged and dizzy instant I imagined she was going to kiss me. Instead, she reached for my throat, gently straightened my tie, and fiddled with my shirt collar.

"There," she said, "that's a little better."

"Thanks, Mom," I said.

"You're welcome," said my new ally. "You know, I've always liked writers. When I was a kid, I even wanted to be one someday."

"So did I," I said.

Chapter 8

She led me through the maze of furniture and rugs and sculptures and vases, and across the threshold of Robert Maxx's enormous office. Off in the distance, beyond the conference area, beyond the palms and ficuses and conversation nooks, Maxx was sitting at his desk. His posture was intent and tight, shoulders cinched, elbows propped. He was listening to another man who had his back to us. All I could tell about the other man was that he had a magnificent head of silver hair.

As we came closer, Maxx looked up at Jenna, and at some point, the other man fell silent. I hadn't heard what he'd been saying, but from the pitch and cadence of his voice it seemed that he had discreetly broken off midsentence, possibly midword.

"Robert," Jenna said, "I'm sorry to interrupt, but Mr. Cullen, Mr. David Cullen, has just arrived . . . from Montreal."

As she turned to leave, he looked at her as if he was a bit confused. Then he half rose, faced me, and extended his rare steak of a hand. "Dave," he said, "good to see you again. Glad you're here. Say hello to Arthur Levin."

I knew the name. Everyone who followed business news even casually knew Arthur Levin's name. He was a real estate attorney, one of those people who generally had the epithet *legendary* appended to his job description. He was always being interviewed on TV or in the *Times,* explaining trends or speaking with faultless tact about difficult pending transactions. By reputation, he was a wizard at mediation, a sort of human lubricant who kept the biggest egos from grinding one another, along with their deals, to smithereens. Moreover, he reportedly achieved this not by gamesmanship or any sort of legal razzle-dazzle, but by the simple expedients of decency and candor. In a milieu where everybody hated someone and was hated in return, Arthur Levin seemed to have no enemies.

We shook hands and I sensed his charm at once. He had an open face, pale and slightly watery blue eyes that drew you in, a rather pink complexion that perfectly set off the silver hair. He was probably seventy, but his tall brow was smooth and unfurrowed.

Maxx waved me toward a chair, then turned his attention back to Levin. But the lawyer didn't resume speaking. He flicked his eyes toward me, then shot Maxx a questioning glance. Maxx said, "It's okay, Arthur, Dave will be working closely with me. There's nothing you can't say."

I sat. I scooted my chair an inch farther toward the periphery, hunched as low as I could without appearing to have some terrible spinal issue, and kept my eyes down on my notebook.

Arthur Levin cleared his throat. "As I was saying, Robert, I'm concerned that there'll be complications, backlash about the naming issue. I'm afraid you're making headaches for yourself."

"Headaches?" said the billionaire. "Backlash? Why? My name has added value to everything I've ever put it on. And aside from that, why is it making headaches if I want to change the name of something I own?"

Calmly, the attorney said, "With due respect, you don't own it yet. And more important, ownership is not the only criterion here. There's also public feeling. Emotion. Tradition."

"Tradition is sentimental bullshit," said Maxx. "Look, Saigon was Saigon for a thousand years, then there was a change of ownership, and now it's Ho Chi Minh City. Things change. To the victor goes the spoils. And the victor happens to be me."

"*If* the deal goes through," said Arthur Levin. "That's why I'm urging you to reconsider your position. I'm concerned that you're putting up a big roadblock to its happening at all."

The billionaire gave a derisive little snort. "Oh, Arthur, please. Three and a half billion dollars on the table, and people are going to walk away because of what we call the place? I don't think so."

The attorney raised a Socratic finger. "Excuse me, but the money isn't on the table yet. That's my whole point."

Impatiently, stormily, Maxx said, "It's as good as on the table."

"I beg to differ. Money's not so free and easy anymore. Credit's tight, and getting tighter every day. People are looking much harder at where they lay their bets, and being much tougher as to terms. There's a lot of negotiating still to be done."

"So negotiate!"

Unperturbed, Levin soldiered on. "Which is why I'd hope to avoid complications, intangibles, controversies. Climate like this, people are afraid, they're happy for a reason to say no. Why give them that reason?"

"Jesus, Arthur, they won't say no. There's money to be made."

"There's also money to be lost. There's substantial risk. And the fact is that public opinion is part of the risk. If the Landmarks Commission—"

"Fuck the Landmarks Commission! A couple of fat-ass old matrons who haven't been laid in thirty years and some silly queens who want the whole city to look like a Busby Berkeley set. They mean nothing anymore!"

There was a pause, a standoff. I melted deeper into my chair, happily inconsequential. Marcie Kanin had urged me to capture the tang and the musk of these confrontations in silk and mohair suits. And in fact I could almost feel the heat, the will, throbbing off of Robert Maxx in agitated waves. As for Arthur Levin, he radiated nothing but a mildly insistent calm.

He laid his pink hands on the edge of Maxx's desk and very quietly said, "Robert, it's ultimately your call. But I ask you, I beg you, to try to understand the implications. Look, especially since 9/11, people feel very attached to, very protective of, certain buildings and certain places. They're not just addresses; they're shrines. There's an affection, an emotional resonance. Maybe it's just nostalgia. Maybe it's silly. That's not the point. The point is that people *feel* it."

I listened to Levin, but I was watching Robert Maxx. He didn't seem to want to hear what the older man was saying. His eyes slid away and his lips tightened into a smirk like that of an unremorseful child being scolded. The lawyer went on anyway.

"Think of the associations people have, memories that go all the way back to childhood, all the way back to their *parents'* childhood. Having hot chocolate next to the rink. Seeing the Christmas show at Radio City. Waiting for the big tree to be lit. Robert, it's always been Rockefeller Center. Keep it that way. You'll be seen as a benefactor. Change it, and you'll be cast as a villain. Trust me on this. Please."

Maxx sat in a kind of furious quiet behind his giant desk. Grudgingly, he said at last, "I'll think about it."

The attorney dared to press just a little further. "The people from Knightsbridge Partners are coming in from London on Thursday—"

"Those tea-sipping ballbusters?" Maxx put in. But he said it with respect.

"We need them. So remember—these are Brits. Big on tradition. They still have a queen, for God's sake. They're not going to be comfortable with a name change."

"All right, all right. I said I'd think about it. Arthur, you're a real pain in the ass."

At this the legendary lawyer smiled. "Your father used to say that, too. Quite regularly. Maybe once a month for twenty years. I always took it as a compliment."

"You would."

"I'm a pain in the ass," said Levin, "who tries to keep his clients from making trouble for themselves. It's a much harder job with you."

Maxx, in turn, seemed to take *that* as a compliment. The lawyer snapped his briefcase shut, rose quite spryly from his chair, and left.

I stayed behind. Maxx took a moment to regroup, then he turned to me and eased into the B smile, the seemingly unguarded one, the one he allowed himself once per session. "See?" he said. "I told you I had big stuff coming up."

I acknowledged that it was in fact big stuff. I don't know why he cared that I acknowledged it, but he seemed to.

Then the smile was erased and he pointed a warning finger at me. "Nothing comes out till the money is raised and we officially announce. Got it?"

Back on the street in the late afternoon, I strolled south on Fifth Avenue. I walked to the plaza with the fabulously corny Atlas holding up the globe. I turned west past the skating rink, still rigged up as an overpriced café this time of year. I skirted the barriers that people stand behind to gawk at the *Today* show, then continued to Sixth Avenue, took shade under the marquee of the Radio City Music Hall. I really didn't give a damn who owned the place. But it would be awfully difficult to think of it as anything other than Rockefeller Center.

Chapter 9

After that brief pilgrimage, I turned uptown, and had got as far as Columbus Circle when I remembered to turn my phone on. There was a message from Claire. One of her students was giving an informal recital at Juilliard, just a little performance for faculty and friends. It was at six-thirty, and I was welcome if I felt like showing up.

I killed some time in the park, then headed over to Lincoln Center. I never missed a chance to go to Juilliard. I'd loved the place ever since the earliest days of my relationship with Claire, when I would meet her there for the standard student lunch—cup of yogurt, eaten with a plastic spoon—or join her in the early evening, to slip without a ticket into Alice Tully, or Avery Fisher, or even the Met if she happened to be ushering.

There was a hivelike earnestness about Juilliard that never failed to touch me. White-bloused Asian girls with violins were always hurrying down the hallways, their soft shoes making no sound whatsoever. Skinny boys who were all thick glasses and Adam's apples hustled past with clarinets. From the warren of practice rooms came the belch of tubas, the bray of horns, the farting razz of the slide trombone. Now and then I'd be treated to the splendidly absurd spectacle of a kid trying to maneuver a bass through a doorway.

There was a remarkable thing about young classical musicians: even in New York, even with the competition and the pressure, they never seemed to be lonely. They all seemed to be pals. Some of them dressed funny. More than a few were socially backward with outsiders. It didn't matter. With one another, they seemed comfortable and close. Maybe it was the habit of playing chamber music. They had a shared and sacred language that didn't require words. They intertwined their talents and melded their emotions with little nods and lifted eyebrows; the sounds they made forged an intimate and seemingly effortless bond. I confess I envied them. I also think that this mysterious form of communication was part of what fascinated me about Claire. She could express so much with a tilt of the head or the slightest change in cadence; she could remain entirely herself while blending seamlessly into an ensemble. Me, I need words and explanations, and I carry a certain loneliness inside of me, because I am by temperament a soloist. There is no such thing as chamber music for writers.

I entered the school and found my way to the smallish room where the recital was being given. It was nothing fancy—bare walls, fluorescent lighting, thirty or so folding chairs set up in rather untidy rows. The pianist was a Polish girl, maybe seventeen. She had stately posture, a wide, pretty face, and a distracting habit of flicking her blond hair back from her neck. But once she started playing, I thought she was sublime.

After the concert, Claire and I went out for sushi on Columbus Avenue. As she was sipping her green tea and I was firing down my sake, I said, "What did you think?"

She glanced quickly around the restaurant to make sure she wouldn't be hurting anybody's feelings. "Only so-so. To be honest, so-so at best."

"Wow," I said. "Hard marker."

Claire was wearing a corduroy jumper, forest green, with a navy-blue turtleneck underneath it. That's the way she dresses—dark colors, soft textures, a quiet, modest style that's a perfect counterpoint to her complete assurance when it comes to matters of music. "The Mozart was a little muddy," she said. "The Beethoven had some good moments but was missing that forward drive."

"The Brahms was beautiful," I said.

"Wishy-washy." Her hair swooshed as she shook her head. "Look, with Brahms, you can play it all restrained and dignified to please the critics, or you can schmaltz it up to wow the blue-haired ladies. In between just doesn't work."

I pulled apart my chopsticks and polished one against the other. "Guess I'm lucky to have an amateur's ear," I said. "I thought she was really good."

"Right," she said. "And I can pick up a random bestseller, and get totally swept up in it and think it's grand. You'll come along, read three pages, and decide that it's a piece of garbage. It just depends on how much you know."

"Seems perverse," I said. "The more you know, the harder it is to enjoy something."

"That's true," she said. "But when it's perfect . . ."

She let the thought trail off. When it was perfect, there weren't any words.

Our sushi arrived, a big platter of it set in the middle of the table. I looked at it, and, weirdly, I felt a sudden pang as sharp as a snort of wasabi. I knew exactly which piece Claire would save for last: it would be the salmon with the little curled-up slice of lemon on top. And she knew which piece *I* would save—definitely the yellowtail. And it ripped at me to wonder why, if we knew each other that well, and still liked each other enough so that we sat here gabbing like sophomores about music and writing and life, and if we were perfectly at ease eating sushi off a shared platter . . . then why weren't we together? Understand, I'd wondered about this a million times before. I believe that Claire had, too. For lack of an answer, we'd each fallen in and out of occasional brief relationships with some perfectly nice people whom we just didn't like as much as we liked each other. So here we were again, knees almost touching beneath the small table, regarding the sushi platter as though it were a chessboard, looking ahead to each other's familiar endgames. It kind of broke my heart.

But it was dinnertime, so we ate. After a while I braced myself and said, "How are your hands?"

She gave a dark little laugh and widened her eyes. "For using chopsticks? Or playing the piano?"

I said nothing.

"They're really about the same," she said. "It's just the strangest thing. Most of the time they're perfectly fine. Then they do something out of control. Now and then I get some tingling, sort of pins and needles."

"Have you seen that other specialist?"

She pushed her tea aside. "I think I want some sake," she said, and she gestured for the waiter.

We clinked our tiny cups, then she went on. "I haven't seen him yet. I've been fighting with the insurance people. They're really assholes, pardon my French."

"What's the fight?" I said, "If you need—"

"They're saying," she cut in, "that they've paid for two opinions and a bunch of tests, and since nothing definite has shown up, they're finished."

"But that's crazy!"

"Funny you should mention crazy," said Claire. "They're sort of suggesting that *I'm* crazy. That it's all in my head. Hysterical paralysis. Just like the ballerina in *Limelight*."

The reference to the Chaplin movie gave me yet another pang. How many times had we seen *Limelight* together? Or *City Lights*? Or *Modern Times*? How many half-price matinees had we gone to together back when our tastes were forming and we were learning why the classics were the classics? How many earnest conversations over cheap student wine? How many bundled-up walks home to make love through an early winter dusk?

"It's almost funny," Claire went on, knocking back her sake. "I didn't have hysterical paralysis at the Tchaikovsky competition, but I have it now that I'm a piano teacher who doesn't even have tenure, who plays the occasional party or chamber-music gig? It makes no sense."

I gestured for more alcohol. "So, where's it stand? The argument, I mean?"

"The argument is over, unless I want to get a lawyer. They won't budge. They're suggesting that I see a shrink. They'll pay for six visits."

"Oh, for Christ's sake! You need to see that doctor."

She put her chopsticks down, smoothed the napkin on her lap. "I will," she said. "I will. But first I need to talk to my brother."

"Your brother?"

This no doubt sounded shrill, because it so happened that I didn't like her brother. Not at all. His name was Chris and he lived in California. He was reckless, grandiose, drove cars that offended me, and spoke a language I simply didn't understand. By his late thirties he'd already made and lost two small fortunes—one in some dot-com flameout, another in speculative real estate. His latest venture was dietary supplements; according to Claire, he was in on the ground floor of a go-go company that struck me as one of those quasi-messianic enterprises that try to make greed sound spiritual. But what did I know? Maybe I just envied his knack of sniffing out where the action was and having the stomach to jump in. Or maybe it was some crazy Hamlet/Laertes competition, the lover and the sibling fighting over who cared more about the damsel in distress.

"What's your brother got to do with it?"

Very softly, Claire said, "He'll be lending me some money. Possibly a lot of money."

This galled me. "*I* can help you with money!" I blurted out. "I'm in business with a billionaire."

She ignored that altogether. "This doctor," she said. "It's a thousand dollars just to see him. He'll probably want to start all over with the tests. Who even knows about the treatments?"

"Let me help," I said.

"David," she said, "forget about it. It's fine. Chris will lend me the money. He's family."

"So am I."

She lifted her shoulders, let them drop, exhaled deeply, then finally locked eyes with me. "No," she said. "You're not. You *used* to be. We divvied up our little joke of a nest egg a long time ago. It's separate now. Let's keep it that way."

I sat there, feeling miserable and helpless, deprived of the honor of offering comfort or assistance. The noise of the restaurant welled up between us—plates being cleared, orders sung out in Japanese. Claire pulled in her lower lip. She seemed to be feeling about as lousy as I was. She reached out and touched my wrist.

"I'm sorry if I sounded harsh," she said. "It's nice of you to want to help. It's my problem if I can't accept."

She gave me a soft and tentative and somewhat weary smile. It was a smile I knew very well. It was the one we used to give each other when we were making up after an argument that neither of us had quite believed in to begin with.

I smiled back. "Consider it an open offer."

She gave the slightest nod. I guess it was as far as she could go.

I picked up my chopsticks and waited for Claire to retrieve hers, but she didn't. There was still sushi on the platter. We never wasted sushi.

"Have some more," I said.

"I'm not that hungry." She pursed her lips, then said, "Okay, maybe one."

She went for the salmon with the little curled-up lemon slice on top.

Chapter 10

That was Monday. I hadn't expected to see Robert Maxx again until Thursday, when he'd be meeting with the Knightsbridge Partners financiers. But, very early on Tuesday morning, while I was still in bed with stale sake on my breath, Jenna called and asked if I'd meet the billionaire at 9 A.M. He was doing an interview with INN—Investors News Network—and wanted me to come along.

"Why?" I sleepily asked.

"Probably because the interview's with Mandy Lockwood."

I propped up a couple pillows and resigned myself to being awake. "Isn't she the one he was going out with two, three years ago?"

"Very good," said Jenna. "Wall Street's answer to Tyra Banks. The woman who put the wow in the Dow."

"Clever," I said. "But I still don't see why he wants me along."

"Who knows? Maybe so you can see how cool he is on television. Or be impressed with how hot his ladies are. Whatever. Be in the lobby at nine. You'll ride over to the studio together."

I dragged myself into the shower, then pulled on a jacket and tie that

I'd always thought made a pretty jaunty outfit but no longer felt very confident about. Jenna had immediately pegged me as a writer, which is to say, a sort of bohemian slob who wouldn't spend two grand on a suit or buy a new one every time a different lapel came into fashion. Well, so be it. Maybe I could turn my relative shabbiness to an advantage. Maybe it would make me seem unapproachably eccentric, help me stay anonymous.

At ten till nine, I was standing at the security desk in front of Maxx's private elevator. They called upstairs to announce my arrival. At nine sharp, Maxx himself came down. Somewhat to my surprise, he was alone. I guess I'd expected an entourage. But in the moments that followed, I realized that he didn't need an entourage; he was an entourage unto himself.

His presence generated a kind of swirl, a crackling vortex of attention. Even in this building, where Maxx sightings could not have been uncommon, there were sideways glances and full-on stares. Companions elbowed one another, shoes scuffed as curious people veered in for a closer look. And it was true that the billionaire had a sort of mysterious gleam about him, as if he carried deep within himself a tiny spotlight that shone from the inside out. Or maybe it was the electricity of other people's glances that lit him up. Which came first—the aura or the fame? At this stage of his celebrity, it was impossible to say.

We shook hands, then moved quickly through the lobby toward the sidewalk. I admit that I took a certain cheap pleasure in feeling the stares that bounced off Robert Maxx then slid, however briefly, onto me. By association, I'd become someone to be curious about, a provisional big cheese. It's galling to say so, but I began to understand and maybe even feel the doglike pride and loyalty of the sidekick, the small man for whom reflected glory is the only glory he will ever know.

The car was a Mercedes stretch, plenty big though not ridiculous. It was parked in a No Standing zone. A beefy chauffeur, who no doubt doubled as a bodyguard, was standing sentry in front of an open door. There was an odd pucker under the shoulder of his polyester uniform, and I assumed that he was armed. Maxx called him Pete; his name was probably Pedro. He said good morning, ushered us in, and off we went.

Once we were moving, Maxx turned toward me and said, "This'll be fun, Dave. Done much television?"

"Some," I said. "Back when I was touring for my novels. Mostly cable, and those crack-of-dawn shows that nobody but farmers watch."

"Ah," he said. But it was clear that he didn't want to talk about my experience in television. He wanted to talk about *his* experience in television. "I do it all the time. Have to really limit it or it could become a goddamn full-time job. These talking heads are just relentless."

I couldn't think of much to say, so I said, "Nice that you and Mandy Lockwood are still friends."

He gave not the slightest indication of surprise that I would know about his affair with Mandy Lockwood. Everyone followed the details of his private life; he just took that for granted. He was leaning far back in the leather seat, but he still held on to the strap that dangled near his shoulder. He was looking very pink this morning. I wondered if he had a guy who shaved him with a freshly stropped straight razor, then lightly slapped his cheeks to get that shade.

"Friends?" he said. "I'm not sure I'd go that far. We have an understanding. She uses me to keep her ratings up, show the world she still has access. I use her for free publicity."

We crawled down Fifth Avenue, half a block per light. Even stretch Benzes with billionaires inside spend most of their time stuck in traffic.

"Don't get me wrong," Maxx went on. "She's a bright kid. Came from nothing. Worked her way up, even with that stoop-sitter accent. We had a lot of fun together. She's feisty as hell, challenged me on everything. Pretty exciting. Got wearing after a while. You know how it is— nice while it lasted."

Eventually, we reached the undistinguished building in Tribeca where INN had its studios. Maxx was duly fawned over at the door, and we were quickly led away to the green room. A guy in a plastic apron carrying a little brush appeared at once to bring the billionaire in for makeup. I sipped some nasty coffee and watched the monitor. Mandy Lockwood was doing her damnedest to make another humdrum day on Wall Street sound enthralling. Stocks were going sideways, bonds were stuck in neutral, but no matter; the anchorwoman flashed her almond-shaped dark eyes, shook her head of strikingly rich red hair, and offered up some cleavage to the camera. She cooed, she purred, she puckered crimson lips and wiggled in her chair; the effect was like the softest of soft-core porn, just a slight whiff of subliminal sex to leaven the weighty financial matters of the day. No doubt it kept a lot of horny traders tuning in.

Maxx was brought back to the green room. His hair was freshly sprayed and his pink cheeks had been toned down to a more camera-friendly buff. An assistant appeared to lead him to the set. Somewhat to my surprise, she invited me to come along.

The three of us walked down a short hallway to a heavy steel door with a "Quiet" sign on it and a red light above the jamb. Inside, we beheld the wildly bifurcated, schizoid world of television. On one side of the studio, beautiful and fake, a disembodied island, stood the brightly gleaming set, all sculptured desks, gracious backdrops, and anchors with capped teeth. On the other side, plunged in a stygian dimness, the invisible world of tangled wires and curling duct tape, fat cameramen with their shirttails hanging out amid the grease-stained doughnut boxes. The yin and yang of entertainment.

The show was on a commercial break. Mandy Lockwood left the set and sashayed over to say hello. She was stunning, in an unabashedly flirtatious, even borderline slutty sort of way. Maybe it was the exaggerated TV makeup that imbued her with a wanton affect, a touch of carnal fantasy. Standing still, she created an impression of swishing satin or of stockings softly rasping. She was more petite than she appeared on camera, but it was a fleshly petiteness, a compactness that seemed ripe to bursting—an hourglass figure compressed to forty minutes.

If she and Robert Maxx had any real remaining fondness for each other, they had a funny way of showing it.

She extended her hand to him and said without warmth, "Hello, Robert."

"Hello, Mandy. You're looking good. Gained a few pounds, maybe."

"Fuck you."

"We tried that, remember? Care for a rematch?"

"Why? Don't tell me your little soap-opera cupcake isn't putting out."

"You don't know the half of it."

"Or want to." She turned toward me, looked me up and down quickly but attentively, like an expert tailor estimating suit size. She said to Maxx, "Aren't you going to introduce me to your friend?"

Before he could answer, she turned to me again. "More money than God, and still he lacks the most basic manners."

Rather grudgingly, I thought, Maxx said, "This is Dave Cullen. He's working with me on a couple things. And if you're so fucking classy, how come you're still on cable?"

Mandy Lockwood gave a cleavage-lifting shrug. "I guess my influential boyfriends weren't all that influential."

An assistant called them to the set. I slipped back into the shadows, amid the wires and the duct tape. Maxx was quickly fitted with a microphone. He checked the drape of his beautiful suit jacket and armed himself with his rictus of a smile.

They were both pros in their respective roles, and once the interview began, all trace of their sparring vanished—for a while. Mandy Lockwood introduced the segment by saying that the lingering slowdown in the housing market had more recently been exacerbated by the crisis in lending—a crisis that now extended far beyond the sub-prime sector. Some experts believed that the malaise in housing, coupled with the global tightening of credit, must inevitably spread to commercial real estate and resorts as well. Here to discuss this potentially troubling prognosis was possibly the nation's leading expert on the realities of commercial real estate, Robert Maxx. "Welcome, Robert," she concluded.

"It's good to see you."

"So," she said, "this worrisome prediction—is it real?"

Maxx racheted up the smile yet another notch. "Absolutely not. The residential and commercial real estate markets are completely different entities. Apples and oranges. The commercial market is going gang-busters."

"But can it continue?" Lockwood pressed. "Won't there come a point when the housing slump, with its big jump in foreclosures and negative impact on the wealth effect, drags down these other sectors?"

Maxx leaned forward, pressed his hands together thoughtfully, and stayed perfectly on message. "Won't happen," he said with certainty. "Businesses are doing great. Space is at a premium. If anything, the commercial and leisure sectors will do even better as the residential bottoms out and the speculative money looks for a safer home with a better return."

"Ah," she said. "But this speculative money—given the worsening credit crunch, is there really so much of it around?"

Maxx tried to strike a lighter tone. "Oh, is there a credit crunch? Listen, not to be unsympathetic to the people who've lost their homes or taken mortgages with crazy rates, but the so-called credit crisis is all about loans that should never have been made in the first place. Unqual-ified borrowers. Irresponsible lenders. For healthy companies with solid results, there's plenty of money around and plenty of growth still to come."

"Very persuasive," she said, and then she paused for just the briefest of pregnant beats. "But if the outlook is so bright, how do you explain these numbers—numbers from your own company?" She looked down from the camera at a sheet of paper on her desk, as if the information on it had come in too recently to be fed into the teleprompter. "Vacancies in your five largest office buildings are up six percent over last year. Occupancy rates in Maxx Hotels are down eleven percent. Casino rev-enues offshore are flat, and domestically they're down in double digits. Revenues are projected to fall short of debt obligations in the coming quarter. How does that square with your argument?"

The camera was on Mandy Lockwood as she said this, but I was watching Robert Maxx. His face seemed frozen, stuck between gears as with a balky shifter. His hair moved slightly, all together, riding a tectonic twitch of his scalp. He attempted a dismissive laugh that came out sounding ugly. "That's just a blip, Mandy. Not a trend. It means nothing. Nothing at all."

Now the camera was on the billionaire, but my eyes were glued to the billionaire's old girlfriend. There was no doubt she was enjoying this.

When the interview was over, Maxx stormed off the set. He barreled past the netherworld of cameramen and wires, through the heavy soundproof door, down the crummy cinder-block hallway, and out into the daylight. His skin had grown livid beneath the TV makeup, and there was a patch of apoplectic purple around the too-tight collar of his shirt. I followed him into the waiting limo, and he never said a word.

Inside the car, he pulled out a cell phone and, fingers trembling with rage, punched in a speed-dial number.

"Jenna?" he said, his voice between a high whine and a growl. "You saw the interview? That cunt shanghaied me! Those numbers should never have come out! Where'd she get 'em? Find out! Whoever leaked those fucking numbers is fired, finished, ruined. Find out!"

He snapped the phone shut, stashed it in a pocket. For a minute or two he just sat there in a seething sulk, tapping his foot like a hopped-up kid. Finally, he swiveled toward me and said, "You see? You *see*? Fucking media. Fucking snoops. They're all like that. They suck up to you, kiss your ass, then turn on you when you're trying to get something done. Something *good*, for Christ's sake! Fucking parasites."

I considered responding to his outburst, but didn't. He seemed so genuinely miserable in that moment that I actually felt bad for him. We continued uptown in his chauffeur-driven limo, back toward his imperial office at the top of the world.

Chapter 11

What do you mean, you can't tell me?" Marcie Kanin said. "I'm your editor!"

"Excuse me," said Paul Hannaford, "but I'm his agent—which is way more important—and he can't tell me, either."

The three of us were sitting in the Gramercy Tavern, spending some of Porter & Kraft's money on tasty things that the likes of me don't get to savor very often—duck risotto, veal sweetbreads, porcini flown in straight from Tuscany. Probably more to the point, we were halfway through our second bottle of Pinot Noir. So much for the dreary and barbaric notion that people no longer drink at lunch. Then again, this was no routine meal, but a celebration—even though it seemed a little dubious to be celebrating the signing of what Paul had called the most one-sided and unreasonable contract he'd ever allowed a client to enter into.

"He can't tell you," Paul said. "He can't tell me. He can't tell anybody. I've never seen such tough disclosure language. One slip and they can fire him, owe him zero, and come after him for damages."

"Takes some of the fun out of it, doesn't it?" said Marcie. "I mean, we throw five million bucks at the guy and we can't even dish about him?"

She was a little tipsy, and I have to say it did her good. Wisps of hair had escaped from the neat pile that she held together with a tortoiseshell clip. They wandered down against her neck, and slightly drunk myself, I wondered if they tickled. Her hazel eyes had gotten soft and sleepy, and her shoulders sagged just slightly, making her bosom look exceptionally comfy. Don't get me wrong. I know that sleeping with your editor is the worst idea in the entire world, plus I still didn't know if Marcie Kanin was single, or straight, or what. And on top of that, there was my tender and romantic and/or delusional and futile relationship with Claire, which kept my heart aching and bewildered while doing nothing whatsoever for my sex life. So nothing was going to happen, and I knew it. I'm just saying that if Marcie had happened to be interested and if the restaurant had happened to have rooms in back, it would have been an awfully pleasant way to spend the afternoon.

But in the meantime, I said, "How do you think *I* feel? I'm getting all this inside dirt—stuff that would make me a star at cocktail parties and maybe even get me a better class of agent—and I can't say a word about any of it."

"There is no better class of agent," said Paul.

"I'll drink to that," said Marcie.

"Bitch," he countered. "That isn't what I meant."

He drained his wine, then refilled for all of us. I must say, the guy was amazing. I've mentioned that he didn't show his age, nor did he ever seem to show how much he'd had to drink. Four, five glasses in, he could have bamboozled a state trooper, then gone off to race a sailboat. "Anyway," he said, "gossip or no gossip, dishing or no dishing, at the end of the day, there'll be a damn good book. Here's to *Maxxed Out*."

We had a three-way clink. Underneath the table, I secretly knocked wood.

But then something strange and unsettling happened. I don't usually have mood swings when I drink, but all at once I had a whopper. Seemingly in a single heartbeat, I grew melancholy and morose. Everything felt wrong, pointless, and unfair. Okay, maybe, just maybe, *Maxxed Out* would turn out to be a damn good book . . . but *whose* book would it be? Not mine. I'd be a footnote, an asterisk. Maybe I'd be mentioned in some grudging, formulaic, patronizing acknowledgment that hardly anyone would even read. *And thanks to David Collins, a sensitive and responsive collaborator.* Collaborator, my ass! *Maxx* was the collaborator, and a largely unwitting one at that. *I* was the author.

I don't know if Marcie could tell that I'd gone into a funk. If so, she made a kind but misguided attempt to pull me out of it. Proposing another toast, she said, "And to the beginning of a long relationship with Porter and Kraft."

I was grateful for the comment and I tried to smile. But I don't think I pulled it off. I was thinking: Long relationship—in *this* business? *These* days? Not too damn likely. And even if it happened, what kind of relationship would it be? A relationship based on more thankless and insulting ghosting work? One that would assure me an ongoing invisibility and would pay just enough to cover my bills and keep me in the game, but never enough to break free of it? Congratulations to the former novelist! I was talented enough to be a sought-after hack who would remain anonymous forever.

It must have become pretty obvious that I was sulking. A glance passed between my editor and my agent. They suddenly seemed to be my parents. To my shame, I knew what they were thinking and I knew that they were right to think it. *The kid's getting cranky. Must be time for his nap. Let's get out of here before there's a meltdown.*

And I *was* getting cranky. But dammit, I felt I had a right to be. I had more at stake in this book than anybody else. More than Marcie Kanin, who had a dozen other titles on her schedule. More than Paul Hannaford, who had a whole stable of clients, and certainly more than Robert Maxx, for whom this was the merest sideline. For me, this book was huge—maybe my last shot at something major. It would be my sweat and even my love that would bring it into being. Was I wrong to believe that it should be mine? By any measure of reason or justice, it *was* mine.

And yet it wasn't. Not according to the contract that we were sitting in this lovely restaurant to celebrate. The contract put it very differently, and the contract was the final word—at least for as long as it remained in force. Which is to say, as long as the parties to it were alive.

Chapter 12

"Okay, people," Robert Maxx said. "Enough bullshitting about your golf scores. No one believes you, anyway. Let's get started."

It was Thursday, the day of the sit-down with Knightsbridge Partners. A dozen or so people were settling in at the enormous conference table in Maxx's office. Jenna was there, stately and efficient in a suit of olive green. Arthur Levin, a gorgeous pearl-gray jacket setting off his silver hair, sat next to the host. Perched on Maxx's other side was his chief financial officer, Carlton Phelps, a twitchy man who wore reading glasses far down on his narrow nose.

As for the Knightsbridge Partners people, they'd brought a fair-size contingent all the way from England. Two senior guys, Jeremy Bostwick and Frank Eaton, did the talking. Bostwick was heavy, gruff, and rumpled; you could imagine him slurping sherry in some dim and dusty room at Oxford. Eaton was natty and lean, his starched collar the snuggest in the room. A cluster of underlings fed them charts and graphs from little portfolios that they kept tucked close to their bodies.

"Okay," Maxx said, "what we're here to talk about today—talk about in strictest confidence—is an amazing business deal. But it's more than that. It's historic. This is going to top the news for weeks. It's going to be studied in business schools forever. It's going to be a touchstone case of taking a property that's already gold standard and bringing it to a whole new level."

I was hunkered down at the periphery, taking notes, trying to stay in the shadow of the plants. I watched Bostwick and Eaton. They were listening politely, but they seemed immune to the colonial hyperbole. Jeremy Bostwick tapped his Montblanc against a yellow pad, and said, "A level where it can still make money?"

"Absolutely," said Maxx, with a salesman's implacable certainty. "Hand over fist. Forever."

"I wonder," said Frank Eaton. An assistant fed him a sheet of data. "The occupancy at Rock Center is running ninety-eight percent. Rents are already among the highest in the city. How much farther can you push it?"

It was a fair question, but Robert Maxx seemed to take it as a bit of an attack. He narrowed his eyes, which gave them that unfortunate piggy look. But before he could speak, Arthur Levin cut in to smooth this first small ripple.

"Frank, Jeremy," he said. "With due respect, leave the management of the property to us. We're pretty good at that. What we want to discuss with you is the financing. We're offering you first position. It's a tremendous opportunity. You'll hold a nice chunk of the equity. With the strength of the pound, it's a bargain for you."

"And if the dollar keeps tanking," said Bostwick, "it'll get to be a bigger bargain still."

"Could happen," Maxx acknowledged. "This is why they call it business. You can make money, you can lose money. If you don't have the balls—"

"Oh, Robert, please," said Frank Eaton. "Leave balls out of it for once. It's not about balls. It's about these rather fanciful projections you've put in place."

"There's nothing fanciful about them," said Maxx.

An assistant slipped Eaton another sheet of paper. "For this deal to make sense, everything has to work just so," he said. "Occupancy has to rise. Retail has to stay strong so you can raise rents on the merchants. Is everything really that peachy?"

"Yes," said Maxx. "It is."

"That's good to hear," said Jeremy Bostwick. "But, you know, your lovely and talented Mandy Lockwood airs on our side of the pond as well. And that rosy picture just doesn't square with her report."

I looked at Robert Maxx. I was getting to know him day by day. I already understood that you couldn't read much in his features. He controlled them almost inhumanly well. But there were other signs that showed when he was getting riled. One of them was the coloring of the flesh around his collar. It was starting to take on the liverish pink of undercooked pork. "Those numbers," he said, "are for our own internal use."

"So, you're disavowing them?" said Bostwick.

"I didn't say that. I'm just saying they should never have been made public."

"Be that as it may," said Eaton, "they've been announced on television and broadcast all around the world, so I suppose it's fair to say they're public now. Are they accurate or are they not?"

Carlton Phelps, the CFO, clearly took this personally. In a high, pinched voice like a badly played oboe, he said, "Of course they're accurate! All our books are accurate."

Bostwick folded his hands and, with a wry and donnish calm, said, "Ah. Then can someone help us resolve this troubling paradox of accurate books showing god-awful numbers in a wonderful market?"

I confess that, in my naïveté, I was thoroughly surprised at how the meeting was going. I had thought that Maxx would dominate. I never expected to see him on the defensive. He was the famous one. He was the host. He sat at the head of the table and had the highest-backed chair. But there was another factor that seemed to trump all this: Bostwick and Eaton had the money, and money talks. Money gets its way. Money, like DNA, puts its own stamp on whatever it touches, and sees to its own interests. My billionaire was suddenly the supplicant, and it was becoming ever clearer that he didn't enjoy the role.

"Look," he said, "you guys are getting your bowels in an uproar about a few unimportant, anecdotal numbers, and you're missing the big picture."

"Which is?" asked Jeremy Bostwick, with admirable terseness.

Maxx took a moment to collect himself before he spoke again. He tugged at the lapels of his suit jacket, jutted out his too-thick jaw. Then he said, softly and slowly, "The value that I add. The value of my name."

There was a silence. I thought I saw Arthur Levin yield to just the slightest wince; his job was to save his clients from themselves, and he seemed to be trying without success to give Maxx a signal. The underlings squirmed. Carlton Phelps squinted through his glasses at his twitchy hands. Jenna kept her eyes tactfully averted.

As if he was suddenly, utterly confused, Frank Eaton said, "But, Robert, this property already has one of the world's great names."

"Right. And, once the deal goes through, it will have another. Maxx Center. For all intents and purposes, the center of the world."

Before Jeremy Bostwick spoke, his head was already shaking. The shaking seemed not to be a conscious action, but a reflex, a gesture of genuine and completely British affront. "No," he said simply. "Terrible mistake."

"Mistake? My name, a mistake? Jeremy, I get paid millions to put my name on things. Nothing more—just to lend the name. It's the ultimate brand. It's money in the bank."

"Not in this case," said Frank Eaton. "With due respect—this is not some midmarket condominium complex or day-tripping coach-tour casino. This is *Rockefeller Center*. Look at the precedents. When RCA bought it from the Rockefeller family, they had the decency to keep the name. When the Japanese consortium came in, they kept the name."

"So what?" said Maxx. "You Brits get so hung up on worshipping traditions, even when they aren't yours!"

"And you Yanks," Jeremy Bostwick shot back, "get so keen on raping traditions—even when they aren't *yours*! Look, it's like . . . like Windsor Castle. Or the Eiffel Tower. Would you change those names, too, if you bought them?"

Maxx's jaw was clenched, his neck an increasingly dark red, and his hands were splayed out on the table in front of him. Through the expensive colognes and lotions there came a smell, not of sweat exactly, but some sort of musk whose precise language we have lost the knack to understand. Through tightened lips, he asked, "Are they for sale?"

Bostwick and Eaton just stared at him.

Arthur Levin cut in gently. "Gentlemen," he said, "please let's not get too distracted over the matter of the naming. We're still in the very early stages. Everything's negotiable. Can we please move on to the financials?"

Chapter 13

The rest of the meeting was a bore and most of it went right over my head. Calculators and PDAs came out. Carlton Phelps took the floor, throwing around some big numbers and arcane accounting concepts. But, once you got past the mumbo jumbo, the gist of the discussion came down to this: Bostwick and Eaton wanted more of Rockefeller Center for less money, and Maxx wanted more of their money for less of Rockefeller Center. At the end of the sit-down, the two sides seemed quite far apart. The avuncular Arthur Levin expressed a gentle confidence that with further good faith conversations, some middle ground could certainly be reached.

The strange part was that once the clawing and the biting were finished, the principals instantly went back to being pals, or at least acting like they were. They fell into easy conversation—about currency hedges, a new resort on Cap d'Antibes—which we peons were not invited to join. I took the opportunity to slip away from the enormous conference table, walking next to Jenna. She invited me back to her office for some Pellegrino and a schmooze. We kept a discreet silence as we navigated the winding hallways.

She closed her door behind us and moved to her desk. I slumped down in a chair facing her. Even though I'd only been a silent observer at the meeting, I felt wrung out and scuffed up, as if I'd been through a bar fight that I hadn't won.

"Wow," I said, "that was rugged. Is it always like that?"

Jenna seemed completely unruffled. I guess those business confrontations are like any other sport where sufficient training brings greater stamina. "That was fairly typical," she said. "The big dogs put their game faces on, snarl a bit, and insist on terms they know they have no chance of getting. The only unusual thing about today is that Robert started at a disadvantage."

"Because of the leaked numbers?"

"Exactly."

"Bostwick and Eaton jumped all over that."

"No surprise there," she said. "Once the money guys start combing through the fine print of a deal, they always find something they can use to beat him up. This saved them the trouble."

"Who leaked the information?"

Jenna stared at me a moment with those astonishing yellow eyes through the hip magenta glasses. She tapped her neat fingers on her desk, then she said, "It's better you don't ask me that."

The coy response only made me more curious. I had a book to write. I needed information. And, aside from that, I'm nosy. "Ah, so you know."

"I never said that."

I plopped my elbows on the desk and leaned across them confidentially. "You know. The first time we talked, sitting right here, you told me that your job was knowing things."

"You remember that?" she said.

"Of course I do. You were wearing a blue suit, you straightened my tie for me, and your perfume smelled of lavender and pine."

She smiled quickly and she flushed just slightly, her mocha skin taking on a comely hint of mauve. "Writers," she said. "Can't even think out loud around them. They notice things. That's sexy."

The comment went straight to my loins. I took a deep breath and continued. "Well, *my* job is getting enough stuff to fill a book. Sometimes by asking questions that would be more polite not to ask. Like about who leaked the numbers."

By now it was a game, of course. Jenna pursed her lips, considered, and flattered me by giving some ground. "Okay," she said. "I think I know who leaked. I think Robert knows, too. It isn't somebody he can fire. And that's all I'm going to say."

"But—"

"That's all I'm going to say. Quit while you're ahead."

One of Jenna's two assistants came in with the Pellegrinos. I sipped some as I looked out the office window at the empty air above Manhattan.

"So what happens now?" I asked. "With Knightsbridge Partners, I mean."

She gave a world-weary shrug. "There'll be more meetings. Smaller ones, without the grandstanding. Arthur will shuttle back and forth with offers, counteroffers. Their bean counters will look more closely at our books."

At the mention of bean counters, I pictured Maxx's CFO, with his pointy nose and tormented squeak of a voice. I said, "That'll give Phelps a whole new set of tics and twitches."

"Yeah," she said, "he's a pretty nervous guy. From what I hear, he's been a nervous wreck for the whole twenty years he's been here."

"Twenty years!"

"He was Robert's very first hire, when he took over from his father. Really kind of a brilliant choice, but surprising."

"How so?"

"They're so opposite. I mean, they're both workaholics. Plenty of nights I leave here at seven-thirty, eight o'clock, and there's Carlton, still at the computer in an empty office. But other than that, they're fire and ice. Robert wings it, Carlton's a grind. Robert thinks huge, Carlton's the ultimate detail guy. Robert's social, Carlton seems to have no life. Lives alone. Never heard him mention family or a date or a relationship of any flavor. He's great at what he does, but he's your basic nerd, married to his numbers."

I was still trying to get my mind around the idea of going to an office and sitting at a desk for two decades. "Twenty years is a long time to be nervous."

"Wouldn't you be?"

"Wouldn't I be what?"

"Nervous," she said. "If you were the head financial guy in an operation like this?"

"If I were an accountant?" I could imagine being an accountant about as easily as being an astronaut or a shepherd. "I have no idea," I said. "But come on. The guy's got a fancy job title, he probably makes seven figures and has a golden parachute. What's he got to be so jumpy about?"

Jenna sipped her Pellegrino and looked at me over the top of her glass. "You don't know a lot about finance, do you?"

I didn't take offense. I mean, what's true is true. "Hey," I said, "I was an English major."

"Do you understand what leverage is?"

"Well, sure. Leverage is . . ." But then I flunked the surest test as to whether one really understands something. I found I couldn't put it into simple words. I fumbled for a moment, then Jenna helped me out.

"Leverage," she said, "is why Carlton Phelps is nervous. Leverage is when you buy something with money you don't have. Like when you whip out your Visa card for a giant flat-screen television that you really can't afford, but you'll pay it off eventually. Got it?"

I nodded.

"Well, multiply that by a million, maybe more like ten million, and that's basically what we do here. We put up pennies on the dollar for a property. It's usual to say we *own* the property—but that's not exactly right. The lender owns it; we control it. And we have to pull enough cash out of it to pay the interest on what we owe—plus a little more, so we can buy a *second* property. Those two support a third. The first three let us wager on a fourth, and so on. You with me?"

I nodded.

"By now we control almost a thousand properties all over the world. Seoul. Glasgow. You name it. Sometimes we put up a lot of money; sometimes just a little; sometimes Robert just rents his name. The structure gets really complicated—which is good."

"Good?"

"That's what lets Carlton do his razzle-dazzle, his virtuoso numbers stuff. But the basic idea is simple. Keep fresh money coming in so the new investment services old debt. As long as the pipeline keeps flowing, we're golden. Understand?"

I tried to. Being an English major, I groped for an image, a metaphor, to help me fully grasp the concept. I visualized a pipeline full of dollars—valves in, valves out—but that didn't clear it up. Finally, I said to Jenna, "Sorry to fall back on an old cliché, but all I can picture is a house of cards."

She pushed her glass away and folded her hands. She almost smiled but not quite, and looked at me from underneath arched eyebrows. "That's what they call it," she said, "when and if it all blows down and falls apart. That's what they said about Bear Stearns—the money pipeline clogged and the house of cards exploded. And I guess the same thing could happen to us someday. Any day. That's why Carlton Phelps is nervous. That's why all of us are nervous. But, *house of cards*—that's what the experts call a big company when it's way too late to fix it. In the meantime, it's known as an empire."

Chapter 14

I went home and made a pot of coffee.

It was too late in the day for caffeine, but I made the coffee anyway. I had notes to transcribe, impressions to record. I didn't want to let a single exchange or gesture or nuance get away from me. And here I should acknowledge something. I try to pass myself off as a pretty blasé sort of guy, and most of the time, I *am* blasé. I'll go further. Most of the time, in most situations, I am a lazy sack of shit, uncommitted, uninvolved, and indifferent as to outcomes. But something happens when I really get my teeth into a project. I get obsessed and a little manic. I wish this didn't happen, but it does. I wish I had some saner, calmer way of working, but I've never had that and I guess I never will.

So, I noodled with *Maxxed Out* until well into the evening. I forgot to eat dinner. But that was okay. I was excited and I was having fun. The voice of the book was starting to talk to me. I was tapping my foot to the particular rhythms and cadences that would give it its momentum. I was in the early, thrilling stage of experiencing suspense. I don't know if civilians realize this—that writers feel the most suspense of all. The writer is also the first reader, the first to discover what happens next, the first to see how things turn out. This is a privilege. A privilege that can drive you nuts, but a privilege nonetheless.

Around midnight, I switched off the computer, then ate some toast and drank some scotch. I went to bed, but was way too wired to sleep. Tossing and turning, close to dreaming then twitching back to wakefulness, I saw Robert Maxx's mean, carnivorous smile looming up before me. I saw his vastly swollen office, as full of pomp and pretense as something Babylonian. I heard the snide and wily voices of negotiators pressing their advantage.

I fluffed my pillow and turned over yet again, but it didn't matter which side I lay on; the story had me surrounded. At length I sprang out of bed and popped the first of many Ambien that I would swallow over the next six weeks or so. While I waited for the drug to kick in, scenes and dialogue kept on tweaking me, chafing me. I may not have owned the story, but the story was starting to own me.

I didn't know when I would next meet with Robert Maxx, but then, on Monday afternoon, Jenna called with a completely unexpected summons. Maxx wanted me to meet him that evening, at seven, at his apartment on Park Avenue.

"His apartment?" I said. "Why?"

"I don't know. He just said he wants to show you something. You're not a vegetarian, are you?"

I told her that I wasn't.

"Good. He wants you to stay for dinner. And all he ever eats is steak."

I had a sudden, dreadful image. I saw myself being squeezed between the ample behinds of two society wives, my ribs cracking and lungs collapsing as I struggled to make conversation. "It's not a dinner party, is it?"

She laughed. "You think you'd be invited to a dinner party? You're just the writer, remember?"

Well, that put me in my place.

"It's just the two of you," she said.

"What's the apartment like?"

Coyly, and maybe with a hint of feigned affront, she said, "What makes you think I'd know?"

I said, "Actually, I was hoping that you didn't."

"Jealous?"

"Maybe."

"It's supposed to be the biggest apartment in the city."

"What's he compensating for?" I said.

"Let's not even go there."

She gave me the address.

Maxx's apartment was around three miles and a universe away from mine.

At around six-thirty I walked over to Broadway and hailed a cab, leaving behind the homeless people, the people who talk funny, the dirty streets with their few scabby trees, and headed for Park Avenue, where everything was perfect.

His building was called the Maxx Uptown, and the first thing I noticed about it was that its doormen—one of whom met my taxi at the curb, and another who ushered me past the threshold—didn't really look like people at all, but like little tin soldiers come to life, or maybe fugitive extras from *The Nutcracker*. They wore immaculate burgundy uniforms, complete with brass buttons, gold braid, and even epaulets. One of them called up to Maxx's penthouse to announce my arrival. Then he walked me to an elevator operated by another toy soldier who was identically dressed, but with the addition of white gloves. He wished me good evening, and up we went.

Call me a peasant, but when an elevator stops and opens in a New York residential building, I expect to look out at a common hallway featuring closed doors with tabs that say things like 7C or 14J. This was not the case in Maxx's building. Since he owned the entire floor—three floors, actually, as I'd learn—the elevator opened onto a hexagonal foyer with terrazzo floors and a no doubt priceless, but rather ghastly chandelier of Venetian glass. A butler stood by, wearing a tuxedo and a British accent. "Mr. Cullen," he said, "welcome. Mr. Maxx will join you shortly. In the meantime, he's instructed me to show you 'round the flat, if you would like to see it."

I said of course I would. Who wouldn't want to see the largest private dwelling in the richest city in the world?

I'm not sure what I expected, but whatever it was, Robert Maxx's showplace of a triplex surpassed it. The top floor, which we reached by way of a dramatic spiral staircase made of intricate inlaid woods, held several guest suites, a gymnasium, a forty-seat home theater, and the servants' quarters, as well as offering access to the roof garden. The garden itself was done up in a Japanese motif, complete with camellia shrubs and ginkgo trees, gravel pathways, and a koi pond; it offered stunning vistas south and west. Luminous in the fading light of dusk, the Empire State Building, the Chrysler Building, and Rockefeller Center seemed to frame a sort of golden triangle, the inmost precincts of Maxx's power.

The middle floor was mostly given over to an enormous ballroom with a coffered ceiling—a place where one could serve cocktails for two hundred, or set up a private casino, or throw one hell of a dancing party. The rest of the space was reserved as Maxx's master suite. We couldn't visit that, the butler informed me, as Mr. Maxx was having a massage.

Back on the entry level, I was allowed a peek at a vast, gleaming kitchen that could have serviced a fair-size restaurant; a formal dining room that seated twenty-four, complete with portraits of the founding Maxxes hovering above the high-backed chairs; a living room with a fireplace large enough to roast a goat, and the rambling layout and stolid leather furniture of a British gentleman's club. Here and there I noticed pictures that, by coincidence, I had also had on my walls back when I was in college—a Modigliani woman, a bath scene by Degas. I'd had the posters. It took me a moment to understand that these were the originals.

Chapter 15

Dave!" said the billionaire, bustling into the study where I'd been seated for a while. "Thanks for coming. Sorry I kept you waiting. And that I haven't dressed for dinner. Who wants to dress up after a massage?"

I rose to shake his hand. He was wearing a dark blue warm-up suit, a towel bunched beneath the collar like a boxer. He was rather pink from being rubbed; his hair was not mussed, exactly, but bent here and there. The odd part, though, was that he really looked no different in sweats than in a business suit. The taut hunch was still there in his shoulders and the aggressive jut still stiffened his jaw. I wondered what it was like for the masseuse to try to coax the knots out of that stubborn, clotted flesh.

"No problem," I said. "I got the grand tour of the apartment. Jenna mentioned that you wanted me to see it."

For a moment he looked puzzled, then he said, "The apartment? No. I told Jenna I wanted to show you something. Something else." He glanced down at his watch. "In just about fifteen minutes. Hungry?"

I was impressed—who wouldn't be?—but by the end of the tour, I was also dispirited and drained, and couldn't quite tell why. Was it just me? Was it envy, pure and simple? Did my shabby background and puny bank account make me reflexively hostile to luxury? Possibly. But the sudden depression that came over me had to do with more than that. There was something very wrong with this place. It seemed less like an actual apartment than like a full-size scale model of itself, still waiting to be breathed into reality, mated to the world beyond it—an urban Xanadu for a magnate who could never be satisfied. It felt like no one lived here, that no one *could* live here, because the pristine and soaring rooms would suck out vitality like the vacuum of deep space. My chest was growing tight, my breathing labored, as if from a sort of claustrophobia in reverse.

Standing in this palace, I felt more than a little like a prisoner. I wondered if Robert Maxx did, too.

A small table had been set for two in the study. It was a handsome room, even cozy—the only one in the whole apartment that was humanly proportioned. The walls were forest green. There was a modest desk with an old-fashioned blotter, a green-shaded lamp, and a rack of antique letter openers. There was a beautiful old globe, some bookshelves, and a television built into a walnut cabinet. I would have bet that this was the room where Maxx spent most of his time.

The butler brought us dinner—filet mignon, baked potato, asparagus with hollandaise. He asked me what I'd like to drink. I said red wine. He asked if Bordeaux would be all right. I said "yes, of course," like I drank Bordeaux every night of my life.

Maxx cut into his steak. "So," he said. "Our book. How's it going?"

"Very early stages," I said. "But I think it's going fine. That scene with Bostwick and Eaton—"

"Sons of bitches, aren't they?" he said. "Brilliant guys. Wait and see. They'll come around."

The butler brought the wine. Maxx didn't have any. I have to say, I tend not to trust people who don't drink. I generally feel that they're hiding something. Sober alcoholics are fine. They've got an excellent excuse. But plain old teetotalers worry me. I always feel they're terrified of some *veritas* that the *vino* might let out. In any case, I drank the wine. It was fabulous.

"Help me understand," I said, "how you can be so sure of that."

Maxx had steak in his mouth. He worked it toward his cheek and pointed at me with his fork. "Deals beget deals," he said. "To get deals, you do deals. And no one does more deals than me. Big deals. Splashy deals. For a money guy, to be in business with me is like the definition of being hot. They'd be crazy not to grab this. How's your steak?"

"Perfect."

"I get 'em from the guy who sells to Sparks," he said. "Mafia meat. The best. It's good to have friends with friends."

Cautiously—but not *that* cautiously, since he'd been the one to raise the subject, after all—I said, "You have a lot of friends like that?"

"Dave," he said. "I own casinos. I've been building in this city for thirty years. Could I do those things without having certain friends, certain understandings? I couldn't get the fucking windows washed, let alone the buildings built. That's just how it works."

He looked down at his watch again. Then he reached for the remote and switched the TV on. "I think you'll find this interesting," he said. "I know I'm going to love it."

I ate and drank through a couple of commercials, then one of those Hollywood gossip shows came on. This one was called *BuzzWorld*. It was hosted by a quintessential L.A. blonde with collagen lips and silicone boobs. As she started to speak, Robert Maxx dabbed beef blood from the corners of his mouth and leaned forward with an almost salacious avidness.

"Leading the news tonight," said the woman on the tube, "a shocker from the world of business journalism. Mandy Lockwood, the glamorous and popular anchor of INN's *Wall Street Confidential,* has been ousted, effective immediately. A spokesperson for the network cited 'philosophical differences regarding Ms. Lockwood's standards and methods of reporting.' No further details are available at this time."

Maxx switched off the television and settled back into his chair. He picked up an asparagus spear, dipped it in hollandaise, and bit off the tip.

I said, "You had her fired?"

"She didn't work for me," he said. "How could I have her fired?"

He cut a piece of filet, but before he brought it to his lips, he shot me that mock-unguarded smile. "Of course," he went on, "I do happen to own that crummy building where they have their studios. So their CEO had a business decision to make. Face the disruption and expense of moving when their lease is up, or renew now on quite favorable terms. He chose to renew."

He ate his steak. I sipped my wine. Before I could catch myself, I said, "Jesus, Robert, she was only doing her job."

"No," he said, seemingly without offense, "she was doing her job in a way that was embarrassing and damaging to me. That's a very different thing. She made me a target. What if I didn't hit back? Other pushy journalists would do the same. Digging, insinuating. I can't have that. Better to send a message."

I held my tongue. What was there to say? I was there to chronicle the great and powerful Robert Maxx, not to give him my opinions. Even so, my silence seemed to goad him on.

"Look," he said, "I don't think you're getting this. I don't think you're getting it at all. If you're so intent on getting this book right, we're going to have to thicken up your skin. This thing with Mandy is not a tragedy. It's a game. That's all it is. A few days ago, she was winning. Now she's not. That's how it goes."

"But it cost her her job," I said.

"For now. Don't trouble your bleeding heart about Mandy Lockwood. She's a smart, tough cookie who fucked her way to the middle, then she made a dumb mistake, and had to be smacked down. Lesson learned."

I pushed some food around my plate. "And she'll recover from this lesson?"

"If she's worth two shits, she will. She'll find a way to use it. Who knows—a public feud with me might even get her off that crappy cable station and onto real TV."

I weighed my words, decided that I shouldn't say them, then said them anyway. "So you're saying you did her a favor?"

Give Maxx credit for this: up to a point, at least, he didn't seem to mind some pushing back.

"No," he said. "I'm saying she pissed me off and I kicked her in the ass. What she makes of the experience is up to her. But never forget that this is showbiz. She's an entertainer. To most people, *I'm* an entertainer. I throw big numbers around, I fuck actresses and models. I keep the paparazzi occupied. The feuds and breakups make good copy, keep people's names in print. So Mandy's had a setback and she also has an opportunity. Get it?"

I nodded, but I really wasn't sure I did. Here was a guy who would hack your leg off if you happened to step on his toe—and I was in business with him, utterly dependent on his goodwill for my next payday, and meanwhile asking a bunch of questions that might piss him off at any moment. It was, I confess, a bit unsettling. I just wasn't accustomed to games being quite this mean, or gestures of revenge being quite so gleeful and remorseless.

A fter-dinner drinks were offered. I couldn't resist an Armagnac. It wasn't until our chatting was finished and I rose to leave that I realized this might not have been the best idea. I wasn't smashed, but I was close. My feet felt somehow independent of my knees. I felt blood coursing in my ears and there was a bluish corona at the edges of my vision. My inebriation lent an aura of even greater strangeness to a peculiar thing that happened as I was leaving the apartment.

Maxx walked me out of the cozy study and back through the lifeless vastness of the other rooms. When we reached the foyer with the appalling chandelier, the butler was greeting another visitor who'd just arrived. The strange part was that this other guest both did and did not bear a remarkable resemblance to Robert Maxx. His features were clearly similar—the deep-set eyes, the mobile lips, the thick, unruly hair—but where Maxx was meaty, this other man was lean almost to the point of looking haggard; where Maxx was ruddy, the visitor was pale; where Maxx seemed always to be leaning forward at you, this man was receding. There could be no doubt that it was Maxx's brother, the troubled and perhaps deranged pariah who had shed the family name and—or so I'd believed—broken off all contact with his famous sibling.

An awkward moment passed—a moment when introductions should have been made, but weren't. The new guest slid into the shadows. My host suddenly seemed uncomfortable and beset. He mumbled a rather clipped good night and hustled me toward the waiting elevator.

Chapter 16

I was braced for a hangover, and certainly figured I deserved one, but next morning I felt surprisingly okay. This was definitely an argument in favor of drinking the kind of first-rate booze served at chez Maxx, as opposed to the dubious wines and iffy brands of hard stuff that my budget generally allowed.

Feeling like I'd got away with something, I made a pot of coffee and got right down to work. This felt very good. I was just reaching the stage of involvement with this book when it was ceasing to seem like a chore, an intrusion on my laziness, and becoming a valued part of my routine, something that filled a vital slot in my day. It was becoming easier to work on it than not to.

I'd been at it for a couple of hours when the phone rang. By then I was happy for an interruption, and even happier when the caller turned out to be Claire. She said she was in the neighborhood and asked if she could come up for a chat. This surprised me—and worried me a little, too. Claire usually doesn't like to come up to my apartment, because at one time it was *our* apartment. It's a longish story, though by no means uncommon in Manhattan, where lives—and not just for the Robert Maxxes of this world—are very often shaped and not infrequently warped by the perennial scarcity and shifting values of real estate.

I'd had the apartment ever since my grad school days. Back then it was a rental, blessedly cheap, and I camped out in it like a typical shabby bachelor. I had bookshelves made of bricks and planks, a torn sofa from the thrift store, oily containers of take-out Chinese moldering at the back of the fridge. I wasn't a slob, exactly, but I wasn't far from one, either. Mainly, I just had a young man's indifference to domestic appearances and creature comforts. I hadn't yet learned that those things matter.

Luckily for me, the building went co-op just around the time I was publishing my first novel. Luckily again, my bargain-basement "insider's price" was more or less commensurate with my puny advance. I bought the place. But pride of ownership didn't change things much; it still looked like a dump.

Then, a year or so later, after we'd been dating around six months, Claire moved in. She'd been living in the place she still had in the West Seventies—the place with the giant piano. She kept it as a practice studio; and no doubt as a safety net in case our relationship headed south; and also because of the real estate paranoia that infected even matters of the heart. If you had an acceptable apartment in a halfway decent neighborhood, you didn't give it up just because you were in love. Prices could too easily pass you by, and you might be frozen out forever. That's life in Manhattan.

Anyway, Claire gradually transformed the place. Don't get me wrong—we were never going to have eight pages in *Metropolitan Home*. But little touches kept appearing. End tables were slid under lamps. Matching dishes showed up on the breakfast table. By the time we got married, we had linen curtains on the windows, a decent rug on the floor, a sofa that was not pre-owned and that actually blended with the rest of the decor. The lair had become a nest. Understand, I resisted all these changes as they were occurring. In my sophomoric stoicism, I thought that furniture was silly and handsome glassware was pointless and bourgeois. But my wife wore me down with comfort and beauty.

She civilized me by the time-honored expedient of bringing the savage into a proper home and letting him learn in his own sweet time to appreciate it.

When the marriage was ending, possession of the apartment might have been a huge, contentious, bitter issue—except that neither of us had the heart to fight about it. This was strange: tormented and diminished by our respective disappointments, we'd somehow lost the knack of being generous to each other in the context of our marriage; but the prospect of divorce somehow took the pressure off and restored to us our better selves. We were both intent on being more than fair, on reaffirming our affection even as we were renouncing it. I contended that the apartment should be hers, on grounds that she had reinvented it. She insisted it was mine, and had been since long before we got together. She had her own place to go back to—and she did. Perhaps to salve my conscience for giving in too easily on this peculiar argument-in-reverse, I stipulated that, when and if I sold the place, Claire would get half of the presumptive profits. She accepted, and that was the end of our battling over real estate.

Still, it didn't seem to be easy for her to return to the apartment, and I doubted she was coming by just for a casual hello.

My doubt was confirmed in the first instant I saw her standing in the doorway. Her skin was pale, her brow was taut; she stepped a bit unsteadily across the threshold, and didn't so much give me a hug as seem to be trying to disappear for a while inside the circle of my arms. I held her a moment, smelled her hair. Her small body expanded then shrank as she labored for a couple of deep breaths.

"You okay?" I said.

Instead of answering, she said, "I hope I'm not disturbing your work."

I waved the notion away, and as I did so a bleak irony occurred to me. I would never have admitted this, but back when we were married—back when I was younger and more naive prey to my own ambitions—in my heart of hearts I'd felt that my work was the most important thing in my life. Only now that we'd blown the relationship did I realize that it wasn't, that it never had been. "Want some coffee?"

"Do you still keep a bottle of Tía Maria around?"

"For emergencies," I said.

"I'll have some."

I went to the kitchen, heated up two mugs of coffee, dosed them with liqueur. When I brought them into the living room, Claire was sitting on the sofa she'd selected years before, stroking its arm like it was an old family pet. She sipped some coffee, then put the mug down on the low table in front of her; it rattled slightly as she placed it. She smoothed her skirt and said, "I've just come from the doctor. The fancy one."

I leaned forward in my chair, propped my elbows on my knees. "And?"

She licked her lips, tried to speak, stopped again. "Okay . . . okay, I'll start with the good news. It isn't in my head. He doesn't think I'm crazy."

This forced me to confront something I'd never even considered before. "Did you for a single second worry that you were?"

Her tall eyes widened. There was anguish in them. "Yes," she said. "I did. That's what people were telling me. Psychosomatic this. Hysterical that. Who knew? Maybe I was having some kind of delayed-reaction breakdown, some kind of flashback anxiety from a million years ago. You don't think I carry a lot of that around?"

I had no answer for that. I felt isolated in my skin and embarrassed that I didn't understand things better.

"Anyway," she went on, "now there's at least a tentative diagnosis. He thinks it's something called chronic inflammatory—"

She broke off and reached for her purse, started rummaging inside it.

"The name's about three octaves long," she said. "I wrote it down." She found the paper and read from it, stumbling a bit on the overloaded syllables. "Chronic inflammatory demyelinating polyradiculoneuropathy."

I swallowed back a bitter taste. I was afraid. Nothing with a name that long could possibly be good. "What's it mean?"

Sounding very brave and clinical and almost calm, she said, "It means something is peeling away the sheath that covers the little nerves that go down to my hands. That's why they misbehave sometimes. They're not getting the information that my brain is sending."

"Why is it happening?" I said. I didn't just mean medically. I meant in terms of the fucked-up justice of the world.

Claire addressed the medical part. "No real way of knowing," she said. "Maybe just overuse. Maybe a virus. Maybe some genetic tendency."

I sipped some coffee and secretly knocked wood as I put down the mug, then I asked the question that I dreaded asking. "Is it fixable?"

It *had* to be fixable. Claire unable to play the piano, to pour herself into the music and thereby to become the music—this was just too cruel to think about, crazy-making cruel.

She sighed and seemed to choose her words very carefully, as if the outcome depended on explaining things accurately, neutrally, without too much weight of hope or fear. "If the diagnosis is right, there's a treatment. It's considered experimental, but supposedly it gets good results. First, though, we have to rule out other things."

Her eyes slid away as she said the last few words; my dread skidded along with her gaze. "What kind of other things?"

"Bad things," Claire said, not looking up, fingers jumpy in her lap. "Lupus. Rheumatoid arthritis. MS. ALS."

"Jesus Christ." I felt dizzy, like the floor had turned to gelatin and the walls no longer met the ceiling. Maybe, as people get older, they become better able to process concepts like sickness, debility, loss of strength, and spoiling of joy; but the first time those things get in your face, it's an overwhelming terror and a devastating insult.

She said, "It's probably nothing like that. It's probably just this inflammation thing. The doc just said I should be aware. There's a lot of tests he has to do. I go in Friday for a spinal tap."

Spinal tap. The term was shocking and horrible; it added a hint of nausea to my fear. I was assaulted and cornered by creepy images. I heard the tiny pop as the needle punctured her thin skin. I saw the point driving closer to the thread of nerve that let her move and feel. "I'm going with you."

I didn't know I was going to say this. The words just came out.

"That's nice of you," she said. "But no."

I sprang up from my chair. I didn't know that was going to happen, either. But my shock and panic suddenly plowed past some threshold and burst forth as exasperation. I was mad at everything—fate, God, doctors, even Claire. "Why? Because you've got to prove that you're a tough, strong, independent woman?"

"No. Because this is my problem, not yours."

My throat hurt from the effort of holding back a scream. "You can't keep shutting me out of things like this!"

"I'm sorry you feel shut out. This isn't about you, okay?"

I'd started pacing. I stopped, pivoted, squatted down almost to the level of Claire's knees. "Then why did you come here? Why did you come to our apartment?"

"It's your apartment."

"Here's what I think. I think you came because, deep down, you feel the same way I do—that you shouldn't have to go through this alone. No one should."

There was a silence. She wouldn't meet my eyes.

"Look," I said, "if the situation was reversed, I'd want you there with me. You know that, right?"

She didn't answer. A long moment passed. Claire was looking around the apartment as if she was just now noticing her surroundings—the dusty windows, the tossed magazines, the breakfast plate still sitting on my desk, dabbed with toast crumbs and jam. Finally, she said, "Been backsliding a little, huh?"

My eyes had followed hers, and I'd seen the bachelor's disarray that usually I wouldn't notice. "I'm a bit of a mess without you," I admitted. "I've never denied it. What can I say?"

She gave her head a little shake. I wanted to believe it was indulgent, maybe even affectionate.

She said, "My appointment's at eleven."

"I'll pick you up at ten."

Chapter 17

"Those assholes!" Robert Maxx said. "Those shortsighted, chicken-shit, nickel-diming assholes. I cannot believe they are letting this deal get away from them. Do you realize how dumb they're going to look? When Goldman or Morgan comes in instead? I think those guys have lost their marbles. Or maybe this is just too big for them. That's it—probably it's just too big. Fucking Brits. Fucking Europeans. They've got this puny little continent with all these tiny little countries, and they just can't deal with something really huge."

It was Wednesday, late morning, and the billionaire, huffing and snarling behind his giant desk, had just been told that his confident prediction about Knightsbridge Partners jumping at the chance to be the lead financiers in the Rockefeller Center acquisition had been absolutely, flat-out wrong. Bostwick, Eaton, and company had passed. Moreover, they had passed without even making a serious counteroffer to the original proposal. They simply wanted no part of the deal.

The bearer of this deflating news was Arthur Levin, who sat across from Maxx, his gorgeous mane of hair unruffled. The legendary negotiator had delivered the message with his usual evenhandedness, in return for which he was made the vicarious target of the billionaire's tantrum. The old lawyer listened placidly as the tirade was winding down, then softly said, "When you're finished, there's something I'd like to say."

But Maxx's face was flushed, his sneer of a smile had hardened into a twitching grimace, and it seemed he had some pique reserved for Levin himself. "Save it," he said. "You're so goddamn predictable. I know what you're going to say. You're going to say something soothing and conciliatory that does no fucking good at all."

"No," said Levin, still speaking quietly but squaring up his shoulders, "I'm not going to say something soothing and conciliatory. I'm going to say I told you so."

Maxx froze at the words. His mouth was half open, his neck was craned at a graceless, awkward angle, but for a long moment nothing moved. I myself—sitting off to the side, as usual, unspeaking and unspoken to—held my breath as I took in this little drama of my tycoon being scolded. I was sure he'd been expecting better news about Knightsbridge Partners; that's almost certainly why I'd been invited to this meeting—so I could duly record that Maxx had been vindicated, that he'd been victorious in yet another skirmish. Well, that hadn't quite worked out. And now, on top of the defeat, he was being lectured by his own attorney.

"You played your hand much too strong," Levin went on, softly but implacably. "You tried to tell the money what to do. That hardly ever works. And this business of the name—I told you it would be a problem. You gave them a simple reason to say no. They took the opportunity. It really isn't that surprising."

The freeze-frame ended; Maxx became animated once more. His neck flushed brick red, his rippling forehead tugged at his helmet of hair, and he pointed a thick finger at Levin. "Listen, Arthur," he said, "you get paid to negotiate for me. You don't get paid to tell me how to do a deal."

"I'm not telling you how to do a deal. I'm *trying* to tell you how not to lose a deal. I thought you would have learned that from your father."

Maxx smirked and looked away. "My father was a wimp and did business like a wimp."

"I respected the man," said Levin. "But let's leave that on the side. The point is I can't negotiate from an impossible position. That's just a waste of everybody's time."

"And you get paid a thousand bucks an hour for wasting yours," the billionaire shot back.

"It isn't worth it," Levin said.

He said it softly but the words made everything stop.

"Are you threatening to quit?" Maxx said, in a steeply rising pitch that conveyed incredulity and affront, but failed to perfectly mask just a hint of panic. Levin had flexed the ultimate kind of power—the power to walk away.

"I'm not threatening anything," said the lawyer. "I'm saying I can't sell this deal the way it is. The numbers aren't great. The timing's miserable. And the naming thing is a major problem. Maybe there's someone else who can sell it more convincingly. If you find that person, hire him."

Maxx dropped his eyes and stared down at his desk; he pushed his lips into a pout. There was something in his expression that was both touching and annoying, some look of genuine disappointment—heartbreak, almost—that was childish but affecting. It was as if, for all his purported savvy about the ways of the world, he simply didn't understand that he couldn't always have his way. He drummed his fingers on his desk and seemed to be trying to make peace with that offensive fact.

"Okay," he said at last. "I'll have Phelps rework the numbers. It'll make him crazy, but he'll do it. And we'll plan on keeping it Rockefeller Center. Happy now?"

Levin was far too skilled to show even a jot of satisfaction. He didn't shift his posture or his tone. He just said, "Fine. So who are we going to talk to next?"

By the time I left Maxx's gigantic office, it was almost noon. On an impulse, I wound my way through the corridors to look for Jenna. I thought I'd see if she happened to be free to grab some lunch. I stood in the doorway of her office while she finished up a phone call, then made the invitation.

"What did you have in mind?" she said. "Nobu? Michael's?"

"Ah," I said, "I'm sick of those places. I was actually more in the mood for a falafel in the park."

"Funny," she said, "that's exactly what I felt like having."

We rode downstairs together, then picked our way through the bustling lobby and out into the day. The weather was mild for early November. On Fifth Avenue, people were streaming forth from every building, spinning through revolving doors before launching themselves like salmon into the swift currents of the sidewalks; this headlong lunchtime rush—to restaurants, delis, health clubs—was another of those workday rituals that I viewed with baffled awe, as though I were a Martian. Why did everyone try to go at the exact same time?

Walking next to Jenna, I realized that she wasn't just tall, she was really leggy. She had a stride that gobbled up distance; I had to take a little skip step now and then to stay even with her. I realized, too, that there was something slightly but deliciously illicit in being with her outside the office—just the vaguest hint of sex and/or conspiracy. Maybe this frisson was one of the things that made office jobs bearable.

We walked through Grand Army Plaza and across to the corner of the park where the horse-drawn carriages waited hours for a fare. Our hips nearly touched as we bobbed and weaved through the hurrying crowds; a couple times I made bold to put my hand on Jenna's back to steer her through the pedestrian ballet. She didn't seem to mind. We found the falafel guy and staked out a vacant bench that faced south, toward the fleeing sunshine and the skyline.

It isn't easy to look dignified while eating a falafel. Shreds of lettuce tend to escape from the corner of your mouth; dribbles of tahini sometimes soak through the pita and the foil and end up in your lap. But

Jenna showed great grace in eating hers. Her long fingers cradled the sandwich; her lips proceeded carefully but without fuss. Between bites she was even able to have a conversation.

"So," she said, "how was your morning with Robert?"

I answered with a question of my own. "You've heard about Knightsbridge Partners?"

She nodded, nibbling her sandwich. Of course she'd heard. It was her job to know things, after all.

"What's your take?"

"It's not good," she said. "Word has a way of getting out. A deal starts seeming like soiled goods. And, in a funny way, there's as much prestige in saying no to Robert as in being in business with him. It's like bragging you turned down sleeping with a movie star. How'd he seem to be handling it?"

"Badly," I said. "First, he decided that Bostwick and Eaton were small-time losers. Then he jumped all over Arthur Levin."

Jenna shrugged. "Typical," she said. "Rule one: When something goes wrong, it's never Robert's fault."

"That part I get," I said, wrestling with my falafel, which had reached a dangerous state of asymmetry. "But the part I can't quite get my mind around is this. He's the boss. He's obsessed with winning. He always expects to get his way. But the times I've seen him in action, he's either begging for money, or getting shot down, and he barely seems to notice. It's like the smackdowns just don't register."

To Jenna this was not at all mysterious. "That's his gift," she said. "That's what lets him do what he does. He's incapable of embarrassment. He doesn't know when he should feel humiliated. He just bulls ahead."

"But with an ego like his—"

"That's the part," she interrupted, "that I don't think you're quite getting yet. You see the big part of his ego—the bluster, the noise. But his secret—and it's a little spooky—is the way he can shrink that ego down to get what he wants. He'll plead, he'll wheedle, he'll make a total fool of himself—and none of it bothers him, because he's shrunk himself down to a dot, pulled in his ego like, I don't know, a clam or something. Then, once he's got what he wanted, he'll puff right up again, big as ever, like nothing ever happened. Takes a special kind of person."

"Yeah," I said. "A sociopath."

"Or a highly successful businessman," she said. "Your sandwich is about to drip."

The warning came a heartbeat too late. A blob of tahini slipped between my fingers and landed on my pants. It wasn't in my crotch, exactly, but it was pretty close. Without shyness, Jenna took a napkin and dabbed at the spot. I shot her a look as her fingers were retreating.

"Just trying to save you the dry cleaning," she said.

We both looked at my stained pants for a moment. It seemed a pretty good time to change the subject.

I said, "But I haven't told you about my evening in the biggest apartment in New York."

"What did you think?"

"I thought if I had to live there, I'd shoot myself."

"Not exactly warm and cozy, is it?"

"Ah," I said. "So you *have* been up there."

Her gorgeous yellow eyes glinted as she turned her head. "I never said I hadn't been. Any sign of the girlfriend?"

"You mean the one Mandy Lockwood refers to as a soap-opera cupcake?"

Jenna gave a chuckle that was not quite devoid of cattiness. "That's a little harsh. A little. Maybe."

"No sign of her," I said. "I hope I get to meet her sometime."

"Oh, I expect you will. That's part of what she's there for. For Robert to show off."

I said, "Speaking of trophy girlfriends, you know what it was he wanted to show me." I didn't even phrase it as a question. By now I took it as a given that Jenna knew everything I knew, way before I did.

"Yeah, getting Mandy axed," she said. "Terrible thing to do."

I assumed she said this out of gender solidarity or sympathy for the underdog. In fact that wasn't what she meant at all.

She went on, "It's a crazy feud to escalate. Mandy has so much more to gain than lose. He has so much more to lose than gain."

I thought about that while balling up the foil that had held my sandwich. "I think I'm beginning to see a pattern here."

"Namely?"

"He makes trouble for himself. Headaches with Mandy Lockwood. Headaches with Knightsbridge Partners."

"His life is headaches," Jenna said. "His life is scrapping and arguing."

"I wonder if it's more than that."

"Like how?"

I half turned on the bench, crossed my legs, and grabbed an ankle. "When I was younger," I said, "I had this idea for a novel. I didn't know enough to write it, but the basic premise has always rung true to me. It's about a hugely successful guy who gains everything he ever wanted. But even while he's gaining it, somewhere inside himself he understands that's only half the story. The other half is losing it again. He *has* to lose it. It's the inevitable ending. Like there's some ticking clock inside of him that will dictate when it's time to piss it all away. Up the mountain, across the summit, and down the other side. It's the shape of his life . . . Maybe it's something like that for Maxx."

I finished speaking. There was a brief pause that was somehow off the beat. Jenna was looking at me with those remarkable eyes. Her face was intent with lips slightly parted, and I was flattered as hell by her attention. She said, "Do you make love like you talk?"

This flabbergasted me, stunned me, slaughtered me. But before I could come up with a suave and clever answer, Jenna continued. "It's not a proposition. Just idle curiosity."

"God, you're a tease."

"And so are you," she said. "You should write that novel sometime." She looked down at her watch. "I have to get back."

She rose without effort, and smoothed her clothes, which had not been at all mussed. We left the park and slipped into the tide of people streaming back to offices. Along the way, I said, "Guess who was coming in to Maxx's place as I was leaving."

"Who?"

The question surprised me. I just figured she'd nail it. "You really don't know?"

"I have no idea."

"His brother."

Her eyes widened but she never broke that graceful stride. "You serious?"

"I wasn't introduced. But it had to be the brother. Looked just like Maxx, but maybe with half the blood removed."

"I can't believe he'd be there."

"Why not?" I said. "They're family."

"They hate each other's guts," said Jenna. "And Robert's furious with Tony."

"Why?"

Maxx Tower loomed above us now; we were almost at the entrance. Suddenly it felt a bit scandalous to be talking as we were, as though the shades were up and the neighbors might be watching. Jenna looked around a little nervously.

I pressed my question. "Why is Robert furious with Tony?"

She bit her lip then looked me in the eye and spoke extremely softly. "Because Tony's the one that leaked the numbers that started all the trouble."

I said, "I didn't think he was even involved in the business."

"He isn't. Not day to day, I mean. But as a family member, he owns a piece, so he has a representative on the board."

"But why would he make trouble?"

"Maybe because he's crazy. Or maybe because he isn't. Who knows? I gotta go."

She kissed me on the cheek, so quickly and so fleetingly that I had to ask myself if it had really happened. Then she disappeared into the building. The revolving door spun an extra moment in the wake of her decisive push.

Chapter 18

I am not ordinarily a reader of the business pages. They tend to bore me to death. This company buys that company; this fallen CEO does the perp walk on the courthouse steps; who cares?

But as I've mentioned, when I really sink my teeth into a writing job, I get compulsive. I become a stickler for homework, a hound for small but telling facts; I hate to be embarrassed by continually being the last to find things out. So, ever since I'd gotten involved with Robert Maxx, I studied the business pages every morning. I read every article, even going beyond the page jump, where everybody stops. I pored over the columns for mentions of his name or accounts of his recent exploits. I even read the little three-inch items buried back among the stock tables. You never knew where a gold nugget might turn up.

On this particular morning, however, a small story caught my eye that had nothing to do with Maxx. It was about a company called Herbjoy, which was based in California, and sold vitamin supplements and natural remedies imported from China. Its founders, a husband-and-wife team, had recently come under investigation for fraud, embezzlement, and running a classic Ponzi scheme. After pledging to cooperate with authorities, they had reportedly fled the country and were believed to be in Bali. The company had ceased to operate, leaving suppliers with millions in unpaid invoices, and franchisees with nothing to sell.

For 99 percent of readers, no doubt, this story came under the "who cares?" category. For me, however, it was of compelling interest. I wasn't sure; I couldn't remember if Claire had ever mentioned a name, but it seemed possible if not likely that this was the company my high-flying, New Age ex-brother-in-law had been working for—the company that was going to make him his next fortune.

I'll be honest here. I couldn't help hoping that it was indeed his go-go, get-rich enterprise that had crashed and burned. This was small of me. I admit it. A better person would not have felt this way, and probably I will roast in hell for it. But what can I say? Have I mentioned that I didn't like the guy? I thought he was a smug, self-serving hypocrite, a con man muttering *namaste*. A world that rewarded people like him was not a world I approved of. It wasn't just pleasant, it was reassuring to see him fail.

Then again, he was still my ex-wife's brother, and I suppose I was a miserable cur for feeling as I did. There were also practical considerations that could not be taken lightly. According to Claire, Chris had plenty of dough and was going to help her with her doctor bills. This deprived me of the rare opportunity to play the white knight; but at the same time, the presence of another benefactor, while it made me feel diminished, also let me off the hook—because the money that with all my heart I offered her was money that I did not have. It was *leveraged* money. I'd have it in nine months or a year, when *Maxxed Out* was written and accepted. But Claire needed it now. If the big-shot brother had in fact gone bust, and if I ended up with the privilege of helping, how was I going to come up with the cash?

There was a simple way, of course, to find out if Herbjoy was in fact Chris's company—call up Claire and ask her. But I felt I couldn't do that. She was having a needle pushed into her spine next day. That was scary and weird enough without further complications. There was no way I would worry her.

So I worried myself instead. I fretted, I paced. Pointlessly, I checked my bank balance, as if funds might have somehow accumulated when I wasn't looking. I scratched figures on a piece of paper; I threw the disappointing paper in the garbage.

And the morning passed in worry instead of work. I could not afford to let this happen, but it happened anyway. It was a tidy formula for failure. Fretting about dough was distracting me from any chance of making dough.

The afternoon and evening were no more productive. Then winter arrived overnight. Next day the sky was white with ugly ocher smudges. My dusty windows were cold to the touch, and ribbons of chilly air somehow slipped between the window frames and the sills. Reluctantly, I pulled on a heavy jacket for the walk downtown to Claire's place.

She was dressed and ready when I got there, wearing nice slacks and a cardigan. She was just finishing some toast and a cup of tea, and when she rose to clear the dishes, there was something in her posture that reminded me of how she used to look backstage before performing—a certain studied slowness in her movements, a certain angular precision in how she held her head and squared her shoulders. This was a mask for nervousness, I knew; but it was such an effective mask that it gave her an aspect that was stately, even regal. Her posture was a victory of poise over anxiety, confidence over insecurity; it was a put-on that could only come from something real and fierce inside. It was the posture that made men fall in love with women onstage, with actresses and opera singers. Seeing her take on that posture once again, remembering how lucky and how smitten I used to feel while watching from the wings, made me want to sit down and weep.

Instead, we both tried much too hard to be cheerful. We smiled; we made trivial remarks about the change in the weather. Claire's appointment was in the East Seventies, directly crosstown. She suggested we walk. I gratefully agreed. It was better to be moving, pacing off some of the fear.

In the park, old people were walking their dogs; squirrels, suddenly urgent, were sprinting from tree to tree. Leaves were raining down in the chilly breeze. Sycamore mostly, brittle and dull brown. They landed in the short, coarse grass and stuck, their stems curling upward like tails.

We skirted the south end of the Great Lawn and followed the path that headed just below the Met. At some point Claire took my hand. She didn't look at me. I didn't look at her. Shy as kids, we seemed to be pretending that neither of us had made a move, that our hands had simply found each other on their own. We walked the rest of the way in silence.

Dr. Simon Gupta appeared to be just around my age. I found this unsettling. Illness, I realized, made us want to be children again, made us want to believe that there were grown-ups who knew everything and had the power to make everything all right. If this was not the case—if even fancy East Side neurologists were people just like ourselves, works in progress, still wrestling with their gaps and limitations and things they hadn't yet figured out . . . well, that was a little worrying.

Even so, Gupta, all in all, inspired great confidence. In his immaculate white coat, he was handsome in a solemn sort of way, with wavy blue-black hair and gray shadows beneath his kind, dark eyes. When we were ushered into his consultation room before Claire's procedure, he explained things patiently and carefully, his soft voice enlivened by just a slight remaining trace of Indian lilt. Claire's problem, he believed, came down to a particular kind of neural damage that was quite rare but not unheard of in musicians, due to all the repetitive motions. If that assumption was correct, there was a treatment that, anecdotally at least, had shown promising results. The treatment involved large intravenous doses of something called human immunoglobulin—essentially a cocktail of natural anti-inflammatories derived from living tissue—that was considered more effective than steroids, and with fewer side effects. As for today's procedure—a lumbar puncture, more commonly known as a spinal tap—it involved the drawing off of a small amount of cerebrospinal fluid so that it could be tested. The tests were needed mainly to eliminate far more serious diagnoses; he believed they would prove negative. If that was not the case, we would deal with things in due course. Were there any questions?

I looked at Claire. She was sitting very still, as in that breathless moment before raising her arms and arching her wrists and touching the piano. She had no questions. Neither did I—except for the same bitter and unanswerable riddle that had gnawed at me all along. Why was this happening to us?

We were shown to an examination room that was all chrome and porcelain. Claire was given a gown to put on; it was soft cotton with faded blue flowers on it; it opened at the back. Without embarrassment, with the strange matter-of-factness that medical settings seem to impose, she slipped out of her cardigan and sat there in her bra.

It had been a long time since I'd seen her body. I glanced at her prominent collarbones and pale tummy, and an avalanche of feelings tumbled down on me. Remembered desire—wildly inappropriate to the moment, but undeniable nonetheless—was part of it, but only a small part, almost incidental. Seeing her unshielded flesh in the harsh light of a doctor's office, mostly what I felt was an excruciating tenderness, a pity that applied not just to Claire, but to everyone who'd ever been born. It was a helpless kind of pity that could drive a person mad. We were all so fragile. Things could so easily go wrong . . . And then, unbidden, came a leap: I understood that all of us would die, that there were no exceptions. I'd known this before, of course; but I'm not sure I'd *really* known it until that moment.

She slipped into the gown and asked me to tie the strings at the back. As I did so, I touched her hair, I smelled her skin. Everything seemed more precious than it had the minute before.

Gupta came into the room, followed by a nurse. The doctor smiled reassuringly at Claire; the nurse looked dubiously at me. "Are you sure you want to be here?" she asked.

I told her I was sure.

Gently, but not without a touch of wryness, Gupta said, "Fine. But remember that your wife's the patient. We can't handle two."

Claire was told to lie down on the table and to curl up in a fetal pose, to stretch the space between her vertebrae. I stood before her and touched her shoulder. The doctor pulled on gloves, then filled a small syringe with local anesthetic. Claire tensed and twitched as the needle broke her skin.

When the place was numb, Gupta bent close over her with a larger needle. "Still now," he said. "Very, very still."

I couldn't watch but I couldn't look away. I saw the needle sink into her flesh between the nubbly bones along her spine. The doctor seemed to adjust the depth of penetration, then very slowly began to withdraw fluid. The fluid looked very viscous, almost like melting jelly, as it was pulled into the syringe. It seemed to take a long time to gather it. Claire was taking tiny, shallow breaths, breathing the way a wounded animal breathes. My vision went very glary at the edges and I reminded myself I was not allowed to faint.

When the procedure was finished, the nurse and doctor left the room, telling Claire she needed to lie still for a while. I stroked her hair and asked if she was okay.

"Not too bad," she said. "Really spacey, though. My brain feels dry. Talk to me. I'd like it if you'd talk to me."

I was more than a little dizzy myself. Also, I had the feeling that if I tried to speak I would probably get choked up. "What would you like me to talk about?" I managed.

"Doesn't matter. I kind of have a ringing in my ears. I'd rather hear your voice."

"Okay," I said. "Okay." In the hard light of the examination room, with its smells of blood and antiseptics, I opened my mouth without knowing what would come out. I heard myself say, "Funny, how you think of things. I think I finally figured out why we split up. Why we stopped being nice to each other. Stopped even looking at each other for a while. After all this time, I think I know."

Claire said nothing. I had no idea if she was really hearing me, if the sounds were resolving into words or just filtering through as vague and simple music.

"We had a wrong idea of what perfect was," I rambled on, "because we had a wrong idea about time. When things got tough, we imagined that everything was ruined, forever. Like the bad stuff would just go on, in a straight line, as far as you could see. That was wrong. Things weren't ruined; they changed. And they could change again, be good again. We didn't understand that: that things can change, *have* to change, because they have an ending. Does that make any sense at all?"

Claire said nothing. Maybe she was thinking, maybe she was dozing, maybe she was in a state for which we don't have words. Maybe I was talking to myself. And maybe that was just as well.

"We broke up," I said, "because we imagined we would live forever."

Chapter 19

That weekend, Claire and I talked a couple times each day. Mainly, I was just calling to see how she was feeling—which was fine, knock wood, except for a lingering dull headache. Even so, those morning and evening phone calls were a lot more frequent contact than we usually allowed ourselves; my Saturday and Sunday seemed to arrange themselves around the times we would talk. Her test results were due in on Wednesday, and apart though we were, it felt to me that we were keeping the vigil together. During that weekend, I couldn't quite tell if we were courting, or just dealing with a crisis—or maybe leaning toward a different kind of crisis. I wondered if there would come a point when Claire would say, "Wait a second, back off, let's remember that we're just old friends." If she said that, I really didn't know how I would answer.

Monday came, and brought with it a different set of preoccupations. Jenna called mid-morning to invite me to a meeting late that afternoon with another financier.

"Who's it this time?" I asked. "Warren Buffett? Kirk Kerkorian?"

"Move a few steps down the food chain," she said. "It's a hedge-fund guy. Name's Trip Campbell. Young, sharp, brash as they come. Runs about eighty billion dollars."

In my naïveté, I said, "Hedge-fund guys buy real estate?"

"Hedge-fund guys buy anything," she said. "They're unregulated madmen. It's all haggle, barter, bluff, and whine. Anything to make a deal. Plus, there's some history with this guy that I think should make it pretty interesting."

"How so?"

She answered with a question, as she often did. "Pardon my French, but you know what a mercy fuck is?"

"Do I ever."

"How about a revenge fuck?"

"Happy to say I have less experience with that."

"Well," she said, "this meeting may turn out to be either one of those."

"But who's doing what to whom?"

"That's the interesting part. See what you think, then come talk to me."

"You won't be at the meeting?"

"Seems to be boys only," she said. "Some weird testosterone thing, I guess. Just Robert, Arthur, the whiz kid, you, and Carlton Phelps."

"Ah," I said, "the nervous guy."

"Come see me later," she said, and hung up the phone.

The first thing I noticed about Trip Campbell was the drape of his suit. It was gorgeous. It was more than gorgeous; it was sculpture in silk and mohair, a classical carving come to life. The suit was no color in particular, but a mysterious heather of taupe and gray and hints of steely blue.

The second thing I noticed about the hedge-fund guy was that he sniffled a lot, and he didn't seem to have a cold. I'm not saying he was hopped up on coke or meth or anything like that, though I wouldn't rule it out, either. I doubted he slept much. He seemed like someone who would be awake before dawn to monitor the overseas markets, then out at the clubs till all hours, sipping Cristal with fashion models.

I didn't think he was more than thirty-four or so. His sandy hair was moussed so that it stood in stylish clumps. He had a dimple in his chin. Everything about him was jumpy and abrupt. His gestures were angular and choppy. He'd brought along no associates or assistants; he wrote nothing down on paper. Now and then he tapped an entry into a fancy PDA. I thought: *If that thing falls down a subway grating, this guy's life is over.*

As the meeting was a small one, it was held at Maxx's desk. Plump, yellowish clouds rolled across the giant windows at his back.

Being the host and the celebrity, my billionaire tried to control the tone and tempo of the conversation; I was just beginning to understand that the tempo was important, maybe even crucial. Every business confrontation, like every prizefight, had a certain pace and rhythm; each rhythm favored one combatant or the other. Maxx's natural cadence was a rather undulating one, a legato that allowed for the occasional digression or flight of grandiosity. Trip Campbell's beat was pure staccato. It was like the difference between tai chi and kickboxing, and it became clear from the start that Campbell's rhythm would prevail. Maxx launched into his leisurely spiel about the historic import of this deal and the need for complete confidentiality, and Campbell cut him off.

"Let's not play games," he said. "It's Rockefeller Center."

Maxx's mouth had not had time to close. His jaw hung slack; in that moment he looked a little stupid. He blinked at Arthur Levin. Then he said to Campbell, "What makes you think so?"

"Come on," said Campbell. "There's been rumors for months that it's on the block. Suddenly you're scraping for cash. It isn't rocket science."

Carlton Phelps squeezed his hands together, then piped in with that pinched and reedy voice of his. "We aren't *scraping*. That isn't accurate at all."

"Whatever," said the hedge-fund guy.

Arthur Levin said, "Yes, it's Rockefeller Center. We see it as a tremendous opportunity. Are you interested?"

Campbell sniffled. "I'm here. So talk to me."

Sitting off to the side as usual, I buried my face in my notebook and scrawled my impressions as fast as I could. When I wasn't writing, I was studying my billionaire. His eyes flickered, his forehead crawled; it was as if there was some physical shifting of gears inside his head as he struggled to regroup. By the time he spoke again, something impressive but slightly spooky had happened. He'd completely retooled his pitch; some hardwired gift of mimicry made him sound like the person he was spieling. With the old-school Knightsbridge Partners, the pitch had mostly been about the prestige of the property, its marquee value all around the world. With new-school Trip Campbell, there was none of that. Now it was a brisk litany about buying in during a trough in the market, using it as a diversification move against the volatility of the derivatives, and a counterplay to short-selling the REITs. I can't say I really understood all this, but I found it virtuosic.

Trip Campbell, however, seemed determined not to be impressed. He didn't even respond directly to anything Maxx had said. He just cracked a knuckle and asked a simple but very rude question. "Why don't you go to a plain old bank?"

Carlton Phelps twitched at that, and said, "We'd prefer not to bring this to our usual lenders."

"Why not?"

Even I could tell that this was disingenuous. And malicious—though I didn't yet know where the malice came from.

Arthur Levin tried to defuse the question, but a new firmness or perhaps indignation had replaced his usual mollifying tone. "That's a strategic decision that's ours to make. It's independent of the terms we'll offer you."

"No, it isn't," said the hedge-fund guy. "I think you're not going to a bank because you *can't* go to a bank. You're finally tapped out. Those giant credit lines—all used up. That's my guess. Hey, no shame in that. We all live on debt. But it means there's more risk in the deal. More risk, more reward. That's basic."

I looked at Maxx. For the first time since I'd known him, he seemed tired, plodding, like a heavyweight who'd been chasing his opponent around the ring, throwing punches that did not connect. With an uneasy mix of petulance and weariness, he said, "There's plenty of payoff in the deal. And there's plenty of other people we can bring it to."

"I'm sure there are. But you invited me."

There was a silence—one of those seething silences in which skin begins to prickle and people notice that the smell in the room has changed. Carlton Phelps toyed with a fingernail. Maxx stuck out his heavy chin. Then Arthur Levin said something that took everyone by surprise.

"And that was a mistake."

Trip Campbell fidgeted as his crackling synapses tried to process what had just been said. He seemed to want to treat the comment as a little joke, but his spasm of a smile soon turned sour as he realized that Levin wasn't kidding.

"You're not serious about this deal," the lawyer went on. "You're not serious at all. You're here so you can make some smart remarks and brag that you were here. It's a bad way to do business."

The hedge-fund guy stiffened and sniffled; his sandy eyebrows pulled together tight and the flesh between them turned dark. With a sneer, he said, "It seems to work for me."

"For now," Levin calmly said. "Because people don't really know you yet. You're just starting to make enemies. I give it two, three years. After that, maybe prison, maybe rehab." He turned away from the jumpy young man and looked at Robert Maxx. "I think we've wasted enough time here. I think this meeting's over."

Even the unflappable Jenna was impressed by Levin's zinger. "Wow! He *said* that?"

"Word for word."

She wagged her head and smiled. But the smile didn't last long. She said, "I love it, but I'm not sure it was the best idea. Guy like Campbell thrives on insults. Give him a kick, he's that much more likely to come back and bite your ankle."

We were sitting at her desk. She was wearing a black turtleneck sweater and big hoop earrings that I hadn't seen before. Behind her, the clouds had thickened and were tinged with orange; she made a pretty silhouette against them.

"What I don't understand," I said, "is why anybody bothered with this meeting in the first place."

"That's what important people do," she said. "They have meetings with other important people so they can remind themselves that they're important."

"But this guy was just so hostile from the get-go."

"No one knew that in advance," she said. "That was the gamble. Reconciliation or revenge fuck. Robert basically ruined Trip Campbell's father."

Her tone was so completely matter-of-fact that the words took a moment to register. "Excuse me?"

"Back in '94. The second bankruptcy scare—no, the third. The court was threatening to freeze domestic assets. So Robert quietly sold off some foreign ones—a huge hotel in Buenos Aires, a residential complex near the Olympic site in Barcelona. The banks got the properties at fire-sale prices. Robert got the cash he needed. The unsecured investors got screwed. Campbell Senior probably lost about twenty million. Never really recovered."

Call me unforgiving. I said, "I can't believe the son would even sit in the same room as Maxx."

Not surprisingly, Jenna took a more pragmatic view. "Business is business. And families are weird."

"And why would Maxx even show this guy his hand? He's making trouble for himself again."

"Possibly. Then again, how many places can you go to raise three billion dollars?"

"Maxx said there's a lot of people he can go to."

"Of course he'd say that."

I leaned closer across her desk, close enough to get a whiff of her pine-and-lavender perfume. "And you're saying there aren't?"

She paused, then made a gesture that I was coming to see as quintessential in the working world: a quick paranoid glance toward the open office door as she was on the cusp of saying something that she probably shouldn't say. "These days? No."

I tapped my fingers on my notebook. "Campbell was guessing that Maxx wasn't going to the banks because the credit lines were all tapped out."

"Not a bad guess."

"It sure made Phelps squirm."

"It would. I mean, that's exactly his department."

"But wait," I said. "Bear with me a minute. English major, remember. If Maxx has all this debt and the banks won't lend him money anymore, why is he still trying to make this big, gigantic acquisition?"

Jenna looked at me like the answer should be obvious. "Because he has to."

"But—"

'"Fresh investment services old debt.' That's the mantra. That's the key. The big new acquisition is made with other people's money. That's how the new cash comes in. It's a process that can't stop. If it stalls, if credit gets too tight, we're toast. This Rockefeller Center thing—you think it's about a property? You think it's about some *buildings*?"

Sheepishly, I admitted that, yeah, I did.

"No," said Jenna. "It's about a transfusion of funds. About finding a deal sexy enough to pull in new investment to cover other bets."

"So, Rockefeller Center . . . doesn't matter?"

"It matters that it's huge. It matters that it's prestigious. Other than that? It could as easily be some giant project in Germany or China. Plenty of other deals could fill the bill."

"So why's Maxx so obsessed with this one?"

"Ah. Now we're not talking business anymore. Now we're talking Robert. He's itching for that property, wants it bad. But that's got nothing to do with business. All the business needs is cash. This craving for a crown jewel in the heart of midtown, that's ego pure and simple."

"Is there a difference? Between Robert's business and Robert's ego, I mean?"

She pursed her lips and thought it over. "Once upon a time there was. There isn't anymore. And that's what scares me."

Chapter 20

Twenty or so years ago, when I first moved to New York, I stumbled across a piece of performance art that has stayed with me all this time.

The concept was as brilliant as it was simple. The artist climbed a stubby flagpole near Columbus Circle, and perched on top, he cheerfully sang out people's names, as if he was hailing long-lost friends. He yelled each name twice. "Nancy! Nancy! Barry! Barry!" Invariably, all the Nancys and the Barrys in the throng would look up hopefully, gratefully, in the direction of the voice, believing for a moment that they were being recognized and greeted. It was a play, of course, on the epic loneliness of Manhattan streets, where most people do most things on their own, and the affirmation that comes from crossing paths with someone who actually knows your name happens a few times in a year.

I thought about this performance, probably for the thousandth time, as I left Maxx Tower and emerged into an early, chilly dusk. As ever, the nameless pedestrians were hustling and weaving, one by one;

but it wasn't the spectacle of isolation that put me in mind of the artist on the flagpole. It was that I heard somebody call my name.

"David! David Collins!"

It was a female voice, vaguely familiar, though not one I could immediately place. By reflex, I looked around to locate its source. I guess I shouldn't have done that. In this neighborhood, I wasn't supposed to be David Collins at all. I was Dave Cullen, anonymous scribe. But how could I not react to the sound of my name ringing out above the bustle?

I traced the voice to a taxi stopped illegally at curbside, cars veering angrily around it. The taxi's rear door was open; a leg extended out from it. It was a nice leg, with a full-muscled calf and a slender ankle. The leg was dressed in a dark stocking—a tad too dressy or provocative for the business day, more suggestive of an evening out.

For a moment I just stood frozen on the sidewalk. Horns blared; buses roared; I struggled to put my thoughts together. Clearly, the owner of the shapely leg had been laying for me outside of Maxx's building. This was bad. But what could I do? Run away? I pictured some grainy, hackneyed chase scene through the streets of New York, skyscrapers blurring in the background as my necktie streamed out behind me. It seemed futile and faintly ridiculous. I walked over toward the taxi.

Connected to the shapely leg was Mandy Lockwood. Aside from the dark stockings, she was wearing a short black skirt and a tight pale sweater that traced out the swell of her breasts like fresh snow on hills. "Hello, David Collins," she said. "How's my old pal Robert?"

I said nothing.

She said, "I know, I know. You're sworn to secrecy. Get in the cab. I'm buying you a cocktail."

"Um," I said, "sorry, but I'm supposed to be somewhere."

This was a lie; it was a feeble lie; and anyway, it didn't matter.

Mandy said, "You're a writer. You're doing a book with him, and nobody's supposed to know. If you want to keep it that way, get in."

She slid across the seat, and patted the warm place where her ass had been. I had no choice, I got in the taxi. She directed the driver to an address way downtown, in the meatpacking district.

As we snaked through the traffic, she said, "I've known Robert a long time. I know how he operates. He likes to have a writer in tow. Like he's the president or something, making history every time he opens his big fat mouth."

I said, "But how did you—"

She pulled a book from her purse. It was *Nowhere Fast,* my second novel, the one the critics hadn't much liked. The jacket still had the remainder sticker on it. Talk about adding insult to injury. I sweat blood over the fucking thing, and she ruins my life with a copy marked down from twenty-four dollars to a buck ninety-eight. She opened it to the author photo on the back flap. "If you're playing it incognito," she said, "you shouldn't have your picture out in public. I described you to some people I know in publishing. It wasn't difficult. Especially for an unemployed reporter with time on her hands."

The taxi lurched and squeaked. Hoping to establish some solidarity, some sense of collegial loyalty, I said, "I think it sucks that he had you fired."

She shrugged. I couldn't tell if the shrug was meant to be coquettish, or if it just looked that way because of how she was built. Given her compact carnality, there was no safe and neutral space between her erogenous zones; her body was like a book with no parts you could skip.

"A lot of things suck," she said. "Where you from?"

"Jersey."

"See," she said, "you know. Me, I'm from Brooklyn and I talk Brooklyn. You don't think I could change that if I wanted to? Well, I don't want to. It's who I am. My father drove a subway. My mother stayed home and sneaked cheap whiskey. Did we know from privilege, power, how things really work? No way. We're outsiders, David Collins. Bridge-and-tunnel. People like us, we have to find a way in, have to improvise."

"That includes kidnapping?" I said.

She let it pass. "But I'll tell you something. I was pretty sick of that gig anyway. That may sound like sour grapes, but it really isn't. I mean, how many years do you want to go on faking orgasms about some company beating earnings estimates by a penny? Problem is, I made the classic mistake of leaving my last job before I had my next one."

"Come on," I said. "You're famous. You're great-looking. You'll get another job."

She gave her thick red hair a shake. "Damn straight I will. And it'll be an upgrade from that stinking cable ghetto. Because I'm going to have something big and juicy to lay at the feet of my next employer. I'm going to have the definitive exposé on Robert Maxx. And you're going to help me do it."

I swallowed. I worked for a deep breath, but it suddenly seemed like the taxi had been shrink-wrapped and all the air squeezed out. I cracked a window and got a faceful of bluish bus exhaust. Trying not to stammer, I said, "There's no way I can do that."

She didn't answer right away. But suddenly her hand was on my leg. I didn't see it move; I didn't feel it land. But there it was, with its painted nails and a ring or two, splayed out on my thigh. "Don't be so absolute," she said. "We'll have a chat, a couple drinks, we'll see if we can work together. Who knows—it might even be fun."

South of Thirty-fourth Street, the traffic thinned; below Fourteenth, it all but disappeared. Soon we were winding through a funky warehouse neighborhood where the streets were still cobblestone and the sidewalks met at crazy angles. The taxi stopped between a Dumpster and a truck trailer that had lost its cab. If there was a bar there, I didn't see it right away. But we emerged into evening air that smelled of blood and fat, and Mandy led me past some garbage cans and toward a door with a single dim bulb and a small sign that said VOID.

"Excellent martinis," she said. "And I don't have to worry about being recognized. This is not exactly a Wall Street crowd."

It's fair to say that was an understatement. In fact, it was a crowd with lots of tattoos, purple hair and shaven heads, and maybe half a ton of facial hardware. There were nose rings and eyebrow studs, safety pins in ears and rivets shot through lips. People slouched at the bar with lengths of steel chain dangling from their collars. The lights were low to the point of semiblindness, and some morbid and funereal techno pop was coming through the speakers. It was a place where one could go mad, die in the bathroom of an overdose, or just riffle through the anguished poses of one's twenties before getting a real job and moving back to Westchester.

We took a small table near the back. A waiter in a dog collar came by to take our order. Hoping to stay reasonably sober and to keep my wits about me, I asked for a glass of red wine.

"Don't be a pussy," Mandy said to me. To the waiter, she said, "He'll have a martini."

"What color?"

"What *color*?" I said.

"He'll have the blue," said Mandy. "I'll take the orange."

Waiting for the cocktails to arrive, I turned to my lovely abductress and put on as stern a face as I could manage. "Listen," I said, "there's nothing I can tell you about Maxx. You know him. He stuck me with a really strict nondisclose. I say one word, I'm fired and I'm sued."

She dismissed that with a wave and a sort of clucking sound. "Come on. *Everyone's* on nondisclose these days. And everybody talks. Leaks. Rumors. Unnamed sources. Makes the world go 'round. Take those things away, and what's left of the news? Spin-filled press releases by frightened little PR flacks. Would that be interesting? Is that a world you want to live in?"

I didn't have to answer, because the drinks arrived. They were served in classic martini glasses, but still, they looked bizarre. Mandy's was the color of leakage from a rusty radiator. Mine, unhappily, reminded me of the toilet-bowl freshener often seen in bourgeois suburban homes. I have no idea what was in the drinks. But we clinked glasses and sipped them. Not surprisingly, I guess, mine tasted really great. Have I mentioned I like alcohol?

Mandy took several sips, then positioned her glass carefully between her elbows. She leaned toward me, and the pressure of her arms squeezed her boobs together so that a cleavage line was clearly visible right through her sweater. "So," she said, "what's Maxx up to these days? What's he working on? Who's he talking to?"

"No idea," I said. "None at all."

"Something's cooking. He only does my show—my former show—when something's cooking."

I just shrugged and shook my head. Trying to convey an utter lack of interest, I let my gaze wander through the dim and hazy room. I would have hummed along with the background music if there'd been a tune to hum along with.

"There's been whispers about Rockefeller Center," she pressed. "You know anything about Rockefeller Center?"

This was getting a little close for comfort. I struggled with my face muscles and turned to my drink to stall for time while considering my answer. Finally, in a tone of capitulation, I said, "Yes. I do."

At that, she leaned closer to me, nakedly avid. Her eyes were coaxing and she squirmed a little in her chair. I don't know if her mouth was watering but she definitely licked her lips.

Softly, I said, "It's the home of the Rockettes."

I must admit, I was pretty pleased with that. Mandy wasn't.

"Oh Christ," she said. "You're going to be an asshole. Okay. Let's have another drink, at least."

"I haven't finished this one yet," I pointed out.

"You will," she said. "And it's the ability to plan for the future that separates us from the lower beasts."

She caught the waiter's eye and ordered us another round.

Then she said, "Okay, you don't want to talk about Robert. Let's talk about something else. Let's talk about you. You married?"

I probably shouldn't have answered this. I probably shouldn't have answered anything at all, but just sat there sullen and grudging until she gave up and released me. But I didn't do that. "Divorced," I said.

After all this time it was still a hard word for me to say. It was a word that seemed to call for drinking. The second martini arrived at an auspicious moment.

"Ah," she said, "too bad. I mean, I guess it's too bad. Maybe it isn't. Who knows? Got a girlfriend?"

At this, for some reason, I gave a little laugh. "Not really."

"Not really? Usually it's yes or no."

I couldn't disagree with that. Then again, I was not about to sit there and explain that my ex-wife was sort of my girlfriend, except for the ways in which she wasn't.

Mandy nipped at her infernal-looking martini, then stared at me over the top of it. "Getting laid?"

There it was—the exact reason why I shouldn't have answered any personal questions in the first place. I had information that Mandy Lockwood wanted, and I should have known that this is where the conversation would go. I couldn't be sure if the rude inquiry was in fact an outright offer. My gonads seemed to think it was; awkwardly, they started to wake from their long slumber. This was bad. I shouldn't have had the second martini; and I wouldn't have, if I hadn't had the first. Then again, why not just lighten up and go for it? I was forty-two years old, and for better or worse I was single. I'd lived in the metropolis for decades, and I'd never had sex with a single television personality, not even cable. What was the harm? Then I remembered that the harm was that I'd probably lose the chance to write this book and my life would be destroyed, all for a measly piece of ass that I'd feel lousy about anyway, since I was really still in love with someone else.

I guess I took much too long to answer. Mandy said, "It's a pretty simple question."

Finally I said, "Not lately. No."

She put on a pouty face and said, "Me neither."

I tried not to look surprised.

"You look surprised," she said. "Well, okay. All you know is that I used to sleep with Robert and now I'm coming on to you. So you think I'm just some slut from Bay Ridge. You're wrong. I'm really pretty picky."

I guess this was a compliment, though I wasn't sure that I believed it, and in any case I had no answer for it. Mandy sipped her drink and went off on a different tack.

"Ever been fired, David Collins?"

"No," I said. "But only because I've never had a job. Not a real one."

"It's humiliating. They lock your desk, confiscate your files, and escort you out like you're a goddamn criminal."

"I'm sorry."

"I could kill the son of a bitch," she said.

That inebriated evening may have left me hazy on a few details, but I am absolutely certain that she said those words.

"Wouldn't it be fun to bring him down?" she went on. "Wouldn't you be *proud* to bring him down?"

I considered that. As Maxx himself had said, this parry and revenge stuff was just a game, and games were meant for winning. If, that is, one chose to play at all. "I'd be happy to be a spectator," I said. "But I can't help you. I just can't do it."

Apparently she didn't take me at my word.

She squirmed a little in her chair, then put her head at an angle suggestive of resting on a nest of feather pillows. She said, "I have a nice idea. Why don't you put your hand under the table?"

This made me slightly dizzy. I pictured the shapely leg in its dark stocking dangling from the taxi door. I saw the short black skirt, the compact and voluptuous thighs with so little safe expanse, barely the span of my fingers, below the loins. My hand badly wanted to go there. It wanted to go there so badly that I feared I'd rupture a tendon holding it back. Finally, instead of groping for her flesh, I made a rather spastic grab for the edge of the table. Not very smoothly, I eased my chair away from it. It made an ugly scraping sound as I stood.

"I'm going now," I said, my voice unsteady and congested. "I just can't do this. Sorry."

She looked at me, she looked away. I stood there in the dimness as the awful music throbbed along; I was waiting to be cursed or threatened. But when her gaze returned, her face had softened. There was something wry in her expression, and also something that was almost tender. She said, "You're a pussy, David Collins." But she said it without rancor.

"You're probably right," I said. "Throw in wimp, weenie, and incurable romantic, too." I extended my hand. "Friends?"

She made me wait a couple heartbeats, then extended hers. I took it, then did something I had no idea I was about to do, and maybe was completely geeky and ridiculous, but it felt right and I'm really glad I did it. I raised her hand to my lips and planted a chaste kiss on her fingers.

I staggered past the pierced and tattooed drinkers at the bar and out into the street.

Chapter 21

Back at home, it was a night for Ambien, and no mistake. I didn't even go through the dreary charade of trying to get to sleep without it, just went straight to the medicine chest. The prescription label said *Do Not Mix with Alcohol*. That was a good one. I fired down a tablet and dove into bed.

The drug was a mercy. The hangover from the blue martinis wasn't. It kicked in sometime during the middle of the night, taking the form of rough thumbs behind my eyeballs, and waking me from a grotesque and feverish dream of Mandy Lockwood on a brightly lit stage set in hell.

I was still paying dues in the morning, but that was okay; it seemed a just and therefore almost pleasurable penance. I had a dull headache and my eyes itched, but some semblance of clarity had returned, and the headache wasn't so bad that I couldn't get to work.

It felt like I had a lot to catch up on. There were my quickly scrawled notes from the thoroughly unpleasant meeting with Trip Campbell, the hedge-fund brat dissing Maxx right to his face. There were the twists and insinuations in my most recent chat with Jenna, her suggestion that far more was riding on the Rockefeller Center acquisition than just a few acres of historic real estate. I sifted through those conversations, and attached words to the residue of hunches and emotions that they left behind. I typed it all into the computer file that was starting to take on an encouraging heft, and even showing early signs of squirming to life and becoming a story.

But every story has its particular difficulties and challenges; and with a story like this one—where the basic facts are widely known, and the ending, therefore, seems inevitable—the trick lies in remaining honest about how much I knew, and when I knew it, and in not claiming credit for more insight or prescience than I had. So let me be clear: in retrospect, it is easy to see that Robert Maxx was already in deep but secret trouble, but I really didn't know it at the time. Maybe I *should* have known it, but I didn't. New to his world, naive about his business, I just figured he was embroiled in a tough and grinding and in some ways ugly part of the process by which he had always made his money and his reputation. I assumed the setbacks would end and he would come out on top yet once more. Who would have imagined otherwise?

And while I'm admitting to things I didn't timely understand, let me confess to another one, a whopper: I don't think I really understood yet whose book I was writing. I believed I was writing Robert Maxx's book, the one I'd been hired to write. But in fact, all I was doing on Maxx's behalf was piling up words; and words alone don't make a book, any more than notes alone make music. A book needs passion and aches and laughs and wild guesses, and those things I was reserving for a different book—*my* book—that would inevitably be a sort of funhouse mirror reflection of the official one, a dark twin, an antibook. Call me schizoid—I was working on one book with my right brain and another with my left. Someone should have paid me double.

In any case, I was working quite happily that morning. I stopped noticing I had a headache; because I didn't notice, the headache went away. I drank more coffee, strung more sentences together, largely vanished into the task at hand. At some point, the phone rang. I picked it up and said a distracted hello.

"Hi!" said a voice that clearly expected to be recognized.

"Hello," I said again, in a tone that clearly expressed no recognition.

A bit exasperated, or certainly puzzled, the voice said, "It's Marcie. Marcie Kanin. Your editor. Remember?"

"Oh, hi, Marcie. How are you?"

"Fine. Just wondering if you'd left the country or something. It's been weeks since we've talked."

"It's been that long?"

"Guess you've really missed me. You don't need a lot of hand-holding, do you?"

"No," I said, "I don't."

In fact, I'm just the opposite. I like to be left alone when I'm working on a book. It's like the book is my own precious egg, and no one else's butt is coming near it till it's hatched. I guess a shrink would say there's some infantile, retentive action going on. But that's how I work—what can I say?

"I guess I should be grateful for a disappearing author," Marcie said. "Most of my others are so goddamn needy. I get calls on weekends, people wanting to read sentences aloud. I get text messages with questions about commas. But still, you'd think there'd be some happy medium."

"With writers? No, you wouldn't."

"So how's it going?"

"Fine."

"Fine? Jesus, don't overwhelm me with details. Is Maxx cooperating? Are you getting what you need?"

"Getting great stuff," I said. "Really kind of amazing stuff."

There was a pause. I don't think it's too far-fetched to say it was a hungry pause. But I added nothing more, and Marcie said, "But you're not going to tell me about it."

"No."

I hadn't set out to be a tease, though I'd realized by now that's exactly what I was being. Teasing and being teased—about information, about sex—seemed to occupy a large percentage of my waking hours lately, and I really didn't know how this had happened.

Marcie said, "Well, if there's anything you'd ever like to talk about . . . You know, just so I can feel I'm earning my meager pay-check . . ."

Her voice reluctantly tailed off, and as it did so, something occurred to me—something quite liberating. I was forbidden to say anything to anyone about what I learned regarding Robert Maxx. But there was no such prohibition about things that happened to *me*. Apparently it had never dawned on Maxx's lawyers that anything that happened to a ghostwriter might be of the remotest consequence.

So I said, "Actually, there's one thing I can tell you. I was kidnapped last night."

"What?"

"By a beautiful woman who ordered me into a taxi, put her hand on my thigh, then plied me with martinis and offered up her gorgeous little body in exchange for things I couldn't tell her."

"You're serious?"

"Entirely."

"Jeez," said Marcie. "And I only offer a nice lunch now and then. So what happened?"

"What happened *what*?"

"About her offer."

"Now you're pushing it."

"I'm not asking for a play-by-play. But who was the woman?"

"It's better I don't tell you that."

She made a frustrated, softly hissing sound. "Okay, okay. But the whole setup is just so cool and sordid. You're putting it in the book, I hope."

Clearly, this was blurted out before she'd thought it through. There's no way that my little escapades and misadventures, not to mention my aches and laughs and wild guesses, would make it into the official book, the one that Robert Maxx controlled.

"I don't see how that could work," I said.

Marcie seemed to take a moment to shift back from enthusiast to editor. "No. I guess it wouldn't." She tried to put a laugh into her voice, but it was a melancholy laugh because it seemed to carry the knowledge of opportunities lost, of stories that wouldn't be told, a perhaps worthwhile book that was dead before it was written. "Oh well. Another good scene on the cutting-room floor."

I said nothing. My headache started coming back, probably because my jaw was clenched.

"Anyway," she said, "glad to hear it's going well. You'll call if you need anything?"

"Sure."

"Lunch sometime?"

"That'd be great. But maybe when I'm a little farther along."

"Right," she said. "And I should just leave you alone in the meantime."

"Pretty much. No offense."

"No offense."

Chapter 22

That evening, I saw Robert Maxx again, though not in person. I saw him on the six o'clock news. This was network, not cable, watched by tens of millions. Maxx's segment ran in the coveted slot before the first commercial—the slot where they show the big stuff, the footage of wars and coups and earthquakes—and he gave a bravura performance, a performance of breathtaking chutzpah.

The anchor, looking earnest and unflappable yet suitably impressed, had reported that a source involved in the negotiations had confirmed what previously was merely rumored—that Robert Maxx, the brash and visionary real estate magnate, was in talks to purchase Rockefeller Center. The sale, if completed, would set a new record for the value of commercial property in Manhattan, and might very well raise the bar on top-tier urban holdings all around the globe. Asked to comment, Maxx seemed to have decided on the characteristically grandiose and theatrical idea of staging an impromptu press conference in the Rock Center Plaza, right next to the skating rink.

So there he was, in my living room, in *everybody's* living room, smiling and gesturing and lying through his teeth.

He did so with remarkable panache. Dressed in a perfect charcoal suit accented with a rich red power tie, he oozed confidence and poise. He was surrounded by the tall and staid and blockish buildings of the Center, and yet he did not seem dwarfed by them; on the contrary, his ego and his presence matched—or even overmatched—their monumentality. With his zestfully pugnacious jaw and endlessly hungry carnivorous grin and crazy head of cantilevered hair, he dominated the camera frame, all but blotting out the cityscape, sending it, vast though it was, into some vague and dreamy background, as in a medieval painting. It was the personality, the will, that commandeered the focus.

With a dozen microphones wagging in his face, Maxx told the world that he was, in fact, on the verge of completing this historic transaction. He was currently choosing among a number of financial partners who were clamoring to get in on the deal—who shared his conviction that the purchase would soon seem an amazing bargain. Under the new ownership, with fresh ideas and almost unlimited capital, these great old buildings would help to usher in a new golden age for midtown. And, because new eras call for new names, and to underscore his personal commitment to making this property his flagship, the former Rockefeller Center would be rechristened Maxx Center, the center of a changing world.

The news went on to other things. I switched off the TV, and sat there transfixed, appalled and awed. I guess that, with every story on the news, there's a tiny subset of insiders who know for sure that most of what is being said is patent bullshit; the rest of us have to decide for ourselves, trusting to intuition and the fine-tuning of our cynicism. But I had seldom had the queasy privilege of the backstage view. Everything Maxx had said was plausible, and I was keenly aware that nearly every word of it was either false or a betrayal of something else he'd promised. Yet, through it all, his gaze had been steady, his voice firm, his gestures sincere and enveloping; as a performance, it was both mesmerizing and disgusting, and I couldn't wait to ask him how he managed it.

A t nine o'clock the next morning, I called Jenna. For the first time since we'd met, I was a little bit annoyed with her.

"Thanks for the heads-up on the press conference," I said. "I really would have liked to be there."

"Me, too," she said.

"You weren't?"

"Almost no one from the company was there," she said.

This surprised me. I would have thought that something as important as a network news announcement would have called for a major team effort, with lots of strategizing and planning and support from the underlings. I would have thought that—and I would have been wrong.

"Robert just pounced on it," she went on. "A couple of calls came in from media, and he decided that's how he would handle it. It was set up in an hour."

"Doesn't that strike you as . . . I don't know . . . awfully impulsive? Maybe undisciplined? Maybe reckless?"

"It strikes me as Robert being Robert. You have to understand how he operates. When he feels like he's losing control of a situation, he goes into streetfighter mode. He doesn't think, exactly; he just reacts. It's all adrenaline and instinct. He'll roar, puff up, charge like a bull—anything to get back on the offensive. Sometimes it's brilliant and sometimes it's reckless."

"Which is it this time?"

She avoided answering by her usual trick of countering with a question of her own. "You coming in today?"

"I'd like to. Will he see me?"

"I'll arrange it. Be here in an hour. You can ask him this stuff yourself."

O n the threshold of Maxx's gigantic office, I crossed paths with Arthur Levin, who was leaving. I caught just a glimpse of the attorney as we passed and said a perfunctory hello; but that quick glance stayed with me. In a setting where people kept their poker faces on, where expressions conveyed bargaining positions but not emotions, Levin looked genuinely sorrowful. His skin, usually pink, was chalky; his blue eyes were without their sparkle and seemed to have turned inward. His posture was labored, as though it was costing him great effort not to hunch.

Maybe it was just a carryover from this troubling impression, but Maxx's office struck me as horribly empty that day. All those vacant chairs; those arbitrary clusters of settees where no one ever seemed to sit. Even the big, lonesome potted plants—what had they done to deserve being yanked out of the ground and exiled to this sterile place fifty stories above the earth?

As for Maxx himself, he was sitting at his desk, alone, and as I approached, he seemed to be reprogramming his face, trying to compose lips and chin and eyes into a dignity worthy of his station. He also seemed to be working on his voice, searching out a tone that was authoritative, unruffled, but also wry. "So," he said, before he'd even said hello, "Jenna tells me you saw me on the tube."

"Impressive performance," I said. "It belongs in our book. I was hoping we could talk about it."

"Sure," he said, waving me into a chair, "but what's to talk about? I had to do it. That dick Trip Campbell leaked the story—that's pretty clear. Maybe for spite. Maybe to earn some favors down the road. Either way, once it was out, it became an opportunity. An opportunity, a pain in the ass, and a risk. They often go together. That's life. So I did what I had to do, and it put things on a slightly different footing."

"Different footing, how?" I said.

He paused, looked down at his fingernails, then pointed with his massive chin toward the doorway where Arthur Levin had exited.

"Well, for one thing, the old lady just quit."

He tried to smile. It didn't work. His face moved instead toward a sort of puffy-lipped frown.

"It's sad to see a guy go soft like that," he went on. "When I first knew Arthur, he was quick as a cat. Things changed, he changed with them. He was always a move ahead. Now he's sluggish, stubborn. Something changes, he's, like, thrown off, confused. *But that wasn't the deal!* No, Arthur, it wasn't. But now it is. Get on board, old lady."

"This was about the naming thing?" I said.

Sourly, Maxx said, "Yeah, the naming thing. He got it in his head that I'd given up on that. Not true. I said I'd reconsider."

Was that what Maxx had said? I wasn't so sure. Frankly, I don't think *he* was sure. Not that it mattered. He needed to justify his current stance. If that meant revising history, so be it.

"So I did reconsider," he went on. "And I decided my first impulse was right. I needed something big to tell the media, a capper. What's going to create more buzz than a name change? Nothing. He couldn't grasp that. So fuck him. What else you want to ask me?"

Maxx seemed eager to move on, but I hadn't quite shaken off the distressing image of the departing counselor. Levin wasn't just some functionary who'd thrown in the towel. He was a man who'd advised Maxx's father, who'd seen Maxx himself grow up through the usual scrapes and errors, and had no doubt eased him through some self-created messes along the way. He was almost family—until, in a heartbeat, he wasn't. I couldn't seem to let go of this.

"Arthur's leaving," I said. "Is it a problem?"

It was clear Maxx didn't like the question. He put on the dismissive tone that he used as a mask for annoyance. "Problem? Lawyers quit or get fired every day. No big deal."

There was the briefest of pauses, the small syncopation that happens when caution makes a failed stand against momentum. I said, "And, um, about the financing . . ."

"What about it?"

"Well, you sort of made it sound like the bankers were fighting to get in."

"And?"

I groped for words, and Maxx laughed. It was a rather operatic laugh, sudden, harsh, and clipped, but I thought some actual amusement and maybe even a bit of relief were hiding in it somewhere.

"Dave," he went on, "you can't have it both ways. If you want to ask hard questions, then stop being so fucking tactful. What you want to say is that the money raising is going badly and my pitch was one big bluff. Right?"

"Well," I said. "Yeah."

"Okay. It was. But there's a logic to these things, a psychology. What am I supposed to say?"

It was a fair enough question, but it begged another; and the question that it begged was anything but tactful.

"What if the bluff doesn't work?"

"It'll work," said Maxx, with a blank certainty that seemed almost religious.

"How do you know?"

He folded his hands and leaned far forward across them. "It'll work," he said, "because it has to work."

I thought: *That's not really a reason or an answer.* But I didn't push it any further. I'd been a ghostwriter before, and I'd learned a thing or two from the experience. One thing I'd learned was that when a powerful person, on whom you were dependent for a payday, told you to put aside tact and say whatever was on your mind, he usually didn't mean it. He might *think* he meant it; he might *wish* he meant it—because everybody knew, deep down, that candor was good medicine. But it was medicine tolerated best in little doses, and not administered too often.

So I thought it best to leave things where they were. I closed my notebook and thanked Maxx for his time. I was halfway out of my chair, my hand extended for the customary shake, when he surprised me by speaking again.

"You'll be around?" he said. "Available, I mean?"

"Sure," I said. "There's meetings coming up?"

He gave a shrug, as if to say, *Of course there'll be meetings, there's always meetings.* Then he said, "Or, you know, just to have a chat now and then, talk things through."

There was something almost shy in how he said this, something suddenly bashful at the outside corners of his eyes—almost like, in his veiled and guarded way, he was reaching for a friend. Don't get me wrong. I'm not saying Maxx was trying to be buddies, or anything as mutual as that. Given his epic self-absorption and the yawning gap in our relative importance, that was never in the cards. Still, I don't think the timing of his tiny overture was a coincidence. Things weren't going well for him; he'd just lost his most trusted adviser, just become a notch more isolated at the top of his empire. In his way, he was looking for connection. I would never be more to him than a witness and a sounding board; but I was getting to believe that in those roles I was valued. Call me a sucker—I was touched by this. It was probably the best that he could do.

Chapter 23

I left Maxx's office with way too much on my mind.

I'm a pretty linear person. I like to deal with one thing at a time. One sentence; one thought; one scrap of understanding bouncing along the track and hoping to join a train of others. But over the past few days it had suddenly seemed like everything was happening at once. There was Mandy Lockwood, with her thighs and wisecracks and undaunted mission of revenge. There was Jenna, who kept me guessing as to whether her indiscreet asides were meant to be subversive or were simply furthering my business education. There was Marcie Kanin, who had unwittingly thrown me back onto my futile resentment of the deal I'd cut. And now here was Robert Maxx himself, threatening to become something like a human being as things got dicier for him, becoming at least a bit harder to dislike as his ramparts showed some cracks and he sent out what might have been the first faint filaments of real engagement.

For better and worse, this jumble of activity had been distracting me—distracting *part* of me would be more accurate—from something that, in my eyes, was way more important than whether Mandy Lock-wood would ever get even, or Robert Maxx would win or go bust, or this book would ever get written; and that was the question of Claire's health. I'd been preoccupied with it at every moment; and yet I'd gone about my business as if the dread existed only in some different world. My fear was like a torn fingernail that I could almost forget about until something rubbed against it.

But today was Wednesday, the day Claire's test results were due, and as I walked uptown against a grimy north wind, I could no longer keep my worry locked up in the background. It moved center stage and gnawed at me. It itched. It made me quietly frantic to realize that des-tiny itself could come down to a few coded lines on a lab form, a terse pronouncement from a doctor. I wanted to call Claire, to ask if there'd been any word, but my superstitions wouldn't let me. I believed it was a bad idea to hurry news, as if the facts themselves were beings that could change their shapes at any moment, and might spitefully turn ugly if they were rushed or prodded. So I just kept walking, knocking wood along the way, hoping at every moment that my cell phone would ring. It didn't.

I slogged all the way home and went straight to the answering machine. There were no messages.

I changed out of my business clothes and made a pot of coffee. I tried to do things very slowly so that time would feel less like it was dragging. Still, the afternoon seemed awfully long. It stretched away, eventless yet cluttered with troubling thoughts; the light changed and grew feeble, and my composure faded with it. I wondered what compo-sure was made of. Was it just a habit? A pose? Did it come from a kind of unearned courage—a false courage that was really just a failure of imagination, a refusal to acknowledge all the things that could go wrong? Whatever it was made of, mine was breaking down, giving way to a secret shivering panic. My nerves seemed, like Claire's, to have molted off their insulation, to be unbearably exposed and crackling, as beneath a drilled tooth.

Finally, around four, she called. I listened to the short version of her news, and I began to cry. She heard my sniffles and whimpers and started crying, too. I bolted out, grabbed a taxi, and headed down to her place.

The cabdriver kept stealing glances at me in the rearview mirror. I couldn't really blame him. It wasn't every day that a grown man got into your cab and sobbed. But the tears were tears of relief. Claire did not have anything that would cripple her or kill her. She had something that could certainly be treated and had a reasonable chance of being cured. My gratitude for this went places that even my superstitions couldn't follow; I felt the nonbeliever's dilemma of being overwhelmed by thankfulness and not knowing who to thank.

The taxi stopped in front of her building. I approached the front door and heard, faintly, that she was playing the piano. It was Bach; it was gorgeous, as complex yet inevitable as the course of water streaming over stones. I didn't ring the bell; I couldn't bear to interrupt. I would have stood there listening for days. Finally, the music ended. I rang and she buzzed me in.

I ran up the stairs and found her standing in the doorway. We hugged; I picked her up off the ground. We were crying, laughing, our eyes were puffy, our noses were running. "So tell me," I said. "Tell me everything."

We moved into the apartment and sat down on the little sofa—took the exact places where we'd been sitting a few weeks before, when Claire's fingers had balked and she spilled her glass of wine. She reached up toward her thick brown hair, pulled it back away from her face. "Okay," she said. "Apparently they've ruled out all the really awful stuff. So it's just this weird inflammation thing. They still don't know what brought it on, but that doesn't seem to matter. It shouldn't get much worse. It might just stay like it is."

She broke off and tried to smile. The smile was soft and tired, tender but clouded.

I said, "But the treatment. What about the treatment?"

Her big eyes slid away. She looked at the piano, the window shades, the floor. Finally, she said, "There's a problem with that. A temporary problem."

"What?"

"It doesn't matter. I can do the treatment later."

"But you just told me that it might get worse."

She bit her lip and flexed her hands. "Oh Jesus, I didn't want to talk about this part. Let's just be happy that I don't have something really bad."

There was a pause. Muffled car horns and a distant siren sounded through the windows.

I said, "Your brother's company. Was it called Herbjoy?"

She flinched. "You know about that?"

"I saw something in the paper. He okay?"

She let out a long slow breath. "He's fine. He wasn't high up enough to get in trouble. But he lost what he invested. He's broke again."

I knew I was supposed to say something sympathetic, but I couldn't quite manage it; this was no time to be petty but it was no time for pretending, either. I just said, "How much will the treatment cost?"

She looked away. But she answered. This gave me hope. I don't think she would have if she wasn't going to let me help. She said, "Twenty-five or thirty thousand, over six weeks or so."

"Let me give it to you."

She said nothing. Her eyes were distant and her skin was getting red along her hairline.

"Look," I went on, "I know it's not the way you wanted it. But it's the way it is. Call it a loan. Whatever makes you feel okay about it. It's not even for you. It's for your hands."

She extended her arms and splayed out her fingers. She looked at them as though they were, in truth, no longer quite a part of her, but more like sick pets or troubled children, helpless things for which she was responsible. She swallowed, brought her eyes back to mine, and said, "Are you really sure you want to do this? Are you sure you can?"

I held her gaze and struggled to keep my own expression definite and clear. Was I sure I wanted to do this? Absolutely. As sure as I had ever been of anything. Was I sure I could? That was not so simple. But I would find a way because I had to find a way. "Yes," I said. "I'm sure."

She still looked dubious. She knew my finances, how little dough I usually had in reserve.

Hoping to quell all doubt and maybe even lighten the moment, I tried a gambit that had failed before. "Hey, I'm in business with a billionaire, remember?"

She raised an eyebrow, glanced at me sideways, and tried to echo my lighter tone. She was about as convincingly light as I was. "Hope you got a big advance."

It was natural she would think that I'd been paid to start this book, that I was flush with the signing money. Book deals almost always worked that way. She didn't have to know that this one didn't. To avoid the sin of lying out loud, I just nodded.

"I'll pay you back," she said.

"Whatever. One thing at a time. Meanwhile, schedule your treatments. I can get you the money in a day or two."

She pulled in a breath that did not come easily but had some little stops in it. "Thank you," she said. "Jesus, I'm embarrassed."

"Don't be."

"I am."

"Would you feel better if I told you I wanted something in return?"

"Maybe," she said. "What do you want?"

"I want you to play me some Bach."

Chapter 24

It wasn't until much later, when the raw emotions of the moment had subsided, that some odd and uncomfortable things about that conversation occurred to me. This had nothing to do with Claire, or with things that were or weren't happening between us. Rather, it dawned on me—to my unease if not horror—that a couple of things I'd said and promised could almost have come from the mind and life of Robert Maxx.

Consider: When I'd asked Maxx why he was so sure his financing bluff would work, he'd answered that it would work because it had to. This reply had struck me as the height of illogic and recklessness; but was my promise to Claire any less rash? I loved her and she needed money. Ergo, I would raise the cash because I *had* to raise the cash; things would work out because I chose not to imagine them otherwise. My leap of faith may have carried me across a much narrower chasm, but it was every bit as blind as his.

Then there was the matter of leverage, of spending money that one did not have. As Jenna had explained to me, when Maxx needed funds, he went deeper into debt on properties he owned—or seemed to own, though in fact the real owners were the financiers who held the mortgages. Well, what could *I* do to raise cash? Only one thing: take out a loan, with my apartment—the only thing I owned, or seemed to—as collateral.

Which is exactly what I did, first thing next morning, at a dingy bank branch on Broadway. I guess someone had to be the last jerk to sign on for a sub-prime second mortgage, and it might as well be me. I took a crazy bridge loan, and the terms were simple; no payments for a year, with two alternatives thereafter: pay up or be foreclosed. I thought little or not at all about this latter possibility; after all, I had a book in progress and a good-size payday coming up. Still, somewhere way in the back of my mind, it occurred to me that in my puny, microscopic way, I had started down the same track as Robert Maxx, gambling on leverage, risking my tiny bit of security and comfort in the name of trying to appear a bigger big shot than I was.

Suddenly I was overextended, and therefore vulnerable, no longer master of my fiscal destiny. I didn't regret it for a second. I did it for Claire's hands, and it was one of the few generous things I've done in my entire life.

Even so, there were aspects of the whole business that struck me as perverse and slightly creepy. I mean, the real issues here were health and loyalty, but those things had now become wrapped up in cashier's checks and promissory notes. Was it just in Manhattan, or was it everywhere, that even the most intimate and lyrical parts of life so often got tossed into the same file as creditworthiness and real estate?

Chapter 25

A couple of days later, I had a call from Robert Maxx.

Not Jenna; not a secretary; Robert Maxx himself. I was so surprised that it took me half a beat to find my voice and say hello.

He was calling to invite me to lunch; there was somebody he wanted me to meet. He said this coyly, as he more than occasionally said things. This was one of the ways in which he could be both winningly boyish and completely infuriating. He was just so utterly fascinated with his own jumbo life, and he assumed that everyone around him was as well. He savored his little secrets, all but rubbing his hands together when he had one; he made a fanfare of his carefully dosed-out revelations. If this was egomaniacal, there was also something incurably nerdy about it. Why did he have to work so hard at sounding fascinating? In any case, lunch was one o'clock at the Four Seasons. Could I make it?

Of course I could make it. I don't think anyone ever turned down lunch at the Four Seasons. Foodwise, there were way better restaurants around, but all in all there was no more amusing place to have a meal. I'd been there just a couple of times, though not in several years. Back when

I was still considered an up-and-coming novelist, someone to watch and maybe even to be seen with, I was taken there by one of my early editors, a fairly famous guy, who was a regular—one of those people who never ordered from the menu. Every visit, he'd have a giant baked potato served with a little cruet of olive oil, for which I think they charged him thirty bucks. But it was a beautiful potato, and the people watching was priceless. You never knew who you'd see at the next table. Hillary Clinton or Kofi Annan, Steve Martin or Philip Roth, Katie Couric or Steven Spielberg or Nathan Lane. The place was a club that, at a certain age and at a certain point in the arc of your career, you could kid yourself that you belonged in, or at least might break into someday. This pleasant illusion generally survived until you'd sipped the last of your espresso and were back out on the street in your cheap shoes and rumpled blazer, at which point it gave way to a slight depression tinged by secret embarrassment. *Just who do you think you're kidding, young man?*

Still, I was happy to be going back, and I dressed for the occasion. Since I couldn't compete in the sheer elegance department, I went arty: a purple shirt under a tweedy black jacket, a tie that didn't match, exactly, but seemed to comment with a subtle irony. At least that's how it seemed to me. Other people might have just assumed that I was colorblind. But I thought I looked good.

I arrived unfashionably promptly, and was shown to Mr. Maxx's empty table. As I scudded through the spacious dining room, other guests glanced up briefly to check out the new arrival. You could almost hear them thinking, *Ah, it's . . . nobody,* before going back to their oysters or their soup.

I was seated on the scallop-shaped banquette. I ordered a mineral water, perused the menu, and tried my best to look comfortable.

Ten or twelve minutes later, a silent, indefinable, but palpable thrum went through the room. Robert Maxx had entered. With him was none other than Caitlin Kilgore, the star of the wildly popular television show *Adrift*. The maître d' led them toward the table, and I noticed that Maxx kept a proprietary hand on her waist; he splayed his fingers, as though to feel as much of her as possible. They seemed to be the most famous people in the room just then; as such, they took on the mysteri-ous, primordial glow that came from other people's shy attention.

But, in that moment at least, her aura far outshone his. Robert Maxx was merely rich and powerful, while Caitlin Kilgore was young, broadcast weekly from Edinburgh to Sydney, and drop-dead beautiful to look at.

She had a quite particular kind of beauty, very contemporary and probably not for everyone, a somewhat androgynous blend of tomboy and vamp. She was tall but not willowy; she seemed to spend more time with her trainer than her cosmetologist. Her shoulders were broad and there were little strands of muscle in her neck. She was underdressed as only the truly confident can manage, in black pants, a white shirt, and a fuzzy blue sweater that seemed quite retro to me but was probably the height of style. Her raven-black hair was short and unfussy. Her eyes were indigo, wide, and stunning; her teeth were a little too perfect. Her makeup was so artfully applied that it was hard to be sure if she was wearing any; maybe just a dusting of mascara and a hint of gloss to make her full lips glisten.

I stood up to be introduced. Maxx got my name wrong but I let it slide.

We settled in around the table, and a captain scurried over to take the drinks order. Caitlin asked for "a glass of something white and French, maybe a Montrachet or something." I wasn't about to let her drink alone, especially if she was drinking Montrachet, so I said I'd have the same. Sober Maxx asked for a Coke.

Spreading her napkin across her lap, Caitlin turned to me and said, "Robert was very keen to have us meet. I understand you're writing a book for him."

Very keen to have us meet? I wondered if there was a shred of truth to this, or if it was just an instance of that glib and habitual L.A. nice-ness that was really quite pleasant in its flagrant yet charming insincer-ity. Then again, Maxx really did seem pretty pleased to be hosting his squeeze and his amanuensis; and why not? He was the nexus, the rea-son we were there; we were the ornaments, he was the tree.

Since my tycoon had clearly spilled the beans already, I said, "Yeah, we're doing a book. But I thought it was a secret."

Maxx leaned thick elbows on the table. "It's a secret," he said, "to the tight-ass suits I work with. It's not a secret among friends."

The comment struck me. Maxx, as usual, was in Armani with a triple-figure tie that cinched his jugular. Did he imagine that he was not a tight-ass suit himself? Was that why he seemed so pleased to be in the company of an underdressed actress and a writer whose tie didn't match—so he could forget his own clothes and his own life for an hour? Or was he just trying to sound all loose and groovy for the benefit of his young, show-business girlfriend?

The drinks arrived. We clinked glasses.

Caitlin said, "It must be very difficult to write a book."

It was another gracious comment, socially appropriate, but I didn't sense a burning interest behind it. Besides, I'd known an actress or two, and I saw it as inevitable that the conversation would soon come 'round to her, so I tried to play along and ease the way. "It's not that difficult," I said, "if you like to work alone. I think it would be much harder to do what you do—working with a big cast, acting in front of all those people."

She nipped at her wine then gave a little laugh. "Acting? You mean when I run through the jungle in a towel?"

"Don't be modest," said Maxx. "Everyone says you're really good. Besides, you look unbelievable in a towel."

I had to agree. I'd watched *Adrift* exactly once, and Caitlin Kilgore in a towel was the only part of it I'd understood. She was running past palm trees and ferns, along with some other very attractive people looking scared. Something was chasing them; I had no idea what. The towel started midway down her cleavage and ended just at the little crescents at the base of her buttocks.

The waiter came over and asked if we were ready to order. My companions hadn't yet looked at the menu, but as I suspected, they didn't need to. Caitlin asked for grilled fish, preferably sea bass, and an arugula salad. Maxx ordered a small steak. When it was my turn, I asked if they had calf's liver today. I knew perfectly well they did; I'd seen it on the menu, though I didn't admit it. Okay, so I was being a pretentious jerk. But what can I say—I was embracing the moment.

The waiter left, and we went back to talking about Caitlin.

"All those years," she said, "of studying Ibsen and Chekhov, so I can play opposite a special effect."

"For half a million bucks a week," Maxx put in.

She shot him a mock-scolding look. "Didn't anyone ever tell you that it's rude to talk about how much money people make?"

"People tell me that all the time," he said. "Interestingly, though, it's usually people who make chump change. But come on. You're a winner. You're a star. Why be shy about it? Your salary's always in the paper anyway."

"Along with all the other crap," she said. She turned her gorgeous face to me. "You follow that stuff? The entertainment so-called news? The gossip columns?"

"Not really," I admitted.

"Good for you. It's dreary beyond words. Completely worthless."

Maxx was sucking Coke through a straw. He abruptly raised his face and said, "Now wait a second. I don't agree with that. If it wasn't for the entertainment shows, I would never have known that you were up for grabs."

"Up for grabs?" she said, with rather theatrical affront.

"Okay, *available*. Whatever. Cut me some slack. I was hankering for you ever since that beauty contest in Bangkok." Turning to me, he said, "She was so much better-looking than any of those sad-ass contestants, it wasn't even funny." Turning back to Caitlin, he said, "And if it wasn't for the gossip shows, I would never have known that what's-his-name was back in detox."

There was a brief silence, and I had the sudden giddy and dreamlike feeling that I had made a wrong turn in some dim hallway and wandered onto a talk-show set. I was no longer making ordinary chitchat with regular people. These were celebrities and there were different rules of conversation here. Privacy was banished, excessive dignity was not invited back; nosiness was encouraged, indiscretions were applauded, confessions were met with eye-dabbing empathy.

So I jumped in and said, "Who's what's-his-name?"

Caitlin said, "Oh boy, if we're going into this, I think I'll have another glass of wine. Join me?"

It turned out to be a longish story, and one that more tube-savvy people than me were probably familiar with already. What's-his-name was Matt Gaston, one of her costars on the show. According to Caitlin's completely indiscreet account, he was a wonderful actor and a truly nice guy, except when he was wigged out on drugs. The problem, however, was that Matt was on drugs most of the time, because he was one of those people who quickly became addicted to anything. He was addicted to cocaine; he was addicted to meth; he was addicted to Vicodin washed down with flavored vodkas; if you fed him milk and cookies two days in a row, he would be addicted to milk and cookies. According to Caitlin, everyone connected to the show knew he was a mess, and no one wanted to deal with it. Ratings were good; he was functional on the set; as long as he didn't die, it was best to leave it alone.

Unfortunately, though, one of the many things that Matt Gaston was addicted to was Caitlin Kilgore, and when she finally told him that she couldn't take it anymore, she was ending their relationship, he flipped out altogether. This was on location, under a full moon in the middle of the night. He'd stormed out of their hut stark naked, screaming, wailing, wielding a machete, threatening to kill her, kill himself, kill anyone who came between them. He was kneeling down and slapping mud on himself when he was finally subdued by other cast members; he was flown off the island in the producers' private plane at dawn and transported straight to Promises, where celebrity maniacs go for a time-out.

It was a harrowing and pathetic tale, but lunch had arrived in the midst of it, and no one's appetite seemed spoiled. Caitlin was working daintily at her sea bass, using her fork to separate the flakes. Maxx was sawing away at his steak. I paused in the savoring of my calf's liver to say, "Poor guy. What a waste."

"Yeah," said Caitlin. "It's really sad."

Maxx was lifting a piece of meat to his mouth. He stopped it just below chin level. "Poor guy. How sad. Come on, he's a junkie with zero self-control and he brought his problems on himself."

Caitlin dabbed her lips on her napkin. "You could at least pretend to feel a little compassion."

Maxx ate the forkful of steak. "Why pretend? Besides, I feel something way better than compassion. I feel lucky. He fucked up, and I'm here with you. Cheers."

He raised his glass of Coke, she lifted what was left of her second Montrachet, and they clinked. The toast did not include me, so I sat there. But something was bothering me—a professional matter. I said, "So what'll happen to his character? On the show, I mean?"

At this, Caitlin feigned exasperation. "You men. Either you're waiting to steal the poor guy's girlfriend or you're just worrying about the stupid show."

"Come on," said Maxx, "it's a multi-billion-dollar franchise."

"Okay, okay," she said. "For now, his character got kidnapped. So the options are open. If the rehab goes well, he escapes. If not, he's killed. They'll decide within a few more weeks."

A few more weeks? Very vaguely, I wondered what might happen when and if Matt Gaston came back to the show, back to the jungle where Caitlin was cavorting in her terry cloth. Would the romance with Maxx survive his return? Would Gaston try to reclaim what once had been his? Would he wig out again and pick up the machete? The situation had celebrity contretemps written all over it.

Caitlin demurely pushed her plate away. Half the food was left on it, and this said to me that maybe she wasn't quite as wholesome as she looked. Yes, she was buff and scant of makeup, but she drank more than she ate, and I would have bet she sneaked maybe half a dozen cigarettes a day to squelch her appetite. Complex, these actresses, and usually tormented. She drained her glass, and by the time she put it down again, she seemed to be in a different mood, like she was tired of being the center of attention but didn't know how not to be. She asked me if I ever wrote for television.

Surprised to be asked about myself, I said, "No, I don't think I'd be very good at it."

"Why not?" She fixed me with those indigo eyes, and a strange chemical reaction took place. Her beauty combined with my second glass of wine to form a serum that dissolved my tact.

I said, "The meetings. The writing by committee. Having to pander to adolescents of all ages. No wonder the shows are awful. Frankly, I'd sooner slit my wrists. No offense."

For some reason Maxx got a big kick out of this. "No offense," he echoed. "I love that!" Then he turned to Caitlin and talked about me as if I wasn't there. "Didn't I tell you he's amusing? So cautious, diplomatic, best behavior . . . then the truth comes out. Then right away he's apologizing for it. No offense! That cracks me up. Anybody want dessert?"

Chapter 26

Maxx made it clear that he wasn't going back to the office after lunch; no doubt the day's agenda called for some postprandial frolicking back at the cavernous apartment. Not that I was envious or anything. Still, when we'd emerged from the restaurant onto Fifty-second Street, and he and Caitlin slipped into the waiting limo, and I was left there standing alone on the cold sidewalk, my breath steaming in the November air, I remembered that old sense of deflation, the painful reentry from a cocoon of glamour and privilege back to my actual life. Pedestrians bustled past me without so much as a sideways glance. No one was the slightest bit impressed that I'd just lunched at the Four Seasons and gotten away with pretending to order without looking at the menu. I was completely anonymous once again.

I should probably just have gone home for a nap, but since I was already in midtown with a clean shirt on, I felt I should make a bit more of the expedition. Maybe I just wanted another half hour of pretending I was really part of the bigger world. So I strolled over to Fifth Avenue and uptown toward Maxx Tower. I thought I'd have a schmooze with Jenna.

Lobby security knew me by now; so did the receptionist on the fifty-first floor. So I breezed right past and wound my way through the corridors toward her office. Her door was open; she was sitting at her desk; I was able to look at her for a moment before she noticed me. There was something in her posture that I hadn't seen before; something I was probably not supposed to see. Her shoulders looked weighted and cinched; her long neck seemed weary, tired of propping up its burden of an alert and smiling face. There was a tightness in her jaw.

She saw me, and straightened, and instantly became the person I was used to seeing—a picture of confidence and poise, with a wry edge to her attention. Still, you can't undo an impression any more than you can unsay an intemperate word, and I would never again look at Jenna without seeing a hint of bravely masked fretfulness behind the smile and the clever comment.

Instead of hello, she said, "So how was lunch?"

"The wine was better than the food, and the scene was better than the wine."

"What did you think of Caitlin?"

"Pretty stunning. But personally, I'd be terrified to get involved with an actress. I mean, they fake emotions for a living."

"You think they have a monopoly on that?" She said this with a flash of yellow eyes and a pursing of the lips that was midway between a mordant, almost mocking pout and a kiss; the delicious ambiguity made it clear that there was no monopoly.

Moving on, I said, "So what's up around here?"

Jenna looked away, pulled her brows together just a fraction, tapped long fingers on her desk. "Nothing good."

Before she said anything more, she rose and walked rather stiffly across the office to close the door. She closed it gently; still, it clicked shut with a sound that seemed strangely sinister and loud, like in a prison movie when they amplify the clang of the closing cell.

Seated at her desk once again, she said, "I just had a call from Arthur Levin. He was giving me a heads-up about what he's afraid might become a media shit storm. Want to guess who's stirring it up?"

I didn't have to think for long. "Mandy Lockwood?"

"Very good. You're learning how the game is played. Yesterday, Mandy called Arthur, looking for an inside angle about what's going on with Rockefeller Center. Arthur told her he couldn't help, he was no longer associated with the deal. Mandy jumped all over that. Why wasn't he? Was the deal in trouble? Did he have a falling-out with Maxx?"

I pictured Levin with his smooth brow and clear blue eyes. I said, "I can't imagine him getting pulled into that kind of gossip."

"Absolutely not," said Jenna. "But it's a no-win situation. Arthur says no comment, and that leaves people free to spin the story any way they want."

"What's to spin?"

A little impatiently, Jenna said, "Come on, you're a storyteller. There's two strands here. Let's start with Arthur. His reputation is impeccable. Robert's is anything but. Robert's known as a cowboy, a rule stretcher, maybe worse. Arthur's the straightest of straight shooters. His involvement is like a big kosher stamp. If he quits in the middle, doesn't that raise questions?"

"I guess. Sure. But—"

"Okay," she interrupted. "If Arthur was the only issue, it would probably be no big deal. There'd be some lifted eyebrows. The problem is there's this other strand as well—which is Trip Campbell blabbing to people that we're having trouble raising cash. What happens when the two strands get wrapped up together? The possibilities start multiplying, taking on a life of their own. You see?"

I guess my blank expression told Jenna that I didn't.

"Maybe Levin left because Maxx is out of dough," she said. "Maybe the financiers are balking because the deal is crooked, and that's why Levin walked. Even Maxx's press conference—doesn't it seem a little shrill and over-the-top in light of Levin quitting and bankers passing? You see? Every little piece of the story reflects back on the others and makes them seem more damning."

"But," I said, "all this stuff is just nasty innuendo from a couple of people with axes to grind. There isn't a single solid fact."

She gave a little laugh, though she didn't seem amused. "You think that matters? Here's how it works if you're a business journalist. You hear something once, it barely registers. You hear it twice, it starts taking on the weight of a juicy rumor. You hear it a third time, it starts seeming urgent, like a story that's about to break. And since no one can afford to be left behind on a breaking story, people start asking questions that they wouldn't have thought to ask before, start looking at things they wouldn't have looked at. It's a nuisance and it's dangerous."

Nuisance I could readily understand. But dangerous? I said, "If there's nothing to hide—"

"There's always something to hide. It's just a question of how and where it's hidden, and how hard someone decides to look for it." She paused, her head cocked at an angle that suggested both fatigue and a sort of genial defiance. "You remember a company called Enron?"

"Who doesn't?"

"Well, I'm not saying we're anything like Enron. We're not. But there's one little piece of the Enron story that almost might apply here."

At this, I could not resist whipping out my notebook from my inside jacket pocket. Jenna told me to put it away.

"Enron was a fraud from the get-go," she said. "Why did it take people so long to figure it out? I'll give it to you in two words: full disclosure. They disclosed *everything*. They disclosed things they didn't *have* to disclose. This turned out to be the perfect camouflage. The books were there—reams and reams and reams of books, documenting an incredibly complicated web of deals—"

"As complicated as Maxx's?"

"Just about. And since the books were there for all to see, and since it would have been unbelievable drudgery to go through them, nobody bothered to look. When people finally *did* look . . . well, you know the rest."

"But fortunately," I said, "this is nothing like Enron."

"No," she said. "It isn't."

She put her hands down flat in front of her. At her back, the blue was leaching out of the sky, being overtaken by a dim and pasty white.

Not quite realizing I was about to speak aloud, I said, "You look a little tired."

"Been a long week," she admitted. "Thank God next week's a short one."

"It is?"

She looked at me as if I'd just dropped in from another planet—an inference that was really not far off. "Thanksgiving," she said. "No one told you?"

"Guess I forgot," I said. "Truth is, I hate the holidays. I just try not to notice."

"You'd sure as hell notice if you had a job and it meant a four-day weekend."

"Doing anything special?"

"Going home," she said.

This was funny in a way. For many if not most New Yorkers, *home* was always someplace else. Where did that mean they were on most nights of the year, when they were asleep in their apartments?

"Where's home?" I asked. I imagined it was Philadelphia, New Haven, someplace like that, someplace with a solid black middle class and plenty of big-city advantages.

"Mississippi."

"You're from Mississippi?"

I couldn't keep the shock out of my voice, and Jenna gave me a gently scolding look. "Ah," she said. "So, you're okay with black folks, but you're prejudiced against the South."

I fumbled for a denial and could not come up with one.

She said, "That's okay. So am I. Especially the rural South, with red dirt roads and schools where they run out of textbooks."

Stupidly, I said, "What happened to your accent?"

She took off her hip magenta glasses, carefully put them down in front of her, then gave her yellow eyes a quick and weary rub. "I conquered it," she said. "Listen, I don't talk about this much, and it doesn't need to matter to anyone but me, but I've had some ground to cover and some work to do. Nothing's easy. That's just how it is."

She shrugged, and for the space of a single breath, she looked around her office—the big granite desk, the pictures on the walls, the luxury of natural light—as if it still surprised her that she'd made it here. Or as if, at the end of a perilous and grinding week, she was realizing that at any moment it could all be taken away. Robert Maxx's company was nothing like Enron; not at all. But collapses kill; that's another part of how it is. And if Maxx's empire were ever to go down, then many hard-won lives would surely go down with it.

Chapter 27

On the way uptown, I slipped into the vestibule of Claire's building and slid a check into her mailbox. I didn't know if she was home or not, but I didn't want to see her just then. I would have felt weird, putting the money in her hand. I didn't want to embarrass her, and I didn't want to be thanked. Feeling oddly furtive, as if I'd taken something rather than given it, I walked quickly down the stoop and along her street, touching the trees for good luck as I went.

Back in my own apartment, a long way from the elegance of East Fifty-second Street, I found the usual toast crumbs and stained coffee cups and tossed magazines everywhere; I also found a completely unexpected message on the answering machine.

It had not occurred to me that lunch that day was in the nature of an audition, but apparently it was, and apparently I'd passed; I hadn't spilled my wine or eaten with my fingers, and I guess I'd been sufficiently amusing. My reward was a summons from the beautiful and famous Caitlin Kilgore. She was calling to ask if I had plans for Thanksgiving dinner. If I happened to be free, she and Robert would love to invite me, with a guest if I'd like, out to Southampton for the holiday. She left a cell-phone number with an L.A. area code, and asked me to call as soon as I could.

I listened to the message twice. I walked around the apartment and listened to it again. The invitation was flattering, of course; but having been a ghostwriter before, and having had occasion to cozy up, in a subservient sort of way, to people who were rich and famous, I was less flattered and more ambivalent than you might imagine.

Not to put too fine a point on it, the rich and famous tended to be a real pain in the ass. Somewhat like retarded people, but without the good excuse, they had special needs, exaggerated needs. They required both an audience and a sideshow, a buffer of unimportant people on their flanks; ravenous for novelty, they went through acquaintances like most of us go through socks. For some odd reason, writers still had a certain cachet in their world; a writer at the table was a species of adornment, a kind of talking floral centerpiece. But this singing for one's supper was both undignified and tedious, and I wasn't sure the dynamic could ever be otherwise. Even when the rich and famous believed they were offering friendship, the best they could do was patronage.

And patronage was fine, was the way of the world—except I had a big fat problem with its fundamental lopsidedness. This will no doubt sound conceited, ridiculous, and maybe even clinically delusional, but here it is: in spite of everything the world had told me about where I stood in the order of things, in spite of the stunning disparities in wealth and fame and recognition, I happened to believe that my own little life and puny struggles were every bit as important as those of Robert Maxx or Caitlin Kilgore or anybody else. Call me American—I demanded to be treated as an equal; and I understood though did not accept that this wasn't going to happen; and that's a big part of the reason that things between Maxx and me ended up going so violently wrong.

But don't let me get ahead of myself.

In the meantime, I had a book to write, and the more I knew about Robert Maxx, the better the book could be; it would be dumb to miss an opportunity to see him in such a different context, out of town, perched, presumably, over a homey plate of turkey. I dialed the number Caitlin had left.

She picked up on the second ring and said hello. It sounded like there was TV in the background.

"Hi," I said. "It's David Collins."

"David!" she said, like I was a dear and long-lost friend. "Thanks so much for getting back to me. Can you come on Thursday? We'd love it if you could."

"I think I can," I said. "I have a sort of tentative plan but I think I can get out of it."

This was one of my pointless little fibs, and I'm not even sure why I bothered telling it, except that the holidays, being false themselves, tended to draw forth other falsehoods. It was unallowable not to have plans for Thanksgiving; if you didn't have plans, you looked like a real loser. The fact that I didn't have plans, and didn't want any, took too much trouble to explain. But Claire and I had decided a long time ago that it was far too melancholy a charade to hang out together on holidays. As for family, let me get that out of the way right here. My parents, some years before, had transferred their unhappiness, perfectly intact, from New Jersey to Arizona, a place for which I had no feelings whatsoever; they didn't like each other much, should probably have divorced decades ago, and were therefore excruciating to be around. I have one sibling, a kid brother who, when last heard from, had taken a Sanskrit name and was living in an ashram in Idaho. Suffice it to say that "home" for the holidays was not an option. Frankly, my preferred recipe for holiday dinners was two or three cocktails, savored quietly alone, and a sleeping pill that would get me serenely to the other side of the hypocrisy and the nonsense.

So it was actually sort of funny that Caitlin Kilgore, who clearly seemed burdened by the bloated expectations of the season, was practically begging me of all people to come brighten up her Thanksgiving. "Oh, *please* come," she said. "I'm afraid it'll be really dreary otherwise. None of my friends are on the East Coast anymore. It'll just be me and Robert, maybe a snooty, boring neighbor or two, and Mr. Happy."

"Mr. Happy?"

"You know. Robert's brother. Tony. You've met him, right?"

"Only in passing."

"He's a real laugh riot," Caitlin said. "Just the sort of cheerful face you love to see across the table."

I assumed that Caitlin was still at Maxx's place. I wondered if Maxx was within earshot, and if that would have made a bit of difference in what she said or didn't say.

"I thought he and Robert were on the outs," I ventured.

"They are. They were. Who knows? I'm pretty new here myself. But I think they're trying to make up. Families are fucked."

There was a tiny pause, then I heard her say, clearly not to me, "Darling, are you and Tony trying to make up?"

I couldn't hear the answer, but Caitlin relayed it. "He says they're trying to reach some sort of accommodation."

Then she spoke to Maxx again. "I love it when you talk like that, all businessy and noncommittal. He's your *brother*, for Christ's sake!"

If Maxx responded, I didn't hear it. I was left to wonder what he might have said; and to wonder, also, if Caitlin had had a bit more wine or other intoxicant since lunch. But of one thing I was now completely certain: I was going to Southampton for Thanksgiving. However much I deplored the holiday, and however contrived and debasing the dynamic between people like them and people like me was fated to be, this was too good to pass up. The dysfunction of a family other than one's own, as narrated by a beautiful loose cannon of a girlfriend—I wouldn't miss it for the world.

back from Long Island. Then there'd be the taxi ride uptown, through streets that always seemed somehow cinematically deserted and unavoidably romantic with so many people away for the weekend. We'd reach her building—then what? Would I simply say good night and continue on alone? Would I pop out for a chaste and friendly good-night kiss? Would she invite me up for a nightcap? Tea or cognac? Would we end up necking on the couch like teenagers, avid yet tormented by the rapidly fading conviction that we really ought to stop? And if I was still there in the morning, would it feel like we'd reclaimed something precious or just made a really dumb and sad mistake?

It was better not to go there. At least I thought it was. At least I told myself it was.

Monday came—the beginning of a truncated, slow-news week—but still, it brought with it some early rumblings of the media shit storm that Jenna feared was on the way. The *Times* and the *Journal* wouldn't touch the rumors about the rift between Robert Maxx and Arthur Levin, and its possible connection to the Rockefeller Center deal—wouldn't touch them yet, at least. But the *Post* had no such hesitation, and ran a Page Six item that was a little masterpiece of innuendo.

Under boldface type that asked the question WHERE'S THE LEVER-AGE NOW?, the piece cited "a leading hedge-fund honcho who'd been offered—but declined—a piece of the Rock Center deal." According to this insider, Maxx's unsolicited pursuit of nontraditional financing clearly suggested that he'd finally used up the patience of his bankers, and therefore had no choice but "to get creative, which sometimes was another way of saying desperate." This "creativity," in turn, took the ultratraditional Arthur Levin well beyond his comfort zone and expertise, and that was why he left. Asked to comment on this version of events, Maxx called it "irresponsible baloney." Levin declined to say anything at all.

I read the brief story carefully, parsed it word by word, and came to the conclusion that while Trip Campbell was a little scumbag who, let us hope, was heading for a nasty fall, he clearly understood the concept of payback. By fine increments, he seemed to be racheting up his anti-

Chapter 28

The weekend passed. I did some writing, played some squash, spoke to Claire a couple times. She thanked me for the check; sure enough, this embarrassed both of us, but I guess it couldn't be avoided. She was starting her treatment on Tuesday—two hours attached to an IV drip in Gupta's office. After that, the regimen would be two sessions a week for six weeks; hopefully, she'd start to see improvement midway through, but there were no guarantees. I didn't love it that the total number of treatments was thirteen, but I kept my unease to myself.

I thought about inviting Claire to Maxx's for Thanksgiving, but reluctantly decided not to. It would have been a pleasure to have her company, but . . . But a lot of things. As I've said, we'd decided some years ago that the holidays were a maudlin, mawkish no-no. Plus there was the ticklish business of presenting ourselves, even fleetingly, as a couple. Most of all, there was the mingled hope and fear as to how the day might end. We'd have a presumably titillating time with the rich and the beautiful, followed by the slow, swaying, mesmerizing train trip

Maxx campaign, threatening, perhaps, to become not just an annoyance, but an actual menace, to the man who'd ruined his father. But smearing Maxx was the easy part. The thing that raised Campbell's malice to a sort of artistry was the way in which he also managed to cast aspersions on the blameless Arthur Levin. I recalled how tersely, deftly, and completely the old lawyer had put Campbell down during the meeting in Maxx's office. Now the brat was getting his revenge by suggesting, not too subtly, that Levin was out of step with contemporary business, that he was rigid, obsolete, that the world had passed him by. Round two of this particular skirmish went to the odious wunderkind.

I tried calling Jenna, to get her take on the new wrinkle. I was told that she was in a meeting. There was nothing surprising about this; executive life was meetings, after all. Nor did I find it especially odd that she didn't get back to me by the end of the day. She was a busy woman; no doubt she had higher priorities than indulging my somewhat salacious appetite for insider gossip.

But she'd always been so responsive and accessible before.

Tuesday, late morning, I tried her again; there was always the possibility that my first message hadn't gotten through. This time, I was told that Jenna had already left for the long weekend.

In itself, this was nothing untoward; plenty of people bolted a day early if they could manage it. Still, there was something about Jenna's early departure that gave me a bad feeling. Maybe it was just the assistant's tone of voice, protective but not quite convincing. Maybe it was a carryover from the weariness and wistfulness I'd sensed in Jenna the last time we'd spoken. But I couldn't help feeling that her early departure was essentially a flight from a situation that was growing ever more stressful and maybe heading toward the unbearable. Maxx's enemies were circling; rumors were festering and debts were coming due; it had been a while since any of the news was good.

But just how bad *were* things in Maxx's empire? At that point I didn't really know. I knew what people told me, and no one told me everything. Maxx himself only told me things that made him look forceful and savvy and suggested that he would eventually be the winner yet again. Jenna gave me a more somber view, but only within the limits of her professional discretion. For every meeting I was privy to, there were probably a dozen where the doors were closed. I was in the loop, and then again I wasn't.

For someone with a story to get, this was both an intriguing and highly frustrating situation. I may not be a real reporter, but still, I don't like it when facts elude me. So I hatched a new idea: Why not speak with Carlton Phelps? If anyone could give me the straight skinny on the state of the empire, it would be him. But how could I best approach him? For that matter, if he gave me a bunch of accountant-speak, would I even understand what he was saying?

Feeling very on-the-case, I made myself a note to reach out to the CFO right after the long weekend. Then I largely forgot about it. Isn't that what holidays were for?

Chapter 29

Thanksgivings are supposed to be sunny and crisp, days when you see your breath while tossing a football against a bright blue sky. This one wasn't like that; not at all. The morning was gray and clammy, unwholesomely warm, almost muggy. Having some time to kill, I walked all the way down to Penn Station, leaving my beloved neighborhood of crumbling mortar and peeling paint, walking through Robert Maxx's fantasy precincts of soaring glass and tinted metal and so-called public spaces that the public generally avoided like the plague. I was sweaty and uncomfortable by the time I neared the terminal. The streets were still mobbed with people who'd gone to the parade; the pavements were sticky with dropped candy and tragic with the heartbreak of busted balloons on snapped sticks. Kids were having meltdowns; parents were getting testy. Welcome to the holidays.

A few blocks above the station, I popped into one of those produce stands that stays open 24/7/365. I don't know much about high-end etiquette, but I do know you're not supposed to arrive empty-handed for dinner at someone's house. So I bought some flowers. They cost eight bucks, and the minute I bought them, they underwent a mysterious and dramatic change. Sitting on the shelf with a couple of hundred other bouquets, they'd looked pretty nice. As soon as I paid for them, they looked chintzy and pathetic. Petals were already curling here and there; there was brown on the edge of the single lily that was supposed to be the star of the show. The stems were ratty and the greens looked fake. I considered tossing them, but didn't.

The train was packed, but only for the first few stops. By the time we'd left behind the archaic clutter of Queens, I had a window seat and plenty of legroom. After the nearest of the tract-house suburbs, I was practically alone in the car. Eventually the ride got pretty. There were fields full of pumpkins framed by long rows of poplar trees; there were sod farms that even in late November were stunningly green. I made myself a mental note to get out of town more often. I told myself that from time to time, and then six months or so would go by without my doing it. I was a prisoner of Manhattan, and I guess I liked it that way.

At Southampton I seemed to be the only person getting off the train. Other than the hired help and maybe some half-share renters, not many people took public transportation to Southampton; Hummers and limos and seaplanes were the more typical means of arrival. So I walked across the deserted platform and went to look for my ride to Maxx's.

Caitlin had told me that someone would be there to pick me up; I'd assumed she meant a servant of some sort. But when I looked around the all but empty parking lot, I saw that it was she herself, perched behind the wheel of a tall and shiny SUV. Enthusiastically, she waved me over, and when I'd climbed into the passenger seat, she leaned across the shifter and, in keeping with our oddly accelerated, showbiz-type alliance, gave me a quick and somewhat awkward hug.

"Thanks for coming," she said. "I'm so glad you're here."

This might have been just another of those facile Hollywood niceties, but in that moment I had the feeling that there was some actual emotion and relief in the words. I don't kid myself that this had much to do with me. But Caitlin looked like she needed some distraction, like she hadn't been having much fun. Oddly, she seemed less relaxed out here in the country than she'd seemed in the fishbowl of the Four Seasons. There was tension at the corners of her indigo eyes; her hands were fidgety on the steering wheel.

My hands were fidgety on the cellophane wrapper of the chintzy bouquet. Sheepishly, I said, "I brought some flowers."

"That's so sweet," she said. She made a point of sniffing them but didn't look at them too closely. Thank God, it was the thought that counted. With a show of caring, she put them gently on the back seat.

She started up the car. "Do you know Southampton well?" she asked.

"Hardly at all," I said.

"If you like, I'll drive you around."

"Sure. That'd be great."

She paused an actor's beat, then gave me a sideways look and said, "It'll be my excuse for staying away a little longer."

She pulled out of the parking lot and we headed through the tidy village. There were lots of little shops, the kind that sold ladies' cardigans with pearl buttons and bright green pants for men. Everything was closed.

"Thing aren't going well at home?" I ventured.

We were heading toward the ocean, on a winding street flanked by huge and scaly sycamores. Even out here, the weather was mild enough to keep the window open; the air smelled of salt and iodine and seaweed. The hedges got taller and the gates got grander as we moved closer to the water.

She said, "Those two are just so weird together."

I nodded sympathetically. "Is Mr. Happy just out for the day, or the whole weekend?"

A look of complete incomprehension flitted across her beautiful face. Then she said, "*We're* the guests. It's Tony's house. Estate, I should say."

Now it was my turn to look confused. Stupidly, I echoed, "Tony owns the house?"

"Yeah. I thought you knew. When the parents died, that was the deal. Robert got the business, or at least the lion's share of it. Tony got the family estate and a big allowance from the business to maintain it. That's what all the weirdness is about."

The road had narrowed, and I tried to process this as we drove through a chute of privet and boxwood that afforded here and there a glimpse of a Tudor facade or massive stone chimney or perfectly weather-beaten shingle exterior.

"It was one of those situations," she went on, "where the parents sort of did their fighting through the kids. Robert was the mother's favorite. The father doted on Tony, the moody and artistic one. The mother wanted to make sure that Robert got the buildings, the offices, the power. That was fine with the father—who actually seems to have been pretty sly—as long as Tony got the Southampton property and the means to keep it up. So the bottom line is that Robert has spent his life working his tail off, taking on all the stress and all the risk, so Tony can live like country royalty."

I said, "But isn't Tony sort of . . ."

Before I could come up with a tactful way of ending the sentence, Caitlin ended it for me. "Crazy?"

"Yeah."

Just then we veered onto a nearly invisible side road that offered grudging public access to the beach. The big tires crunched over strewn sand, and Caitlin stopped the car. We climbed out, slipped past a splintery wooden gate, and stared at the Atlantic. It was a rich but lusterless gray green, viscous looking. The waves seemed to be squashed down by the weight of the muggy air. They rose languidly, not more than a foot or so, then didn't really crash, but just gave up, as if they themselves were somehow drowning.

"The thing with Tony," Caitlin said, "is that no one really knows how crazy he is. He's been in therapy forever. He's been institutionalized four or five times—Robert isn't even sure how many. But the thing is, the doctors never agree on what the diagnosis is. One time they think he's bipolar. Another time he's paranoid. A different doc says borderline schizophrenic. It's so all over the place that Robert thinks maybe he's been faking it."

"Faking it?"

A little way up the beach, halfway to the water's edge, there was a broad and absolutely irresistible driftwood log. We started walking toward it, our footsteps pleasantly labored in the cakey sand.

"This is Robert talking, okay? Not a trained psychiatrist. And maybe *faking it* isn't exactly right. More like going with whatever works. Tony has a really easy life. He's got an endless supply of spending money and he's never had to work. He paints. He flies around the world to art openings and museums. When he needs a rest, he checks into a nuthouse that's basically a Ritz Carlton with sedatives. He gets his way just like in childhood—by being helpless, spaced out, unable to cope. Not a bad strategy if you're from a really wealthy family."

I said, "But an easy life is different from a happy life."

"Oh, big-time different," she agreed. "Don't get me wrong. I'm not accusing him of being happy. As far as I can tell, he's miserable, frustrated as hell. All he ever wanted was to be recognized as a painter. Did you know he changed his name?"

I vaguely remembered reading that. "Went back to McDermott, right?"

"Right. He did that so people would forget who he was and just look at his work. The problem is his work doesn't seem to be very good. So I'm not saying he's thrilled with his cushy life. I'm just trying to explain why Robert is so resentful of him. He's sick of paying the bills."

I thought that over as we neared the silvery log. It seemed to me that sibling resentments were nearly always mutual—mirror images of active and passive, bully and runt, prodigal and goody-goody—eternally linked by the stubborn ligaments of family. I said, "And making Robert pay the bills is Tony's way of getting even, right? Making Robert pay extra for his success, his recognition, for being a big, important person."

"I guess," said Caitlin, sitting down, slipping off her moccasins, and letting her toes play in the sand. "I mean, the resentment definitely cuts both ways. And it shows. Constantly. That's why I'm going to have a couple hits of this."

She reached into a shirt pocket and came up with a joint. It was expertly rolled in pale blue paper and was about the girth of a Tiparillo. "Want some?"

I was tempted but I passed. It had been a long time since I'd smoked pot, and truthfully, I'd never liked it much. It had occasionally made me giggly and loose, but more often I just got inward and morose. I watched Caitlin light up. With the first deep drag, her face took on an expression of pleasure and release that worried me; her last boyfriend was an everything addict, and I'd grown a bit suspicious that maybe Caitlin herself was a bit too cozy with the substances. But she limited herself to two big tokes, and as she held the second one, she stubbed the j out in the sand and put it back into her pocket.

Letting out the musky smoke, she said matter-of-factly, "Twenty-five million."

"Excuse me?"

"That's what Robert pays for Tony's allowance and the upkeep on the estate. Year in, year out. Whether the business is going well or badly. It's worse than alimony."

"Dad's revenge on Mom," I said.

She shrugged and did a half swivel on the driftwood log, facing out toward the empty ocean. Lithely, she drew up her knees and hugged them with her forearms. I don't know if she knew this about herself—as an actress, probably she did—but many little things about her were achingly perfect: her suntanned ankles above her sandy feet, the way her turned-up shirtsleeves lay just so and set off the sinews of her arms.

I heard myself say, "Not that it's any of my business, but you and Robert seem an unlikely match."

Without hurry, she turned back toward me. "Oh," she said, "we are. Definitely. But I like him. I mean, he's not the love of my life. I'm not the love of his. But this isn't just for the convenience of the press agents. We mostly have a lot of fun together."

Gulls wheeled; sandpipers chased receding foam. I weighed my words, then realized that I probably didn't have to. Celebrities were used to questions that most of us would find bizarrely inappropriate from near strangers. I said, "Tell me what you like about him. I need to understand."

She didn't take offense; she hugged her knees a bit more tightly and pushed her lips out thoughtfully. "His intensity," she said. "His will. When Robert wants something, he *really* wants it. Like nothing else in the world would satisfy. If you're what he wants, it's flattering, it's exciting. He's a bit of a caveman. I guess that's good and bad. He can be a real jerk, a boor, a show-off. Then there are these moments—not often—of the most unexpected and amazing tenderness."

I confess this last revelation surprised me. What did he do—get all kissy-face, make baby talk? I guess I'll never make it as a daytime television host, because I couldn't bring myself to ask for more details. I really didn't want to know.

After a silence, Caitlin said, "What about you? You in a relationship?"

For some reason, the question made me giggle. Maybe I had a contact high or maybe I'd drunk in a few too many molecules of Caitlin's exhalations. I said, "You know, you're the second beautiful woman to ask me that this month, and I didn't have a good answer the first time, either."

"Why not? You gay?"

"Not that I know of. No. I seem to be in love with my ex-wife."

My companion seemed intrigued by that. She put her feet down on the beach, crossed her arms against her midriff, and put a compassionate yet probing expression on her face. I vaguely realized that the tables had instantly been turned, that I was no longer the talk-show host but the guest about to be stripped naked. "That's so cool," she said. "In love again, or still?"

"Good question," I admitted. "I'm not really sure. It's hard to tell if you're still in love when you're feeling lousy about a bunch of other things."

"Other things?"

"You know. Work. Career. Success or failure."

"Ah," she said, "that shit. But you feel okay about that stuff now?"

I heard myself give another nervous laugh. "Let's just say the pain has receded. I guess my attitude has changed about a lot of it. I've met a lot of successful people through my ghostwriting. They're not any happier than I am."

"Fuckin' A," said Caitlin. "And your ex—is she still in love with you?"

"I wish I knew."

Caitlin jumped all over this. She brought her legs up effortlessly into a tailor pose, and fixed me with a blue-eyed stare. "Come on. How can you not know? You were married to this person."

Rather feebly, I said, "We're friends now. There are certain lines we just don't cross."

"David, no offense. That's bullshit."

"But—"

"I don't buy this 'certain lines' stuff. If you're in love, there are no lines. And if you can't tell whether or not she's in love with you, it's because you really don't want to know."

"But why wouldn't I—"

She cut me off, barreling along in full loose cannon mode. "It's so obvious! Come on, you're a writer. You supposedly have a lot of insight into other people's stories. How can you be such a knucklehead about your own? You don't want to know if she's in love with you, because if she is, you've got to shit or get off the pot. Either take the plunge and get back together, or let go of this romantic little fairy tale and get on with your life. I don't think you really want to do either."

I sat there on the log. I pride myself on having quick and ready answers for most things, but for this I had none whatsoever. I had no answer because I knew she was right. Boy, was she right. I didn't even need a brain to grasp this; the truth of it went straight to my pores and spine and heart with a suddenness that made me sort of dizzy. I felt like . . . I don't know, a peeled grape, a soft-bodied critter caught by headlights between one skin and the next.

My unease must have been obvious. The relief that went with it was probably less so. Caitlin said, "Jesus, I'm sorry. I've upset you."

"No," I said. "It's fine. It's really fine."

"I talk way too much. I say what's on my mind." She lightly slapped the pocket with the joint in it. "Probably the herb was not the best idea."

"It's really okay. You got me. You nailed it. I should pay you for a session."

"Group therapy on Thanksgiving. Beats watching football." She glanced down at her watch and frowned. "I really should be getting back. I'd feel guilty if they killed each other without me there."

We rose and headed up the beach. The waves hissed against the stony sand.

When we were halfway to the car, Caitlin stopped and said, "Can you do this?"

She was wiggling one ear, the left. I told her that I didn't have that talent.

"How about *this*?"

She pulled her eyebrows closer together without moving anything else. That I thought I could manage.

"Great," she said. "That'll be our high sign. Do me a favor. If I start running my mouth at dinner, look at me and do that. It probably won't help. But try, okay?"

Chapter 30

Caitlin hung a U-turn that did nothing good for the foliage that bordered the narrow access road, and we got back onto the street that paralleled the ocean. After a bit, she pointed to a place where the high hedges were interrupted by a big wrought-iron post with an *M* on top, and said, "This is where the property starts."

And we drove. And we drove. And we drove.

"Jesus Christ," I said. "How big's this place?"

She shrugged. "Don't really know. Some hundreds of acres. There's stables, a steeplechase course. There's swimming pools, tennis courts, croquet lawn. A couple guest cottages, servants' quarters. But the big thing is the oceanfront. Almost half a mile. Biggest in the Hamptons."

Before I could catch myself, I said, "They'd have to have the biggest, right?"

She shot me a look that was more conspiratorial than cautioning, and said, "Now you sound like me. Don't start making trouble."

At last we came to a gated driveway. The gate was less grand than, say, the one in front of Buckingham Palace, but it was impressive enough. Dozens of gleaming black spindles were topped with golden spears; it must have been a bear to paint. Caitlin hit a gizmo on the dashboard and the gate swung open, slowly and with pomp.

Inside, all was order and serenity. Majestic oaks and beeches lined the drive. The outbuildings hugged the dunelike contours of the land and were roofed in restful green. Columns and fountains defined a formal garden. Ahead, in the slightly hazy distance, the main house loomed, enormous and symmetrical. It was made of limestone and had those graceful eyebrow curves above the windows. I counted nine chimneys. Nine, to me, was a lucky number, but this did not strike me as a lucky place. Maybe it was just my peasantish unease with too much luxury; maybe it was the freakishly heavy weather that cast a humid pall, but there was something lugubrious and stifling in this presumptive pleasure palace behind the hedges. Not a single fallen leaf stained the lawn; not a piece of gravel strayed from the drive; things seemed too perfect and settled to be anything but dead. Ridiculously, the theme song from *The Addams Family* flew into my head, and I wouldn't be able to get rid of it all afternoon. *"Their house is a museum . . ."*

Caitlin parked. A butler appeared at the front door while we were still some yards away. He greeted her as Miss Kilgore; she handed him the flowers that I'd brought and asked him to put them in a vase. He glanced down at the cheap bouquet with evident disdain. It's always the servants who are the biggest snobs.

We walked through a foyer with a coffered ceiling, then down a broad corridor completely lined with paintings. On one side were portraits of the Maxx forebears: the patriarchal great-granddad with his bristly whiskers and the twinkle of the joyful scoundrel in his eye; his wife, somehow both elegant and bovine beneath the extravagant folds of her satin gown. The next generation seemed to have kept the sharpness but lost the zest. Then there were Maxx's parents—the father, mild and soft-chinned for all his obvious and poignant effort to appear imposing; the mother, regal and severe, her gaze as hard as the diamonds at her throat.

On the opposite wall were a dozen or so abstract canvases that I imagined to be Tony's.

I said to Caitlin, "I think some of these are really good."

"Which ones do you like?"

I pointed out a couple.

"Those aren't Tony's. One's a Rauschenberg, one's a Larry Rivers. *These* are Tony's."

She steered me toward a group of pictures that, even in the well-lit gallery, were a little hard to see, mainly because they were almost black. One was purplish black, one was blackish midnight blue, one was a dull and liverish red that seemed to be turning black from the inside out. Tony painted a universe whose batteries were dying.

The corridor spilled into an enormous living room that faced out through twin picture windows toward the beach. As we entered, I saw three men deep in conversation—or rather, two men talking, and the third, our host, looking distractedly out toward the ocean. Before Tony McDermott could greet us, Robert Maxx got up from his leather arm-chair and said, "Ah, you're back. Thank God. Hal and I were just boring each other to death, talking about our money."

The second man had stood up as well, though it took me a moment to realize this, because he was extremely short. He had a big head, bald on top with a monklike tonsure around the dome, and darting eyes that seemed to lick at things, as though the world were made of ice cream. He held out a soft neat hand, and said, "Hal Lazar. Nice to meet you."

I knew the name and face from the business pages. Harold Lazar owned a huge cosmetics company. He made the paper maybe once a month on average, for buying up new brands or fighting with the FDA or parrying the complaints of the anti-animal-testing people. I shook his hand, and for a brief and absurd moment I could not figure out how to introduce myself. Was I Dave Cullen or David Collins? And did my uncertainty constitute an identity crisis, or was it just a measure of my unimportance, since probably no one would remember me anyway? I said, "David Cullen. Nice to meet you, too."

To Lazar, Maxx said, "Dave's writing my next book for me." He said it like he owned not just the publication rights, but the author, too. Then, to me, he said, "Maybe Hal should be your next victim. He could tell you great stuff about the unconscionable margins in his business and how great it is for *shtupping* supermodels."

"I don't do that anymore," said Lazar.

Maxx said, "If that's your story, you stick to it."

Not until this bit of badinage had played itself out was our host able to get a word in. Without hurry, he wandered over from his lookout near the picture window. He was wearing a tweed jacket with leather patches at the elbows; very arty, very English. He seemed not offended, but maybe darkly amused, that even here, in his own house, the assumption was that his older brother would take the lead, control the meeting, play the big shot. The alpha, it seemed, was everywhere the alpha.

Or was he? I'd never doubted it until the moment that Anthony McDermott extended his hand, fixed me with a cool but somehow sardonic gaze, and welcomed me. Instant by instant, syllable by syllable, his greeting defined one of the densest and most surprising moments I can ever remember.

I think it was Joseph Conrad who observed that, often, a single glimpse is the surest way to judge a character; all further impressions serve only to obscure and complicate. And in that moment of shaking hands with Robert Maxx's brother, I felt without a doubt that I was seeing him clearly, and that everything I'd thought I knew about him was wrong. Because he was passive, I'd assumed he was weak; because he was quiet, I'd imagined he was gentle. He was neither. He was passive like a fort is passive, and he was quiet because he didn't care to tip his hand, to give up a possible advantage. His self-effacing manner was in fact a way of playing defense against his brother's unrelenting offense, and I suddenly understood that he played it just as formidably. When he seemed to be retreating, it was only a strategic pause. He didn't recede; he lurked. The handshake was actually a little scary.

We had a few flutes of champagne, nibbled some caviar served up on an ivory spoon, then moved into the formal dining room. In the course of chitchat, I'd learned that Hal Lazar owned the mansion next door, and that he was on his own because his wife and two young children had gone to Paris for the holiday weekend. He'd been planning to go with them, but was stuck at home while he concluded a complicated little acquisition.

He didn't say what the acquisition was, but it was clear he wanted to be asked. So as we settled in around the table, where our starter course of foie gras and pears was waiting, I helped him out and inquired.

"I'm buying the ad agency that does most of our stuff," he said.

In my naïveté, I said, "It's better to own it than just to hire them?"

"Actually," said Lazar, "it'll be a pain in the ass to own it. But I have no choice. I hate the guy who runs it."

"So fire him," said Robert Maxx.

Lazar was spreading foie gras onto a triangle of toast. "Then I lose the agency, and they happen to do great work. Besides, if I fire him, I can only do it once, whereas if I buy him out, I've got him under me every day."

The foie gras was served with a small glass of Sauternes. Caitlin ignored the food and went straight for it. "Oh," she said, "that's nice. Buy his company so you can torture him."

I flashed her the high sign of the pulled-together brows. If she noticed, she ignored it. But it didn't matter; Lazar didn't take offense.

"Until he can't stand it anymore, and quits," he said. "Then I've got the agency, and he's got capital to start a new one. Everybody wins."

"Absolutely right," said Maxx. "Still, if you really don't like the guy, it must've been awfully tempting just to fire him."

To everyone's surprise, Tony McDermott spoke up then, albeit very softly. Twirling his small crystal glass, he said, "Probably irresistible to you, Robert. Because you lack subtlety. You always have. Even as a child."

Our host paused, sipped some wine. His gaze turned to Caitlin and Lazar, and he went on in a mild, mock-genial tone, camouflaging the attack in the guise of a fond family reminiscence.

"His favorite toy? A bulldozer. His favorite tool? The hammer. You should have seen him with a box of crayons. Colored so hard he broke them half the time. Not a subtle lad, my brother."

Maxx was trying to smile through this; the effort was painful to watch. His face was slightly flushed, the telltale purple was rising at his neck. I was waiting for him to strike back with something clever, something wilting, something dead-on mean. But he didn't, and I didn't yet know why.

I found out over the main course, which, thank God, was not turkey, but a magnificent prime rib—Mafia meat, most likely. The slabs of beef called for serious cutlery, and each of us was presented with a shockingly heavy sterling knife whose ornate and oversize handle was stamped with a Gothic *M*. Hal Lazar commented on the handsomeness of these heirlooms, and that gave Maxx the opening he'd apparently been waiting for.

Holding his own knife like a scimitar, he said, "Glad you like them. Great-Granddad had them made in Germany, just around the time he bought this land. Got it for a song. Of course, everything was so different then. The Hamptons weren't the Hamptons. No one around except some Polish potato farmers."

We were drinking Clos Vougeot by then—everyone but Maxx, that is. Caitlin put her glass down briefly and blurted out, "Once again, the robber barons get in on the ground floor."

I flashed her the high sign; she flashed it right back as if to say *who cares?*

But Maxx openly agreed with her. "Yup, that was a lucky generation. Got in before the clutter."

I sipped my wine, and vaguely wondered why Maxx, who'd worked so hard at burnishing the myth of being a self-made man, was suddenly playing the ancestor card. Probably it was because ancestors were the only thing he had that Hal Lazar didn't.

He looked at the short man with the hungry eyes, and went on, "No one could afford this property now. Well, hardly anyone."

Tony McDermott said, "Makes no difference. It'll never, ever be for sale."

Ignoring that, Maxx said, "I'm guessing it would have to fetch at least three hundred million."

Caitlin said, "Christ, it's Thanksgiving. Do we have to talk about money at the dinner table?"

I didn't even bother with the eyebrow thing.

Maxx said, "It's a shame, really, how little use the place gets. Tony's here—what?—eight, ten weeks a year? It wants a family. That's what these old estates are for. To be the seat of an important family."

Hal Lazar had a reputation as a tough and cool negotiator, but at the thought of someday being master of the Hamptons' biggest old-money oceanfront estate, he could not quite keep his avidity from showing. He licked his lips, his bald head took on a hint of rutting gleam. He said, "If it ever comes onto the market—"

"It won't," said Tony. He smiled. For the first time all day he seemed to be really enjoying himself, and I realized that Maxx had put him in a passive person's dream scenario. He had something other people wanted, and all he had to do was say no.

But his brother, of course, had a knack for never hearing *no*. He said to Lazar, "Combine your little parcel with this place. Get rid of the right-of-way in between. Wow. That'd be a property."

"Yes it would," said the makeup magnate. "Well, keep me posted. Price wouldn't be an obstacle."

"I'm the obstacle," said Tony. "My brother's being nice to me these days, hoping that I'll change my mind. But it isn't going to happen."

"We're still talking about it," Maxx said to Lazar. "We'll keep talking. I hope he'll see the sense of selling sometime soon."

Caitlin said, "Yeah, it would be nice to shed that twenty-five-million-dollar nut."

Maxx quickly turned his face toward her. I'd noticed that in business meetings, he had lots of different stratagems for masking or deferring anger; but now he didn't bother. This was a girlfriend, and it was clear that he was pissed.

Caitlin didn't flinch; she squared her buff shoulders and met his annoyance head-on. "What?" she said. "You can talk money at the dinner table, but I can't?"

Before he could reply, she'd hidden her famous face in her wineglass once again.

Chapter 31

Boy, was I glad to get home.

I almost always felt that way after one of my brief forays into the world of the rich and famous. It always seemed that I heard things I really didn't want to hear and saw things that I really didn't want to see. Like the apparently lifelong tug-of-war between Robert Maxx and Tony McDermott—the elder's dismissiveness pitted forever against the younger's spite, in a white-knuckled stalemate that went on and on like something out of Dante. Then there was Caitlin—probably, at the end of the day, a rather helpless victim of her own beauty. Basically a nice and honest person, she'd been thrust by her world-class looks into a milieu of falseness and artificial choices. It was hard to blame her for leaning on the reefer and the booze; where else could she look for comfort, not to mention love? Either to a drug-addict colleague or a tycoon twice her age, with whom she had nothing in common except having reached a similar stratum of the celebrity pyramid.

You might think that these up-close glimpses of the rich and famous being miserable would at least make me more at peace with my own modest means and professional obscurity. But no, it doesn't work that way; human nature is far too perverse for that. If anything, seeing the unhappiness and neuroses of the people at the top made it rankle still more that I was mired somewhere in the middle, because I knew in my heart that I could do such a better job of being filthy rich and wildly successful. I would appreciate it more, savor it, and never take it for granted. I wouldn't let it change me or deform my basic values. I would bask in my good fortune without becoming arrogant or greedy. In short, I'd be that rare person who could be rich and famous without also being a complete and utter asshole.

At least that's what I told myself. Then I went to sleep.

Over the rest of the long weekend, I got a fair bit of writing done; I played squash with the other strays and exiles who'd stayed in town for the holiday; and I brooded about my relationship with Claire.

I couldn't squirm out of acknowledging that Caitlin, in her unbridled straightforwardness, had nailed it. When it came to Claire, I was being a chickenshit. Friends. Right. Here was the woman with whom I'd been lovers for a dozen years, with whom I'd come of age into a world of fleeting success and lingering heartbreak; the woman who had nursed me, and been nursed by me in turn, through a decade of New York winter colds and bellyaches and funks that felt like they would never end. After all that, we were pals; just pals. It was sweet—but what it mostly was, was convenient and safe. My romantic but sexless loyalty to Claire gave me a high-sounding excuse for avoiding other commitments. It kept my loneliness at a manageable level without jeopardizing my stubborn independence.

At the same time, holding on to that platonic closeness also spared me from confronting a terrifying and even sickening question: What if Claire's and my love affair was really, truly over? It might sound strange, but I don't think I'd ever really accepted that idea. We'd divorced, okay; the marriage had stopped working. But we still cared deeply for each other, were central to each other's lives, had a clear, clean reservoir of affection we could draw upon. That was an article of sustaining faith. What if we put it to the test and found that time had drained it of its meaning, had twisted it into a lie? That would be way worse than divorce. That would be a death.

I called her a couple times that weekend. She'd had her first treatment a few days before; except for a bit of faintness when they implanted the IV port, she'd had no discomfort at all. She just sat there for a couple of hours, watching the mysterious fluid drip into her veins. She had no idea as yet whether the treatment was helping.

We talked about getting together, but it didn't quite work out. She had plans with various musician friends. One evening a group of them were going to Brooklyn to hear a colleague's recital. Another evening she was having people over to play piano trios. I couldn't help wondering if maybe there was something a bit contrived about her busyness, if maybe she was growing shy of me . . . if maybe she was feeling, as I was, that we were in some small danger of sliding toward a delicious crisis.

Or maybe it had nothing whatsoever to do with me. Musicians were sociable, after all. They had that easy camaraderie of the beautiful chord, the shared pleasure of the shapely phrase that they could only bring to life together. Have I mentioned that I envied them that?

O n Monday I was awakened a bit too early by the telephone.

It was Paul Hannaford, my agent. He sounded very chipper. Sounding chipper well before 8 A.M. was yet one more thing I might have held against him, along with his refusal to look his age or to show how much he'd had to drink. We hadn't spoken in a few weeks; he knew me well enough to leave me alone when I was on a project.

He said, "David? No time for chitchat right now. Just thought you'd like to know that your boy's about to be crucified on the *Today* show. They just did a teaser and went to a commercial. Check it out and call me later."

We hung up. I fumbled for the remote and switched on the TV. When the advertisements ended, there was an exterior shot of the Rockefeller Center Plaza, just outside the studio.

A demonstration was in progress. It was small—maybe a hundred people—orderly, and anything but ragtag. Judging by the Hermès scarves and Coach handbags and close-cropped gray haircuts and blue button-down oxford shirts, I'd say it was composed mainly of society matrons and architects—just the sort of Landmarks Commission types who had long been Robert Maxx's nemeses. A few people carried placards. Some said ROCKEFELLER, SÍ! MAXX, NO! Others were emblazoned with the slightly clever acronym PORCH—PRESERVE OUR ROCKE-FELLER CENTER HERITAGE.

Matt Lauer was doing a voice-over, reminding viewers that, as they'd probably heard, billionaire developer Robert Maxx was in talks to purchase this famous property, and planned to change its name to his own. Not everyone was happy about this. These protesters felt strongly enough to form an ad hoc organization to publicize their concerns.

Cutting back to the studio, Lauer was shown on the set, along with two guests. One was a man whom I did not recognize. The other was a woman whom I did. I suppose I should not have been surprised to see her there. But I was.

The host introduced the man—who was wearing a splendid flannel suit and had a handsome cleft in his chin—as Kenneth Hotchkiss, curator of the urban planning department at the Cooper-Hewitt Museum of Design, and president of PORCH. Then he introduced the group's vice president, Mandy Lockwood, the anchor, until just recently, of the influential financial news show *Wall Street Confidential*. She was wearing a suit as well. Its color was aubergine, and though the skirt was of a modest length, it had a slit in it that drew the eye. If the purpose of business suits for women was to play down the differences between the genders, it didn't work on Mandy. She looked just as kittenish and sensual as ever.

Lauer began the interview with a hanging curve. To Hotchkiss, he said, "What's in a name? Why is it significant to your group if Robert Maxx wants to rename something that he owns?"

"Two reasons," Hotchkiss said. A poised and practiced interviewee, if maybe a little bit stiff, he seemed to have rehearsed his answer. "First," he said, "the name itself is part of history. It evokes an era. You can't just undo that with some new signage and a change of stationery. More important, though, is what the name change says about Robert Maxx's whole approach to development. He seems to think that the owner of a property can do absolutely anything he wants."

"Well, can't he?" Lauer said. "I mean, property rights are taken pretty seriously in this country."

"Right," said Hotchkiss. "And if we're talking about a ranch in Montana, fine. But this is a city of almost nine million people. Prerogatives must be balanced. Ownership also implies stewardship. Our concern is that Maxx doesn't really understand that concept."

With the sure instincts of a popular entertainer, Mandy Lockwood seemed to realize that the professorial Hotchkiss was in danger of losing the audience, that the conversation was growing a tad too rarefied for morning television. She cut in and imposed a more demotic tone.

"Look," she said, "we all know what Robert Maxx's buildings look like. Can we talk? The man has a thing for chrome, dark glass, and fake gold paint, for seeing his name in great big lights. He makes everything look like a casino. That's why we're here this morning. We don't want Rockefeller Center to look like a casino or some cheesy condo in Miami."

The temperate Kenneth Hotchkiss looked more than a bit uneasy at his colleague's tirade, but Matt Lauer seemed nothing but grateful for her animation. He swiveled toward her and said, "But, realistically, there are safeguards, there are rules in place—"

"Right. And Maxx breaks rules all the time," said Mandy. "It's in the paper every other week. He does what he wants, and applies for permits afterward. He takes down trees, puts up giant flagpoles. He reduces access, cuts back on public spaces—"

"And public spaces," Hotchkiss said, "are one of Rockefeller Center's glories."

"Look at the skating rink," said Mandy. "An amazing public space. You don't think a developer could make a lot more money using that for something else?"

"You're not suggesting that Robert Maxx would take away the skating rink?" said Lauer.

Mandy Lockwood did her remarkable shrug—the one that lifted her breasts up toward her collarbones as if she could toss them right over her shoulders. "No one knows what Maxx would do. That's why we're on guard. And that's why we're hoping that the buzz about a competing bidder is for real."

Lauer jumped all over that. "Competing bidder? Now, wait, this is breaking news."

"Just a rumor," Hotchkiss said.

"Who's the bidder?" Lauer pressed.

Mandy said, "Stay tuned."

The segment ended. I made some coffee and then called Paul Hannaford.

"Wow," he said. "Rockefeller Center. Let's hope this stays in the news awhile. How's the book going?"

I knocked wood and said, "Going okay. Going better than things seem to be going for Maxx."

"Can you tell me?"

I sipped some coffee and weighed what I could safely pass along. "Let's just say he seems to be at some kind of pivotal moment. He's scrambling to raise money. He's chased away his closest adviser. He's sleeping with a woman whose last boyfriend was a violent madman. And he's locked in some kind of almost biblical battle with his own brother."

"Sounds fabulous. For the book, I mean."

"It better be," I said. "I mortgaged my apartment."

I'm not sure why I told him that just then. Probably it popped out because I was more nervous about the situation than I admitted to myself. A book deadline was one thing; a deadline for losing the place I lived in and the only thing I owned was something else.

"You did what?"

I told him briefly about the problem with Claire's hands. He got it at once. He knew Claire. He'd been my confidant over the whole looping, convoluted arc of our relationship; if anyone understood our peculiar but persistent bond, it was him.

He gave me some well-intended if generic reassurance that I shouldn't worry, it would all work out, this was a project that just couldn't miss. Then he passed along what is the only truly useful advice that an agent can bestow upon a client.

"Write fast," he said. "Let's get this out there while the son of a bitch is still hot."

Chapter 32

I waited till shortly after nine, then called Jenna. I was still concerned, or certainly curious at least, about her unannounced and early departure for the holiday weekend. I had to believe there was more behind it than a sudden burning desire to get home to Mississippi.

An assistant put me through. Jenna said hello—a little wearily, it seemed to me. Not being that familiar with the world of work, I wasn't sure what to make of this. You'd think a long weekend would make people sound refreshed. But maybe that was canceled out by the oppression of returning, that back-to-the-salt-mine sort of feeling. I really couldn't tell. But then it dawned on me that Jenna did not, in fact, sound weary; she sounded southern.

"Oh hell," she said, when I mentioned this. "My drawl comes back a little whenever I go home. Takes a day or two to shed it."

"Your holiday was nice?"

"Great, if you like sweet potatoes. Let's leave it right there. How was yours?"

"Bizarre. I spent it in Southampton with your boss."

"Really?" she said. "You're more upwardly mobile than you look."

I let that slide. "See the *Today* show?"

"One more thing we didn't need."

"Know anything about a second bidder?"

"I know that Robert's bullshit about it, and picking brains all over town to see if it's for real. Hopefully it's a one-day rumor. We've got enough to worry about without some competitor coming in with wads of cash."

I said, "Speaking of worries, I had a thought right before the holiday. I thought I should interview Carlton Phelps, try to understand this finance stuff a little better. Whaddaya think?"

There was a silence. I think it's fair to say it was a stunned silence. Then she said, "I think it's about the worst idea I ever heard. Carlton doesn't talk to anyone. Robert doesn't want him talking to anyone. And if Carlton had his way, Robert wouldn't talk to anyone but him. And aside from that, your timing couldn't be worse. Carlton threatened to quit last week."

"What?"

"Hold on a minute."

The line went quiet and I understood, of course, that Jenna had gone off to perform that emblematic ritual of third-millennium insecurity, the closing of the office door. When she returned to the phone, she said, "That's why I bolted early. Things were really a mess."

"What happened?"

"Who knows? For years the guy sits quietly in his office, then last week he just explodes and throws a hissy fit."

"So he's leaving?"

"Remains to be seen. But I'll tell you this. A CFO quitting is the granddaddy of all red flags. If he left, you could kiss the Rock Center deal good-bye. The press would be all over it. And it wouldn't just be a business-section item anymore. It'd be front-page news. Robert asked him please to take the weekend to cool down. They're meeting again this afternoon."

"I need to be there."

I said this without hesitation and without thought. It was a reflex, a storyteller's twitch. This happens sometimes when instincts are aroused. We become servants or maybe slaves to the stories we are telling; we chase them like dogs chase cars, and after a while it becomes pointless even to wonder if we have a choice in the matter.

Jenna gave a quick and nervous laugh. "I don't think that's going to fly. This is very touchy stuff."

"Exactly. Touchy is good. Can you put me through to Robert?"

"You're serious? You're going to try to crash that meeting?"

I assured her that I was.

"What's going on," she said. "You didn't hear it from me, okay?"

I need to take a moment to explain what happened next, because, in retrospect, it was crucial. It changed my whole relationship with Robert Maxx. It ushered in a subtly but fundamentally different phase— a phase that lasted right up to the night he died.

Up until this point, Maxx had always led and I had always followed. He summoned; I came. He set the agenda; I scribbled down the minutes of the meeting. Now, up to a point at least, I was taking charge. This was a somewhat surprising development. I am not an aggressive guy; I think that's clear by now. But in service to the story, I found an assertiveness that I never could have mustered on my own behalf. It was a little like those anecdotes of mothers lifting cars off children; when you care, you somehow find the muscles that are needed.

I suppose I could also put this in a slightly different, harsher light. From our very first meeting, I was pissed off at the idea that Robert Maxx was exploiting me. Finally, I was embracing the notion that, fuck it, I could exploit him back. He had a better story than he knew how to tell, and probably a sadder and truer story than he wanted told. Too bad for him. I was going to find a way to tell it.

In any case, I got through to Maxx and, after the tersest of chitchat, told him that I wanted to be at his meeting with Phelps that afternoon.

"How the hell you know about that?" he asked.

"It's my job to find things out," I said. "Anyway, it doesn't matter how I know. It sounds important, and I'd like to be there."

He thought it over, not for long. "I don't think that's a good idea."

I steeled myself and said, "Can I tell you, at least, why I think it *is*?"

"Okay, tell me why you think it is."

He said this grudgingly, more than a little condescendingly, but there was something else hidden in his tone—something I would come to recognize over the next few weeks, as Maxx's problems grew only deeper and more overwhelming. This other thing was hope. He was a man who could not ask for help, but who, behind a veil of self-sufficient gruffness, seemed always to be hoping that help would somehow come unbidden and not need to be acknowledged, that someone would say or do something that would rescue him.

Rescue, of course, was not my line of work. I was only talking about the book I had to write. Still, I took the opportunity to go into my dance.

"First," I said, "a confession. The whole time we've been working together, I've been collecting impressions, gathering scenes . . . but have I really known what our book was *about*? No. Now I think I do."

The bait dangled there a moment. Finally, Maxx said, "So what's it about?"

"Guts," I said. "Brinksmanship. Grace under pressure. Look, you don't want to be presented as a nice guy, but a winner. Fine. But what's the big deal about winning, when winning comes easy? It's a big deal when it comes hard. When you've got to fight your way off the ropes, summon up the courage, and pull out all the stops."

He thought that over, then said, "Rocky in a business suit."

"Let's hope a little better than that. But yeah, that's the general idea. Not Rocky the underdog. Rocky the guy who's been champ so long that lots of people are just dying to tear him down. So the battle isn't against just one opponent. The battle is against all the pressures and demons that go with being on top. *That's* what our story's about."

He liked it. I could tell he liked it, even though he didn't answer right away. Finally, in a tone that I was pretty sure was meant to be facetious, he said, "But what if I don't win the fight?"

I said, "Do you believe for a second there's any chance you won't?"

He didn't answer that. Maybe I imagined it, but I couldn't help feeling there was just the slightest whisper of doubt in his silence.

Then he said, "Phelps isn't going to like your sitting in. Be here at ten to three."

Chapter 33

Carlton Phelps truly looked like hell that day.

Other times I'd seen him, he was already rather pale and jumpy, but in the past week or two he seemed to have taken a quantum leap into neurasthenic misery. The skin around his eyes was parched and papery. His fingernails were chewed. It had been a long time since I'd seen chewed fingernails on a grown man; the flesh beneath the stubs was a raw and obscene pink, like some part had been amputated. On his wrists, chafing against the stiff cuffs of his shirt, was what appeared to be an eczema rash.

He clearly wasn't pleased to see me sitting there in Maxx's office. I don't know if his resentment came from paranoia or possessiveness; either way, he didn't try to hide it. Honestly, I couldn't blame him. If the situation were reversed, I wouldn't want a stranger on hand, either. But what can I say? I had a job to do.

To Maxx, he said, "I thought it would be just the two of us."

The tycoon said, "Dave's okay. There's nothing you can't say."

That earned me another blaming glance. Maybe it wasn't jealousy.

Maybe it was just that he'd figured out I was a writer. During his long tenure, after all, half a dozen other ghosts had passed through the office, no doubt looking as awkward and out of place as I.

The accountant licked his dry lips with a whitish tongue. "I really don't think—"

"Carlton," said Maxx. "Lighten up a little bit. Try to relax."

It was odd, the way he said this. The words were soothing but the tone was not. There was something smug and taunting about it, like a strong kid urging a weaker one to grow up and not wet the bed. He gestured the nervous man toward a chair opposite his desk.

"So let's talk," he went on. "This craziness about your leaving. It's out of the question. You're too good. You're too valuable. I hope you've calmed down and reconsidered."

The accountant had got into the chair, but he wasn't seated, exactly; he was perched, very lightly, as if expecting an electric shock. "I haven't," he said.

Maxx frowned and pushed out his lips. "Is it the salary? You need a raise, a bonus? You want an extension on your contract?"

"It's not about that. And we both know it."

"No," said Maxx, "we *don't* both know it. Maybe you know it. All I know is that we've worked together a long time. I hired you. I've trusted you. I've made you wealthy. And now suddenly you want to screw me."

I wasn't sure, but I thought I saw just the fleetingest smile flicker at the corner of Carlton Phelps's tight mouth as the nervous underling realized he had a little power after all, that he could now and then inflict anxiety as well as feeling it himself. The look of satisfaction, if it was ever there at all, was quickly replaced by the more usual beset expression. "This isn't about you, Robert. It's about me. I haven't been able to sleep. I haven't been able to eat. You've put me in a completely untenable position."

"What's untenable?" said Maxx. "I'm asking you to do your job at what happens to be a challenging moment."

Phelps bit his lip and squirmed. He seemed torn between throwing himself against the back of his chair or springing out of it like a grasshopper. "No," he said. "It's not a moment. It's years and years. Hiding debt. Masking liabilities. Look, the accounting rules are pretty flexible. But there are limits, after all. There are lines that can't be crossed."

Maxx's tone grew suddenly judicial. "Have I ever instructed you to cross those lines?"

The accountant didn't quite answer the question. "That's the point," he said. "I don't work from *instructions*. I work from what's there. And if what's there doesn't add up, there's only so much I can do to make it look like it does."

Maxx looked away, drummed fingers on his desk. He sighed, blew air out very slowly. "Carlton," he said, "listen. I hear what you're saying. I know it's been tough. But if you'll bear with me till the end of the quarter—"

And that's when the guy snapped.

"No!" he piped. "No. I've been hearing that too long. Wait for this, hang in for that. Wait till the currency hedges come right or the market bounces back. Wait till the troubled casinos get sold, till the fancy golf course opens. And in the meantime, make it look like minuses are pluses. Log in money we don't have yet. Push losses back another quarter. It's bullshit, Robert. I just can't do it anymore."

He broke off suddenly, and I really thought he might start to cry. I can't claim to really understand the man's profession, but in that moment I think I understood a thing or two about his torment. Numbers were at the center of his universe; he believed in their elegance and truth, their sanctity. Their violation was a double-edged affront, both moral and aesthetic. Numbers that didn't add up were ugly, jangly, jarring, as maddeningly un-serene as a piece of music that failed to return to the key it started in. Phelps's whole world had been yanked out of tune.

In the wake of his outburst, there was a hush. I heard a dull electric hum that I'd never noticed before. Someone's chair squeaked.

Then Robert Maxx said, very softly, "Okay. You win. Leave."

The words could not have been simpler or more definite. They seemed like a complete surrender. They also left Carlton Phelps speechless and immobile. I had the impression that he wanted to get up from his chair but his muscles wouldn't let him.

Two or three breaths later, Maxx raised a thick finger and went on. "But when you go, consider this. The company's in dicey shape. Your leaving will make it a whole lot dicier. And if things ever get so bad that the D.A. or the SEC starts combing through the books, I promise you that I will pull a total Kenneth Lay. I knew nothing. I saw nothing. I did my job—strategy and planning. The books were your department. If they're cooked, you cooked them. If they're a mess, they're a mess you made, right up till the day you bolted. And by the way—why did you pick just this moment to leave? Was it because you were afraid the fudging was about to be found out? You might want to start thinking how you'll answer that."

It was hard for Carlton Phelps to get more pale, but he did. Color drained from his lips and eyelids; his nostrils trembled and their creases went white. Struggling for quick sharp breaths, he said, "You fucking bastard. That's blackmail."

Maxx actually smiled at that. "No, it isn't. It's accountability. All I'm saying is that you're responsible for what you've done, whether you're still here or not. So, as I see it, you have a choice. Leave now and take your chances. Or stick around another quarter or two, till you can clean things up and walk away with a clear conscience. Either's fine with me. Why not go home and think it over?"

Phelps left the office. His eyes seemed unfocused and his knees didn't bend as he walked.

When he was gone, Maxx took off his game face; or rather, he put a different game face on—the one he used with me. This was an expression of wry and partial frankness, intended to convey mastery and calm. But today the tycoon's agitation showed right through it. He waited until his tortured accountant was out of earshot, and said, "Christ, what a neurotic pain in the ass."

"Will he quit?"

There was no hesitation in Maxx's answer. "He'll stay. Of course he'll stay. He'll stay till things get turned around, then I'll fire his disloyal ass. I mean, how can I trust him after this?"

I rubbed my chin, weighed my words, and ventured on. "But what he said about the books . . . ?"

"What about 'em?"

"What's he so upset about?"

Maxx's eyes slid off of mine. Suddenly he seemed evasive. This was new. Usually, he answered or he didn't; there was no prevarication. Now he said, "That's really more technical than you need to know."

I waited. Silence sometimes draws out more than questioning.

"Bottom line," Maxx resumed, "he's shitting bricks about our debt. Small people get nervous about borrowing. My father was that way. Drove me crazy. Me, I love borrowing. It's how you make real money. Always has been. Is the cash flow always as smooth as you'd like? Of course not. That's life. You deal with it. Stall a little, rearrange a little, get a next deal done. You don't just whine and go to pieces."

Hoping to keep Maxx talking, I said, "You fight back off the ropes."

"Exactly. Now there's this credit crunch. Plus the dollar's a piece of shit. That makes things tougher. Sure it does. But listen, I've been here before. And there's something I've learned. If you're one poor bastard going down, losing your house or whatever, forget about it, no one cares, you're dead. But if you're big enough so that your going down would take a lot of people with you, they'll find a way to bail you out. Why? Very simple. Because people would rather throw good money after bad than look like idiots for being in business with you in the first place."

I said, "But if they bail you out—"

"They're just getting in deeper," Maxx cut in. "Right. And if people were logical, they probably wouldn't do that. But people aren't logical. People would rather look smart than be smart. That's the dirty little secret."

He leaned back in his enormous chair, rubbed his meaty hands together, then gestured toward the empty place where his CFO had recently been sitting. "Except for accountants, maybe," he went on. "Accountants tend to be pretty logical. I guess that's why they're usually miserable. Why they get rashes. Neat freaks in a messy world."

He seemed to be groping for a compassionate tone, but he never quite got there, it was too much of a stretch. What came out sounded much more like contempt and a closing of the iron door. No less than Arthur Levin, Carlton Phelps was out now, never to be welcomed back.

"It's sad in a way," Maxx went on, as if talking about someone he'd never liked much who had died. "A really bright guy who just doesn't get it."

Chapter 34

By the time I left Maxx's office, I was feeling really wired and maybe a little bit soiled. Cooked books, allegations of blackmail, a human being dissolving before my very eyes—the meeting had presented both business and life as more low-down and brutish than I liked to think they were. The spectacle, I had to admit, was gripping and somewhat titillating; but titillating in an unwholesome, pornographic kind of way, thoroughly mixed in with creepiness. It made me feel a little desperate for some light and air. I couldn't wait to get out of the building.

Out on the sidewalk, however, the light and air I found were nothing to write home about. It was only four o'clock or so, but a grainy, bluish twilight was already setting in along Fifth Avenue, and I was reminded of something that kicked me in the stomach every single year: there came a time, somewhere near the cusp between November and December, when, in a heartbeat, every pleasant and bracing thing about the fall seemed finished, and all that lay ahead was the long and dreary slog of winter. Head colds and slush puddles. Delivered Chinese food arriving at a melancholy lukewarm temperature that somehow pointed out how long the evenings were. It was a crummy time to be alone.

I should have censored that last thought, because of course it made me think of Claire. The early dusk; the damp chill moving in; the naked trees and shriveled grass at the south end of Central Park; even the meanness of Robert Maxx's world that made the solace of a loved one seem an absolute requirement for sanity—suddenly *everything* was ganging up to make me think of Claire. A feeling assailed me that I tried to squelch but couldn't. All at once I was aching to see her; really, bodily aching, in a way that you feel in the place between your chest and stomach when you draw in breath.

It had been a while since I'd felt that ache so strongly—or maybe just since I'd acknowledged it. I lived with it for a block or two; I studied it and I suppose I wallowed in it. It had some of the sting of hunger pangs, but it wasn't exactly in the belly; more between the ribs. It seemed to draw its power from a thousand little tokens of goneness that were too vague and swift to count as memories; just images and fragments—a dented pillow, a blouse left on an empty chair, a coffee cup abandoned on a counter. The ache had a smell like hair after sunshine.

I took out my phone and called her up. I had to.

I asked if she could meet me for a drink, though I was hoping she'd invite me over, as she had before. I was hoping she might be playing the piano when I arrived. I was hoping we would be alone, would sip wine by candlelight, our shins against the low table.

She didn't invite me over. But she did agree to meet. She suggested a place on Columbus, just south of Lincoln Center.

I got there first and staked out a small booth at the back. A waitress came over to take my order. I wanted something with enough bite and burn to balance the extremes of all I'd seen and felt that afternoon. I asked for a Laphroaig, neat. It tasted of rage and the fellowship of the tavern and I loved it.

Claire arrived maybe ten minutes later. It was almost fully dark out-side, not quite, and from my vantage I could see her silhouetted in the doorway before she noticed me. For just an instant, I had the weird sensation of being on a blind date and seeing my companion for the very first time. I thought she looked beautiful. She wore a short, snug jacket over a turtleneck sweater; the collar showed off the grace of her neck and the lushness of her curls as they trundled down around it. Her features were generous and mobile; there was dignity in her posture and her walk.

I waved. She saw me and came over. She gave me a warm hello and sat down across from me, but without the kiss on the cheek that I was used to. I tried not to notice the omission. But of course I noticed it. It worried me.

The server came by. Claire asked for a glass of cabernet. I said I'd take another scotch.

"You're going big," she said.

"I've had a wild afternoon with Maxx."

"Anything you're free to talk about?"

"Nothing that I really want to. Too mean and ugly. How are you?"

She said she was fine. She'd coached a chamber group that afternoon; played some Fauré and really enjoyed it.

"And your hands?"

She shrugged. "Had a treatment this morning. I brought a score to read but couldn't really concentrate. Sat there and tried to visualize the IV stuff coating my nerves, like honey or syrup or something."

The drinks arrived. We clinked and drank.

Claire said, "Seems weird, doesn't it?"

"What?"

"Talking about medical stuff, health stuff. Like we're middle-aged all of a sudden."

I didn't really have a comeback for that, and the conversation lagged. This, in a low-key way, was shocking. Between Claire and me, conversation never lagged. I'm not saying our chatter was always witty or profound; just that we seldom had a problem keeping it going. If conversation was stalling, it could only be because there was a blockage somewhere, some unsaid thing that was damming up the words behind it.

I looked down at my golden whiskey, then back up at Claire. There was something veiled and uneasy in her wide dark eyes; her smile was without its usual playfulness. Suddenly I knew what was making both of us feel awkward. No—that's wrong. I'd probably known it all along, but I was finally ready to voice it. I said, "Can I ask you something? Were you avoiding me this weekend?"

Her eyes moved away. This was as surprising as the lapse in conversation. Claire never shrank from my gaze, nor did I from hers. That's not how we were together. If anything, our problem was the opposite. We tended, in the name of modern honesty, to be too unflinching, too direct. We said things even when they hurt; when the truth was barbed, we took it in our flesh.

But now she was deflecting me. Unconvincingly, she said, "I was busy. I had plans."

I heard myself sounding petulant, and it embarrassed me. "Every evening? Every lunch?"

I was overstepping. I knew it. I wouldn't have blamed her if she told me it was none of my business. But she just kept quiet. It was a silence with nothing coy about it, but I couldn't let it be.

"Claire," I said, "listen, you don't owe me any explanations, but I'd like to know what's going on. Are you seeing someone?"

For some reason she seemed to find this darkly funny, or maybe just a stupid question. She twisted up her mouth and shook her head. "I'm not seeing anyone. I was out with friends. It's a busy time of year." She sipped her wine and looked down at the table. Then she raised her eyes and fixed me with her more usual head-on stare, intimate and brave. "And, yes," she went on, "I've been avoiding you."

First things first: I was thrilled to hear she wasn't seeing someone else. Jealousy is primal, and if I've ever made it sound like I wasn't jealous when it came to Claire, I was lying. But that still left the question of her dodging me. "Why?" I said. "Did I do something? Are you mad at me?"

She gave me an appraising look, as if she suspected I was being deliberately obtuse. And maybe I was. Sometimes dumb questions are the only way to get an answer that you're aching to hear. She toyed with the stem of her wineglass and said very softly, "I'm a little scared. I've been feeling really close to you lately. I don't know if it's my illness. I don't know what it is. But it scares me."

I thought that over. "Would it help if I told you I'm scared, too?"

"I guess that's nice. I don't know if it helps or not."

She swept her hair away from her neck, like she did when she was sitting down to play; I wondered if she even realized she was doing it.

"We had so much work to do, splitting up," she went on. "So much work at trying to be honest, trying to be fair, trying to figure out what happened and to get over being angry. I can't stand the thought of having to do that work again."

I listened hard to that. She was right. Our breakup had been excruciating, exhausting, a cruelly slow passage through every disappointed hope. We'd been lucky to emerge with our lives and egos more or less intact. It was like a close escape from a burning building; you had to be a little crazy even to consider going back in. Either that, or you had to believe that something irreplaceable had been left behind among the charred rafters and ashy floors. With no great confidence, I said, "Who says we'd ever have to do that work again?"

"David, don't," she said. "Please."

I squeezed my lips together. Words pried them apart again. "You don't believe in second chances?"

She flushed a bit; her voice was pinched. "I just don't know too many happy stories of people getting back together. Do you?"

I didn't. But what did that matter? This wasn't about figuring the odds, and it wasn't someone else's story. This was Claire and me. I said, "You know, when we first got together, I had this cockiness—definitely a young man's cockiness—that I'd get everything just right the first time through. Marriage, career, everything. But hardly anyone gets anything right the first time. Things are complicated. You don't know enough. You haven't learned to bend. Now I think that, without second chances, life would be pretty hard to get through."

She didn't answer that. Her posture stiffened, she grabbed her cocktail napkin and dabbed her lips, and said, "I really have to go."

She was halfway out of the booth by the time I managed to mumble an apology for upsetting her.

"No," she said, "it's fine. It's really fine. I just need some time to think."

She slipped around the table, and before I quite knew what was happening, she kissed me. It was a quick, shy kiss; it seemed entirely unplanned, and it landed by design or accident at a deliciously ambiguous place that wasn't quite cheek and wasn't quite lips, but just at the very corner of my mouth. I had no idea what it meant.

Her face still very close to mine, she said, "Don't call me for a little while, okay?" And she headed for the door.

Chapter 35

I toyed with the idea of having one more drink, just for the romantic exercise of sitting there lonely and bewildered; but the place was starting to fill up with noisy preconcert people in suits and jewelry, so I left.

I walked home to an empty refrigerator and a message from Jenna. She said that if I happened to be free tomorrow evening, there was something she thought I might like to attend. I should call her in the morning.

If I happened to be free. That was a good one. What did she imagine my social calendar was like? In fact, I didn't have a social calendar; what I had instead—right next to the phone, where some people might keep an engagement book—was a small stack of Chinese take-out menus. I called a Hunan joint and ordered up some noodles and some twice-cooked pork. Sure enough, they arrived lukewarm, and it wasn't even winter yet.

I called Jenna first thing next morning.

Since neither of us could resist a chance to gossip, she asked me about Maxx's meeting with Carlton Phelps. I told her it was brutal, beastly, horrible; a front-row seat at a stranger's nervous breakdown. "I just can't see a happy ending here," I said. "If Phelps stays, he goes insane. If he leaves, Maxx is screwed. And if Maxx is screwed, so's he. I don't see a solution."

"Money," she said. "Money's the solution. Fresh cash. Smoothes things over just like new asphalt. Fills in the potholes, covers the seams."

"Fine," I said, "but I don't see this nice new money pouring in. Am I missing something here?"

"Only Robert's relentlessness," she said. "That great ability not to be embarrassed. He's like the guy who'll proposition every single woman at the bar. Doesn't matter how many shoot him down. If the fortieth one says yes, he's in. But about this evening . . ."

"Yeah, what's up?"

"They're lighting the tree at Rockefeller Center."

For a moment I said nothing. This was because I so completely didn't give a shit about the lighting of the Christmas tree at Rockefeller Center that I just couldn't find any words. Chop a tree down; bring it somewhere else; tart it up with lights and doodads, and everybody oohs and ahhs. Have I mentioned I don't like the holidays?

Through the silence, Jenna heard my lousy attitude loud and clear. "Listen, Scrooge," she said. "I'm not saying you need to wear a Santa hat, okay? But Robert's going to be up on the dais with the mayor and a bunch of VIPs, and we've got seats in the bleachers just behind. Might be interesting."

"Fascinating," I said. "Will there be any elves?"

"Don't be such a snob."

"Can we have a drink before, at least?"

"Only if we have it in my limo."

I said, "You have a limo?"

"I'll have one for the evening."

"Jesus, why didn't you say so? That sort of changes everything."

"May as well live large before the expense account runs out. I'll pick you up at six-thirty. Where do you live?"

own in midtown, they're common as dirt, but on my funky street that was lined with archaic Nissans and rusted-out Chevys, a chauffeur-driven limo was still a bit of a novelty. Waxed and spotless, the big car pulled up in front of my grimy building like an apparition from some mythic Crystal City far away—or at least from Robert Maxx's empire, a few miles to the south. My slob of an evening doorman pretended to be suitably impressed when the chauffeur scampered around to open up the door for me. A garbage picker at the corner of Broadway deigned to look up from his recycling bin as we passed, and a Middle Eastern produce guy, sitting on a crate and peeling fava beans, peered intently toward the smoked-glass windows, as if convinced some big American celebrity must be behind them.

Inside, Jenna and I were soon sipping Veuve Clicquot from graceful flutes. She looked smashing. I'd never seen her in anything but business clothes. Now she was wearing a shimmering gold dress that hugged her endless thighs and was topped by a long and elegant tunic that made her look about seven feet tall. She wore a topaz necklace and earrings, and gave off just a hint of that crisp, outdoorsy perfume I'd noticed the first time we met.

We drank our way down toward Rockefeller Center, but a few blocks above it the traffic just stopped. Streets were blockaded; sidewalks were glutted with hordes of people made bulky by their winter coats. We climbed out of the limo and entered the crush, eventually escaping into a privileged haven beyond a red velvet rope. Jenna gave our names; we were welcomed into a gracious lobby right next to Radio City Music Hall, then escorted through the building to the plaza, where a different usher showed us to our places midway up a bank of heated bleachers with little plastic cushions for our butts. The general public, by contrast, filed in off the street, jostled for space against the barricades, and were left to freeze their asses off as the night got colder. Then again, our bleachers weren't quite prime seating, either. We flanked the action, but the center of it was the dais itself, which had comfortable chairs and elaborate displays of poinsettias and wreaths, and was closest to the enormous

unlit tree. There was something Versailles-like about the whole arrange-
ment, an unstated but carefully calibrated architecture of rank, a legible
geometry of prominence and favor. Where you sat was who you were.

And that, as it turned out, made it a really bad evening for Robert
Maxx.

The plaza grew packed; the throng that flanked the skating rink was
bathed in the somewhat ghoulish blue light that reflected off the ice. The
bleachers filled around us with people of middling importance or con-
nections. Then, just after seven, the VIPs were shown to the dais as a
group.

It was, at least in terms of the city, a decidedly A-list gathering. There
were powerful people known only by their titles—the parks commis-
sioner, the culture czar, the tourism chief. These august presences were
leavened by the requisite celebrities—Patti LuPone, David Letterman,
Tony Bennett, Derek Jeter. It was not immediately clear if Maxx
belonged to this clique of famous people, or if he was part of a third
contingent—a group associated with the venue itself.

There were two immaculately suited Japanese, clearly being shep-
herded by a pair of silver-haired CEO types. I asked Jenna if she had any
idea who these people were; not surprisingly, she did. They were principals in the consortium that was the current owner of Rockefeller Center.

Not far behind them came, of all people, Kenneth Hotchkiss and
Mandy Lockwood, the officers of PORCH.

Ushers showed the big shots to their seats. When the tableau was
complete, the owners and the PORCH representatives were huddled
close together to one side of the podium. The stately Kenneth Hotchkiss
was shaking hands and bowing to the visitors from Tokyo, although
these gentlemen seemed more interested in the famous and fetching
Mandy Lockwood.

Maxx was sitting on the other side of the stage, sandwiched between
an aged crooner and the shortstop of the New York Yankees.

I gently elbowed Jenna and asked her what she made of it.

"A picture's worth a thousand words," she said. "Robert's going to
be bullshit."

Spotlights came up. The mayor made some welcoming remarks; from my vantage behind him, I could see that he stood on tiptoes as he spoke. There was a choir down from Harlem; they sang a carol and some gospel. The cast of a Broadway show did a production number. I kept an eye on Robert Maxx as the festivities proceeded; his shoulders were tight and he kept up a frozen smile that must have taken enormous discipline and stamina.

Finally, the big moment arrived. The lighting of the tree was announced. The plaza and the city around it went almost silent. Then the lights were all switched off. The effect of this was stunning. Darkness in Manhattan—true, deep, velvet darkness—is not like darkness in other places. It seems not like the natural, original state of things, but like the rarest form of an eclipse, an event so strange that what you cannot see becomes, itself, the spectacle. Vanished intersections; invisible buildings; blocks without edges. Put this darkness in a context not of threat and fear but of safety and celebration, and it can really make you giddy. The lights stayed off just long enough for eyeballs to throb and pupils to open greedily, hungry for light . . . then the big spruce was lit up, thousands of twinklies reflecting off the tinsel and the foil and the spangly metal snowflakes.

And here I have a confession to make. It's embarrassing as hell, but I've been trying my damnedest to be honest so far, and I'm not going to back off now. The lights came on, and I got a lump in my throat and felt an itching at the corners of my eyes, and I thought, *You sucker! You sentimental jerk! What is* this *about?* It wasn't that I gave a damn about Christmas. It wasn't that the breathtakingly sudden appearance of the gleaming tree coming out of total darkness swept me back to a child's unquestioning wonder, or reminded me, if only for a heartbeat, of a time when I still had the untested belief that all surprises were good surprises. No, it wasn't anything like that. I got choked up because the lighting of the tree was very well-done theater. That's my story and I'm sticking to it.

The party broke up quickly after that. The VIPs were led from the dais. The plaza began to empty out. Jenna and I climbed down from the bleachers and walked back through the lobby. Our limo was parked in a long row of others; they were crammed as close as shopping carts at the supermarket. It was only around nine o'clock, and I was just asking Jenna if she'd like to grab some dinner, when her cell phone rang. She flipped it open, said hello, and I could tell at once that it was Robert on the line. I couldn't make out the words, but I could hear his tone of voice. It wasn't happy and it wasn't calm.

She snapped the phone shut. "He wants me at the office. Now. Guess I can't offer you a lift home. Sorry."

I said, "I'll go up there with you." I said it without thinking. It was that pushy reflex to get the story.

"Not a good idea. He's really pissed."

"If he doesn't want me there, he'll kick me out. But I'll bet you a dinner he doesn't."

"What makes you so sure?"

The funny part is that I wasn't sure at all . . . until the moment that I made the comment. Then a slightly intoxicating thought occurred to me. Maybe I wasn't the only one who had become a slave to this book; maybe Maxx himself, in a somewhat different way, was also in its thrall. Maybe, right alongside his insistence on controlling his portrayal, on dictating what could be revealed and what could not, there was a contrary yearning, reckless but redeeming, for exposure. Maybe he was sick to death of the posing and the feints and the spin. Maybe, in his rise to fame and power, he'd become such a stranger to himself that he was looking to a story to remind him who he was.

Jenna and I shook hands on our wager and climbed into the limo. The last of the champagne had gotten rather warm and mostly flat. We drank it anyway as we crawled the few busy blocks to Maxx's office.

Chapter 36

That little prick," said Robert Maxx. "That waffling, whiny, sneaky little prick."

We were in his office, Jenna and I perched lightly in our chairs. Maxx was behind his desk, though he wasn't sitting down; it was more like he was using the furniture as a barricade, a sentry line behind which he was pacing. His stiff hair was slightly mussed; I couldn't remember ever seeing it move before. It was getting on near 10 P.M., and he was talking about the mayor of the city of New York.

"Why'd he put those people right up front?" he went on. "Who the hell are they, anyway? They have no standing."

"Now they do," Jenna quietly observed.

"That bitch Mandy and that faggot Hotchkiss," he raved. "I can't believe they're getting all cozy with the owners while I'm sitting next to an ancient pop singer and a guy who makes his living with a bat and ball. The little prick!"

He paced; he tugged his tie; he raked his hand along his desk.

Jenna said, "With due respect, Robert, I know the mayor's a bit of a micromanager, but I really doubt he made the seating plan."

"Then who the hell did?"

"Maybe it was an innocent misjudgment. Maybe it was someone Mandy got to—"

"That would be like her—"

"Maybe it was someone you've pissed off along the way."

The comment stopped Maxx in his pacing. I studied him and tried to parse his reaction. He didn't seem offended. He knew he stepped on toes; he knew he *crushed* toes, and he liked having the power to do so: the pleasure showed. What galled and surprised him seemed only to be the rude fact that smaller people might eventually have a means of getting even. "Like who?" he challenged.

"Who knows? Some woman with a friend on the Landmarks Commission. Some investor in a failed casino. Who knows?"

"Find out," Maxx ordered.

Even I could tell that this was a petulant and futile command. If Jenna was able to track down the information, then what? Would the damage be undone? And how much time and effort did it make sense to devote to striking back at every affront and bit of opposition? Where was the line between a useful toughness and vigilance, on the one hand, and a potentially deranged, exhausting paranoia on the other? I'd seen Maxx lash out at enemies before, but now he seemed to be conjuring antagonists out of the blue, and for the first time it occurred to me to wonder if he was really losing it. Maybe Phelps's threatened departure was gnawing at him. Maybe it was the rumored competing bidder that was pushing him toward the edge. Whatever it was, he seemed to be reaching that perilous point where rage blurred tactics and strategy was overwhelmed by desperation.

"And another thing," he said. "The Japs. How long are they in town? Find out. I want a meeting with the ownership consortium ASAP."

Jenna looked down at her hands. "Are you sure that's a good idea?"

He glared at her for questioning him. When he spoke again, his voice was no louder, but higher in pitch and with a sort of strangled hiss to it. "I don't think you understand. These PORCH assholes are inside now, and it seems I've got another buyer breathing down my neck. I can't just sit still—"

"I do understand," Jenna dared to interrupt. "But if there's a meeting, they're going to ask about progress on the financing—"

"Right!" Maxx said, and slapped his desk. "And we'll give them progress. We'll give them lots of progress. We're close on the money. Closer than anybody else could be. Remember that."

Maybe it was the flagrant emptiness of this bluff that suddenly made me acutely, uncomfortably aware of the emptiness of the nighttime building. There we were, fifty-one stories up, way on top—but on top of what? There was nothing under us but dark cubicles, sleeping computers, abandoned desks; nothing but dim and tiny indicator lights as security cameras panned across a softly thrumming vacuum. Suddenly everything seemed terribly tentative and fragile. I'd never before been nervous in a tall building; now I was; I thought I felt it sway.

Softly, Jenna said, "Robert, can I ask a question? Where do things stand on plan B?"

Maxx looked away and puckered up his mouth, almost like he was getting ready to spit on the floor. "Forget plan B."

Jenna said, "The hotel complex in Milan? The condo city in Shanghai? The backups for pulling in fresh currency?"

"I said forget it. Everything's stalled. Those projects aren't happening."

"But—"

"Jenna, let it go." He broke off, paced a couple of steps behind his desk. Then, through tight lips that seemed unable to hold back a terrible admission that maybe he'd made a mistake, he said, "Those projects, the financing, forget it. I'm putting all my clout right here. In New York."

I thought: If that was in fact a blunder, at least it was true to his personality. While he fancied himself a global figure, New York was where his ego lived, and for someone who needed always to be the big shot, being the big shot in his own neighborhood counted double.

For the first time since I'd met her, Jenna seemed rattled, slow on

the uptake. This was her future, too, after all. She said, "So it's Rockefeller Center . . . or nothing?"

That made Maxx feisty again. "No, it isn't Rockefeller Center or
nothing. It's Rockefeller Center or some other goddamn thing. But I
can still save this deal. Don't doubt for a second that I can. Set up that
meeting with the Japs."

Without enthusiasm, Jenna said she'd get on it first thing in the
morning. She started standing up, looking to escape.

I rose, too, and as I was doing so, Maxx looked at me, like it just now
registered that I was in the room. "And what the hell are you doing
here?" he asked.

His eyes were flicking back and forth between Jenna and me. Before
I could answer, he said, "Oh great. A fucking office romance. Just what
I need."

Jenna said, "Don't make trouble, Robert. See you in the morning."

The two of us headed out, leaving Maxx alone in his enormous
office. Jenna dropped me off at home. Riding the limo was not so much
fun by then. We kissed on the cheek and said good night. This was very
pleasant, but an office romance it didn't seem to be.

Chapter 37

The tree-lighting ceremony, as it happened, took place on December 1—the first day of the last month of Robert Maxx's life (and also, by my superstitious reckoning, an unlucky day, as 12 plus 1 equals 13). Call it coincidence, but the opening of the year's final phase seemed also to usher in the final and climactic stage of Maxx's downfall.

That December, nearly every day seemed to bring a fresh discouragement; the pace of dissolution seemed to accelerate, cascade, snowball. Maxx wouldn't make it to New Year's Eve—not even close. He wouldn't live to Christmas, not even the solstice. And for all that, I *still* believed—at least for a while longer—that *Maxxed Out* would turn out to be a story of improbable triumph, of a gutsy victory against steep and daunting odds. If I appear doltish for so long remaining blind to the actual outcome, keep in mind that no one else seemed to see it coming, either. With his boundless aggressiveness and history of dodging bankruptcies and wriggling out of failures, Maxx had created around himself an aura of invincibility. No one seemed to realize that the aura had already long outlived the fact.

Besides, I *had* to believe that things would come right for Maxx, because that's the story I thought I was writing—the story I'd get paid for. He was a winner and a comeback artist; I was a guy with no cash flow and an onerous mortgage. If he in fact went down in flames, where the hell did that leave me?

As early as December 2, a barrage of damaging coverage started appearing in the media. Jenna had been absolutely right—the presence of the PORCH representatives on the Rockefeller Center dais had conferred on them a legitimacy far beyond a one-shot *Today* show segment. Kenneth Hotchkiss and Mandy Lockwood were at once sought out by NPR as well as local television to comment on the property's historic significance and the possible implications of its purchase by a developer of Maxx's known proclivities. Kenneth Hotchkiss was quietly impassioned in these interviews; Mandy Lockwood never missed an opportunity to murmur something snide and scary about Maxx's taste for glittering kitsch or his tendency to import Atlantic City style to midtown.

Once the topic was established as newsworthy, careful outlets like the *New York Times* and the *Wall Street Journal*—which had declined to touch the earlier rumors about Maxx's trouble raising money and his rift with Arthur Levin—found themselves with a journalistically respectable way of entering the fray and digging deeper. Enterprising reporters started to connect the dots, and the picture that emerged was decidedly unflattering. It was a portrait of a tycoon whose own house was in disarray, and who was now seeking to control and put his stamp upon a landmark that, emotionally if not legally, belonged in some measure to everyone.

Against this background of negative and nasty buzz, Jenna had—as ordered, and against her own best judgment—set up a meeting with the ownership consortium. I asked her to tell me a bit about this group, which had always struck me as rather shadowy and mysterious. It turned out that that was not the case at all. The current owners were simply quiet, discreet, and diplomatic—in a word, everything that Robert Maxx was not. Insofar as the ownership had a public face, it was the principals of Whipple, Smith, and Landis, a midsize but decidedly white-shoe investment bank. But the majority stake—some 80 percent of the equity—was held by a Japanese conglomerate called Shizeki Industries. Its chairman was a gentleman named Tanaka; the CEO's name was Nakamura. These were in fact the men who'd been at the tree lighting. By reputation, they were extremely powerful but modest and self-effacing people—what the Japanese approvingly referred to as heroes in the dark.

The meeting was scheduled for the afternoon of Friday the fourth—the last day that Nakamura and Tanaka would still be in the States. As was by now my habit, I invited myself along. No one objected. After all these weeks of hanging quietly around, my presence seemed to be expected, maybe even welcome. I was like . . . what? A pet? A mascot? The king's fool? Maybe more like a good-luck charm who had so far failed to bring good luck.

In any case, I arrived at Maxx's office ten minutes early, and saw a side of him I had never seen before. He was flitting around like a nervous host before a dinner party, obsessing over the sort of small details I'd never realized that he even noticed. On the conference table around which the meeting would be held, there were vases of fresh flowers; he fussed with them. "Camellias," he said. "Japanese flower. Very traditional."

An underling bustled in with a silver tray on which was perched a handsome ceramic tea service. "No," he said. "The tray looks like shit. Get a different one. Not metal."

Then, to me, he said, "That bitch Mandy is telling people I've got vulgar taste, that I only like shiny things. Bullshit. I give people what they want. They want shiny, they get shiny. They want understated elegance, I can do that, too."

He messed with his tie, fiddled with his collar. He sidled around the conference table, making sure the chairs were evenly spaced.

Stupidly, needing something to say in response to his jumpiness, I said, "Pretty important, this meeting."

He stared at me as if he was trying to decide how much weakness it would show, how vulnerable it would make him look, simply to acknowledge what was already so clear. Finally, in a tone of capitulation that carried with it a hint of relief, he said, "Yeah. It is."

Without really thinking, without bothering to notice that the question was both presumptuous and ridiculous, I said, "Anything I can do to help?"

For just an instant I thought I saw something like gratitude in Maxx's face. It was quickly erased by his more usual sardonic and insular expression. He said, "Got three billion dollars you can lend me?"

Jenna came in, along with a few midlevel people I recognized by now but didn't know. Conspicuous by his absence was Carlton Phelps; I had no idea if he was boycotting or if he'd been banished because of his recent outbursts, if his spectral pallor and his eczema had made him so unpresentable that he'd been ordered to stay in his own office amid his ledgers and antacids.

Just a minute or two past 3 P.M., the visitors were shown in. Maxx rose from his place at the head of the conference table and put on his meatiest smile to greet them. First came the two silver-haired WASPs who'd been at the lighting ceremony. Then came . . . no one. No Tanaka. No Nakamura. No one else at all.

For a long, pained, and rather absurd moment, Maxx suspended his greeting—arm reaching out, mouth half open—and seemed to be peering around the shoulders of his present guests, as if wondering whether the Japanese had somehow been left behind in the men's room or taken a wrong turn in the hallway.

Finally, one of the bankers said, "Tanaka and Nakamura send their regrets. They were called back to Tokyo on an earlier flight."

Maxx absorbed the news like a body blow. He didn't wince; he didn't wobble. But there was just the slightest slackening in the muscles of his face that showed that damage had been done, some starch and swagger had just been belted out of him. I don't claim to know much about how the Japanese do business, but I know what everybody knows: the Japanese are famously polite, attentive people. Unlike Americans, who often give offense out of clumsiness or ill-considered informality, they are sticklers for proper form and ritual. When the Japanese do something slighting, then, it generally isn't by accident; it's an oblique though not gentle way of passing on a message. The message clearly seemed to be that Robert Maxx was no longer as important to them as he once had been. Studying my tycoon, I wondered if this insult-by-omission had caused that rarest of injuries—the diminishment, in his own eyes, of a supremely confident person.

Trying to rally, Maxx began the meeting. After introductions and the most grudging of warm-ups, he said, "Okay. I want to clear the air about this crap you've been hearing about all the terrible things I'll do to Rockefeller Center. It's nonsense. What do these lunatics think? That I'll put slots in the lobby? Poker tables in the skating rink? Nothing's going to change."

Here he paused for effect, then added, "Not even the name."

One of the bankers—Todd Whipple, a grandson of a founding partner—said, "But you've been saying publicly—"

"That calling it Maxx Center would add value and create excitement," said the host. "I still happen to believe that. But I'm a sensitive guy, what can I say? I will bow to public opinion, however ill informed. They want Rock Center, it'll stay Rock Center."

The other visitor, whose name was Miles Hardy, and who, I would learn, was the bank's general counsel, said, "There would need to be some very specific covenants in place on that. The Japanese are very firm about the name."

It was hard not to look toward the two empty chairs where Tanaka and Nakamura were supposed to be sitting.

Maxx said, "I just told you nothing would change. My word isn't good enough?"

"Don't get testy," Whipple said. "You know how it is. These people are really big on reputation, on the whole corporate citizenship thing. Toyota, Honda—look how hard they work to protect their image. They're serious about this stuff."

"How quaint," said Maxx. "But okay, they're Japanese. What's *your* excuse for not trusting my word?"

"Experience?" quipped Hardy.

Whipple said, "Let's not argue, because all this might be academic anyway."

"Academic?"

The banker cleared his throat and said, "Listen, Robert. I'm sure you've heard the rumors. They happen to be true. We're entertaining another offer. A better offer."

This was said very mildly, almost blandly, but at the words, Maxx's face grew instantly puffy and splotched with red, like he was having big trouble swallowing a piece of steak. "What do you mean, another offer? We have a deal, remember?"

Quietly but precisely, Hardy said, "We don't have a deal. What we've had is a good-faith understanding, which you yourself have violated by bringing so much controversy into the sale and being so tardy in raising the funds."

Maxx was leaning far across the table so that his suit jacket bunched up and bound him in the armpits. "You can't back out!" he said. "I'll sue you!"

Whipple didn't rile, just shook his head, almost sadly. "If Arthur Levin were here," he said, "he wouldn't let you make these crazy threats. You have no grounds and you know it."

There was a standoff. Angry glances panned around the conference table but never quite connected.

Meekly breaking the silence, trying to help, an assistant reached for the elegant pot that had been placed so carefully as an homage to the Japanese, and said, "Would anybody like some tea?"

"Fuck the tea!" said Maxx. "Who's the fucking offer from?"

"We can't tell you that," said Hardy. "It's quite preliminary and rather complicated. A hedge-fund situation."

Too fast for thought, definite as instinct, Maxx blurted, "It's that little cocksucker Trip Campbell."

"We never said that," said Todd Whipple.

"He knows nothing about real estate!"

"He knows something about money," Whipple countered. "He'll hire someone to manage the property. Interested?"

"You son of a bitch," said Maxx. "You think I'd work with someone who just screwed up my deal?"

"To repeat," said Hardy mildly, "it is not your deal. I hope we're clear on that by now."

Again there was a silence; its feel and nuances were remarkably different from those of just a few moments before. In the intervening heartbeats, Robert Maxx had been knocked off the top of the hill. Chest thumping from the level of the common dirt would be clownish, ineffectual. Other strategies were suddenly called for—working the angles, making nice. Seeming to strive for a tone that acknowledged being chastened but stopped well short of pleading, Maxx said, "Okay. Fair enough. But I'm not ready to give up on this. What can I do to get back in?"

Conciliatory in turn, Whipple said, "We'd welcome a sweetened offer from you. But do it soon. And have the money ready."

"How soon?"

Whipple looked at Hardy. "Two weeks at the outside," said the lawyer.

"Jesus Christ."

"Robert," said Whipple, "you've had a head start of a couple months. The truth is that the Japanese have stopped believing you can pull this off."

"They're wrong," he said, and he jutted his chin toward the empty chairs where Nakamura and Tanaka weren't sitting.

Chapter 38

That eventful Friday afternoon led on to yet another weekend that figured to feature no events at all—just another forty-eight hours in the companionless, sexless limbo I'd been living in for too long now.

Claire had told me not to call her for *a little while*. Fine, but what the hell did *a little while* mean? Three days? A week? Two months? Could any exceptions be made, say, for clinical reasons? Claire would have had another treatment or two since I'd seen her last; could I call to ask about her hands, or would that just seem a transparent excuse for contact? I was willing to try my best to play by her rules; I just wished the rules had been clearer. I didn't want to scare her away and I didn't want to be a pain in the ass.

At the same time, I was vaguely aware of an obsessive tug that seemed to strengthen with each day I felt I couldn't call; an unreasoning and potentially overwhelming impulse to pursue her, if for no other reason than that she was unavailable to me. Don't get me wrong. I'm not stalker material—much too passive and aloof—and I was in no danger of getting crazy, still less criminal, in my odd courtship of Claire. I'm only saying that, maybe for the first time in my life, I thought I understood the frustration and bewilderment and helplessness behind the stalker's impulse. It came from some prerational imperative, maybe more animal than caveman. The rabbit runs; the fox pursues; it's an ancient game that neither party is at liberty to call off; and at some point, it's not even the object of his desire that the fox is chasing, but only the flash of retreat itself.

As it happened, this fleeting and decidedly uncomfortable glimpse into the mind-set of a stalker would come in handy, as a stalker—in the guise of a jealous madman—would soon be added to Robert Maxx's long list of increasingly unmanageable problems. But don't let me get ahead of myself.

That weekend, I mostly mastered the impulse to chase after Claire. Friday evening—the time of hope and possibility—passed by; I didn't call. Saturday night—the fulcrum of the weekend, when anticipation either flies up toward fulfillment or sinks toward resignation—came and went; I didn't lift the phone. Finally, on Sunday afternoon, I called her. Sunday afternoon seemed safe and neutral. Hearing some music on a Sunday; having a quiet drink after the rambunctious promise of the weekend had already died—those things did not feel like a date. They were things you did with a friend, not a lover.

So I called her up. She was either out or screening her calls. In any case, I left a message that might have been the dumbest in the history of answering machines. I said, "Hi, it's me. I'm calling to ask if I'm allowed to call. If not, sorry, you don't have to call me back. I miss you."

I had not intended to say that last part. It just slipped out. I didn't hear back from her that evening.

Monday morning, bright and early, Robert Maxx called to ask if I liked helicopters. I wasn't sure I'd heard him right.

"Helicopters," he repeated. "Choppers. Whirlybirds. You like 'em?"

"I've never been in one," I admitted.

"Meet me at the heliport at ten," he said. "The one on the river, south of the U.N. Don't bring a notebook. Don't bring a pen. Don't ask any questions. This isn't for the book."

"Then what's it for?" I asked, but he'd hung up by then.

I showered, dressed, and caught a cab downtown. I found Maxx already in the lobby of the heliport, which seemed less like an airport than the anteroom of a private club. Everyone looked rich; everyone seemed to know everyone. The pilots all had neat creases in their pants, and names like Skip or Chip. They called their passengers Ms. this or Mr. that. Maxx and I shook hands, and I asked where we were going.

"Nuh, uh, uh," he said, and wagged a thick, pink finger in my face. He was savoring one of his little secrets, hoarding a surprise, being a tease.

Ordinarily, this might have annoyed me; on that day I found it reassuring. It was an aspect of a person I thought I knew fairly well by then. In other ways—ways I found unsettling—Robert Maxx seemed changed that morning. If you didn't look too closely, his swagger seemed intact; yet a certain zest was missing, a certain cocky directness was gone. In the past, you could say that Maxx was a bully and a boor, but not a conniver or a sneak. He plowed straight ahead; when he wanted something, he went for it with a minimum of guile and never an apology. Today there was something furtive and cagey at the corners of his eyes; something cunning rather than forceful, more devious than determined. Maybe the nonappearance of the Japanese had so deeply dinged his confidence that this new slyness was needed to cover up the scrapes. Or maybe he was putting on yet another kind of game face for the errand we were heading out to do.

We went onto the tarmac and climbed into our chopper. Maxx sat up front, next to the pilot; I climbed into the only other row. The engines were started with a whir and then a deafening clatter; the big rotor added a whoosh that was less a sound than a slamming pressure on the ears. We took off at a vertiginous angle that made the skyline lean and the horizon rumple up like a wave about to break. Then we were out over the East River, heading south.

I watched the city slide by—the gold-topped Met tower at Twenty-third Street; the somber Con Ed clock at Union Square; the low, crammed swath of the East Village, its flat roofs level as a prairie. We topped the Brooklyn Bridge, skirted Wall Street, could not look away from the horrendous vacancy of Ground Zero. The city looked both very grand and very tiny, and almost unbearably poignant in its smallness. From sidewalk level, everything appeared so big, so solid, so important; things mattered, life felt large and consequential; a life like Robert Maxx's seemed nothing short of monumental and historic. Yet, from even just a few hundred feet up, the city became a miniature, a snow globe, a tableau in which people the size of Barbie and Ken played their trivial games and lived out their dinky lives. Mighty Manhattan was behind us in hardly more than a minute.

We flew above the harbor—a great world crossroads, also tiny. Very soon we were over Staten Island, the forgotten borough. Except for the bridges that splayed out from it like spokes, and the expressways that knifed across it here and there, it appeared from the air not just suburban but rural, with ball fields and parks dotting a mostly uncluttered landscape. We headed for the hilly center of the island, then eased down toward what seemed to be a sprawling private compound. I saw giant hedges backed by metal gates; big bare sycamores arrayed on rolling lawns; a very large white house whose columns and arches came into focus as we dropped gently toward a concrete landing pad.

The engines were cut. My ears still rang. Maxx said, "Remember, you're not a writer, you're an associate of mine. That's all we need to say. Don't speak unless you're spoken to. Have coffee if it's offered. Got it?"

A man appeared at the helicopter door. He was a large fellow and he wore a quilted nylon vest. It did not occur to me till later that the vest was bulletproof.

He led us from the pad to a gravel walkway that wound through trees and brittle grass, and eventually brought us to the house. We were on the south side of the building; there was a solarium made of curving panels of greenish glass. Entering, we felt a sort of Floridian humidity, and saw an older man, whose back was to us, carefully spraying orchids with an atomizer bottle. In no great hurry, he turned to face us, then he slipped his gardener's apron over his mane of silver hair and put it aside on a bench. "Hello, Robert," he said. "Good to see you again."

"Hello, Victor," Maxx said. "You're looking well."

"Bullshit. I'm looking old and fat and my liver's acting up. Who's your friend?"

"Dave Cullen. A trusted assistant."

The man with the spray bottle welcomed me and offered us coffee. Maxx said he'd love some. I just nodded. I was having a tough time getting my voice to work. I was also having a tough time getting my feet to move and keeping my bowels from rumbling or melting. This was because I recognized the man with the orchids—though the newspaper pictures I'd occasionally seen of him were always of a younger, harder, meaner man; they didn't show the age spots on his hands or the slightly jaundiced cast of his skin.

His name was Victor Magnola and he was, by most accounts, the Godfather of the New York Mafia—or what was left of it, at least, after decades of rubouts and prosecutions. Still, it was a pretty damn intimidating job title, and it cost me great effort not to blubber or tremble in his presence. Not that the man himself looked frightening; he didn't, not at all. He had a wise face, with a broad forehead, and extravagant eyebrows that threw tangled shadows over dark and thoughtful eyes.

"Come on," he said, "we'll go into the kitchen."

He led the way. I followed on stiff legs. The funny thing about the kitchen was how ordinary it was, just like anybody else's kitchen. There was a microwave, a toaster oven. There was a small Formica table in a breakfast nook; that's where the three of us sat down. The only unusual thing was a professional-grade espresso machine. The man who'd met us at the helipad now served demitasse. It was fabulous coffee; like being in Europe.

The Godfather raised his little cup and said, "So, Robert, what can I do for you?"

"Maybe nothing. Maybe a lot. I'm in a bad financial bind."

"How bad this time?"

"Bad. Worse than ever before."

"Worse than '94?"

"Way worse. Plus, now there's a lot of people I can't go back to."

Victor Magnola said, "Yet you feel you can come back to me." This was not said harshly; it was almost humorous, though it clearly seemed meant to establish an edge, to remind Maxx of a debt.

Deferentially, Maxx said, "I think we've always done right by each other."

"Yes. We have. So talk to me."

Maxx took a tiny sip of his espresso. "I've been trying to buy Rockefeller Center—"

"I'm aware of that."

"Exactly. Everyone's aware of it. I've made sure of that. Why? To make it seem like acquiring Rock Center is the most important thing in the world to me. But you know what? It isn't. I really couldn't give a shit about owning Rockefeller Center."

At this, I hid my skepticism behind my coffee cup. Had Maxx been faking his ardor for the flagship property all along? I doubted it. As Jenna had said, his ego craved those big and famous buildings. More likely, then, this was a monumental case of sour grapes, of denigrating the prize he probably wasn't going to get. I don't think the turnabout was conscious dishonesty; I think it was something more visceral, instinctive. For someone like Maxx, with his relentless drive to win—to be *seen* as winning—there were necessary fictions and denials without which it would have been impossible to carry on.

"No," he continued, "Rock Center was just a means to an end. I kept the focus on it to distract attention from the real reason I need to raise those funds."

The Godfather stirred his coffee with a tiny spoon. "Which is?"

Maxx looked down, squeezed his lips together, then seemed to muster the nerve to look full on at the other man. "Victor, my books are a disaster. My CFO's flipping out and threatening to bolt. I've got hundreds of millions in losses that I just can't hide much longer. The casino business is completely in the toilet—"

"Other operators are doing fine."

"Yes. They are," said Maxx. His tone was embarrassed and contrite. "We've fallen behind. I admit it. Other places have upgraded, passed us by. We haven't had the cash to keep up."

Close to scolding but not quite, the Godfather said, "Where's the money been going?"

Maxx gave a clenched little laugh. "Name it. Golf courses where no one plays golf. Empty condos that we built back when it looked like the housing boom would last forever. Retail space sitting vacant for six months, a year. It's all been going sour, Victor. Little by little. That's the bitch of it. The decline has been so slow and steady that it's almost been invisible. But I can't keep it invisible much longer."

The Godfather folded his hands and considered. While he did so, I tried to get my mind around a certain warped and disturbing irony. How was it possible that Robert Maxx had no trouble bullshitting his bankers and investors, but would come here and confess the hard and painful truth to a mobster? Was it just that there was something priestly in Victor Magnola's bearing, some gravitas that made it seem that lying would be futile? Did Maxx trust him more than he trusted the experts with the MBAs? Or was it that misleading investors didn't seem to have real consequences, whereas misleading the Mafia would?

At length, Magnola said, "I'm concerned about jobs. It sounds like jobs are going to be lost."

"That's true," said Maxx. "Casino jobs. Construction jobs. If I can't hold it together, there's going to be considerable pain."

The Godfather frowned and twirled his miniature spoon. "How much do you need?"

"Minimum? Three hundred million, by the end of the year. That's what I have in obligations as of January one. I was planning to skim it off the top of the Rock Center deal—"

"But it sounds like that deal isn't happening."

"It doesn't look good. Lenders are scared." He glanced down at his espresso. "Plus, there's another bidder. With ready cash, I think. Unless they decided to withdraw—"

The Godfather pulled his remarkable eyebrows together. "You've seen too many movies."

"Victor, hey, I wasn't suggesting—"

"No. Of course you weren't." He settled his espresso spoon against his saucer and looked around the kitchen. "Three hundred million is a lot of cash."

"If I meet the payments, everybody's happy, it buys me another quarter to turn things around. Given a little more time, I can do it. I know I can."

Magnola showed neither confidence nor doubt. "And in the meantime, what's the payback? What are you offering?"

"An additional ten percent of all the AC holdings."

"Which are in the toilet anyway."

"Then tell me what you want, Victor. I'm obviously not in a real strong position to negotiate."

"No, you're not," said the Godfather. He said it very softly, but the power came through loud and clear, because it was the money that was talking. "Let me think it over, talk to some friends. I'll get back to you within a week."

Chapter 39

We walked in silence to the helicopter.

On the ride back to Manhattan, the engine noise made it impossible to talk. So I stewed. I was angry. The anger was the residue of the fear I'd felt at being thrust, without warning, into the presence of the Godfather. That wasn't fair; not fair at all. Then again, underlings were often subjected to unfair treatment by the people who signed their paychecks, and had to be careful about how vigorously they protested. So probably it was just as well that we couldn't talk for a while.

By the time we landed alongside the East River, I'd cooled down considerably. My anger had mostly mellowed into curiosity; and this, I guess, is a useful progression that makes writing stories both possible and worth the bother: trying to understand what pisses us off. When Maxx offered me a lift uptown in his waiting limo, I accepted, and took it as an opportunity to ask him just why the hell he'd done that to me.

"Done what?" he said absently. He seemed very wrapped up in his own thoughts, and they didn't seem to be happy ones. Clearly, he'd dealt with Victor Magnola before; he could read him in a way that I could not, and he didn't seem thrilled with how the sit-down had gone.

"Brought me to that meeting," I said. "Without even telling me, giving me a choice. Now I know all this stuff I really shouldn't know, and it isn't even stuff I can use."

Maxx looked surprised. "Who says you can't use it? It's great material. Of course you'll use it. Just not in the book that you and I are doing now."

The comment stopped me in my tracks; I've thought about it many times since. What was he really saying? Was he trying, in his awkward way, to give me a gift, to hand me the makings of a real story? Did he have a presentiment of where things were heading for him, a sense that I might soon be free to tell that story? Or was it just that what he wanted from me had changed—that he'd revised our relationship to suit his own convenience, just like he'd revised his feelings about Rockefeller Center?

He'd hired me to be his ghostwriter; but ghostwriting entails a lot of bullshit, a lot of dissembling, giving voice to a persona, not a person. These days, bullshit and dissembling were not what he seemed to be asking for. He seemed to want something more intimate and scary—an honest witness. I'd been amazed at how straightforward he'd been with Victor Magnola, turning to him as an improbable confessor. But wasn't he doing something similar with me? By letting me see so much, by blurring the line between what was on and what was off the record, he was flirting with far more exposure than he'd bargained for. Part of him, at least, seemed to yearn for that exposure—for the catharsis of stripping off the mohair suits and shaking out the rigid hair and unclenching the jutting jaw, and presenting himself naked and unguarded, inviting, perhaps, some simple human sympathy for the difficulty of his life, rather than the grudging awe, nearly always tainted with ill will, that attached to tycoons and celebrities.

As his remark had silenced me, he himself went on after a moment. "I thought you'd find it interesting," he said. "He's an amazing businessman. Like an outlaw Warren Buffett. Sorry if it made you uncomfortable."

I tried to remember if I'd ever heard him apologize before—to anyone, for anything. He seemed to mean it, seemed almost sheepish, and I suddenly felt bad that I'd raised the subject.

We were on the FDR Drive by now, crawling along next to the river, tunneling under grimy, overhanging buildings. Maxx's cell phone rang. He answered it and was on the line, I'm guessing, five or six minutes. During that time he barely got a word in—a phrase here and there that always seemed to get interrupted. Now and then he frowned or winced. Whether it was the bad reception on that canyon of a highway or what he was hearing in the conversation, I couldn't tell.

He snapped the phone shut, slipped it into a jacket pocket, and stared out at the river; the tinted windows of the limo gave the water a black and sheenless look. Finally, he exhaled rather loudly through pushed-out lips, and said, "That was my brother, Tony."

"Ah," I ventured. "Family."

"He seems to be flipping out again. Sounds completely manic and paranoid."

"I'm sorry."

"He was planning to go to Paris for an art show. Had his ticket, hotel, everything. Then he decided that something way more important was happening in Hong Kong. Then it was Venice. Definitely Venice. Now he's decided that he better not go anywhere at all, because someone's been trying to break into the house. He's sure of it. Someone's trying to break in, take the paintings, the furniture, the silver and the dishes, everything. He's heard noises, like someone trying the locks. He stayed awake the past two nights, with a big knife in his bathrobe pocket, waiting. He's sure the thief is coming tonight . . . Jesus Christ. The poor guy's a fucking lunatic."

I searched for something to say, something that might help. If there were such words, I couldn't think of them.

"He'll end up in the nuthouse again," Maxx went on. "I feel it coming. And I hate to say it, but it's where he belongs and it's probably best for everyone."

He shook his head, pressed his fist against his jaw, and turned back toward the black river as the limo crawled uptown.

Chapter 40

I got home to a ringing phone, and dashed across the apartment to pick it up before the machine did. In answer to my slightly breathless hello, Claire asked if I was all right.

"I'm fine," I said. "I just got in. I was hoping it was you."

"That's nice," she said. "You can be very sweet some of the time."

I said nothing. Partly because I get flustered at compliments; and partly because I was wondering what she thought I was the rest of the time.

"I got your message," she went on.

"I didn't know if I should call. This game we're playing, I don't have any experience at it."

"It's not a game."

"Sorry. Bad choice of words."

She said, "I'm just trying so hard to be smart, to do the right thing."

I understood that—sort of. I shrugged into the phone and looked around the apartment she had done so much to civilize. Did it make sense to feel nostalgic for an end table, a picture in a frame, a bookshelf that was actually built into the wall?

"I've been putting myself through a difficult little exercise," she said. "I've been trying to imagine that you aren't in my life, not even as a friend. Then I try to imagine that we're lovers again. I can't decide which possibility is scarier."

At her use of the word *lovers,* a strange thing happened. Or maybe not strange, maybe the most natural thing in the world. Maybe the part that *was* strange was that, until that moment, my yearning for Claire had not been primarily fleshly. I'd wanted to be in bed with her again; of course I did. But my desire had been—how can I put this?—almost schematic. There were certain boundaries I wouldn't cross, not even in my mind; I allowed myself no imagery, few details. There were certain sensual memories—the feel of her thighs around my waist, her breath on my cheek when her breathing quickened—that were just too excruciating to revisit. That one word, *lovers,* was enough to demolish my prudish reserve and turn a mere notion into flesh and skin and heat again, to change sex from a vague and abstract concept to a vivid, wriggling presence with a rhythm and a texture and a taste.

Through a rather dry throat, I said, "Now you're being a tease."

"If I am," she said, "I'm doing it to both of us."

"I guess that's a consolation. Or even more of a tease. When can I see you?"

She hesitated. Her voice shrank back, lost some of its boldness. "I don't know," she said. "I'm sorry, but I don't."

"Tell me about your hands, at least. Are they getting better?"

"I like to think so. It's hard to tell. It's pretty frustrating, to be honest."

"Maybe it would be better if I kissed your fingers."

"Don't say stuff like that."

"When can I call you?"

"I think it's really better if I call you. Is that okay?"

I said it was. What else could I say?

After we'd hung up, I paced around the apartment for a while. I sat down on the sofa, then got up and paced some more. At some point it dawned on me to wonder what might have happened if I *had* said something else . . . If I'd said, *No, it's not okay. I'm still in love with you and I'm dying to take you in my arms this very minute.* What would have happened? Would I have won her back or chased her away? And in *not* saying that, was I being grown-up and respectful, or just a wimp?

This was idle speculation, because I am who I am; my natural mode seems to be to sit around with a wry expression, waiting for life to come to me. Maybe that's why, at the age of forty-two, I was still nagged by a sense of prelude more appropriate to a younger man—a suspicion that life in earnest hadn't started yet. I tended to observe other people as they grabbed the gusto; false modesty aside, I wasn't too bad at describing the process, maybe even understanding it; why did I have such a tough time grabbing some myself?

Then again, I suppose that everyone has times when life just seems suspended, when everything is hanging fire, out of one's control. Even Robert Maxx, who, by temperament and habit, could hardly have been more different from me, now seemed to find himself at such a juncture.

The next few days felt very weird. I tried to work, but my momentum was suddenly gone. That fraught Monday morning had seemed to promise a week of tumult and perhaps of resolution—and then everything just sort of stopped. Make no mistake—there was nothing serene or reassuring in the pause; it was more like the uncanny and unwholesome stillness that is said to settle on the ocean before a tsunami gathers itself for a charge.

Suddenly there were no more meetings in Maxx's office. Who was there to meet with? His lead attorney had quit and his chief accountant had tried to. He'd worked his way down the food chain of financiers, and been rebuffed at every level. He'd been reduced to meeting in secret with the Mafia, the lender of last resort; now he could do nothing but wait for an answer from Victor Magnola.

At the same time, the media seemed, for the moment at least, to have lost interest in Maxx. If he was no longer the front-runner in the pursuit of Rockefeller Center, what was the story? Mandy Lockwood, having done her part to mess things up for her former boyfriend, retreated from the limelight. As for Trip Campbell, he now had his own deal to put together—if he was the least bit serious about consummating it, rather than just playing the spoiler.

On Wednesday, troubled and made jittery by the quiet, I called Jenna, just to ask how things were around the office. She said that everyone seemed to be sleepwalking—either that, or hunkered down behind closed doors, making phone calls or polishing résumés in preparation for a next job search. Carlton Phelps, meanwhile, had become an object both of serious concern and cruel humor. He'd apparently used up all his tantrums and his threats, and now just skulked around the fifty-first floor with his pallor and his rash, seeming less panicked than unmoored.

In all, then, the week took on a funereal feel, the somber tone of a deathbed vigil. Maxx was going down. The hints had been accumulating for many weeks; the details had finally come clear. Three hundred million, due on January 1. No way to pay it and no way to continue hiding it. My tycoon had at last run out his luck and exhausted his nerve and overplayed his many bluffs. His former charisma had become grotesque; it repelled where it used to attract. The former magic name had turned to poison.

It was fitting that it was December, a time of endings. Through that dreary week, each day got shorter and dimmer than the one before; life itself felt pinched and drained of color, vitality was ebbing away. Friends had been exiled. Maxx's last remaining relative was going mad on the family estate. The buildings were wobbling and the empire was set to implode.

In the midst of the general gloom, I felt plenty sorry for myself. I'd laid a heavy bet on a comeback artist who wasn't coming back this time. I'd wasted months on a book that no one would read, since who the hell wanted business secrets from a loser? Gradually, though, and with no satisfaction whatsoever, I realized that if Maxx went belly-up, I'd be no worse off than thousands of other people. I'm not talking about the investors. Fuck the investors. But what about the secretaries and black-jack dealers, construction workers and the guys who mowed the golf course, waitresses and window washers and desk clerks and janitors? How many would lose their jobs? Their homes? Their chance to send their kids to college? How many lives would fall into the sinkhole left by the collapse of an important maniac like Robert Maxx? I got gloomier and gloomier and madder and madder as I thought about it.

Then, just around five o'clock on Friday afternoon, I got a phone call.

Before he even said hello, Maxx issued forth a lusty, barking laugh. "Dave?!" he said. "Davey boy?! Great news! Fabulous news! Our friend from Staten Island has come through. We're whole again. Back in business."

"Back in business?"

"Back on top. Fuckin' A. I knew I'd work it out! Your brinksman-ship story—there it is! Perfect! Head-butting my way right back off the ropes. We need to talk. Not at the office. The apartment. I'll explain it all. I'll see you there in half an hour."

Chapter 41

The elevator guy with the ridiculous white gloves brought me up to Maxx's triplex. When the door opened onto the foyer with the hideous Venetian chandelier, Maxx himself was there to meet me. He shook my hand and caught me looking around him for the butler.

"I fired him," he said. "The pressure I've been under, I just couldn't stand having someone fluttering around all the time. And another thing, this fucking apartment—I've decided I hate it. Who needs all this shit?"

He gestured dismissively around the cavernous and lifeless place, and for a moment I thought he'd finally seen for himself the pathos of it, the unfillable hollowness. I was wrong. He was only talking about the dozens of pieces of ponderous furniture.

"When things settle down," he went on, "I'm going to have it entirely redone. Less clutter. More modern. Come on, we'll talk in the study."

He led the way toward the reasonably scaled comfort of the dark green den—the place where we'd had dinner on the evening of Mandy Lockwood's firing; the place where he very soon would die.

On the small table where we'd eaten our steaks—Mafia meat, he'd called them—there was a bottle of Bordeaux, one glass, and two cans of Coke. Waving toward the wine, he said, "I seem to remember you like that. Help yourself."

It was the same wine the butler had served before. It was nice of him to remember—one of those surprising things that almost made me fond of him at isolated moments, and invariably set me up to be appalled anew at what a relentless and solipsistic prick he ultimately was. That didn't stop me from sitting down and drinking his wine.

Still standing, he picked up a can of Coke and took a swallow. He didn't seem to need any more sugar or caffeine. He was wired—so much so that I thought about his brother's mania, and wondered if maybe there was some family tendency to leap out of one's skin. In Maxx's case, the jumpiness seemed to be pasted like lumpy, tortured wallpaper over a base of emotional exhaustion. He was still in business clothes, but his shirt collar had been sprung, the tie yanked askew. There were twitches at the corners of his eyes.

"So, Dave," he said. "It's amazing. Just amazing. It's turning out just like you said. Grace under pressure. Back from the edge. The old champ taking his lumps and slugging away. How did you know?"

I hadn't known, of course. In fact, when I'd proposed that scenario, I was bullshitting entirely—trying to flatter Maxx so he'd give me more access, groping for a facile outcome to a formulaic book. Now that, by a fluke, things actually seemed to be working out according to that pat and mediocre story line, I should have been happy; act three was taken care of, my job was a whole lot easier. But I wasn't happy; I felt deflated and somehow personally embarrassed. Maybe this was because I just couldn't, in my heart of hearts, root for Robert Maxx; professionally I should have, but I couldn't. And besides, this upbeat ending, the tycoon a winner yet once more—it just felt false, unsatisfying, wrong. Endings that work are endings that are earned; you don't just stumble across one and say, "I think I'll go with that."

Hiding my ambivalence—which Maxx, in his epic self-absorption, would not have noticed anyway—I brushed aside the praise and said, "So what happened? What did Magnola say?"

Maxx swigged some cola, did an odd half pirouette, and finally sat down. "He said we've known each other far too long, and there's way too much at stake here, for him to just sit by and watch me crash and burn. So, if I accepted certain conditions, he said he'll get me three hundred million bucks by Christmas."

"Wow. That's a lot of guys with briefcases full of cash."

"Wired from an offshore bank. Discreet. In fact, invisible."

I sipped some Bordeaux and tried to sound extremely worldly and unshockable. "He want more of the casinos, the skyscrapers?"

Maxx sprang up again. He paced the short distance between the small table and the desk with its handsome globe and rack of letter openers. "No. His conditions are really pretty interesting. He wants nothing in Atlantic City. Nothing in Manhattan. What he wants is a controlling interest in the crappy old properties my father liked so much. Crummy office buildings in second-rate cities. Old brick apartment houses in blue-collar neighborhoods. Down-market stuff that no one ever heard of. That's what he wants. Funny, huh?"

Maxx didn't really seem to find it funny. I didn't, either. I found it, rather, to be an astonishingly terse and total repudiation of everything that my tycoon had spent his life working at. No one doubted Victor Magnola's savvy as a businessman. Here he was, in a position to take his pick among the pieces of Maxx's threatened empire, and he wanted no part of the glittering, glitzy properties that had made Maxx a celebrity and even something of a culture hero. No, he saw value in exactly those things Maxx had shunned, the things that hadn't met his personal criteria of shininess and scale—solid things that had been bought with solid cash.

"He wants," Maxx went on, "the below-the-radar stuff, the stuff that won't attract attention."

This seemed a credible way to spin the Godfather's rejection of his monuments—and no doubt it was partly true. Because the other condition that Magnola insisted on was that Maxx lower his profile for a while, keep his face off the television and his name out of the papers.

"The media attention freaks him out," said Maxx. "I mean, what could be more foreign to the way he handles things? So I just have to lay low, keep my mouth shut for a few weeks. Then, *boom,* the cash comes in, the creditors get paid, the books get balanced. Everything's dandy again. I get my world back, you get your story. Cheers."

He took another big pull on his soda. I poured myself some more Bordeaux. After a deep breath, I said, "Robert, this is all great news. But I do see one small problem with it."

"Yeah?"

"This triumphant ending. I don't imagine you want me to tell the world that the Mafia bailed you out."

"Well, no. Of course not. Obviously not. That's just between us."

"Then how do I get from yesterday to today? How do I explain your comeback?"

He knitted his brows and pursed his lips a moment, then seemed to decide that plausibility, still less truth, was not his headache. "Dave," he said, "what the hell am I paying you for? You're the writer. Make something up."

Great. So now I had an ending that not only felt emotionally wrong and morally unsatisfying, but that, even in terms of the simple facts would turn out to be some weak and arbitrary lie.

Even Maxx could see that this did not sit well with me. He softened his voice and threw me a bone. "Dave, listen, I really appreciate your work on this book. Your involvement. The questions you ask. It's different from how I've ever worked before. You've been like . . . like a friend. A friend in a difficult time."

He almost, not quite, met my eyes as he was saying this.

"I appreciate it," he went on. "I'm excited about this book. I want you to be excited, too. And I want you to benefit from its success. I know how tough it is to make a living as a writer. You think I'm not aware of that? You deserve something extra, some security, for the work you're doing here."

I sat there and tried to keep my face neutral and serene. I suppose I should have been offended by Maxx's characteristically seamless segue from talk of appreciation and even friendship to the vulgar ploy of dangling money in front of me, offering me a tip. But I'm a working stiff; I can't afford such rarefied emotions; like most folks, I just hope to get well paid for the indignities I'm subjected to. So, what was Maxx about to offer? Would he finally come clean about his own advance and multiply my fee by five? Would he slip me at least a tiny slice of the windfall that was about to come his way?

Greedy himself, he knew how to play on other people's greed. He let the moment stretch, and I confess that during the pause I was completely in thrall to my own puny avarice. I imagined being able to pay off my mortgage ahead of schedule. Maybe afford a romantic getaway with Claire. Maybe even, with some money in the bank, take another shot at writing novels.

Finally, crossing his arms against his chest as if to control the outpouring of so much magnanimity, he said, "So here's what I'd like to offer. Right here, right now, I'll commit to having you do my next book. With a raise. Ten percent. So you've got your next gig all lined up. That's a luxury, right? What do you say?"

I said nothing. I couldn't. I was stupefied. Ten cents on the dollar? *This* was my reward? The chance to do the same shit over again, with no hope of escape, for a cheap bastard I liked about one percent of the time?

Maxx seemed to regard my silence as a token of being overwhelmed with gratitude. "It's an open offer," he said. "Think about it. I mean, who knows what the next book will even be about. And this one'll be hard to top, right?"

I was still speechless. Maxx picked up his second can of soda, took a pull, then glanced down at his watch. "Shit. I've got to get ready. Can you give me five minutes?"

"Get ready for what?"

"Dinner. Did I forget to mention dinner? Christ, I'm running on fumes. I thought I mentioned it. Caitlin's getting into town. TV actors get a Christmas break, just like all the other children. We're going someplace nice. You'll like it."

"Thanks," I said. "But come on, you two haven't seen each other for weeks."

This, I hoped, was a polite way of saying I really wanted to go home. I'd had quite enough of Robert Maxx for one evening; and the night would have turned out so much better if I'd stuck to my guns and bolted.

Maxx said, "We'll see each other plenty. More than enough, between you and me. The honeymoon's over, if you catch my drift. Besides, she especially asked if you would come along."

"She did?"

"She likes you. Don't ask me why."

Hearing that Caitlin Kilgore liked me made me feel just slightly giddy. Such is the power of celebrity. I agreed to join the two of them for dinner. Maxx went off to freshen up.

To keep myself company, I had one more glass of wine. Savoring it, I saw in my mind's eye a preposterous tabloid headline: STARLET DUMPS BILLIONAIRE FOR GHOSTWRITER. I'm not saying this was anything I actually wanted or believed for a second would occur. My heart was elsewhere. Still, abstinence breeds daydreams, and this one just flew into my head to amuse me for the few minutes I was waiting. Network, not cable. What was the harm in imagining?

Chapter 42

A limo brought Caitlin straight from JFK to Maxx's building. Saying she was famished, she didn't even bother coming up to the apartment. She just had the doorman take her luggage; then quick hugs were exchanged, Maxx and I climbed in on either side of her, and off we went.

Once again, she was underdressed for a fancy New York restaurant, and once again it was clear that she could pull it off. It wasn't just her beauty—the violet eyes, the classic cheekbones; it was a certain unstudied West Coast informality that defined a different kind of elegance—an elegance based on ample sunshine and year-round tans, toned lean muscles and skin that glowed from the benign effects of pricey emollients made from herbs and flowers. She wore black slacks, a black T-shirt, a tan suede jacket with a zipper, and maybe just a hint of lipstick.

But despite the informality, she didn't seem relaxed. Maybe she was just antsy from sitting on the plane, keeping those well-toned muscles idle for too long. Maybe—though God knows why—she was more upset than Maxx seemed to be that their affair wasn't going well. Whatever the reason, she seemed on edge. Combined with Maxx's caffeine-laced jumpiness, this made, at first, for awkward, disconnected chitchat.

We crawled across Central Park South to Columbus Circle, then stopped in front of an oddly rural-looking blue door embedded in a thoroughly urban-looking skyscraper. Ah, so this was the famous restaurant Per Se; three Michelin stars and a two-month wait for reservations; except that Maxx seemed to sort of show up on the fly.

We went up to the fourth floor and entered a dining room so marvelously tasteful that it almost disappeared, like a cloud once you've flown into it, or maybe the inside of a feather pillow; it was all soft grays and muted blues that blended into a delicate haze of nuance. Tables were far apart; there was a hush about the place. It felt like we had left New York, and it occurred to me—as it had when I'd first beheld the spectacle of empty air beyond Maxx's office windows—that the ultimate Manhattan luxury was respite from Manhattan. We were shown to a table that looked across the Circle to the park. In front of us, almost precisely at eye level, was the usually unnoticed statue of Columbus himself, perched atop the once-grand column that was now thoroughly dwarfed by the corporate monuments all around it.

Champagne was served. Caitlin lost no time reaching for her flute. She raised it and the three of us clinked glasses. Maxx took a token sip. Caitlin drained about a third of hers. "Ah," she said, with a breathy sigh, "that's better. Much better."

"Welcome to town," Maxx said. "How's work? How's the show?"

She shrugged, using nothing but her eyebrows. "It is what it is. Our ratings are down double digits, and the suits keep saying we're right on track. You gotta love the networks. I mean, they've got absolutely everything figured out. They've got projections for exactly how many viewers we should lose from season to season, month to month. As long as we don't prove them too far wrong, they're happy."

She went back to her champagne. Almost before her glass had touched the table, a waiter appeared to top it up. Not surprisingly, he also found room to top up mine. Maxx asked for an iced coffee. I could not have imagined a more bizarre or outré request, but the server didn't flinch.

"And how are things," said Caitlin, "in Robert-world?"

"Fabulous," he said. "Terrific." He stretched his lips into a spasm of a smile that put crinkles at the corners of his eyes and made his scalp shift just slightly, all together, like a floating island. "Been through a tough time, really tough, but found some of the old magic when I had to. Found it in the nick of time."

"Great. I'm happy for you."

Christ, but actresses are hard to read. They can sound heartrendingly sincere when they are feeling absolutely zip; even more impressive, they can manufacture doubt when they're being seemingly straightforward. There was something just very slightly cockeyed in Caitlin's simple utterance. I couldn't tell if she was trying to mask a hint of foiled schadenfreude, a traitorous participation in the all but universal hope that Maxx would fail. Or if—perhaps even more perversely—she was being perfectly honest in her good wishes, but didn't want him to have the satisfaction of believing it.

"So what's the magic?" she went on. "How'd you turn things around?"

Maxx had invited the question, but he didn't seem quite ready with an answer. He waved his hands a bit, then said, "New investors."

And he turned to me. I was the writer. I was supposed to make something up. I figured I might as well start working on my story. "A European group," I said. "Mostly Dutch and Belgian."

I thought Belgian was a nice touch. Whoever thought about the Belgians?

"They've been wanting to get into business with Robert forever," I went on. "Now, with the euro so strong and the markets here a little undervalued, it just seemed like the perfect time. Worked out really well."

There. That was easy. I doubt that Caitlin was convinced. It's hard to kid a kidder, as they say. But she didn't question the story. She just looked from me to Maxx and said, "Do you think we could switch to red now?"

The waiter brought Maxx's iced coffee. He ordered a bottle of Chambertin.

Then food started to appear. Didn't these people ever use menus? The food was both amazing and preposterous. Oysters and tapioca. A crayfish holding a grape like it was a beach ball. A tiny lamb chop carved into a perfect question mark, as if posing some eternal riddle. As for the wine, it tasted of mushrooms and leather and soil, and kept on tasting that way a good while after I'd swallowed it.

At some point, Caitlin said, "So the book is almost finished?"

"Everything except writing it," I said. "But in a funny way, that's the easy part. Once the thinking's done, once you know what it's about—I mean *really* know, like in your bones—the words just sort of come."

She looked at me through widened eyes. "Easy for you to say. I think that's really impressive."

This was flattering, of course, even though I think she said it mainly to annoy Maxx. It worked. He seemed to feel compelled to remind her that she was wrong to be in any way impressed with me, to find anything at all noteworthy about what I was doing with my little life.

"Come on," he said. "It's all right there in the material. Look at what he has to work with."

She gestured with her wineglass, as if getting ready to argue the point, but then there was a distraction—a small commotion at the podium of the maître d'. The commotion was not loud; in most Manhattan restaurants, it would have gone unnoticed. But here in this temple of gastronomy, where any lapse in decorum seemed a rude and rattling intrusion, even a mild contretemps was enough to make heads turn and conversation stall.

Slow on the uptake, benumbed by food and wine, I did not immediately realize that the commotion had anything to do with us. I realized it only when I saw the change in Caitlin's face. Suddenly she didn't look like an actress anymore. She looked like a flesh-and-blood woman with a nasty problem right in front of her. Very quietly, she said, "Oh no." She closed her eyes just for a heartbeat. "No."

By now the commotion was sweeping toward our table like a gust of dirty wind. A man, in jeans and a black V-neck sweater over a plain white T-shirt, was striding our way, the fretful, pleading maître d' dogging his heels. Waiters scattered before his momentum; other diners paused to watch. He moved very close to us, put his hands on his hips, and said, "Hello, Caitlin."

I looked at the man. There was no doubting who he was. He was absurdly handsome, with a dimpled chin, the square jaw of a comic-book hero, and one of those carefully calibrated Hollywood physiques, seriously buff but never bulky. He had a two-day stubble beard and black eyes set far back in their sockets.

"Matt," she said. "Go away. Just go away."

"Is that nice?" he said. "After I've come all the way from California? And tracked you from the airport? I don't even get a hug, a nice hello?"

She ignored him.

"And this is the famous Robert Maxx," he went on. "I've been wanting to meet you. Curious to see what kind of person steals another man's girlfriend while he's in rehab. That's kind of scummy, don't you think?"

Maxx said nothing, just looked past the intruder at the helpless maître d'.

"Sir," he said, "you'll really have to—"

"Chill out, Pierre. I'm just visiting some friends."

Caitlin said, "If you were my friend, you wouldn't do this. Please leave."

"Leave? But we had plans for this hiatus, remember? Saint Bart's? That sweet little villa with the drop-dead sunset view?"

"Enough," said Maxx. "Call the police."

"Yeah, great idea," said the intruder. "Have them drag me out in the middle of dinner hour. Maybe kick over a few tables in the struggle. Great publicity for your restaurant."

At the mention of publicity, Maxx flinched. Only hours before, he'd promised the Godfather that he'd shut up and avoid the media. Was he already in the middle of a scandal? That could scotch the whole deal. More than that, Victor Magnola might feel personally insulted by Maxx's almost instant breaking of his pledge, and insulting a man of honor was never a good idea.

So Maxx hesitated; the maître d' hovered indecisively; and Gaston sensed he had an edge. He said to Caitlin, "Okay, no Saint Bart's. But I hope we'll get to see each other. I'm staying right in your neighborhood, at the Plaza Athénée. You get bored with Old Moneybags here, maybe we can have a drink or a snort or something."

She didn't even look at him. By this point, no one could look at anybody.

I stared out the window—and, amid the ceaseless swirl of traffic around Columbus Circle, I saw one of those broadcast vans with the crazy antennas and the satellite dish on top. It was probably just coincidence; one saw a lot of those vans in midtown. But I found myself becoming a little paranoid on Maxx's behalf. The ratings for *Adrift* were slipping. Would it be beneath a Hollywood publicist to contrive fresh buzz by putting out the word that one costar was now desperately stalking another? I imagined a clot of paparazzi and reporters pushing and shoving in front of Per Se's blue door. I pictured an undignified dash to the limo, flashbulbs capturing guilty and abashed expressions.

"But hey," Matt Gaston said, "don't let me disturb your dinner." To Maxx, he said, "Just one quick question before I go. Fuck is with your hair?"

He turned and left. The maître d' stood there, mumbling apologies. Disgustedly, Maxx waved him away. After a silence, the genteel hum of the dining room set in once more.

Caitlin reached for her wineglass. Her hand was trembling.

Maxx ran his napkin across his lips. His neck was red and his eyes were squeezed between their little pads of fat. In a voice that was all scolding and no sympathy, he said, "Caitlin, I can't have this."

"Can't have *what*?" she lashed back, every bit as angry. "You think I liked that? You think it's my fault?"

He backed off, but not enough to notice that this wasn't about him. "I don't care whose fault it is. I can't have scenes. I can't have gossip. Things are at a really delicate place for me right now."

"That's funny. Just a few minutes ago you said that everything was fabulous, terrific."

"It *will* be. I've just got to get over this next hump. I can't blow it. And I can't let some wacko ex of yours blow it for me."

Just then there was a burst of light below our window. It was too close to the building to see what caused it. Strobes greeting the emergence of Matt Gaston? It was impossible to say.

"I don't think you should stay at my place," Maxx went on. "It's just not a good idea right now. You should go to a hotel."

"Oh, that's a *great* idea!" said Caitlin. "That'll really keep things quiet. Like I won't be recognized? Some reporter'll slip a concierge a hundred bucks, and everyone, including Matt, will know exactly where I am. Fabulous idea."

There was a standoff. Caitlin drank more wine. Maxx tapped his fingers lightly on the tablecloth. "Got a better one?"

She didn't answer right away. Her skin flushed beneath the December tan. Her jaw tightened and sinews stood out in her throat. Finally, she said, "Yeah, I do. Fuck this and fuck you. I'm going back to California tomorrow."

At this, however tardily, Maxx seemed to gain a glimpse and maybe even feel a bit of empathy for the world beyond his stunning self-concern. Almost tenderly, he said, "Now wait a second—"

"Too late, Robert. You're a selfish bastard, and I've already got one too many jerks in my life. Forget it. Good luck with whatever it is that's so important for you to deal with."

She drained her glass, put it down a little unsteadily, then, to my complete surprise, she turned to me. "Could you stand a roommate for one night?"

Chapter 43

Let me be clear: it was never in the cards that Caitlin and I were going to sleep together. It just wasn't. On both sides, there were compelling reasons why it would have been a terrible idea. She was on the most immediate and syncopated of rebounds, having dumped Robert Maxx while still hearing the footsteps, so to speak, of the pathetic but menacing Matt Gaston. She had every reason to be disgusted with men, love, sex, the whole idea. As for me, I was still carrying my torch, and even though there were moments when the torch felt pretty goddamn heavy as I trudged along in my sexless marathon, I sensed that maybe the finish line was coming near. In the meantime, call me corny: I felt good about the purity of my quest. Should I give it up or soil it just because a stunningly gorgeous woman whom I really liked was spending a Friday night at my apartment after drinking lots of wine?

Then again, the whole night was crazy; the kind of night when the rules had a way of breaking down.

Mere seconds after Caitlin had told off Maxx, the poor unsuspecting waiter had appeared at our table with another round of tiny plates dotted here and there with miniature food. Maxx waved him huffily away and just asked for the bill. I was still hungry and found this a shame. Had the others lost their appetites just because their love affair was finished? Not me. Caitlin and I polished off the Burgundy, at least.

A few moments later, the maître d' came over. Apologizing yet again for the disruption of our meal, he said of course there was no charge. I thought: *Isn't that always the way? Billions of people could never afford to eat here, and the ones who can, get it for free.* That said, I would not have traded places with Maxx for all the tea in China. He looked wretched, unhealthy, doughy, as if being fired by his young girlfriend had suddenly made him old. His skin had gone slack around the bones of his face; it seemed he'd all at once burned through the last of his caffeine and was drooping like a fallen cake.

The maître d' had more bad news as well. Apparently there were a number of photographers, quite a few, waiting outside the restaurant. He was sorry about this, though of course it was beyond his control. However, if we wished to avoid them, he would be happy to help us do so.

And that was how it happened that we left Per Se by walking through the immaculate tiled kitchen, past the locker room where the employees changed into their whites, along a prisonlike hallway lit by bare lightbulbs, and down a service elevator to an alley. The alley was lined with garbage cans and Dumpsters, and stank to high heaven of rotting food and cat piss. Through the darkness came scratchy, scuffling sounds that could only have been rodents. I give Maxx credit for taking one last stab at lightening the mood. Stepping gingerly around the oozing garbage, he said, "Don't say I never take you anywhere."

"Took," corrected Caitlin. "Took."

That was as close as they came to saying good-bye.

The alley met the sidewalk maybe thirty yards from where the paparazzi were gathered. Two ordinary taxis were waiting at the curb. A gentleman to the end, Maxx sprinted into the first one. Caitlin and I took the second, turned our backs to the cameras as we made our escape past the blue door, rounded the Circle, and headed north.

For a few blocks we were silent. Then I said, "Do you think the lamb chop was the main course?"

Rather than answering, Caitlin said, "Why do I attract such scumbags?"

Not really meaning to flirt, I said, "You attract everyone. The question is, who attracts you?"

"Fair enough. I should think about that, I guess. Got any brandy at your place?"

"How about scotch?"

"Even better."

Caitlin seemed to really like my apartment. It seemed to make her feel nostalgic—which was an odd reversal, of course, since she was ten years or so my junior. But success and notoriety had changed the scale of things for her, transformed dwellings into showplaces, substituted luxury for coziness. My place, with its scatter of books and papers and coffee cups, its makeshift desk set up in the living room, seemed to take her back to a time when the place you lived was no one else's business; it reflected truly who you were and what you valued and what you dreamed of doing with your life.

I showed her around. She touched things a lot. She touched notebooks, throw pillows, picture frames. I don't think she was aware how much she used her fingertips. I found this very sweet and very sexy. Not as in seductive, don't get me wrong. Just sensual, tactile, experiencing a new place through her skin.

I went to the kitchen, reached deep into a cabinet, past the cheap crap I usually drank, and found my treasured bottle of Laphroaig. I poured out two big snifters.

Back in the living room, we clinked glasses and had a sip. Then Caitlin said she felt really icky from the plane ride and would it be okay if she had a quick shower. I said sure. But all her luggage had been left at Maxx's place; did I have a shirt or something she could put on afterward? So I went to my closet, found a big old corduroy shirt, and gave it to her.

She went off to the bathroom and I went back to the kitchen. I scavenged a desiccated hunk of cheddar cheese, lopped off the really crusty part, and put it on a plate with some soggy crackers. It was quite a comedown from Per Se, but I was starving. While I was there, I figured I'd bring the scotch bottle into the living room. It might save steps later on.

A few minutes later, Caitlin reappeared. She looked . . . she looked like a vision that every poor bastard should have the privilege of seeing in his apartment at least once in his puny little life. Her short black hair was wet and combed straight back; droplets still collected at the ends. Her skin glowed and seemed almost to pulse from the heat of the shower. Her collarbones described a beautiful arc beneath the open neckline of my corduroy shirt; the shirttails came down nearly to her knees in the front and back, but were scooped out at the sides to reveal a stunning length of fit, tan thigh. Saying that she felt much better now, she retrieved her glass of whiskey; we clinked again and she sat down on the sofa.

"I have a question for you," she said. "About Robert, if you don't mind."

I said I didn't mind.

"In all the time you've spent with him, have you ever heard him hum?"

"Hum?"

"Hum, whistle, sing. Whatever."

I thought about it, and realized that I hadn't.

"Most people," she went on, "you spend time with them, at some point you hear them singing in the shower, whistling in the elevator, something. Not Robert. He has no music. I find that really sad."

She leaned forward and grabbed a cheese-and-cracker. I sipped some scotch and thought over what she'd said. It rang true, and it suggested a lack that went well beyond music. Other than a rare and bleeding steak, what did Maxx actually take pleasure in? What was the refuge? Where was the delight? The money, the deals, the fame—what were they really buying him? What were they *for*? In that philosophic moment, something else occurred to me as well. Maybe I shouldn't admit this, maybe it'll make me sound like an adolescent jerk. But what can I say, this is how men are, and I'll tell you flat out that every straight guy in the world would have been thinking the same thing. At the exact moment I was thinking about Maxx's deepest values and motivation, it also occurred to me to wonder if Caitlin was wearing panties. I mean, think about it. She only had the one pair with her. She'd said she was feeling icky from the plane ride. Would she have put the same ones on again after the shower?

I was wondering that when we heard a knock on the door.

It wasn't a loud knock, but it was firm, it had resolve in it. I looked at Caitlin. Her face had instantly tightened, her shoulders lifted. She must have reached the same distressing conclusion I did: that this unwanted visitor could only be the lunatic Matt Gaston. Presumably, he'd stayed lurking in Columbus Circle after skulking out of the restaurant. He'd had a taxi or more likely a limo follow the cab in which we'd slipped past the paparazzi. He'd bided some time, then sweet-talked his way past my very lax doorman, just as, with his famous looks and confidence, he'd trampled the authority of the maître d'.

But what now? Should I answer the door? Try to ignore it?

The knock came again, louder now.

Caitlin whispered, "I should probably talk to him."

I whispered back, "Why? Why do you owe him that? He's out of control. Maybe he's dangerous."

She bit her lip. "He's someone I've cared about. He's not a bad person. I can't just hide like this."

"Why not?" I said, but Caitlin was already rising from the sofa and heading for the door. This put me in a hell of a dilemma. I hate confrontations. I am not very brave. Then again, nor am I completely devoid of gallantry, and there's no way I could let my guest face off alone against a wigged-out stalker. So I pushed myself up from my chair and strode on unsteady legs beside her.

As we approached, the knock came a third time, and there was an unmistakable frustration and insistence in it now. For a heartbeat,

Caitlin and I stood close together in the narrow entryway. We shared a deep breath and a reassuring glance, then I put my hand on the knob and, intent on showing strength and courage, yanked the door swiftly open.

In the suddenly vacant doorframe, backed by the dim yet glary light of the hallway, stood Claire.

She looked at me. She looked at Caitlin. She blinked. All she said was "Oh."

"Claire!" I said. I fumbled and squirmed and could feel that my face looked incredibly guilty. Which was crazy. I hadn't done anything. I hadn't even *intended* to do anything—at least I don't think I had. True, I'd wondered about the panty thing, but where was the harm in that? Wrestling my voice into something like a normal register, I said, "Please, come in. Come in."

"No," she said, "I don't think I will."

So we stood there in the doorway: me, my ex, and a half-naked stranger. I said, "This is Caitlin Kilgore. Friend of Robert Maxx's. She needed a place to stay."

I realized an instant too late that this made no sense whatsoever. Maxx controlled thousands of condos and hotel rooms and lived in the biggest apartment in New York. A friend of his would need a place to stay?

Claire said to Caitlin, "I guess I'm supposed to say it's nice to meet you."

Caitlin said, "It isn't how it looks. It really isn't. Your husband's being very kind."

"He's not my husband."

"He's told me all about you. I root for your relationship. I really do."

"How nice that he confides in you. Sorry to interrupt your . . . conversation."

She pivoted on the threshold and turned to go. She stopped just long enough to say, "Did he also tell you I bought him the shirt you're wearing?"

Shit. I hadn't even thought about the shirt.

She started walking away. I chased her out into the hall. The grainy light and vague echo reminded me I'd had a lot to drink. I said, "Claire, I really can explain all this."

"I'm sure you can. Explaining things is what you're good at. But you don't owe me any explanations. You're a single man."

As she was pushing the button for the elevator, I said, "I don't want to be a single man. I want to be with you."

Claire's face changed when I said that. She no longer looked angry. Instead, she looked sad and disappointed and embarrassed—embarrassed for herself, for me, even for Caitlin. It was much harder to take than when she'd just looked mad.

She said, "You've got a really peculiar way of showing it."

The elevator opened and she slipped away.

Chapter 44

Back in the apartment, I sat down heavily, topped up my scotch, and gulped some.

"Jesus," Caitlin said, "I'm so, so sorry. I really messed that up for you."

"Not your fault," I said. "It could have been any half-naked woman wearing a shirt that was a present from my wife."

I picked up a cheese-and-cracker. I put it down again. I felt jittery and awful and was having trouble with the simplest decisions about what I wanted or didn't want.

Caitlin said, "She was coming to make love with you."

That made me feel even worse.

"Definitely," she went on. "A woman can tell. Wow. Unannounced. Out of the blue. That's bold. Really sexy."

"Okay, okay," I said.

She drank. "I think it'll come right in the end. The way you two care for each other—I'm envious. You'll explain. She'll believe you. If you want, I'll call her up myself."

"That's all right. You've done enough."

"Anyway, a toast: to you and Claire getting back together and having a good laugh over this sometime."

We clinked and drank. I appreciated the good wishes but had a tough time believing they would ever come true. I'm not sure if I was totally depressed or suddenly just very tired. "Sorry to be a bore," I said, "but I think I need to go to sleep."

As if on cue, Caitlin yawned. It was a big yawn, undisguised and intimate, like we really were old pals and roommates. There was a tenderness in it that made me feel a little better. Not much. She said, "Got a blanket? I'll sleep right here on the couch."

"No way. Take the bedroom. Please."

She protested, but I won the argument and showed her to the empty and none too tidy bed where not one TV personality had ever slept before.

I settled in on the sofa, but tired as I was, I couldn't get to sleep. My mind was racing; my gonads were irritable, resentful, and entirely confused. I was haunted by the abashed look on Claire's face as, ludicrously, the three of us had stood there chatting. Sometime around two, I caved and took an Ambien. I probably shouldn't have, on top of all the booze, but that had never stopped me before. After that I slept like a mummy.

By the time I woke up, Caitlin was gone. She'd left a thank-you note with her cell number on it; for all I knew, she was already airborne, heading west.

I took a shower, made coffee, and tried to tell myself I didn't have a hangover, I was just a little logy. But what I was feeling was more than simple sluggishness; for that matter, it was different from a plain old hangover, too. I was feeling a kind of creeping gloom that I couldn't put my finger on. I'd call it dread—but that's probably giving myself too much credit for clairvoyance, given the avalanche that was about to come roaring down. No, what I was feeling was more a kind of general and useless pity, tainted by reluctant mockery; I felt this for everybody, starting with myself. It was a sense that human beings never quite knew what they were doing or why they did it, and that of all the lies we told ourselves to get through the day, probably the farthest-fetched and most widely believed was that we could foresee and control what happened in the next heartbeat.

In any case, I was making toast when the phone rang. It was Jenna. All she said was "Have you heard?"

The way she said it made me think someone had died. "Heard what?"

She sighed. I could almost feel the exhalation through the phone. "Our offices have been raided."

"What?"

"Pretty slick operation. Bright and early on a Saturday morning. Federal marshals. Seized the books, the laptops, the hard drives from the servers, everything."

My hazy brain tried to grasp this and didn't have much luck. "Wait. Why now? I thought Maxx had till January to get things straightened out."

"You know about that?"

"I know about a lot of stuff. Some stuff I wish I didn't know. I can't tell if he's opening up, breaking down—"

"Breaking down just became way more of a possibility."

"But I don't see how—"

"They could raid us? 'Credible information suggesting serious malfeasance.' That's all they're saying. Whatever it was, wherever it came from, it was enough to get the warrants."

I didn't notice that I'd sat down on a kitchen stool. "Have you spoken to Robert?"

"Very briefly. He's off scrambling with lawyers, trying to reach the mayor, the governor, anybody, hoping to call in favors. But no one's going to touch him now. I think he knows that."

My toast popped. I tried to figure out what I was supposed to be feeling, but my emotions were as fuzzy as my thoughts. Should I feel sorry for Maxx? Should I be happy that his bluffs and frauds were finally coming back to bite him? How could it be that I was feeling both at once?

"Listen," Jenna went on, "I'm heading down to the office. I don't even know if they'll let me in the building, but I'd like to check it out. Meet me there if you want."

I couldn't help remembering that last time Jenna invited me somewhere, she'd picked me up in a limo. Now it seemed that the days and nights in limousines were abruptly finished. She'd be arriving by subway, just like me. I said I'd be there as soon as I could.

Chapter 45

The scene outside Maxx Tower reminded me a bit of the aftermath of a coup d'état, like when the celebrating masses pulled down the statue of Lenin or Saddam.

The milling crowd, by New York standards, wasn't large—mere hundreds, I would guess. But strangers were greeting one another, laughing, joking, swapping news and rumors. There was an excitement in the air that seemed in equal parts comradely and cruel. People who could not possibly have known Robert Maxx seemed somehow to regard his troubles as a personal victory, a vindication.

The media were there in force. Broadcast trucks glutted the curb. Cameras panned across the mute building. Stylists touched up correspondents, who then stood solemnly in front of the yellow police tape, repeating endlessly the few known facts about the raid.

I zigzagged through the crowd, hoping to find Jenna. Instead, I literally bumped into Mandy Lockwood. Of course she'd be there, given her revenge obsession, which, in its virulence, was not so different from a desperate, fatal love affair. She was playing it at least somewhat incognito, wearing sunglasses against the weak December sunshine. She had a silk scarf wrapped around her luxuriant red hair; a somewhat baggy coat obscured her remarkably close-packed torso.

"David Collins," she said. "I thought I might see you here."

"And vice versa," I said, though the truth was that I hadn't given a thought to Mandy until that moment. I had way more pressing things on my mind. Events suddenly seemed to be coming at me hardest and fastest just when I was least equipped to process them.

She gestured toward the building with her chin. "What do you know about this?"

"Absolutely nothing."

"You're lying as usual."

"And you're still looking for a mole for your big exposé."

"It's the best card I've got to play," she admitted.

"You got him pretty good with the PORCH thing," I said.

She allowed herself a brief smile. "Yeah, I won that round. But in the meantime, he's still news and I don't have a job."

I looked down at my shoes.

"Come on," she said, "help me out here. Something like this, it doesn't just happen. Something triggers it. That's the key question: What triggered it? I'll bet you know."

In fact, I did know—or at least I thought I did—and the knowledge scared the living hell out of me.

Since the phone call from Jenna, I'd been working hard to clear my head, trying to connect the dots. Maxx's books had been a mess for months and months, very possibly for years. Why had the warrants come down now? Who was the source of the "credible information" that justified the subpoenas?

The more I thought about the timing, the clearer it seemed that the source was none other than Robert Maxx himself; and that the information had been unwittingly conveyed at Victor Magnola's kitchen table, when my tycoon had confessed his business woes and transgressions to the Godfather.

Magnola's house was bugged. Why not? The feds had done this at least once before—back in the eighties, to Big Paul Castellano, who'd thereby lost his street cred and was rubbed out by John Gotti, throwing the whole Mob into disarray. With a past success like that, why wouldn't they try it again? And if the operation netted a supposedly legit tycoon along with the mobsters and goombahs, so much the better.

But I'd been sitting at the kitchen table, too—sitting there as out of place and clueless as Forrest Gump, accidental bystander to history. I knew things that could certainly be used against Robert Maxx. Probably they could be turned around and also used against Magnola. The position I was in did not feel like a healthy one. I'd spent my whole career and life feeling like I knew too little; the danger, suddenly, was that for once I knew too much.

Mandy said, "You're thinking. Tell me what you're thinking."

I said, "I'm thinking it's a really lousy day to have a hangover."

"Bullshit. That isn't what you're thinking."

"No, it isn't. Look—no promises. Give me your number. Maybe I'll be able to help you out sometime."

I shook loose from Mandy Lockwood and finally found Jenna as she was emerging from the clot of onlookers and heading toward the barricade of yellow tape. I called out to her and waved. We moved toward each other, and without even really slowing down, she fell into my arms. It was the kind of heedless and completely unself-conscious hug that usually only happens at a funeral. We came out of the clinch and I asked her how she was.

"Dazed," she said. "Numb. Like I knew this had to happen sometime, and at the same time it's unthinkable."

I looked at her. She looked very different today. She was wearing jeans and a turtleneck sweater, and without the armor of business attire, she just looked heartbreakingly young. She looked like a grad student in English or philosophy, someone with her ideals intact and endless possibilities in front of her. Except suddenly they weren't.

We walked closer to the building and went up to a cop—a regular

NYPD guy in a uniform. "You can't go in," he said, before we'd even asked.

"We work here," Jenna said.

"What floor?"

"Fifty-one."

At that, the cop looked at her a little harder and, not unsympathetically, said, "Too bad. Hang on a minute."

He withdrew a couple of steps and spoke into a walkie-talkie. Then he lifted up the yellow tape and let us pass. "Don't be shocked," he said. "It won't be pretty."

The lobby was deserted except for maybe a dozen marshals. Two or three wore crummy suits; the rest were in military-looking khaki. It seemed that the computers and most of the files had already been hauled away, but here and there, like forgotten remnants of an ordinary moving day, were cardboard boxes with dates and codes scrawled on them, loose papers sticking out the tops.

We walked toward the special elevator that served our previously privileged floor. In place of the private security guard, a marshal now stood at the podium in front of it. He asked us for ID; I produced my Dave Cullen pass card, and could not help thinking that it would make a resonant if melancholy souvenir someday. The marshal looked at us for longer than was polite, as if memorizing our faces so he could testify against us later on. Then he allowed us to go up.

On the fifty-first floor, the door opened in front of the handsome rosewood desk where the receptionist with the British accent used to sit, and the sense of violation was palpable at once. It was like coming across a picked-over shipwreck. Not that the physical damage was egregious; the marshals hadn't overturned desks or dumped out whole file cabinets or yanked wires out of walls. The invasion had been more subtle and more lewd than that. Everywhere, there was a sense of fingers probing, private places plumbed by strangers' hands, innocent secrets as well as guilty ones laid bare. Moving through the maze of offices, we saw family pictures pushed aside and smudged by the marshals' hurried grasp; shelves with vacant places where personal effects had been swept away or taken; desk drawers yawning open, their contents rifled through and ravaged.

I hung back as we neared Jenna's office. Some delicacy or more likely cowardice told me that I shouldn't be there when she confronted it. At the last turning of the hallway, I veered off. I went to look at Maxx's place instead.

His office had always been extreme in many different ways—extremely big, extremely showy, extremely intimidating, and damn well meant to be. On that Saturday morning in December, it also seemed extremely sorrowful. There was an unnatural hush about the place; a hush like the inside of a pyramid. The air was stale, floating silver dust was visible. Here and there, for no apparent reason, furniture had been pushed around; it stood at jarring angles that somehow suggested that these things would never be used again—that, as in some archaic ritual of waste and cleansing, the possessions of a fallen potentate would be buried with him. The wall where Maxx had displayed the many photos of himself with other billionaires and politicians had been turned into an abstract pattern of discolored rectangles. I wondered if the marshals had seized the pictures in order to shield the powerful from possible embarrassment, or to scan them for associates they could implicate or squeeze for information. Maxx's desk seemed strangely undisturbed; but then, he'd never been one to bother himself with the sort of details that required pieces of paper or even a computer. His desk chair had been swiveled and faced out through the giant window, as if some func-tionary had been unable to resist the impulse to sit in it a moment and take in the imperial view: to imagine what it felt like to be Robert Maxx.

I don't think I breathed much as I stood in his office. I couldn't stand to be there very long. I went back through the maze of hallways toward Jenna's place. It seemed that she couldn't quite take it, either; she was already back in the corridor with nothing but a couple of framed photos in her hand. Maybe she'd been crying; I couldn't tell for sure and she would not have wanted me to know.

We headed for the elevator, and on the way, through the open doorway of a big and pillaged office, we caught a glimpse of another shell-shocked visitor. It was Carlton Phelps. He was dressed as if it was just another business day—neat gray suit, pale blue shirt, bright red power tie. His skin was pasty, his posture as rigid as a sleepwalker's. Just then his long stiff fingers were reaching toward a file drawer that seemed to have no files in it.

Jenna held onto the doorjamb and leaned in. "Carlton," she said, "you okay?"

For a moment it was as if he hadn't heard. Then he looked up and blinked with his papery eyelids. His gaze meandered, and finally settled not on Jenna but on me. "You again?"

He said it bitterly, accusingly, and in some crazy way it hurt my feelings. I wasn't an enemy. What had I done to offend him, other than be present to see the mess? Fumbling for something to say, I said, "Hey, I'm on your side here."

"You're not on any side," he said. "You're just passing through. You have no stake in this."

I started to object. He cut me off.

"You just sit there taking notes. You're clever with words and so you think you understand. But you don't understand, because you can walk away. In a few months you'll be doing something else."

He dropped his eyes and went back to the phantom files.

Very gently, Jenna said, "Carlton, is there anything I can help you with?"

"No, there's nothing to help with. Nothing I can think of. Not much to be done here anymore. I'll just straighten up a bit."

Chapter 46

I went home. I had a nasty headache and a crick in my neck from sleeping on the sofa, and all I really wanted was to get into my bed, preferably with Claire, and have a good long nap. The Claire part wasn't going to happen—certainly not until and unless I could explain last night's debacle. Still, some rest and some oblivion seemed called for. But first I had two phone messages to deal with.

The first was from Arthur Levin, who left a cell number and asked me to call him as soon as I could.

He picked up on the second ring. I heard a confusion of voices in the background. He seemed to move farther away from them, then said, "We need to talk about Robert. In absolute confidence, of course."

This surprised me. Levin, with more than ample justification, had fired Maxx some weeks ago. Maxx had responded by slamming the iron door on Levin. "You're working together again?"

"I'm an old family friend," he said. "You don't just walk away."

"A lot of people would."

He let that pass. "We're at the courthouse now," he said. "Waiting to go before a judge. We'll try to have the subpoenas quashed, the books returned."

"What are the chances?"

"Slim to none. But at least we can try to find out what the warrants were based on, what information they have, and where they got it. In the meantime, we need to talk about your book."

I said nothing, because the book was supposed to be a secret. Why wasn't it turning out that way?

"I know he's been confiding in you," said Levin, "that you've been witness to certain conversations. I need to stress that it's absolutely essential those things remain private."

I said, "A book is kind of public."

"Right. A book that Robert approves, and that is published at a more opportune time. Who else knows you're working together?"

"Hardly anyone. The editor. My agent. My ex-wife. Jenna. Caitlin Kilgore. Oh, and Mandy Lockwood seems to have figured it out."

"Shit," he said. The brief letdown in his decorum was strangely refreshing. "But you haven't told her anything."

"No. Of course not."

"Good. If anyone tries to question you—the media, the authorities—please make no comment and refer them to me. If at any point you need legal representation of your own—"

"Now wait a second," I cut in. "Why would I need legal representation? I haven't done anything—"

"These things have a way of getting complicated. It's possible that you'll be interviewed. It's possible that the prosecution will want to see your notes—"

"My notes? My notes are a mess, and anyway, they're private."

"That's the position we will take," said Levin. "Judges lately have seen it otherwise. A few reporters have done jail time."

My head was splitting. I felt just slightly nauseous. Jail time? I thought: *Wait a second. I'm not even a real reporter, still less a First Amendment poster boy. I'm just a guy who's been hired to ghost a silly-ass*

*puff piece for a billionaire. I don't count for diddly. How is it possible I'm
in trouble?*

Arthur Levin said, "But let's not get ahead of ourselves. Hopefully,
none of that will happen. In the meantime, please stay calm and
quiet."

Calm. Sure, no problem.

We hung up, and suddenly a hair of the dog seemed like a good idea.
I'm not saying it *was* a good idea, just that it seemed so at the time. I
poured myself barely enough scotch to wash down a couple of aspirin.
One of the tablets sort of stuck at the back of my throat, so I had to have
a little more. Then I dealt with my other phone message.

It was from Marcie Kanin, my long-lost editor. I called her back at
home in Connecticut.

We exchanged some pleasantries, but she sounded nervous from
the start. "David, listen, I know you've got your nondisclose and all, but
I really need to know what's going on with Maxx."

I said, "Great timing. I just got off the phone with his lawyer, who
told me not to talk to anyone."

"I'm not *anyone*. I'm your editor, and we've got five million bucks
invested in this book."

I tried to see it from her perspective, but other people's problems
have a way of looking trivial when compared to one's own. "Right," I
said. "And I've got a mortgage coming due, and my ex-wife is furious
with me, and I've just been told I might be grilled by the feds."

"Really?"

"Really."

"So it really is as bad as the news is making it sound."

"Looks that way," I said.

There was a pause. I could feel Marcie thinking, fretting. At length
she said, "Well, let me share an interesting editorial dilemma with you.
Tell me what you think. Our lead nonfiction title for next year's all-
important Christmas season is a compelling inside look at America's
savviest, most charismatic businessman, a visionary deal maker and
tactician, who here reveals the strategies and insights that have kept

him at the top. Except that, by the time the book comes out, the guy is bankrupt, disgraced, and possibly in jail. How do we promote that book?"

I said, "Maybe we call it *Ooops!*" And I gave an abrupt and unseemly little laugh.

Unamused, my editor said, "Have you been drinking?" It was around eleven-thirty in the morning.

I said, "I've had a really rough couple of days."

"Well, that's just great. Maybe when you sober up we can talk about a way that this can work."

Trying to reclaim my professional dignity, trying to reassure her, I said, "Don't worry. It'll work. It'll work because it has to work."

Then I thought: *Oh shit, that's what Maxx would say. He's going down the tubes and I'm starting to sound just like him.*

"Say Maxx does crash," I went on. "Doesn't that make a better story?"

"Sure. Fabulous. Except it isn't the book we contracted for, and it isn't a book that Maxx will sign off on."

"Yes, he will," I said, with way more certainty than I felt.

"Even if he loses in the end?"

I said, "You're forgetting that he actually needs the money now. Besides, I've gotten to know the guy. He's a control freak who's dying to be relieved of control. I can get him excited about a different way to do the book. I know I can sell him on it."

Sounding intrigued but not convinced, she said, "Maybe you better sell me first."

And so I started winging it. Life is a moving target, after all, and if the book kept changing in response to evolving circumstances, so be it. I'd already gone from primates-in-suits to grace-under-pressure. What I heard myself pitching now was more of a King of Siam scenario, the thousand dreams that won't come true. There was stature, maybe greatness, in trying to do as much as Maxx had tried to do, in wanting things so badly. If it all came crashing down in the end, so what?

Midway through my spiel, a strange thing happened. I realized I was talking about the book I had always wanted to write, the story that I felt in my gut was the truest: the one about gaining everything and losing it again, climbing up one face of the mountain and tumbling down the other, tracing out a destiny in all its symmetry and completeness. Amazingly, life seemed finally to have handed me the chance to write that book, had even given me my flawed and perhaps tragic protagonist.

Marcie heard me out, then said, "Wow. That's sure not what we thought we were getting."

"No," I said. "It's better."

"You really think Maxx will go for it?"

"Yeah. Because all three of us are screwed if he doesn't."

"And this new take—you're really sure you can write it?"

I said, "I was born to write it."

Chapter 47

Talking with Marcie just then was both very good and very bad for me.

The good part was that I was wildly exhilarated about the new direction the book was taking. Events had turned the story into a cautionary fable on themes that obsessed me. Suddenly it seemed not only possible but necessary to produce a book I might actually be proud of. It was one of those Eureka moments that happen a few times in a writer's life, and that serve as compensation for many, many hours of slogging and frustration.

The bad part was that this exhilaration was laid right on top of extreme fatigue and a hangover. So now I was jumpy and exhausted all at once. My talk with Marcie had completely undone the soothing effects of the scotch I'd had after my talk with Arthur Levin, so I felt I owed myself a little bit more.

I took the drink into the bedroom, sat down on the bed, and took off my shoes. I should have just gone to sleep, but I couldn't yet. I had to call Claire. This was not a good decision, given how frazzled and hyper I was. I got her machine and ended up leaving a long rambling message about how the reason Caitlin had been at my place was that she'd broken up with Maxx right after she'd had to deal with a crazy old boyfriend who was stalking her, and she couldn't go to a hotel because of the paparazzi. All this happened to be true, but even to me it sounded like one of those overly elaborate explanations that generally masks a lie. I told her I was dying to see her and asked her to call when she could.

Then I finally lay down. I didn't bother setting an alarm, and I didn't bother undressing. I was only going to nap for half an hour, an hour tops.

It didn't quite work out that way. I slept around four hours, and woke up just as it was starting to get dark. My headache was gone, but I was completely discombobulated. To my body, it was morning, so I made a pot of coffee. I felt totally sober and alert. If anything, I felt too alert, as though, like Claire, I'd shed the insulation around my nerves. Thoughts were crackling, and I was eager to start noodling around with *Maxxed Out,* take two . . . or three . . . or whatever take this new version was.

I went back to the very beginning of the story. Understand, what I had at that point was not much like a book. I had scenes; snatches of dialogue; bullet points to keep in mind. I had no flow, only moments.

Still, as I read through the fragments, something began to dawn on me; something so surprising and exciting that I found myself bolting from my chair and pacing laps around the living room. I began to see that the new book—the real book—had been there, as a kind of embryo, right from the start. Not to get all woo-woo about it, but there are definitely times when the story itself knows things that the writer doesn't know. In everything I'd set down about Robert Maxx, there was a strand of darkness, a hint of foreboding, a veiled suggestion that, at the end of the day, he was as little in control of his fate as even the smallest of us are masters of ours. That part of the story, subliminally but insistently, had told itself.

It was the story itself that had prompted the brinksmanship idea—the time-honored rooting opportunity of a bloodied champion fighting back. But the story also held another twist that I myself was only tardily discovering: coming back from a particular brink only *seemed* to be the climax. Maxx needed $300 million. He was promised it. He'd won. Right?

Wrong. Because beyond that brink was *another* brink. And if that one was survived, there would be another, and another after that. That was the truth of a life lived on leverage; and that, finally, was the pathos and the jumbo irony in Robert Maxx's story. For him, every victory was only a prelude to a next and bigger crisis; being who he was, there would never be an end point in his grasping, and without an end point there could be no peace. Maxx, at every moment of his life, had been the victim of his own relentlessness. If he deserved any sympathy, if his flame-out even came close to the stature of tragedy, that was why.

I dove back to my desk. My hairline itched and my fingers all but trembled. My eyes flicked back and forth between the computer screen and the ratty notebook I'd toted around for months. I stitched together thoughts, fashioned transitions, ventured guesses. I worked for hours and joyfully lost track of time. It was easier to keep writing than to stop.

At some point the phone rang. Coming out of a long and concentrated silence, the ringing seemed very loud and made me twitch in my chair. For a few heartbeats, I brooded about whether to answer it. I didn't want an interruption. But I was sure it was Claire. I ached to talk with her, to clear things up and win another chance to be her lover. I picked up the receiver.

It was Robert Maxx. To my complete amazement, he sounded drunk. His voice was thick; consonants were sloppy; the tone was sing-song in a bitter and failed attempt at sounding humorous and hale. "Dave!" he said. "This wine you like—it's not half bad."

I was off guard and off balance. As in some cheap special effect, Robert Maxx seemed to have suddenly gone double on me—I had one version living and breathing on the page and now his twin was coming through the phone. At a loss, I said, "I didn't think you drank."

"I don't. Except when I do. Like now. A little celebration."

"Things went well in court today?"

"Things went shit. Things went fucked. I'm toast. I'm screwed."

Gingerly, I said, "So what's to celebrate?"

"What's to celebrate," he slurred. "Lemme think. Must be some-thing. You're the writer—think of something."

"Robert—you okay?"

He gave a quick, barking laugh, a laugh from hell, then said, "This is something you never need to ask. I'm fine. I'm Robert Maxx. I'm fine."

I really wanted to get off the phone. "Well, glad to hear it. I'm kind of working now—"

"Working on our book?"

I said I was.

"You're a diligent little pissant. You might even amount to some-thing someday."

I let that slide. What was the point of not?

"But about our book," he said. "That's why I called. We have to talk."

I waited. We *were* talking.

He said, "In person. Face-to-face."

"Okay. Like, tomorrow?"

"Okay. Like now."

"Do you think that's such a good idea?"

"Now you're telling me what's a good idea? Dave, I'm still the boss here. You're doing a job for me. Remember that. Come on over. We'll have a glass of wine."

Chapter 48

It must have been just eleven when I got to Maxx's building; the doormen's shift seemed to be changing, and the white-gloved guy who brought me up to the apartment greeted me a little sullenly, like I was keeping him from going home.

The elevator door opened onto the foyer with the monstrous chandelier. No one was there to meet me, but every light in the place was burning brightly. If this was meant to be cheerful, the effect was just the opposite. There was something bleak and desperate about the artificial radiance; it seemed a futile fighting back against the night by a child frightened of the dark. I moved through the lifeless rooms, dodging heavy furniture. I found Maxx in the small green study, where I knew I would.

He looked awful. His stiff hair had collapsed into oily bundles. Alcohol had loosened his skin, and the excess flesh around his chin and jowls was bloated, pink, and pebbly. His eyebrows seemed to be slipping downward, and his eyes looked shadowy and cruel. He was watching TV news when I walked in. He called the anchorman an asshole and switched off the remote.

To me, he said, "Well, my little writer friend. Have a drink. You like this stuff."

On the small table where we'd first had dinner together, there were three bottles of Bordeaux. One was empty; one was half gone; the third was uncorked and ready. Say this for Maxx: he planned ahead. He poured me a glass. A bit of wine slopped on the table.

"Siddown," he said, "siddown. And let's talk about this brilliant book, your great idea for how the old champ comes out on top."

I sipped some wine. "Robert, it's been a hell of a day. You sure you want to do this now?"

"Shut up," he said, "and talk to me. My story. Tell me how you're gonna tell it."

He briefly closed his eyes and almost smiled. For a second he looked like a kid about to hear a favorite bedtime tale. Very cautiously, I said, "Well, it's different now."

"No shit."

"It's better. It's truer."

He snorted; people don't like it when a soothing and familiar bedtime story changes. "Truer? Why? Because I'm getting my ass kicked? Because all the jealous little scumbags who wanted to see me go down are finally getting their wish?"

"No," I said. "Because now it's really about how much you tried to do, how much guts it took, how hard it was."

He turned away. "No one gives a shit how hard it was."

"I don't agree with that."

"No one gives a shit how hard it was, and no one gives a shit I *tried*. Losers try. Winners do. It's that simple."

"It's not that simple."

He paused long enough to refill our glasses, though neither one was empty. Then he said, "You know, Dave, you had an easy job to do. Just a slightly different version of the same book guys have done for me half a dozen times. But you had to make it complicated. You had to give me all this crap about making it a real book, like it was gonna be important, maybe last awhile. You should've been a goddamn salesman. You hooked me on this fucking book. You made me give a shit about it."

"Am I supposed to be sorry for that?"

He ignored the question. "Except I hate the way it's turning out. I look like one more jerk who overdrew his bank account, blew right past his credit limit. The ending's a disaster."

"What can I say? Who knew this was coming? But I can make it work. I know I can. I made you care about the story? Other people will care, too."

"I don't want them to care!" he said. "I don't want anybody's fucking sympathy. And you know what? I don't want this book. I just don't. Forget about it. It's done. It's finished."

He stared at me then. I stared back. There was an extraordinary disconnect between his angry words and the look that briefly crossed his face. The look was all tenderness and sorrow; I think it called forth the same expression from me. In some crazy way it was like we were grieving together for the loss of an unborn baby, except that he was ready to let go and I was not.

Struggling for calm, I said, "Why don't we talk about this tomorrow?"

The tactic didn't work. Maxx dug in.

"We're talking about it now," he said. "My mind's made up. The book is off. That's that."

I still didn't quite get it. I *couldn't* get it; the book filled up too much of my head and heart to imagine it gone in an instant, just like that. Though I suppose that Maxx's pulling the plug should not have come as a surprise. What was the very first thing he'd said to me? That he wanted to be portrayed not as a nice guy, but a winner. Life was writing a different ending; of course he wouldn't go for it. I was a sucker and a fool for ever imagining that he would, for wasting time and passion trying to find something redemptive in what he saw as mere humiliation. But I wasn't just any fool; I was a fool with a mortgage coming due.

Trying not to sound pathetic, I said, "Robert, please don't do this."

Something ugly started happening to him then, something that, in turn, made me begin to seethe in a way I hadn't seethed for many years. He was enjoying my discomfort and my powerlessness; he was rubbing my face in it. He put his fingertips together and gave a little smile. "I already have, *David*. You're fired."

He finally said my name. He said it, the bastard, just to let me know he'd known it all along.

"You can't do this to me."

"Oh yes I can."

"It isn't fair."

"Fair. That's a good one."

"Pay me for my work, at least. Pay me for my time."

Maxx smiled insufferably. Bullies will always be bullies, and if they lose a big fight they'll go out and find some smaller person to beat up on. But I really didn't like being the last guy Robert Maxx could push around.

"Read your contract," he said. "You don't work for wages. You get paid when the book is done. If the book doesn't happen, you get zilch. That's the way it goes."

I didn't remember getting to my feet, but suddenly I was standing. "I'll lose my apartment!"

"'I'll lose my apartment,'" he mimicked. "How many apartments, Dave? One? I'll lose hundreds of apartments. I'll lose hotels, casinos. You think I give a rat's ass about your one apartment?"

I paced in no particular direction, and ended up standing very close to where Maxx was sitting. He didn't like that—me standing over him while he still sat. Awkwardly, he stood up, too. We were crowding each other, almost chest to chest.

I said, "You know, Robert, you're right about one thing. I could never have made you human in a book. I couldn't make anybody root for you. It's true—everybody wants to see you fail. Not because you're rich and famous. Because you're a crude, obnoxious, selfish prick."

That was when he tried to hit me. At least I think he did. His hand curled into a fist, his arm started coming up. It happened slowly—he was plastered and probably not much of a fighter anyway. Not that I am, either. But when I saw him raise his hand, I realized all at once just how badly I wanted to take a swing of my own; realized that I'd wanted to hit him for a long time, to strike back for every slight and power play and hint of condescension, to flail against my lousy contract and my helplessness. I pulled my arm back and loaded up. Wimp that I am, I couldn't bring myself to hit him in the face. I punched him in the chest. In truth, it was probably half a punch and half a push—nothing elegant or really decisive or even wholly satisfying about it.

But Maxx was off balance. He stumbled backward, started to fall. Then he did a reeling half twist as he tried to right himself, and finally sprawled facedown, arms flung wide, across the desk. The antique globe went flying. The rack of vintage letter openers clattered and jangled and disappeared beneath him. And he lay, passed out, where he had landed.

Chapter 49

I stormed out of the study and through the oppressive, overlit rooms. In the hexagonal foyer, I rang for the elevator. It came up unattended. I rode it downstairs and bolted through the lobby, where a single doorman seemed barely awake.

I started walking uptown on Park Avenue. For a few minutes I felt absolutely nothing, then I noticed that my scalp was prickling and there was a faint sting in my lungs; the weather had finally turned cold. I hailed a taxi and gave my home address. Halfway there, I changed my mind. I was too wired to go home. I got out of the cab on Ninety-sixth and Broadway and went into a quiet bar where I had sometimes been a regular.

I ordered a Jack Daniel's. I don't really like Jack Daniel's; to me it's always tasted sour and angry, and that's probably why I ordered it. My nerves were shot and my thoughts were muddled. I hate violence, and I was a bit disgusted with myself for losing my temper and hitting Maxx. At the same time, I was disappointed that I hadn't done a better job of it, hadn't had the balls and the wholeheartedness to deliver a clean, stiff right to that thick and overbearing chin.

The second drink neutralized the leftover adrenaline, and a different set of thoughts, more maudlin and more practical, set in. Bottom line: I was fucked. I'd agreed to a deal I never should have taken, spent months working on a book that was not going to get published, and for which I wouldn't be paid a nickel. God knew when my next gig would come around. In the meantime, my apartment would be foreclosed; I'd be squeezed out of Manhattan just like countless other losers who came there with big dreams but weren't quite talented or savvy or lucky enough to make the city work for them. Worst of all, at some point Claire would have to know the real story of where the money for her treatments came from. She'd feel terrible about it, and I'd feel terrible that she felt terrible, given that it was my own rash decision and not her fault at all.

I ordered one more round. I didn't really want it, but I drank it. It seemed to move me beyond self-pity and into some strangely impersonal realm, a hovering-above-myself perspective from which I could see a kind of morbid entertainment value in how badly things were going. Mere hours before, I'd been joyfully noodling with a manuscript full of promise. Now I was sitting in an empty bar, facing utter ruin and coming down with a fever. It was almost wonderful how quickly everything just fell apart.

I think it was around two when I settled my tab and wobbled out. Back at home, I had no choice but to notice my computer, still switched on, still holding the unborn corpse of *Maxxed Out*. I thought of doing something dramatic, like sweeping it off the desk in a rage. But those grand, expensive gestures just aren't me. I settled for closing and tossing aside the tattered notebook that I'd carried around for months.

I went to the medicine chest and took some aspirin for the chills that were getting gradually worse. While I was there, I bit off half an Ambien. This was getting to be a bad habit; I was well aware of that. But this was a crisis; and crises pass; and when this one was over, I'd cut back on the drinking and go cold turkey on the sleeping pills and get back to living cleaner. At least I told myself I would. Then I fell into bed and conked out.

I was awakened by a knocking on the door. It was a firm and steady knocking, and for at least some moments I thought it was part of a dream. When I realized it was actually happening, I dragged myself out of bed with great resentment, pulled on a robe, and went to answer it.

Sounding plenty annoyed, I said, "Who is it?"

A voice said, "NYPD. We need to ask you a few questions."

For a moment I made nothing of this. Understand, I was groggy, badly rested, a little ill, a little drugged. Besides, this was New York. Old ladies got mugged in hallways, quarreling lovers called 911; cops occasionally knocked on neighbors' doors for information. In any case, I opened up.

Glutting the frame were two plainclothes cops. One was white and paunchy, the other was black and tall, just like in the movies. They showed me their badges. "David Collins?" said the black guy.

"Yeah. What's the problem?"

"Robert Maxx," the white guy said.

This only confused me more. Arthur Levin had warned me that I might be contacted by the authorities in regard to Maxx's business problems. But why would that be city cops? And why would it have to be so early in the morning?

"What about him?"

"He was killed last night."

"What?"

Very politely, the black guy said, "Can we come in? This might take a few minutes."

I staggered more than stepped back from the door, and led them to the living room on feet that didn't quite feel connected to the rest of me. It was just barely getting light outside; the windows looked purple. I switched on a lamp, sat down, and gestured for the cops to do the same. They didn't.

Standing over me, the white guy said, "We've been through Maxx's phone records. You're the last person he called. Last night, around ten-thirty. Why?"

"I'm writing a book for him," I said. "He wanted to talk about it."

The black guy said, "It was a two-minute call. Was that all the talking you did?"

I licked my dry lips and begged my mind to wake up. I told myself I had nothing to hide. Why, then, did I feel like I did? A creepy thing began to happen; I started thinking the way a criminal must think. I lost interest in the truth and focused instead on what would wash, how much I needed to reveal, where I could get tripped up.

"No," I said. "He wanted to get together. I went over to his place."

The cops could not resist sharing a quick glance. I couldn't tell if it was a look of surprise or of confirmation. Maybe they'd already heard me described by the doorman or the elevator guy. Maybe they'd been waiting to see if I would lie.

"What time?" the white one said.

"Just around eleven, I think."

The black cop said, "And your talk with Maxx—where did it take place?"

I told them.

"What was it about?"

"He's having—was having—serious business problems. I'm sure you're aware of that. We talked about how the book should deal with what was going on."

The white guy said, "How long did you talk?"

"Half, three-quarters of an hour. It was kind of a rambling conversation. He was drunk."

"Was that unusual?" the black cop asked.

"Yeah, very. I'd never seen him drink at all before. He'd been under a crazy amount of pressure. It was like he was finally letting go."

"So you talked. Then what?"

Then came the part I couldn't tell them. The part about Maxx ruining my life, abusing and belittling me once too often. I couldn't tell them that I'd gotten blindly furious with him. I couldn't tell them about the clumsy, halfhearted, one-push fight that left Maxx sprawled chest down on his desk amid a shambles of sharp objects. Had he twitched when he fell? Had he moved at all after hitting the desk? Was he bleeding? I hadn't stuck around long enough to know.

I said, "Then I left."

The white cop said, "You came straight home?"

"No. I went out to a bar. The Hub, down on Ninety-sixth Street."

The tall black cop finally sat down. The heavy white cop followed his lead. This made me feel a little better, though it shouldn't have.

The black one said, "Mr. Collins—"

"David."

"David, you knew Maxx pretty well?"

"I worked with him pretty closely over the last few months."

"Do you know anyone who was mad at him?"

"Everyone was mad at him. He was kind of an awful guy."

The white cop said, "That doesn't really narrow it down."

I shrugged. I suppose I could have mentioned some names. Mandy Lockwood, over martinis, had announced that she'd like to kill her former lover. Trip Campbell was clearly bent on destroying him. Victor Magnola apparently had reason to be annoyed. I said nothing.

The black cop said, "Do you know an actor named Matt Gaston?"

At this first quick mention of the name, I felt an almost violent stab of hope. I thought, *Yes! Of course! Crazy Matt Gaston is the killer, this has nothing whatsoever to do with me.*

"I know who he is. I've met him once."

"When?"

"Just this past Friday. He made a scene in a restaurant where Maxx was having dinner."

"What kind of scene?"

"There were three of us. Me, Maxx, and Caitlin Kilgore, the TV actress—"

"We know who Caitlin Kilgore is."

"Gaston barged in. Said Maxx stole his girlfriend while he was in rehab. Said he'd followed her from Los Angeles, hoping to get her back. He was pretty insulting, pretty edgy."

The black cop said, "He tried to get into Maxx's building on Saturday afternoon. Maxx say anything about that?"

I wished I could say yes. "No, he didn't mention it."

"Any sign of Caitlin Kilgore being at Maxx's?" the white cop asked.

"She wouldn't have been," I volunteered.

He asked me how I knew that.

"She dumped Maxx over dinner. She spent Friday night right here."

"She gets around, this Caitlin."

"It was nothing like that. She was upset. She was avoiding paparazzi. She just needed a place to hide. I think she went straight back to California in the morning."

"No," the black cop said, "she didn't." It was clear he wasn't going to say more.

The light outside the windows had turned a sickly pink. My eyes itched with returning fever. The cops looked at each other, then stood up and thanked me for my time.

I walked them to the door. I should have kept my mouth shut, but I couldn't. As casually as I could manage, I asked them when and how Maxx had died. I was thinking, *Please let it be a bullet, a blunt object at 4 A.M.; anything to get my conscience off the hook and my ass out of the sling.*

"That isn't public yet," the black cop said. "The body's with the coroner. He'll make an announcement sometime later."

Then the white cop asked me if I had a passport. I said sure I did.

"Don't try to use it," he advised. "It won't work."

"Now hold on a second—"

Very calmly, very evenly, the black cop said, "You met with Maxx in the room where he died. That's not good. Maybe someone came in after you, maybe not. If you have a lawyer, it's probably smart to give him a call."

Chapter 50

When the cops left, I was wide-awake, but still, I crawled back into bed. It was the only thing I could think of to do. It was just after seven on a Sunday morning. For what it's worth, it was also the thirteenth day of December.

I don't know if I was technically catatonic. If I wasn't, I hope never to come closer. I lay there staring at the ceiling. I didn't want to let my eyes close, because when they did, I saw, over and over again, in excruciating slow motion, Robert Maxx doing his drunken pirouette, his ribs and lungs and heart slamming onto the detritus of his desk. So I stared until my eyes went out of focus, the ceiling and the walls blurring where they met. Fever came and went; it was like puffs of hot wind that left me damp and chilly when they stopped.

Time slipped by. At some point the phone rang. The phone was on a nightstand, two feet from where I lay, but it took all my will and energy to reach for it.

It was Claire. She'd just turned on the news and learned of Maxx's murder. The report revealed only that the body had been found by a doorman who was bringing Maxx his Sunday *New York Times,* and that robbery did not seem to be a motive. Claire said, "This must be so weird for you. Are you okay?"

At that I started to cry. I'd had no idea that it would happen. But the crying instantly rose up in a swelling surge that closed my throat and pushed hard behind my eyes. I tasted salt and iodine. I tried to speak but managed only a slurred word now and then amid the childish sobs. I blew my nose, composed myself; I immediately broke down again.

Claire said, "I'm coming over." And she hung up the phone.

I waited, blinking at the ceiling, the covers pulled up tight beneath my chin.

After a while there was a soft knock on the door. I padded to the hallway and opened it. Claire stood before me. Her dark eyes were tender and a little tired. Her head was tipped at an angle of close observation and concern. The first thing she said was "You look sick."

She put a cool hand on my forehead.

"You're burning up. Let's get you back to bed."

She plumped my tormented pillows, settled me between the sheets, sat down next to me. I said, "Thanks for being here. Thank you. This whole thing with Maxx . . ."

I started welling up again. She shushed me, said I didn't need to talk about it just then.

But I did need to. I started, and it all came out. It came out randomly, messily, punctuated by sobs and recourse to the handkerchief. I finally told her the truth about my deal with Maxx; that there had never been an advance; that I'd mortgaged the apartment. I told her how I'd suckered myself into believing the book could work, even with Maxx suddenly the loser. I told her about the confrontation of the night before, my helpless rage at being screwed and taunted, the finally unbearable anger at being the last victim of Maxx's bullying. I told her about my clumsy punch and Maxx's twisted fall, and about the visit from the cops and my shameful furtiveness in answering their questions.

I expected her to recoil in disgust from all of that. She didn't. She held me. She eased me back against the pillows and lay down next to me. She murmured that everything would be okay. There was so much still to be found out. I hadn't meant to hurt him. She knew I hadn't. It would turn out fine. We'd work it out. Everything would be okay.

I stopped hearing words. I listened to her voice as music. Her hair was soft against my burning cheek. Her breath was cool on my neck. She stroked my shoulder as I quaked and shivered. It wasn't anything like the passionate reunion I'd fantasized about for many months. But it was pretty wonderful.

With Claire next to me, I managed to sleep for an hour or so. I woke up in a tangle of sweaty sheets, but the fever seemed to have broken. I felt drained and weak but oddly calm. I'd confessed to Claire and been absolved. She believed I'd meant no harm to Maxx, and so I believed it myself. Or almost believed it. I'd hit him in anger; there was no dodging that; and when anger takes over, bad things happen. But murder was not in me; about that I was at peace. If in fact I'd killed the man, it had been nothing but a gruesome accident, a fluke both tragic and absurd. If there were consequences from what had happened, I would accept them as a penance.

Claire and I had tea and toast in bed. I felt pampered as a child home from school; in spite of everything, I made the most of it. I watched her spread jam onto my toast. Her hands were strong and steady; I took delight in looking at her wrists, her fingers, the wounded parts that, astonishingly, seemed to be healing. I watched her eat, sitting sideways on the bed. A toast crumb briefly caught at the corner of her mouth; her tongue flicked out and captured it. How had we ever not been together? It seemed crazy and perverse and pointless and stubborn.

Drinking tea, I grew gradually more awake and alert. As I did so, I revisited my thinking about this consequences business. Consequences . . . like, prison? Seven to twelve for manslaughter, or whatever they would call it? Being dragged away from my little life that once again felt precious, now that Claire was next to me? For what? For one clumsy and entirely justified push that happened to have an unforesee-able and catastrophic outcome? Fuck that. If there was penance to be done, I could do it quite well in the comfort of my own apartment.

On legs that were still a bit unsteady, I sprang out of bed and went looking for Arthur Levin's phone number.

When he answered, I didn't bother with niceties, just reminded him that he'd told me I should call if I needed legal help, and asked if I could speak to him in confidence.

Sounding like a man with way more important things on his mind, he said, "Yes, of course. But the books, the subpoenas—with Maxx dead, it's just dry business stuff now. You have no reason to worry at this point."

"Yes, I do. I visited with Maxx last night. The cops were here first thing this morning."

This seemed to throw even the unflappable old attorney. He started to speak, stopped, then stammered slightly. "David, you're not telling me—?"

My conscience screaming, I said, "I'm telling you that he called and asked me to come over. We had a talk and a glass of wine. He was drunk and a mess but alive when I left."

Levin asked me to hold on. Through the muffled phone, I heard a chair scrape, a vague exchange of voices. When he came back on the line, he said, "What time were you at Maxx's?"

I told him.

"Was there anybody else in the apartment?"

It was a reasonable question, but it took me completely by surprise. It had never even occurred to me that anybody else was there, though any number of people could have been stashed around the cavernous place. "I didn't see anyone. An awful lot of lights were on. Why?"

"I'm sitting here," he said, "with someone who also visited with Maxx last night and who's ready to confess to the killing."

Before the words had even settled firmly in my ears, my knees went weak with relief and my throat clamped down with gratitude. Numbly, breathlessly, I echoed, "Ready to confess?"

"More than ready," Levin said. "Desperate to confess. The problem is that I don't for a minute believe he did it."

I tried to mouth a reply to that; no sound came out. I sagged right down to my soul. I felt like I'd been thrown a lifeline, then had it yanked away before I'd been able to grab on.

"Why don't you come down here," Levin said. "I really think the three of us should talk."

Chapter 51

Claire said I was in no shape to go out. She was right, but it couldn't be helped. I dressed warm and fired down more aspirin. Before I left, I asked her if we could be together later. She looked at me for a moment, then almost shyly brought long lashes down across her eyes and said we could.

I took a taxi to the address that Arthur Levin had given me. It was a narrow but elegant town house on one of those European-looking blocks in the East Seventies. I rang the bell and was greeted by a handsome woman with a striking silver streak in her thick black hair. She introduced herself as Sylvia Levin, murmured something about how terrible and upsetting all this was, then ushered me into a tiny elevator that brought me up three floors to her husband's office.

The elevator didn't have a solid door, just one of those old-fashioned metal gates that stretch into diamond-shaped openings. Through the gaps, before the elevator had even stopped, I saw Anthony McDermott, Robert Maxx's sporadically crazy brother, pacing around a book-lined room. He paced in random patterns, like a fly deciding where it might be safe to land. Arthur Levin, sitting calmly at his desk, moved only his eyes to track the flitting.

The elevator stopped with a tiny thump; I opened the gate. Levin rose and stepped forward to shake my hand. McDermott stopped pacing and stared at me, seeming to strain for recollection. Levin said, "I believe you two have met."

"Thanksgiving," I said to McDermott. As I looked more closely at him, something unsettling occurred to me. His previously pallid complexion was flushed with exertion or mania; his posture was headlong and his attitude reckless: he resembled his brother much more closely than he had when Maxx was alive, as if by some mysterious process he'd slipped into the dead man's suddenly vacant niche. Fending off my discomfort, I went on, "I was at your house for Thanksgiving."

Rather theatrically, he said, "Ah. When all the horror started."

I had no idea what he was talking about. Then Arthur Levin steered my eyes toward a dark green blotter on his desk. On it were a number of medicine capsules; half capsules, actually, one side white, the other a pinkish beige. Among the opened pills were little piles of white powder.

Levin walked back to the desk, resumed his seat. Still weak in the legs, I sat down opposite. Indicating the powder, Levin said, "Taste it."

I licked the tip of my pinky, gingerly dipped it in. "Sugar," I said. "Powdered sugar."

"Correct," said Levin. "But it's supposed to be lithium carbonate. Tony's medication. Someone tampered with the capsules. Probably Robert. Probably on Thanksgiving."

McDermott had started pacing again, from window to bookshelf, from bookshelf to doorway. In a soft but shrill voice, he said, "*Definitely* Robert. *Definitely* Thanksgiving."

Calmly, Levin said, "Robert badly wanted to sell the old estate. He had a buyer ready, a neighbor. It would be a cash transaction that would bail him out. But Tony wouldn't sell. The only way to get around his refusal was to have him declared mentally incompetent. So the presumption is that Robert wanted Tony to have a severe enough episode to get him put away for good."

I considered that scenario. I'd heard Maxx hawking the estate, sensed the lifelong tug-of-war between the brothers. The assumption seemed both appalling and believable.

McDermott paced over and stood close to me, a hand on the back of my chair. His eyes were wild and there were tiny beads of sweat at his hairline. "I started having a dream," he said.

I knew the dream. It was the one he'd rambled on about to Maxx when we were in the limo, coming home from Staten Island.

"I dreamed about a burglar, a thief," he went on. "Coming to rob my house. Trying to take everything. I wasn't going to let him. I stayed awake, I carried a knife. Finally, I realized the thief was Robert."

Slowly, as if I were talking to a child, I said, "And how did you figure that out?"

McDermott paced a couple of steps, then swooped back close to me. "You know things when you're going crazy. Because you don't go crazy all at once. That's what people fail to understand. It's back and forth. Sometimes you imagine impossible things. But other times you see straight to the heart of something true. I had a moment when everything just seemed so clear. I knew exactly what was happening to me. I knew exactly why. I shook out my pills and broke one open. That's when I called the feds about my brother's books."

"*You* did that?" I said.

He didn't answer; he'd resumed pacing, bouncing off the walls. But I needed confirmation. I needed to be sure that the tip-off hadn't come from a bug in Victor Magnola's kitchen, from the sit-down to which, terrifyingly, I'd been an inadvertent witness. I assumed that Levin had to know of Maxx's dealings with the Godfather. Cautiously, I said, "So the information didn't come from—"

He cut me off before I said the name. "No, it didn't. It came from Tony. We learned that at the hearing yesterday. Robert was devastated."

"Yes, he was," said McDermott, circling back with a demonic gleam in his eye. "I'd got him back. He was furious. And helpless. He called me yesterday evening. He sounded drunk, pathetic. But he still thought he had the power. He mocked me, told me that I thought I'd won, but in fact I'd lost. If the business failed, if he went to jail, I'd lose the estate for sure. He'd make certain that the creditors got it, that it would be the first thing to be sold off. I'd be out on the street or in some horrible state nuthouse. That's when I knew I had to kill him."

I tried to keep my eyes on Anthony McDermott's. I couldn't do it. For respite, I looked to Arthur Levin. He said nothing.

"I got a taxi to the city," the brother went on. "I took my knife. I slipped into Robert's building. It was easy. It was very late, the doorman knew me. I went up to the apartment, to his bedroom. He wasn't there. The bed was made. I found him in his study. It was a mess. Wine was spilled, bottles toppled. We didn't talk, we didn't argue. I just walked up and stabbed him in the heart. I killed him."

He broke off, ran an unsteady hand through his hair. His face held so many different things—triumph, horror, guilt, bewilderment—that I thought it would fracture and come loose from its bones.

After a moment Arthur Levin said, "You didn't kill him, Tony. Maybe you wanted to. Maybe you would have. But you didn't. Why didn't you talk? It makes no sense that you would come all that way, with so much on your mind, and not talk, not argue. I'll tell you why you didn't talk. You didn't talk because your brother was already dead when you got there."

McDermott raised a finger, as if to protest; he shuffled a foot, as though to launch himself on another round of pacing. But he did neither. He seemed suddenly wound down, exhausted. He exhaled noisily and slumped into a chair.

Levin opened up a desk drawer, came out with a pair of rubber gloves like something from a doctor's office. He slipped them on as he rose, then went over to a bookshelf and swept away some leather volumes to reveal a wall safe. He spun the lock, reached into the cavity, and came out with a knife—an ordinary kitchen knife, the blade maybe seven or eight inches long. He brought it back to the desk and laid it on the blotter next to the opened capsules.

He said, "There's no blood on it, Tony. None at all. And it's not consistent with the autopsy report."

McDermott looked down and chewed his lip.

I said, "Autopsy report?"

"It isn't public yet. But I've spoken with the coroner. Maxx was stabbed to death, yes. The weapon pierced a lung and severed a pulmonary artery. But Tony didn't get to the apartment till after three, and Maxx died earlier than that. And the wound didn't come from a blade like this. It came from something double-edged."

Double-edged . . . like a letter opener? I swallowed. I tried to hold my face together as my mind was running for cover. Say it *was* a letter opener. I'd never touched the weapon, never held it in my hand. Besides, I was a mild-mannered writer, the unlikeliest of candidates for any sort of violence; and if I kept my mouth shut, why couldn't my motive remain forever a filthy secret? I'd be viewed as nothing more than a bit player in someone else's vendetta and someone else's tragedy, a bystander at a newsworthy event. Trying to sound offhand, conversational, I said, "What time do they think he died?"

Levin looked at me. I wondered if there was something in his gaze that wasn't there before. Probably it was nothing; just my guilty conscience making me a little paranoid. I told myself that what I saw was not suspicion.

The telephone rang before he answered.

Chapter 52

I t was Jenna on the line.

Levin said hello to her by name, but after that, his side of the conversation consisted mostly of things like "I see" and "of course." From moment to moment he grew harried, fretful; his usually steady eyes blinked and darted, as though charting a course through multiple hazards. Finally, he said, "Listen, I would join you, but I'm in conference here with Tony McDermott and I really can't break away right now."

He paused. Maybe he was weighing certain misgivings; no, I probably just imagined that he was. In any case, he said, "David Collins is with us. Shall I ask him to go?"

He hung up. Before he spoke again, he scrawled an address on a piece of paper and pushed it across the desk to me. He asked me if I'd meet Jenna there right away.

"What's it about?"

He didn't answer. He flicked his eyes very quickly toward McDermott; apparently, he no more wanted to discuss it in front of the fragile, raving brother than to leave him unattended. "Just go, please. It might be important."

I took the tiny elevator down and left the town house. Outside, it was a crappy day; in my guilt, I felt it had to be a crappy day. The sky was white, tinged with an unpleasant yellow, like a water stain or residue of nicotine. My fever was threatening to return; I felt fluctuating waves of heat along my spine. The address I'd been given was at Lexington and Sixty-ninth, just a half-dozen blocks away. I pulled my neck down into my collar and walked there as quickly as I could, trying not to shiver and trying not to think.

From some small distance I spotted Jenna. She was standing in front of a tall residential building, 1960s vintage, blue with stark aluminum windows. No doubt spiffy in its day, it now looked dated and mediocre. In twenty, thirty years, Robert Maxx's monuments would look like that as well. I wondered if he ever considered that when he was building them.

I waved to Jenna. It was probably too hearty a gesture for the occasion; she didn't wave back. We fell into a brief hug. She quickly pulled away but then she squeezed my hands. She looked like she had missed some sleep. Her eyes were red at the rims, her golden skin was sallow at the temples. "Thanks for meeting me," she said. "I really didn't want to come here alone."

She turned abruptly and went into the building. I followed. She gave her name to the doorman. He said she was expected and should go right up. We rode the elevator to the eleventh floor. Exiting into a long and narrow corridor, we turned left, then doubled right, looking for a certain name in its little slot beneath the peephole.

At length we found it: *Phelps. 11G.*

Jenna rang the bell. The door opened immediately, as if the accountant had been lurking right behind it, a hand on the knob. As ever, he was dressed in a business suit, with an immaculate shirt and tie. He looked less pale today, almost pink. But it was not a healthy pink; it was splotchy, as if long-choked capillaries had finally burst open, spilling into a secret flood beneath the skin. There was something fixed and distant in his eyes. When he saw me he scowled, then turned to Jenna and spoke to her as if I wasn't present.

"Why's he here?"

"The truth, Carlton? You sounded really strange on the phone. I wanted someone with me."

Phelps took that in, chewed his lower lip. "This is nothing to him. He doesn't belong here."

Jenna stood her ground. I stood mine. Phelps looked dismayed if not disgusted, but then his expression became sardonic and resigned. "All right," he said. "Fine. The observer will observe. Perfect. What the hell's the difference anyway?"

We stepped into a narrow entrance hall, then passed into his living room, which was sparsely but elegantly furnished, all blond wood and right angles. We moved past a spotless kitchen with every pan in place. We peeked into a bedroom whose bed was made as crisply as at a fine hotel. Then we came to Carlton Phelps's study.

On his desk, squared up with its corners, was a single old-fashioned ledger book. It was bound in brown leather and had the heft of the Manhattan yellow pages. Gesturing toward it, Phelps said to Jenna, "There it is. I'd like you to bring it to the authorities. My masterpiece."

He moved closer and opened the book very carefully, reverently, as though it were a sacred text. I saw tiny handwriting arranged in perfect columns.

He said, "It's a running tally of every accounting irregularity and malfeasance I've committed over the past twenty years. Every time a lender was misled or investors were defrauded, there's an entry. It'll make the prosecutors' job quite easy. And it finally makes the numbers add up right. Combine this with the official set of books, it comes out to the dollar. I'm pretty proud of that."

Jenna was staring at the ledger. She said, "You should give it to the feds yourself."

Ahead of the beat, with the same sort of jumpiness with which he'd yanked open the apartment door, he said, "I'm afraid that won't be practical."

"They'll see," continued Jenna, "that you tried to do the right thing, that you were forced to do the other."

"I wasn't forced," Phelps said quietly. "I made a bad decision early on. Too eager to please. Dazzled by Robert, maybe. Who knows? But I made a bad decision and it led to twenty years of bad decisions."

Almost pleadingly, Jenna said, "But you're coming clean. You were remorseful all along. The prosecutors don't want you. They wanted Robert. This hardly matters now."

"I'm afraid it does matter. Accounts must be balanced. I was saying that to Robert just last night."

I heard myself say, "You spoke to Robert last night?"

Dismissively, Phelps said, "What do you care? You've got nothing on the line here."

"Oh yes I do."

He looked at me then. It was the first time he'd ever really looked me in the eye. Other times, his glance had barely raked across me before it slid away, resentful and annoyed.

I went on, "I also spoke to him last night. I met with him, in fact. Did you?"

Phelps said nothing. His fingers fretted with a corner of his precious book.

"We argued," I said. "He was drunk. And nasty. And bullying."

Phelps stared at me another moment, and then an odd thing happened; he almost smiled. Just for an instant, his gaze softened, went from me to Jenna and back again. He gave us both a look, if not of kinship, then at least of fellow suffering. He said, "Yes, he was a bully, wasn't he? Start to finish."

"He taunted me," I said. "Sort of like the way he taunted you when you tried to quit. Let me know he still had the power. Seemed to get off on my helplessness. Finally, I lost my temper with him. Maybe you did, too. I mean, you have so much more at stake in all of this."

He licked his lips and sat down in his desk chair, splayed his long thin fingers along the edge of the desk. He didn't speak.

I said, "What time did you visit with him, Carlton?"

He turned toward Jenna. "Wait. This is all wrong. This isn't how it was supposed to go. You're supposed to take the book and leave me here."

"What time did you visit with him?" I said again.

He didn't answer, so I went on.

"I left around midnight. I believe Maxx was alive. But here's the weird part. I don't really know. Someone dies and you don't know if you killed him? That's not logical and that's not tidy. I think you can clear it up. Like you cleared the numbers up. Let's get it right, Carlton. You saw him later, didn't you?"

Before he spoke, he looked down at his lap, then slowly opened his top desk drawer. Carefully, he reached in with both hands. Holding it by the end of the handle and the tip of the blade, he produced one of the antique letter openers that had stood in a silver rack in Maxx's study. The blade was smeared with what looked less like blood than drying varnish; the stain had a rich, golden sheen. Phelps said, "Yes, I saw him later."

He spoke so softly that the words were hardly more than a mumble. But when I heard them, I felt something ease between my stomach and chest. There was a burn of dry tears at the edges of my eyes.

"Around one," Phelps went on. His voice seemed automatic but precise. "I went to his apartment. I had a key to the private elevator—a number of the senior people did. He was a mess, slurring, sloppy, but still, I had to talk with him. About a legal strategy. About how to share responsibility."

He paused, and I said, "Except Robert didn't want to share it."

"No. Not at all. The books were my doing. That was his position. The more I protested, the more he dug in. I started getting agitated. That was my mistake. He saw that I was angry, and he fed on it. I don't think he could do otherwise. It was a game with him, an instinct. He teased, taunted, tried to break me down one more time. But he didn't break me down. I only got angrier."

He looked at the murder weapon on his desk. His hand started moving toward it, then pulled back, as if newly horrified.

"His study was a shambles. Things were scattered everywhere. A light glinted and I saw this on the floor. I don't remember picking it up. But at some point it was in my hand. I lunged at Robert. He fell forward against me, mouth open, his face against my neck. He was heavy and hot. I stepped back and he hit the floor."

He broke off, immobile and spent. I looked at his distant eyes and tightly hunched shoulders. I'd never been so close to a killer before, but I felt neither outrage nor fear, only pity . . . and a queasy but genuine gratitude. If Phelps was guilty, I was not. He'd freed me. I could never do as much for him, but hoping to offer at least some faint solace, I said, "It could as easily have been me."

He gave one of those dry and joyless half smiles. His eyes were accepting, past resentment. "But it wasn't. And besides, that wouldn't have added up. You're just passing through."

Jenna leaned down very close to him. "You didn't mean to kill him. We all know that. There's lots of people who'll vouch for you. Let's go to the police—"

"No!" he said. "No. That's what the book is for."

He turned it to the final page. It was a confession, written in that same small, neat, steady hand.

"Everything's explained. It's all quite clear. Please. Take it and leave me here."

Jenna glanced at me, then back at Phelps. "I can't do that, Carlton."

"Afraid I'll run away?"

"I'm afraid you'll hurt yourself. And I won't let that happen."

A look of panic slid across his face; the look of a man whose fondest plan was being thwarted halfway to its climax. "Jenna, please, you have to let me do this my own way."

"No, I don't."

"I killed someone."

"You didn't mean to do it."

"And how are you so sure of that? I hated him so much in that moment."

"Of course you did. Who wouldn't? But I've worked with you a long time, Carlton. I know you better than you think I do. You protected Robert all along. You gave up your peace of mind for him. What more could anybody do? You're a good man."

He blinked down at his ledger book, ran his fingertips along its binding. His face flushed, all his features seemed to swell. He said, "I used to think I was. I really did." And he began to cry, silently at first, then with racking sobs.

Jenna leaned down and put her arms around him. Unused to being held, he was rigid and unyielding in her clasp. I called 911. She rocked him like a baby as we waited for the cops.

Epilogue

I slept a long, long time that night, and didn't stir until the phone rang shortly after 9 A.M. The phone was on what had once again become Claire's side of the bed. She picked it up and said hello.

Then she said, "Oh, hi, Paul. It's Claire . . . Yes, *that* Claire."

She handed me the phone. My agent, Paul Hannaford, went through a brief round of niceties, then told me he had just had an interesting conversation with Marcie Kanin.

I was not yet fully awake. Absently, I said, "Oh. I guess she's looking for a graceful way to tell us that the book is off."

"Off?"

"With Maxx dead and all. I mean, without his name on the cover, what do we really have?"

There was a brief pause. Then he said, "I hope you're kidding. Otherwise, you're really disappointing me. I thought you were a pro. What do we have? We have the exclusive inside story of the decline and fall and death of America's biggest business celebrity. You were there. You're the only one who can tell it. A lot of authors would kill for an opportunity like this."

It was an unfortunate figure of speech, but I let that slide and thought it over. The thing is, during the past thirty-six hours or so, I really hadn't thought about the book. Too much had gone on; I was more concerned with staying out of jail, not to mention escaping the purgatory of my own conscience. Besides, Maxx had nixed the project, and I was in the habit of believing that the tycoon had power over me, power over everyone. Only now did I have leisure to reflect that, Maxx or no Maxx, we really did have something to say and something to sell.

"So Marcie wants a book by *me*?"

"She's salivating for it."

"Did she make an offer?"

"She tried to. I told her to save it for the auction."

Auction. Syllable by syllable, it's not a lovely word, but to an author it's among the sweetest in the English language, right up there with *best-seller* and *royalty check*. To have publishers line up in a pissing contest, staking ego and corporate prestige on a bidding war for your next book—it just doesn't get any better than that. "You really think there'll be an auction?"

Instead of answering, he said, "Can you give me fifty drop-dead pages by early January?"

And so I got to work. It was a rich and marvelous few weeks, roiled only by the news of Carlton Phelps's death. He'd been arraigned for second-degree murder, but the judge seemed sympathetic, especially in light of the killer's detailed confession, clear remorse, and invaluable assistance in solving the crooked maze of Robert Maxx's finances. He would probably have served around eight years, but the case never got to trial.

Left alone in his cell, Phelps managed to tie some strips of bedsheet into a perfect double Windsor knot, and to hang himself from an overhead pipe. Reasonable minds may differ on the question of suicide; I happen to believe that in this case it was for the best. Prison would have been unbearable to someone so fastidious. And the most hellish eight-year penance—even added on to the twenty-year term he'd already served as CFO—still would not have satisfied his obsession with balancing accounts. By taking his own life, Phelps finally made it all add up just so; everything canceled out to a serene and perfect zero.

In any case, through that late December, I wrote in a sort of placid frenzy—a seeming oxymoron, but that's how it was. I was more confident than I had ever been. I knew I had great material. I knew, as well, that if this book was to be more than salacious, wallet-sniffing gossip, then it couldn't be about Robert Maxx alone. It had to deal with the collision between his raucous, outsize life and the lives of others; the lives of smaller, more obscure people whose dreams were just as precious and whose struggles just as worthy of recounting. Even a pushed-around and disappointed ghostwriter had a place in the story.

During those weeks, Claire and I were together almost every night and morning. Now and then, maintaining independence, she slept at the apartment with the huge piano. I guess what we were doing was the mirror image of a trial separation; it was a trial un-separation, somewhere between intensive dating and a full-on renewal of our vows. We talked, made love, ate sushi. She finished up the treatments for her hands; miraculously, her ravaged nerves seemed to be cured. And I thought: If damaged body parts can be healed with time and care and vigilance and patience, then why not relationships? Why not a marriage whose only real flaw was that it joined two lives that turned out not to run as smoothly or as effortlessly or as perfectly as young people, in their greenness, imagine that their lives should run?

So as not to cast a pall over the holiday season or interfere with the Caribbean vacations of the wealthy, Robert Maxx's memorial service was put off until the second week of the new year. Because Maxx had died in bad odor with the authorities, and because a massive legal and financial cloud still hung over the remains of his empire, the event was considerably less grand than it might otherwise have been. Bankers showed up, but they tended to be vice presidents, not chairmen. Hypocritical as ever, the politicians who had previously courted Maxx now stayed away; the mayor and the governor sent representatives armed with brief and carefully modulated eulogies.

Still, bad people get splashier send-offs than unimportant ones, and

Maxx's memorial was splashy enough. It was held at St. Bartholomew's, the beautiful Park Avenue church that, fittingly, was just across the street from the Four Seasons. Stained glass and organ music brought at least a hint of the sacred into the profane and racing heart of the city. There was a short sermon whose theme was the fragile and fleeting nature of all things human—lives, accomplishments, ambitions. Then, as if they hadn't heard a word, a number of speakers praised Robert Maxx for his lasting impact on the world around him.

Weary of the platitudes, Claire and I discreetly scanned the mostly filled-up nave, looking for famous or at least familiar faces. It was Claire who spotted Caitlin Kilgore. She whispered, "Isn't that the naked woman in the shirt I bought you?"

Across an aisle and two pews forward, Caitlin was sitting with Matt Gaston. I caught her eye, and she waved; but it seemed a wave to keep me at arm's length rather than to draw me closer. Maybe she thought I'd disapprove of her getting back together with her addictive costar. And frankly, I did disapprove. The guy had seemed like a narcissistic nut job, and he'd stalked her, after all. Then again, at least he was a gracious winner. When Caitlin left my place on the morning of that pivotal Saturday, she didn't go to California; rather, as the gossip magazines duly reported, she went to the hotel where her former lover was bivouacked, and had, one imagines, a memorable reunion. And when Gaston tried to gain entrance to Maxx's apartment that same afternoon, it wasn't to kill him but to apologize for his behavior of the night before. So who knows: maybe the television stars were meant to be together all along. Maybe Gaston was the love of Caitlin's life. Maybe Maxx had meant nothing to her. Who could tell with actresses?

The service ended; people streamed out into weak but welcome sunshine. Among the crowd on the sidewalk I saw Jenna. She was with a woman I didn't recognize—white, dark-haired, outdoorsy-looking. We made our way over to say hello.

I introduced Claire. Jenna said, "And this is my partner, Kathleen Daly."

I couldn't help doing a double take.

Jenna read my face. Then, more to Claire than to me, she said, "No one at the company knew anything about my private life. Why should they? I mean, hey, I'm black, I'm female, how many more headaches do I need?"

I said to Kathleen, "I think you should know that your girlfriend used to flirt with me in a major way."

Jenna laughed. "I didn't flirt with you. I was *nice* to you. Not my problem if you can't tell the difference."

"Definitely a guy thing," Kathleen said.

Claire nodded in agreement. I felt a little ganged up on, and I loved every second.

That same evening I did my first television interview about my time with Robert Maxx.

The interviewer was Mandy Lockwood. I'd promised her an exclusive a couple of weeks before; she'd used it as a bargaining chip in negotiating terms for her new job, a step up from cable: business correspondent for the New York affiliate of one of the major networks.

Not that I'm trying to take credit for getting Mandy back to work. In fact, she brought her new employers a scoop to which my little story was not much more than a sidebar. She was the first to break the news that Rockefeller Center would not be changing owners after all, as Trip Campbell, citing deteriorating market conditions, had pulled out of negotiations.

This begged a couple of questions: Had the Campbell bid ever been sincere, or had he just jumped in to muck things up for Maxx? No one could say. Equally murky was the process by which Mandy had gotten the scoop. Were martinis involved? Was there a fleshly quid pro quo? I don't know and I don't want to know. As Mandy once told me, we outsiders and strangers to privilege had to play by our own rules to have any chance of winning.

Besides, I'm hardly in a position to judge, as I exacted my own quid pro quo from Mandy. In exchange for the first interview, I received a promise of plenty of coverage when my book was published. In the meantime, this first TV appearance was part of a small but well-choreographed campaign to ramp up interest in my proposal, which was going to auction the following morning.

I spoke with Paul Hannaford many times that day. Each phone conversation was followed by hugs and a recap with Claire, along with a no doubt unseemly and adolescent reveling, not to say cackling with glee, at the progress of the bidding. It would be uncouth—Maxx-like, in fact—to brag about where the numbers ended up; suffice it to say that my billionaire proved to be a far more generous benefactor to me in death than he had been in life, and that I was easily able to get my apartment out of hock. Shortly before the close of business, the winning bid came in from the estimable firm of William Morrow, publishers of the volume you now hold in your hand.

The underbidder was Porter & Kraft, Marcie Kanin's company. When the dust had settled, Marcie called to congratulate me, which I thought was awfully classy of her. In turn, I thanked her for everything she'd done to help conceive and shape the book. In an ideal world, she would have been its editor, but in this world money talks, and that's just how it is.

Acknowledgments

Without the gentle persistence and faultless tact of my agent, Paul Hannaford, this book would not have been written. Thanks are due, as well, to Jenna Cole, Mandy Lockwood, and—not least—Robert Maxx himself. Their words and hard-earned wisdom gave the story its life.

Finally, I am indebted to Laurie Chittenden, my editor at Morrow, for her careful stewardship of this project and for being its most consistent and persuasive champion.